LOOKING FOR LYNNE

John L. Moore

DEDICATION

To those who rode
when the riding was real:
the late Lynne Taylor,
the late Denny Looman,
and Gary Crowder,
who rides with us still.

ACKNOWLEDGMENTS

Many readers will notice the similarity between the fictional Barney Wallace and Miles City's own cowboy cartoonist, Wally Badgett. Yes, Wally rode saddle broncs, but his one appearance at the National Finals Rodeo was in bull riding. Wally's father, Kirk, rode for the CBCs, as did his uncle, Wallace, for whom he's named. (My father, Johnny Moore, rode for the Chappel Brothers as well.) Because of the similarities between Wally and Barney, there was concern Wally's wife, Pam, would be insulted by the name of Mrs. Wallace: Henrietta. Pam said not to worry. Anyone who lives with Wally is used to being offended. Wally's cartoon is called "Earl" and he is an artist of exceptional talent and wit. I thank Wally for inspiring the character, Barney Wallace.

I have many others to thank: Katie Andraski and Becky Kennedy McLendon, for editing and proofreading the manuscript; Cathy Jones and Kami Ellen Moore for reading, encouraging, and praying; Tom and Kim Peila and their family for helping with winter chores, which allowed me time to work on the manuscript; Scott and Joy Brady for the same; Tony Harbaugh and Sue Stanton for select technical help;

Ray Hughes for a lifetime of teaching on praise, worship and the science of sound; John L. Sandford for his groundbreaking work in the healing of the earth; Christy Suits for a beautiful cover design and invaluable computer assistance; my lovely wife, Debra, for loving forbearance; and a special thank you to the loyal *Ezra Riley* fans who have urged me for years to bring this character back and supported me through the process with encouragement and prayers. Many thanks to all of you.

This novel is dedicated to three cowboys, who among other things, rode for the Kramer Ranch. Lynne Taylor, Denny Looman and Gary Crowder. But a secondary dedication is due our grandchildren: Creed, Selah, Ryann, David, Autumn, and Redmond. May they someday read and, perhaps, understand.

John L. Moore April 2014.

INTRODUCTION

*L*ooking for Lynne is written as a stand-alone novel, but is the fourth book featuring Ezra and Anne Riley, so some background will be beneficial to first-time readers. The debut novel, *The Breaking of Ezra Riley*, first appeared nationally in 1990 and was an award-winning coming-of-age story, with flashbacks to Ezra's father's era as a cowboy riding for the CBCs, the Chappel Brothers Cannery of Rockford, Illinois. Ezra, sensitive and poetic, returns to the family ranch in 1979 with his wife, Anne, and their baby, Dylan, following his father's death. He's forced to adapt to the cowboy ways he'd rebelled against, while coping with a bereaved mother, skeptical sisters, two surviving uncles, drought, bad markets, blizzards, and a call of God that he fights desperately.

In book two, *Leaving the Land*, Ezra is reunited with a former hitchhiking partner who's become a charismatic evangelist with a shadowy past in a study of conflict between talent and character.

In book three, *The Limits of Mercy*, Ezra, now a published writer, is pursued by a beautiful seductress and harassed by a bullying poacher, while he and Anne shelter the poacher's abused girlfriend.

In *Looking for Lynne* some real people and real events are fictionalized. Everett Colburn and Gene Autry were partners as rodeo producers. In 1959, the last of the original Madison Square Garden rodeos was held. Also, that year, the first finals for the Rodeo Cowboys Association was held in Dallas. The Kramer Ranch, owned by Bud Kramer and his famous cowgirl wife, Bobby Kramer, did run up to 3000 horses north of Miles City, Montana. Two saddle broncs mentioned in this book, Desolation and Sage Hen, were real horses. Desolation began his career with Feek Tooke and ended up with Cervi Championship Rodeo. Sage Hen was owned by Harry Knight. Charles Snell is a horseman and saddle-maker in Oregon. The Oswald line of Quarters Horses was developed by Montana rancher Bob Shelhamer in the 1950s, but Oswald himself was born in Oklahoma, and used in Kansas and on Rosebud Creek in Montana before being acquired by Shelhamer. This line, though less concentrated, continues today through Leroy Hauerland of Sealy, Texas.

All the government programs mentioned exist, with the exception of EEEP. The Enhanced Environmental Easement Program is made-up.

It is said the CBCs began when its founder, P.M. Chappel, rode a train through eastern Montana in the mid-1920s and saw loose horses everywhere. In 1920, the horse population in the United States was estimated by some sources at 25,000,000 and horses of many breeds -- Thoroughbred, Shire, Percheron, French Coach, Cleveland Bay, and Belgians among them -- were raised in massive numbers in eastern Montana. Some ranches ran 5,000 to 15,000 head and Miles City was also a national center for the Army Remount Program. Because of mechanization and drought, many of these horses were abandoned or escaped and became feral. In 1926, Montana became the first of several Western states to pass legislation demanding loose horses be rounded-up and sent to slaughter. Chappel and his two brothers owned the Ken-L-Ration dog food company, and capitalized on these developments. The CBC horse operation began about 1928 but faced a setback with the passing of the Taylor Grazing Act in 1934, a law that put an end to free and unregulated grazing in the West. At its height, the CBC operation was a wild, strenuous, and extensive affair that handled some 60,000 horses, most of them in eastern Montana. While purging the plains of unwanted animals, the Chappels did so with a timeliness that benefited their own enterprises. Besides dog food, these included exporting horse meat to Europe for human consumption. By 1938, the CBC horse operation in Montana was finished.

A CBC cowboy, especially one who lasted for more than one season, was expected to be the toughest of the tough and the most daring of the fearless.

Today, the nation is experiencing a glutted horse market as it did in 1920s and '30s. The recent horse population in the U.S. peaked in 2007 at approximately 10,300,000 animals, up from 3,000,000 in 1960. A national economic downturn since 2008, and the closing of U.S. slaughterhouses, has created an excess of animals resulting in a depressed horse market and many cases of abused and abandoned animals.

The number of federally-protected "wild" horses in the West has also soared, causing denuded wildlife habitat and the forced containment of mustangs in confined holding facilities.

The Greater sage grouse is up for consideration as an endangered or threatened species. The court-set deadline forcing the U.S. Fish and Wildlife Service (USFWS) to make a decision is September, 2015. This decision will effect 186 million acres in 11 Western states. Ironically, hunting and predation are not considered primary factors in the decline of sage grouse numbers.

PROLOGUE

"Behind every beautiful thing, there is some kind of pain."
-- Bob Dylan.

1959

Sunday Creek. North of Miles City, Montana.

"Ezra! Get in the house!" His mother's scream pierced the morning air and she hurried on worried feet across the ranch yard's hardpan. She saw her six-year-old where she thought he'd be, on the south side of the bunkhouse staring, entranced, at the flowers he'd been told to pull up. Pearl Riley broke into a run, her slender legs wheeling beneath her cotton dress and apron.

The mother grabbed the boy by an arm and spun back toward the tiny tarpaper house, half-dragging him as she ran. It was then that Ezra saw the horses, boiling from the west through clouds of dust, their hooves splattering gravel. He glimpsed a palette of horseflesh: two paints, a black, a buckskin, three sorrels, a roan, and in the lead, its head high and nostrils flared, a line-backed dun. Behind them, shouting, a stiff lariat coiled in his right hand, rode his father on a lathered bay.

A glass-eyed paint, seeing the corrals, peeled from the bunch, galloped behind the house and was quickly ensnared by a netting of clothesline and white linen. It burst through the crisp, clean laundry, broke the poles at their bases, and rejoined the herd dragging behind it a tangle of sheets and pillowcases. The horses swirled into the stout corrals with more fury than fear. Johnny Riley pulled his bay to a strong-armed stop, swung from the saddle and closed the heavy gate behind them. Captured.

Pearl stared through the window with 13-year-old Diane, Ezra, and Lacey, a toddler, beside her. "This is a big day for your father," she warned them. "Everett Colburn, the rodeo man, is up from Texas to look at those broncs. If they buck good they might end up in Madison Square Garden."

But, the little boy wasn't thinking about horses and rodeos. He was thinking sadly about the morning glories; how they opened at sunrise and followed the sun like tiny trumpets of prayer.

His mother bent down and whispered to him. "You pull those flowers up later, when you won't disturb those horses," she said. "You don't want Everett Colburn to know that Johnny Riley's boy grows flowers."

That afternoon, the flowers still untouched, Ezra's face pressed against stiff woven wire that circumscribed the rodeo arena his father had built on Sunday Creek. On the knoll above him, people began to appear. His mother stood, holding Lacey. Diane, however, was not there. She'd refused to come, and Pearl was too weary to fight her. Ezra sensed his uncles' arrival through the odors of tobacco, sweat, and soiled clothes. From the corner of one eye, he watched the six bachelors climb from an old Willys station wagon. They assembled on the hill like a murder of crows. Ezra glimpsed pulses of faint color emanating from them: a storm of muddy yellows, pungent browns, and a wispy blackness punctuated by tiny strikes of red and green.

Commotion crackled at Ezra's left: the sudden rumble of wild horses being jostled from pen to alley by his father and Charley Arbuckle. To Ezra, the horses were fearsome with their long, tattered manes; tails, tangled with burs, dragging to their fetlocks; eyes and nostrils flaring red; and heavy, feathered hooves striking the ground. The herd thundered into a holding pen and a gate slammed shut.

"Where'd ya get that bay?" Ezra's father asked Charley, pointing to the handsome horse the older man rode.

"Got him down on Rosebud Crick," Charley said. "He's by a runnin' horse named Oswald. A good sum-beech."

A pickup pulled up with a tall paint horse in the back and a saddle cinched tight to the stock rack. A young boy spilled from the passenger door and bounded down the hill, snorting, jumping and slapping his behind loudly. "Yee-haa, yee-haa," he yelled, before falling and rolling in a dusty heap at Ezra's feet.

Ezra stared incredulously at the pile of hair and clothes.

The boy bounded up. He was Ezra's age but taller and skinny. "I'm Barney," he said, offering his hand.

Ezra took it tentatively. "Ezra," he mumbled.

"Wanna play rodeo?" Barney asked. "I'm Casey Tibbs and this is the Madison Square Garden." Before Ezra could answer, the boy crow-hopped to the top of the hill, stopped, pivoted and looked down. "Ladies and gentlemen," he announced through cupped hands. "Coming out of chute number one… Casey Tibbs on Warpaint!" He jumped in the air, slapped himself on the butt, mimicked a horse fart, and kicked his way down the hill.

"Ezra!" Pearl Riley yelled. "You boys come back up here. You're going to spook the horses." But, Pearl's shouts were overridden as everyone's attention turned to the sound of an approaching vehicle. From a cloud of dust, a long, black car pulled up.

"Everett's here," Charley said.

Johnny nodded, his weathered face as hard as a carving.

From the driver's side of the Cadillac stepped a lean, gray-haired man in a black hat and western sports coat. While the group studied Everett Colburn, the passenger door swung open and a silver hat emerged. Beneath it was a short, stout man in a tan jacket, western dress pants and ostrich skin cowboy boots. His short-cropped hair was a blend of blond and gray. With a gasp, Pearl Riley brought a hand to her mouth. Her little bird frame trembled. "Its Gene Autry," she whispered to the boys.

Ezra cocked his head and stared. He'd heard the name before.

Barney Wallace looked up at Mrs. Riley with wide-eyed confusion. "Who's he?" he asked.

"Shush," Pearl said quietly. "He's a movie star."

In the corral, mounted on his Oswald gelding, Arbuckle tipped his hat back. "By God," he said. "Everett brought Autry with him."

Johnny Riley's dark Irish face showed a subtle scarlet flush. Knowing Colburn was an honor, but he never suspected he'd also meet his business partner.

Colburn and Autry came down the hill to a man-gate in the alley. Johnny and Charley dismounted to meet them. "Johnny, Charley," Colburn said. "I want you to meet my partner, Gene Autry."

Arbuckle thrust his hand forward first.

"I've told you about Charley," Colburn said. "He was the wagon boss for the Sunday Creek CBC."

"Nice to meet you," Autry said.

"And this is Johnny Riley," Colburn said. "He's the one that sent us the bronc that bucked off Marty Wood in the Garden."

Johnny was nervous. "Ga-ga-ga-good to m-m-meet you," he stuttered.

Jingle-bobbed spurs chimed and a cricket bit chirped from behind them. The men turned to see Avery Wallace leading his paint.

"This here's Avery Wallace," Johnny said. "He'll be helping me pick up. Avery rode for the CBCs, too."

"Did you work Charley's wagon?" Autry asked.

Wallace shook his head. "No, I rode for the Sweeney Creek wagon."

"It's good to meet three CBC cowboys," the movie star said. "You rode when times were wild, but those times will never be seen again."

"Times are changing for me, too," Colburn said. "I'm retiring from the rodeo business. Gene will continue, but this is the last year for the Garden so it's time for me to take a bow."

"No more Madison Square Garden rodeo?" Arbuckle asked.

"I'm afraid the eastern love affair with the cowboy is over," Colburn said. "The Garden won't be crowning champions anymore."

"But we'll still need good broncs," Autry said. "So, Johnny, you and Charley keep sweeping those badlands. We'll take a look at everything you gather."

Charley Arbuckle and Johnny Riley exchanged worried looks. The badlands had been all but swept clean.

"Who do you have coming to get on these broncs?" Colburn asked.

Johnny nodded to the west. "We got a good one, and I think that's Lynne coming now."

A yellow convertible pulled up on the hill. A woman with flaming red hair was driving and a cowboy sat beside her. He stepped from the car smiling.

Ezra stared. The car was so new and bright it looked as if the young cowboy had emerged from the sun.

The cowboy reached into the backseat, grabbed a bronc saddle and swung it easily onto his shoulder. Dressed in a crisp western shirt and new denim jeans, he seemed bathed in blue as if God had drawn outside the lines in creating him. He waved goodbye to the redhead who flew away in the canary-colored car.

The cowboy turned and looked straight at Ezra. Ezra saw sparkles of color -- blues, yellows, greens -- spilling from his eyes and forming like a pool around him.

The young cowboy moved down the hill with a graceful, catlike athleticism. Intent but relaxed.

Ezra continued to stare until his mother gripped him by the neck and whirled him around. "You're imagining things again, aren't you?" she said.

He was too scared to talk.

"I've told you not to imagine things. Christian people don't see things. You go home, Ezra." She pointed north, up the creek. "Follow that cow path home and pull up those flowers."

He ran. He ran until he doubled-over in pain, but as soon as was away from them, he was okay because he was alone with the hills, trees, rocks, and brush. He knew his mother would lie about why he was sent home. She'd say she'd caught him swearing or sneaking a pinch of tobacco and his father would chuckle, secretly proud.

He didn't go straight home. He left the creek and followed a mysterious drainage that led uphill through narrow cuts and washes to a plateau thick with sagebrush. There he flushed a flock of sage grouse that beat the air heavily as they rose in flight.

He walked to a hill that overlooked the creek. Below him was his home. Upstream was the big house where his uncles lived. A dark, dense fog seemed to enshroud it.

He had to quit seeing things. It only got him in trouble. He would quit, he decided.

Ezra moved down the hill to the quiet creek where the saddle horses stood in shallow water, fighting flies.

Resolved to meet his mother's demands, his thin chest lifted with a heavy sigh, and he went to the side of the bunkhouse where the morning glories grew. Their heads were dipped. He knew they sensed his intentions.

Ezra forced himself to do what he had to do. He didn't cry. He thrust his little fingers into the damp soil -- soil moistened from creek water he'd packed each morning -- and gripped the vines' tenacious roots. Sometimes things had to die, his mother said, because that's the way life was.

So he pulled them up. One by one. All the little trumpets of prayer.

PART I

"Riding a horse is not a gentle hobby, to be picked up and
and laid down like a game of solitaire. It is a grand passion.
It seizes a person whole and once it has done so, he will
have to accept his life will be radically changed."
-- Ralph Waldo Emerson

CHAPTER ONE

"Are you comfortable, Mr. Riley?"

The woman had a soothing voice and sweet face.

Comfortable? Who could be comfortable lying on a flat, cold table in a hospital gown?

"I'm fine," Ezra said.

The radiologist positioned the earphones on his head, placed a hard mask over his face and fastened it securely to the MRI table.

Ezra had not expected the mask.

"Okay," she said. "You're going in. You should hear music in the earphones. I picked Johnny Cash. I hope that's okay."

The big machine purred and sucked Ezra slowly in on its tongue. The chamber ceiling was but inches above his face. A liquid fear squirmed in his stomach, coiled liked a snake, and aimed at his heart. "Get me out," Ezra said desperately. "Get me out."

The machine whirred again and the table reemerged. Ezra felt clammy. "I didn't think it would bother me," he confessed. Beads of perspiration glistened on his forehead.

"That's okay," the lady said. "It happens every day. Are you sure you don't want Valium?"

"No, no. It's the mask. I can't take the mask."

"Okay. We can try it without the mask, but you'll have to lie absolutely quiet the whole time."

"I can do that."

She removed the mask.

Ezra closed his eyes and felt the machine retrieve him. Faint music rattled within the earphones. A loud pounding began as the machine blasted his molecules with x-rays. *Okay*, Ezra told himself. *Thirty-two minutes. I am going to keep my eyes closed and escape into my imagination.*

He'd always been good at imaginative detachment -- his childhood had forced it on him -- and his martial arts training, now decades behind him, had added layers of concentration and poise.

Imagine. In his mind he saw miles of rolling prairie beneath a canopy of dappled sky. He was on his ranch north of Miles City, Montana and horseback on…

On which horse? The decision was pivotal and he had to decide quickly.

His life had been defined by horses: Ribbon Tail, the bad blue roan of his youth; Gusto, the Paint redeemer; the charm of Shogun; the warrior's heart of Shiloh; and so many more, a parade of working ranch horses, some good, some bad, a few great. And now, in this cold diagnostic tomb, he must forget the horse Pedro, the bad Oswald, that put him here. He imagined himself on Simon, the good Oswald, but could he trust Simon? Could he ever ride again?

Imagine. Be the writer, the seer, the poet. Be the child running to the hills.

I am in the hills. The prairie grasses, colored like cured oats, sway softly in the breeze. Blue-gray sagebrush dot the coulees. A hawk, buoyed on a thermal, circles above me.

In his imagined world he was alone. His wife, Anne, was not there. Nor his grown son, Dylan, daughter-in-law Kristen, or his granddaughter, Gabriella. His friends Barney and Joe were not there.

There were no ghosts there, either. Not his father, Johnny Riley, nor his six bachelor uncles, nor his friend Lynne. Just himself, a horse, and solitude. Land, and the wildlife and livestock it nourished, was his solace. The weather was pleasant but not ideal. A cool breeze fingered the edges of his silk scarf. His cheeks were flushed pink. He looked about for his cow dog, Casey, but couldn't see him.

He must be lying in the brush.

The bay horse shifted nervously beneath him and Ezra's hand went instinctively to the saddle horn.

The machine burped and shook, rattling Ezra's mind, dispelling the prairie images and forcing a conscious return to the tube. There was a quiet pause and then the metallic hammering began again.

He returned to his imagined world. Horseback again. On a blood bay. But which bay? Simon was a bay, but so was Pedro. In fact, most of the horses from the Oswald line were bays or browns.

Why did I agree with Lynne to breed those horses? Why Oswalds?

He remembered the incidents that put him here.

Bucked off twice in five days, it'd taken a miracle to survive the first wreck; the second was worse.

He remembered a horsehide explosion, fierce snorts, and squeals of anger. His neck had whipped left, then right, then left again before Pedro slipped on the frozen ground and Ezra's head and shoulders struck the creek bank and slid onto cracking ice. Water, so cold it burned, covered his head and twelve-hundred pounds of horseflesh pinned his bottom leg. The horse's hooves thrashed wildly above him.

Why did I get back on him after the first incident? Wasn't one wreck enough?

He knew why. Because that is what Lynne would have done.

He was tempted to open his eyes and touch the closeness of his confines.

Don't do it. Don't panic.

"How are you doing, Mr. Riley?" The voice in his ear calmed him.

"Okay," he lied. "Can you turn the music up? I can't hear it."

"Certainly."

He heard a distant, tinny echo.

Think about something else.

He thought about Anne home calving heifers. He thought about their granddaughter, Gabby, and her crayon drawings of horses. When they talked on the phone she always asked about the horses. He hoped to watch her grow as a horsewoman but she was only five and the family lived in Seattle.

Don't get nostalgic, he warned himself. *Don't think about Gabby.*

He felt the tube pressing in on him. Ezra had been claustrophobic since childhood. He couldn't stand being held, squeezed, or pressed upon. He needed room.

Endure it. Your fingers are numb, your thumbs throb, and your neck aches. You must find the reason and the remedy if you want to remain horseback.

He took a deep breath. His nerves needed oxygen. It seemed he'd been in the tube for hours. Maybe days. What if an earthquake hit or the power simply went off? He would have felt safer in Miles City but he was in Billings. Billings was not home.

"Are you okay, Mr. Riley?"

The sound of a voice made him want to shout for joy. "Yes," he said. "Are we done?"

"You have eight more minutes, Mr. Riley."

Eight minutes!

When it was finally over the radiologist took him to an examination room. He waited five minutes before the doctor breezed in. "Good morning, I'm Dr. Robinson," the man said, shaking Ezra's hand.

The doctor was trim and fit. Ezra imagined him riding mountain bikes.

"How are we doing today?" The doctor's tone was purposeful, like milk warmed for a kitten. He seated himself on a small black stool and glanced through Ezra's paperwork. "You're a rancher," he said, more to himself than to Ezra. "Sixty-one years old," he added.

Ezra did not like the implication in his voice, it read: *You're an old cowboy. Of course you're all busted up.*

"It says here you had an accident." He gave Ezra a glancing appraisal.

I know what you are thinking, Ezra thought. *You are noting my salt-and-pepper hair, the creases in my brow and crows-feet at the eyes. You see the wind-burnt complexion of my face and hands. You think life has about used me up.*

"What type of accident did you have?" the doctor asked.

"A couple horse wrecks."

"And your main symptoms are in your hands?"

"Yes, sir. My fingertips are numb and my thumbs really hurt."

The doctor got up and slapped two X-rays on the light board. "You recently broke two ribs on your left side and separated all the ribs on the right."

"I was wondering about that. I had some rib pain through the winter."

"According to your report these accidents were five months ago. Why weren't you in then?"

"The wrecks were in November and then the winter blew in. I had cows to feed and couldn't get away."

The doctor tested Ezra's arms and hands for nerve response then moved to his laptop. "Let's take a look at the MRI."

As the images appeared the doctor pointed out details with his pen. "There's compression and degeneration in C-four-five and C-five-six. The discs are bulging. Nothing appears to be broken. I suspect a bruised spinal cord but there's no white spot." He tapped the keyboard and the images changed. "No white spot," he confirmed. "I'm going to write you a couple of prescriptions. There's nothing here that requires surgery, but, your spine shows a lot of abuse which isn't unusual for a rancher your age. You really need to avoid further trauma. No more horse accidents. Your neck can't take another *wreck,* as you call it."

"The pain in my hands?"

"We'll see what the scripts do. If the pain doesn't diminish you might need to come back and get cortisone injections in the thumb joints." He glanced back at the notes. "I see you're a writer, too. Does typing bother you?"

"My fingers on the keys feel like brook trout slamming against a rock."

"There's new software you might try that transcribes your voice onto the screen."

Ezra didn't react. *Technology. Everyone's answer was more technology.*

The doctor closed Ezra's file. "Good luck, Mr. Riley," he said. Then he left the room.

Ezra sat for a moment and stared at the floor.

He left Billings thinking he'd spent $3000 on an MRI, prescriptions, and an opinion that he didn't need surgery. Maybe that was worth it.

Interstate 94 was dense with traffic -- the result of the Bakken oil boom in North Dakota -- and Ezra couldn't relax while he drove. Shiny new pickups whizzed by. Oil patch workers from western Montana, Idaho, and Washington rushing to work. Ten days on, ten days off. Long commutes.

In Miles City he pulled into a convenience store to fuel-up because having fuel delivered to the ranch was expensive. He winced as the pump price rolled past $135. At the till he handed a check to a tired girl wearing dark eye shadow and a frown.

"I need identification," she said.

Ezra sighed with frustration. Miles City did not used to be that way. "I left my wallet in the truck," he said.

He walked to the truck quickly, head down, paying no attention to anyone when suddenly a cold, dark force, denser than a sudden breeze, stopped him. He turned and saw two young men getting into a battered truck. One was as thin and wispy as a shadow. The other was huge, tattooed, and glared at Ezra with malevolence. The truck had Nevada plates.

Oil field workers, Ezra thought. The truck rattled away.
Miles City didn't used to be like this.

At the ranch he first strolled through the corrals with a flashlight checking heifers -- the cattle stared at the light dumbly; none were calving -- then walked to the house with Casey trailing at his heels.

A lovely sound roiled from the basement -- a softly thunderous cacophony, like hoofbeats on sod; water rippling over rock; breezes playing in leafed trees: the wondrous talent of Anne on the piano. Grace, power, beauty, majesty rolled from her fingertips. Hers was a talent equaled only by her stage fright, but while she trembled before audiences, she was the music of his life.

The music stopped.

She met him at the door. "How did it go?" she asked.

He showed her the prescriptions, told her what the doctor had said and mentioned he'd nearly panicked in the MRI machine.

"It's good you don't need surgery," she said hopefully.

"Yeah. I guess."

"Have you had supper?"

"No, I'm too tired to eat. I'm going to bed."

"It's too early, Ezra. You'll be up at four."

"I'll read for awhile. I need to unwind." He began taking off his shirt -- he wore only western shirts with snaps because he had trouble with buttons.

"Need help?" She peeled the shirt off his shoulders. Her blue eyes were set in a face formed with character. Her hair, golden blond when Ezra met her, was now platinum and at five-ten she equaled his height. "Things will be okay," she said. "If we have to we'll get a second opinion."

"I know. I'm just tired."

"I'll let you rest." She went to the kitchen.

Ezra pulled on a nightshirt and crawled into bed with two pillows propped behind him and a large pillow on his lap like a table. He reached for a book on the nightstand but it slid through his numb fingers and fell to the floor. He cussed softly.

"Oh," Anne called from the kitchen. "Do you know a Garcia Jones?"

"A what?"

"Someone named Garcia Jones called. A young guy. Says he works for NRCS or something like that."

Oh God. The Natural Resources and Conservation Service. He'd forgotten they had a meeting with them in the morning. "That's the office you called," Ezra said. "Remember?"

"No, I forgot."

Ezra struggled to turn pages.

Anne came to the bedroom door. "Are you mad at me for calling them?" she asked.

"No, I just hate the idea of doing business with the government."

"What else can we do? We'll need money to buy your sisters out soon. They have no attachment to this land anymore."

Land. You work for it. Fight for it. Sweat, bleed, and almost die for it. You love it, you hate it, but in the end it's real value is in passing it on. Legacy.

"Ezra?"

"It's fine, Anne," he said. "I guess it doesn't hurt to talk to them."

Pain was relative. How painful was it to talk to a government employee?

What could it hurt?

CHAPTER TWO

The next morning Anne answered the door to a pleasant-faced young man in a tan jacket, USDA cap, and a disarming grin. He had a pile of folders in his arms.

"Mrs. Riley?" he asked. "I'm Garcia Jones of the NRCS."

She welcomed him in and led the way to the kitchen table. Ezra stepped from the living room and the young man stretched out his hand. "Garcia Jones," he repeated. Ezra took a grip that was firm but not finger-crunching, for which he was thankful.

Ezra thought Jones looked like a modern Huckleberry Finn. He was about six-feet tall, weighed maybe 150 pounds and sported a wispy strawberry-blond goatee. When he removed his cap he loosed a thatch of bristly red hair. They seated themselves in unison.

"So, where are you from, Garcia?" Anne asked. She had unique people skills. The home itself, well-lit with windows and jungled in house plants, reflected her nurturing gifts. People felt comfortable in the Riley home.

"I was raised on 80 acres in Oregon and went to college at Montana State. I interned in Great Falls before moving here two months ago."

He looked at them through pale blue eyes. "I might as well explain my name," he said. "My parents were hippies."

"Deadheads?" Ezra said.

Garcia grinned. "You got it. I was named for Jerry Garcia of The Grateful Dead. My parents never really left the Sixties. They didn't have me until '89 but they must of thought it was '69."

"What do your folks do?" Ezra asked.

The young man's blush loosed a flurry of freckles. "My dad's involved with the medical marijuana industry --"

"In Oregon?" Ezra interrupted.

"No. Here in Montana."

"So your dad's a pot dealer?" Ezra said.

"He calls himself a provider of herbal relief."

"And your mother?" Ann asked, changing the subject.

"She raises alpacas and charts horoscopes."

"Well, I'm sure they're good parents," Anne offered.

"They're all I have." Garcia laughed and his hair shook like a pile of carrot shavings. "I'm the black sheep of the family. I like rodeos, hunting, and working cattle. My mom hardly speaks to me sometimes. She's a vegan and a PETA activist."

"So," Ezra said, nodding at the folders. "You have some government stuff to explain to us?"

"That's right. Are you familiar at all with our programs EQIP, WHIP, and CSP?"

They shook their heads.

"Okay. Well, the one I want to show you is actually a brand new one. You would be part of a pilot project if you qualify. It combines a little of all the others."

"What are the others?" Anne asked. "I mean, what's behind the letters?"

"EQIP is the Environmental Quality Incentives Program. WHIP is the Wildlife Habitat Incentives Program and CSP is the Conservation Stewardship Program. Each is a little different. Under the new farm bill we now have EEEP, Enhanced Environmental Easement Program."

"EEEP?" Ezra asked.

"Yeah, EEEP. I don't know who makes these acronyms up. Probably one of my dad's customers." He waited for laughs that didn't come.

"So, in a nutshell, what is this EEEP all about?" Ezra asked. "What does it involve and what's required of us?"

Garcia Jones transitioned into a relaxed, professional manner. In the next 40 minutes he laid out the basic program of pasture rotation, water development, prescribed burns, stocking rates, and a general list of conservation do's and don'ts. "To be honest," he concluded. "The main thing is to maintain sagebrush populations. No farming, no overgrazing, no rotary mowing or burning of sage, and mostly, no oil development."

"This is a sage grouse deal, then," Ezra said flatly.

The young man smiled wryly. "Officially, no. Unofficially? Let's just say a certain big, gray-colored wild fowl, *Centrocercus urophasianus*, may have some importance in the program goals. And we like to think of this program as a reward for producers who've not eradicated Big Sage."

"Big Sage?" Anne asked.

"It's what we call black sage," Ezra explained. "The little sage."

"Then what's the tall sage we have up and down the creeks?" she asked.

"Silver sage, *Artemisia cana Pursh*." Garcia said. "It's helpful. It makes your overall inventory look good, but it has no real value to sage grouse. We are most interested in *Artemisia Tridentata Nutt*, big sage. *Artemisia filifolia* and *Artemisia frigida* are also helpful. That's sand sage and fringed sage."

"You say it's an easement," Ezra said. "That means we would be giving up some rights?"

"Yes. During the contract period. Of course, you have to qualify through a ranking assessment first."

"I suppose we would have to do some stupid things like put flags on our fences so sage grouse don't fly into them?"

"That is a very real possibility."

"Is predator control promoted?"

The boy's eye's widened. "No. Absolutely not."

"Then nothing else will work," Ezra said.

"How long is this plan?" Anne asked, breaking the tension.

"The contract is seven years," Garcia said. "The pay rate is $50,000 a year, but you'll have some expense through the cost-sharing of water improvements."

Anne's eyebrows raised. That figure was considerably more than their lease payments to Ezra's sisters.

Ezra added seven years to his present age. Sixty-eight. *Good grief.*

The young man waited patiently for the next question.

"And if we do this," Ezra said. "Will we be working with you personally?"

Garcia grimaced. "Yes and no. I'm your range conservationist and I will do some of the range inventory and oversee implementations, but this program is so new the NRCS offices are understaffed for it. We're buried in paperwork, so outside consultants, working through our Technical Service Provider Program, are being hired for EEEP."

"Whose our's?" Ezra asked.

Garcia Jones gave him a cautious look. "Have you heard of Dr. Adrienne Doyle?"

"Doyle! Ezra exclaimed. "Adrienne Doyle?"

Anne looked at Ezra nervously. "Who's she?"

"She's a troublemaker," Ezra said. "She started out with the BLM where she worked with mustangs. Then she went to the U.S. Fish and Wildlife Service. Somehow she's managed to go private and get these government gigs. She's said to be in the pocket of the most radical environmental groups."

"We're not crazy about her, either," Jones confessed. "I've never met her, but I hear she rips through little offices like ours like a bitch in heat--" He caught himself and looked at Anne. "I'm sorry," he said. "I didn't mean--"

Anne shook him off. "That's okay. I've seen a bitch in heat before."

"We have to have Doyle?" Ezra asked.

Garcia nodded. "It's her or nothing. That part is out of our hands."

"I don't get it," Ezra said. "How could she even get on with the government with her track record?"

Jones shrugged. "I assume the present administration in Washington leans in her direction."

Ezra quietly bit his lower lip and looked at Anne out of the corner of his eye. He knew more about Adrienne Doyle than he wanted to say -- had actually met her once. But Ezra saw hope in Anne's face. In spite of a spider web of regulations, this program seemed a possibility for keeping the ranch. *Saving the ranch!* He smiled to himself. It seemed like a trite phrase from old movies. The new reality was Montana was being bought up by billionaires who built trophy homes, hunted trophy elk, and bred horses they never used. And it appeared the oil boom in the region was not going to help the Riley ranch. The oil formations were to the east and north and the boom was only driving up expenses, burdening infrastructures, increasing land values, and flooding the region with workers who didn't understand or appreciate rural values.

The young man watched the rancher carefully.

"Doyle and sage grouse," Ezra said. "That sounds like a recipe for disaster."

"I can't officially comment," Jones replied.

"Is it that bad?" Anne asked.

Ezra rolled his eyes. "If the government puts the sage grouse on the Endangered Species List, ranching and farming as we know it could be over," he explained. "And Doyle could tip the balance. She could help wipe out agriculture on millions of acres."

"Approximately 186 million acres in 11 western states," Jones added.

"I thought your office already had a sage grouse program," Ezra said.

"Yes, we do. SGI. The Sage Grouse Initiative. Unofficially, this is a last-minute supplement to that program."

Ezra turned his head and stared out the window.

Anne watched her husband's haunted withdrawal and knew she needed to break the spell. "So, Garcia," she said. "Did I hear you say you like to ride?"

"Oh yeah, I'd ride every day if I could."

"Ezra always needs help riding. Don't you, Ezra?"

Ezra was deep in a sage-colored fog.

"Ezra."

He broke from his thoughts to Garcia's face shining bright with eagerness. "Uh, what?"

"You need help riding," Anne said. "Like tomorrow?"

"Tomorrow's Saturday. I can come out," Garcia said.

Ezra hesitated. Volunteer help often required babysitting. He'd call Barney, he decided. Barney Wallace was a good babysitter. "That'd be fine," Ezra said.

"I can be out by ten."

"Ten?" Ezra asked.

"Well, it's my day off," Jones explained. "I like to sleep in."

Sleep in? Ezra hadn't even heard the term in decades. "Ten might be a little late."

Garcia reddened. "How about nine?"

Ezra agreed. For him, half the day seemed over by nine, but if he was going to work with this young man he needed to know him.

"Okay," said Garcia, rising from the table. "I will leave you this EEEP information to look at. It's quite a bit to go through, but when you're done give me a call at the office and let me know what you think. Do you have any other questions?"

Ezra and Anne shook their heads.

"Okay. I have your land line number. I should get your cell phone number, too, just in case."

Ezra frowned. "I don't have a cell phone."

The young man stared at him curiously. "Cool," he said. "I've never met anyone who didn't have a cell phone. I guess you don't Tweet or text."

"Tweet?" Ezra asked. "Do I look like a bird?"

Anne nudged her husband softly. "Ignore him, Garcia," she said.

Jones noticed a television set in a bookcase. "Well, at least you have TV."

"It's not hooked-up," Ezra said. "We only use it for DVDs of British television programs we get through Netflix."

"You're kidding?"

"No. British television is more thoughtful. More subtle and nuanced than American television."

"You do have a computer, don't you?"

"Yes."

"Good. I will need to email you things from time to time."

Ezra recited his email address for him.

"Okay," Garcia said, glancing toward his pickup truck. "I'll see you tomorrow morning at nine. Take your time looking over the EEEP application. The deadline isn't until July."

"So what happens between now and then?" Ezra asked.

"I'll do a preliminary range inventory and help you with the application. Then we wait for her."

"Her? You mean..."

"Yes," Jones said. "Dr. Doyle. If you decide to apply she will determine your ranking. In some ways, your future is in her hands."

Our future in the hands of Adrienne Doyle?

Ezra had already seen what she'd done to Lynne. She'd cost him his job with Pryor Mountain wild horses.

And she had tried to do more.

17

CHAPTER THREE

Early the next morning Ezra went to his bunkhouse to write. Or to pretend to write. Most mornings he simply sat before the computer terminal and stared.

Shelves of books surrounded him -- including his two: *The Land* and *Days of Big Circles* -- and copies of magazines containing his articles were stacked in corner piles.

One reviewer had described Ezra Riley as "A writer of imposing but unpolished talent, who writes beautifully from the heart." The critic went on to say that should Riley's heart become wounded he was likely to not write at all.

Ezra felt wounded and unable to write and he didn't know which wound was most crippling. Drought? Blizzards? Family fights over land? Church conflicts? Trouble with publishers?

The many photos on the walls gave no inspiration either. Photos of ranch landscapes; scenes of friends -- Lynne, Barney, Joe -- horseback; Gabby sitting bareback on the gelding, Big Jack. The displays captured good memories but left Ezra feeling empty. How did one continue the lifestyle? Through a government program? He'd lived a rugged and independent life and had earned the scars of an uncompromising individualism. How did that square with a government contract?

It didn't.

He left the bunkhouse, knotted a black silk scarf around his neck brace, and pulled leather gloves over his taped hands. He could disguise his physical liabilities, but covering the defaults in his mind was something else. He was drowsy from codeine, cortisone, and nerve medicine. He saddled Simon and tied Big Jack outside the corral for Garcia Jones, should the young man bother to show up, then Ezra dropped to his haunches, removed his hat, and leaned back against a railroad tie. The May sun felt warm. He'd just nodded off when the slamming of a truck door awakened him.

"Sorry I'm late," Garcia said. He wore new chinks, a large, flat-brimmed straw hat, and held a shiny saddle and a crisp saddle blanket in his arms.

"The sorrel is yours," Ezra said, rising to his feet. "His name is Big Jack."

Garcia laid his saddle and blanket down and began sweeping Big Jack's hide with a new brush.

"Spend a little money at The Saddlery?" Ezra asked.

"Had to. When I left for college my mom sold all my gear."

A rattle of gravel announced the arrival of a silver Dodge pulling a small gooseneck trailer. Barney Wallace had arrived. There was a clatter and bang as Wallace unloaded his black-and-white paint, White Crow. Barney ambled toward Ezra and Garcia in his size 12 boots, Carhartt coveralls, heavy Carhartt coat, black felt hat and a crooked grin made puffy by a pinch of fake chewing tobacco. A gray mustache sprouted above his lip like a clump of dead greasewood.

"Morning, gents," Barney said cheerfully.

"Barney Wallace, meet Garcia Jones," Ezra said.

Barney broke into a gulch-wide grin and gripped the youngster's hand. "Good to meet you," he said.

Garcia said a friendly hello then went back to saddling.

Barney turned back to Ezra. "Are we riding from here or trailering?" he asked.

"Riding from here," Ezra said.

"Dog day or no-dog day?"

"I suppose your dog will be okay," Ezra said. "Casey's tied-up so he won't learn any of your dog's bad habits."

Wallace turned and yelled back at the truck. "Kitty," he yelled. "Here Kitty, Kitty." A mottled mongrel spilled from the truck and trotted over.

Garcia looked at Barney. "You have a dog named Kitty?" he asked.

"Yup," Barney said over his puffed lower lip. "I prefer cats but I can't get 'em to work a cow."

Ezra pulled the cinch tight on Simon. He was nervous about riding but was determined not to show it. Simon was springtime fresh and fat from green grass. He'd never bucked, but he was an Oswald and Ezra had little trust left in Oswalds.

Garcia struggled to mount the big sorrel. Once aboard he took a deep breath and shifted his legs to see how the stirrups felt. Ezra watched him with interest. For a skinny guy Garcia seemed soft, as if built from broomsticks and bubble wrap.

"Brand new rig?" Barney asked the redhead.

"Yeah," Garcia said. "Just got it."

"You might want to take the price tag off," Barney suggested. "Its still hanging on your D-ring there." He turned his head so the youngster could avoid further embarrassment. "What are we doing today, boss?" he asked Ezra.

"Moving the two-year-old heifers and their calves. We'll drop 'em off the divide and into the Red Hills."

Garcia studied Barney Wallace, something many had done without arriving at any conclusions. "Your voice sounds really familiar," he said finally.

"It should," Ezra interjected. "You are in the presence of Barn Wall Wallace himself, bard of the badlands, orator of outhouses, and bane of broadleaf weeds."

Barney nodded shyly. He loved attention but hadn't learned to accept it.

"The radio commercials!" Garcia noted. "You're the voice on the radio."

"He's a cartoonist," Ezra corrected. "He's only on the radio to pay his bills. Besides, he has a face for radio."

"You're a cartoonist?"

"I draw a little," Barney admitted. *"Graffiti on a Barn Wall."*

"I've seen your calendars."

"Yeah, shoot..."

"Bull sales, credit unions, used car lots, and pesticide salesmen have made him regionally famous," Ezra said. "Only ambition and talent have kept him from real success."

Barney barked a laugh. "I thrive on sarcasm," he told Jones. "Especially Ezra's."

Kitty yipped and the three turned to see an SUV drive into the yard and park behind Barney's trailer. A slender young, mid-thirties with a trimmed black beard and curly hair, stepped out. He wore tan khakis and a red pullover. His vehicle had Billings plates but looked like a rental. "Excuse me," he said. "I'm looking for Ezra Riley."

"You've found him," Ezra said.

The man approached and offered his hand. "My name is Peter Landau," he said. "I'm a freelance journalist from New York. I understand you are a person to talk to regarding horses."

"What about horses?" Ezra asked.

"I'm doing a series on the changing role and demographics of the horse in America, and in particular, in the West. I would like to get some background information from you."

"We're a little busy here."

"I understand," Landau said. "I didn't mean right now. I'll be in and out of this area for several weeks. I will certainly be around during the Bucking Horse Sale."

"I don't know that I would be that much help," Ezra said.

"I think you would be, Mr. Riley. In my preliminary research I've come across articles of yours a number of times."

Garcia's mouth dropped. No one had told him Ezra Riley was a writer.

"What's your slant?" Ezra asked.

"My slant?"

"Your angle. How are you approaching the story? What's your theme?"

"That's a fair question. Have you heard the term *husband horse?*"

"Can't say that I have." Ezra looked at Barney. Barney shrugged.

"It's a term you hear back east," Landau said. "If a horse is especially gentle and safe it is called a husband horse because most of the riders are women."

"We'd call that a kid's horse," Barney said.

"The feminization of the equine industry?" Ezra asked. "Is that your theme?"

"A main thread," Landau said. "There are other threads as well."

"You realize how volatile that subject will be?"

Landau's dark eyes steeled. "I've spent the past 12 years in the Middle East," Mr. Riley. I've made Israel my second home. I am very accustomed to volatility."

"Well, call me sometime," Ezra said. "We'll see what we can get done."

The two shook hands again. This time the New Yorker's grip made Ezra wince.

As he turned to leave, Landau stopped and looked back at the tall fellow in the black hat. They'd not been introduced, but the man was smiling at him happily.

When he got into his SUV Landau quickly scribbled in his notebook: *Interview Riley's big friend. He has a face like a welcome sign.*

22

The riders left the yard with Jones sitting tall in his new saddle on the biggest horse he'd ever ridden. His posture and expression suggested he had arrived. He was a cowboy riding with cowboys. Then Big Jack noticed a cottonwood stump glowing white in the morning sun and stopped suddenly. Jones tipped over the horse's right shoulder and landed face-first in a puddle. Mud covered his face and his new hat was bent.

"You okay?" Barney asked.

Jones sputtered an affirmative.

"You gotta watch out for those horse-eatin' stumps," Barney told him. "They're everywhere."

They worked mostly in silence. When Ezra was out of earshot Barney rode over to the youngster. "There's probably one thing I should warn you about," he told him.

Jones, already covered in mud, was apprehensive. "What's that?"

"Well, I think Ezra likes you."

"I don't understand."

"If he likes you he'll hang a nickname on you. A modifying moniker, he calls it. Do you have a nickname already?"

"No."

"Have you ever had one?"

"No."

Barney smiled. "If you hang around here enough you'll get one and it'll be so real to you you'll want to have it tooled on the back of your belt."

Barney rode off to turn a recalcitrant heifer.

Nickname? thought Garcia. *What would it be?*

The rest of the three-hour job was uneventful. Ezra rode sluggishly. Barney and Garcia visited when they weren't busy. Kitty varied from being a nuisance to being non-existent.

When the job was done they rode back to the corrals and Jones unsaddled quickly and excused himself. He wanted to get home and take a hot shower.

"I don't think he's used to being dirty," Ezra said as Garcia drove off.

"Good kid, though," Barney said. "I like him. How did you meet him?"

"Anne met him," Ezra said. He didn't want to mention government programs.

Barney glanced at his watch. "Shoot, I need to get home. I'm making supper tonight."

"Barn Wall, aren't you forgetting something?"

"What?" He felt his pockets for his glasses and cell phone.

"Kitty."

"My dog. Where's my dog?"

"He left us some time ago," Ezra said. "I was going to mention something but you were too busy chatting with Jones."

"Shoot. I guess I better go find Kitty."

"You do that. I have to ride down the creek and check my south water gap."

Barney rode up the creek until he found the dog lying exhausted in a pool. "C'mon, Kitty, let's go home," he coaxed. The dog wouldn't budge. Finally, Barney tip-toed into the water, lifted Kitty out, and set him in the saddle. The dog lay stretched across the seat dripping water down both saddle fenders. The paint didn't mind. It had carried the dog many times before. Barney led the horse back to Ezra's yard, put Kitty in the back of his pickup, and loaded the paint in his trailer.

It was dusk as he left the Riley place but light enough to see an older pickup parked on the shoulder of the highway. A large, bald-headed man with an orange goatee waved Barney down.

Barney slowed to a stop and got out. "Having trouble?" he asked.

"Run outa gas," the big man said. In the truck's cab another man was slumped against the passenger door. "Gotta get my cousin to the dentist."

"The dentist? It's after six. They'll be closed."

"'Mergency. They waitin' for us. We come all the way from Williston." A pink scar stuck to the left side of his face like a pinworm. Tattoos covered his neck in a rash of blue ink.

"Shoot, you got a gas can?" Barney asked.

The man rummaged in the back and came up with a red plastic container.

Barney took it from him. "My buddy lives just back there. I'll be right back." Barney turned his pickup and trailer around, pulled up to Ezra's bulk tank, filled the container and drove back to the strangers.

The bald-headed man emptied the gas can into the truck's tank. "Thanks," he said, not offering to pay. He got in, tromped a few times on the pedal, and the truck sputtered to life and rattled away.

Barney shrugged. "I guess some people just don't like to visit," he told Kitty. Barney saw the best in people but he also had an artist's eye for detail. The man stood stood two inches taller than him and was 50 pounds heavier. The truck was an '84 Ford half-ton Crew Cab two-wheel drive and the mud on its Nevada plates looked applied as if to obscure the numbers. Barney guessed the driver's age at 25. He didn't get a look at the passenger. Barney suspicioned the two were living out of the truck.

"Kitty," he warned. "I don't want you playing with those boys. I think they're probably trouble."

His own generous nature corrected him. "Well, maybe not trouble," he warned the dog. "But they certainly bear watching."

Kitty whined in agreement.

25

CHAPTER FOUR

T he alarm buzzed. Garcia rolled over and cracked an eyelid to spy the clock. He wanted to slam the snooze button but didn't dare. He'd already done it twice. For his second Saturday at the Riley Ranch he wanted to be on time.

He looked at the clock again. It was later than he thought. He fought from the covers and dressed in a panic, the clothes on the floor flying up and landing on his skinny frame like cranes alighting on a bare tree. He shouldn't have stayed up late playing *Call of Duty 4*, but he said that every night. If it wasn't *Call of Duty* it was *Counter-Strike* or *Battlefield*.

A drive-through espresso booth provided breakfast.

When he pulled into the Riley yard he saw that Simon and White Crow were already saddled. Wallace was sitting on his truck's tailgate with Kitty's head in his lap.

"Morning," Barney said. "Beautiful day to be horseback."

Garcia hustled to get his horse saddled.

Ezra came from the tack room wearing his silk scarf and leather gloves though the morning was warm for May.

"Bet you really miss Lynne on a day like this," Barney said.

"Actually I miss him on the cold days when I can't get you to leave your house."

Barney chuckled. He was unashamedly a fair weather cowboy, warped for life by childhood days riding in frigid weather. "When we branding?" he asked.

"When you find me a crew."

"Shoot, I'll find you a crew," Barney said. "I already have some people in mind."

"From that subdivision you live in?" Ezra asked.

"Maybe."

"What subdivision is that?" Garcia asked.

"The one just over the hill," Ezra said. "I border it for two miles. Barn Wall lives on 40 acres. He's tucked up into the cedars like a magpie."

"Has the writer been back?" Barney asked.

"Who?"

"The New York guy."

"No, I haven't seen him."

"Shoot. I hope he comes back and makes you famous, Ez. Then maybe people will hear about your books and make one into a movie."

Garcia frowned. He didn't know Ezra had written books. He thought he'd only written magazine articles.

Ezra ignored the movie comment. *Days of Big Circles* had been optioned twice without going into production. "The writer is legitimate," Ezra said. "I checked him out. Very good credentials. Not a blogger. He writes for major print publications and a few Jewish periodicals."

"Jewish?" Barney said. "What's he doing in the West writing about horses?"

"Who knows?" Ezra said, swinging up onto Simon. "Everyone's looking for something. Maybe he always wanted to be a cowboy."

"I always wanted to be a cowboy," Barney joked.

Ezra reined Simon to the north and left the yard at a trot. "Well, let's go practice," he called back to Barney. "Maybe one of us will make it yet."

It was early evening. Barney had unsaddled and grained White Crow, poured himself a tall glass of sweet tea, and was settling into his favorite chair to do some cartooning when a knock came at his door. He was surprised to see the New York writer.

"Mr. Wallace, I'm Peter Landau. We weren't introduced the other day."

"Come in, come in." Barney was delighted. If he'd had a tail he would have wagged it. "Tea?" he asked, leading the writer to the living room.

"Yes, thank you very much."

They settled into chairs in a cathedral style room with Longhorn steer skulls and western art decorating the off-white walls. "What can I do for you?" Barney asked.

Landau took a sip of tea to clear his throat. "As you heard me tell Mr. Riley, I'm working on a series of articles on horses in today's culture. I know Mr. Riley is a good lead but he doesn't seem very approachable. I thought you might be able to give me some insight."

"Shoot, what do you want to know?"

"I haven't read Mr. Riley's books yet, but I've read a number of his articles."

Barney reached to a bookcase, pulled out Ezra's two books and handed them to Landau. "You can borrow these," he said.

"Thanks. I'll get them back to you. The articles I've read were historical but not about the Old West. They focused on a period from 1890 to 1960."

"The modern horse era. As opposed to this post-modern horse era we're in now."

"I don't follow."

"Ezra writes about the days before horses became toys. Back when they were real ranch horses. Working partners."

"Okay. I think I can follow that, But he also writes about people who aren't well known. The piece he did on this fellow, Lynne, for example ---"

"Oh, shoot, yes. We sure miss Lynne."

"So you knew him?"

"Knew him for years. Used to watch him ride broncs when I was a little kid. He was one of my heroes. He was always one of the matched bronc riders at the Bucking Horse Sale."

"One of the articles about this Lynne mentioned a Kramer Ranch?"

"Yeah. Lynne worked for the Kramers. Then he got hired by the BLM to gather loose horses out of the Missouri Breaks. After that he took the mustang job in the Pryors." That ended somehow so he cowboyed for day wages and raised horses with Ezra."

"He must have been an interesting fellow."

"Sure was. Sort of a rascal with flavoring, but a gentleman at the same time."

"I couldn't find any record of him on-line."

"Oh, he wasn't anybody famous. Well-liked but never famous."

"Never a champion bronc rider?"

"No," Barney said. "He rode well enough but he never won the world or anything."

"But he was obviously the type of man who left an impression on people."

"Shoot, yeah. In fact, before Lynne passed away he got a phone call from a woman from back east who'd met him when he rode at the Garden in '59 ---"

"The Madison Square Garden?"

"Yeah, that's right. This gal tracked him down after all those years. She'd been widowed and called hoping he was single."

"I guess he'd left an impression with her."

"Yeah. I think her call left an impression with Lynne's wife, too. Want more tea?"

The reporter waved him off. "Thanks, but no. This name Oswald that Mr. Riley writes about so often, I take it to be a line of horses? It kept coming up in the articles on Lynne."

"Yup. Ezra could tell you more about those. That bay he was holding the other day is an Oswald and he still has a band of Oswald mares. The Oswald line has been around a long time."

"Are they different or special somehow?"

"They're cowboy horses," Barney said, sipping his tea. "Tough. All-day horses. Especially smart, Ezra says. But, he's into pedigrees, not me. I just want them short and gentle."

"A husband horse?"

"Yeah. If you say so."

"So, tell me. What's hurting him?"

"Hurting him? Hurting who?"

"Mr. Riley. He grimaced when I shook his hand."

Barney thick eyebrows raised like cedars boughs in a windstorm. "I don't know," he said. "I heard he went to a doctor recently. It probably has something to do with the two horse wrecks he had last fall."

"Horse wrecks? You mean, he was bucked off?"

"Yup. I wasn't there. He was alone both times. They happened about a week apart I guess. Pretty bad wrecks, I suspect."

"What happened? Don't you know?"

"Another Oswald," the cartoonist said. "A bad one. One that he and Lynne had raised." Barney gave the reporter a long look. "So, what's this all got to do with Ezra, this story of yours?"

"I don't know, yet. I'm following the story to see where it leads."

"Well, if you want to know about horses and history, Ezra's your man."

"Is he? He doesn't seem to like journalists."

Barney chuckled. "Don't take it personal. Ezra loves the West and he hates what most city writers write when they come here."

"It's that bad?"

"Ezra says so. I don't read papers much. Except for the comics."

Landau softly rattled the ice in his glass.

"Shoot. You need more tea?"

"No, no. Just a habit."

Barney poured him more anyway.

"Thanks." Landau took a sip. "I Googled you, too, Mr. Wallace."

Barney smiled. "I've always wanted to be Googled."

"Because Ezra didn't introduce us, I described you to a waitress in town to get your name and she knew who I was talking about right away."

Barney beamed.

"She said you always forgot something when you dined there. Your phone, your wallet, your sunglasses."

"Yeah, well, I am famous for that."

"You and Ezra are an interesting pair. You're both artists, but in different ways." He nodded at Barney's sketchpad. "You're a cartoonist. I've seen your work in stores downtown. But he's very serious. You two must balance each other."

"Balance? I guess it could be called that, but I think more in terms of water."

"Water?"

"Yeah. Ezra likes the deep end of the pool. He swims with the sharks. Not me. I'm scared of deep water. Can't swim. The ripples and the trickles, the chuckles and the giggles. Those are deep enough for me."

Landau smiled almost imperceptibly. Barney Wallace was toying with him. "You're rather arcadian," he said.

"No, I'm American. The only time I was in Canada was for rodeos. Say, are you going to be in this area for awhile?"

"Yes, for a week or two."

"Well, shoot, you can stay here. No sense wasting money on a motel room."

"But--"

"I insist. I'll help you pack your stuff in. Mrs. Wallace loves company. 'Course, she's not here. She's at a conference in Helena for a couple days, but Kitty and I love company." He looked at the reporter earnestly. "You have met Kitty, haven't you?"

"Yes, I have. Now, back to Mr. Riley's articles if I may. He writes about the CBC organization."

"Yeah. Chappel Brothers Cannery. His dad and my dad both rode for 'em."

"It's hard to find information on-line about them, too."

"I suppose. I don't use computers much. The CBCs were special but they weren't unusual, if you know what I mean."

"No. I can't say that I do."

"Well, that was the Thirties. The Great Depression. The whole West was flooded with feral horses. States passed laws requiring their removal. The Chappels just figured out how to make it profitable."

"They ran a dog food company."

"Yup. They put those horses in a can. Of course, they did more than that. They also exported them to Europe and Russia for human consumption."

"In my travels I've seen horse meat on many menus."

"Yup. But not in America. It's banned here and the slaughter plants closed down."

"How do you feel about that?"

"It's bad for the horse business. Too many horses in the pipeline."

"These CBC cowboys, Mr. Riley writes about them with a certain respect."

"Sure. They were the best of the best. Handling horses, especially wild horses, isn't like handling cows. It's fast, wild, and dangerous."

"This Bucking Horse Sale that's coming up, does it derive from the CBC days?"

"No. Well, maybe in spirit, I suppose, but that's more Ezra's deal."

"You mean, history?"

"No, spiritual things."

"Spiritual things?"

"Yeah. He's been a minister off and on. More off than on lately."

"A minister?"

"Some sort of minister. I don't really understand it. He interprets dreams for people, I know that much."

"So, he's not simply a strait-laced older cowboy?"

"Strait-laced? Shoot, Ezra's an old hippy. He once had hair below his shoulders and wrote hippy poetry. It never made much sense to me."

"So the two of you have been friends for a long time?"

"Yes and no," Barney said. "We went our different ways when we were young. I followed the rodeo trail and he went hitchhiking and spent a little time in jail."

"In jail? What for?"

"I can't say I remember. Something that happened on his travels."

"Like this Lynne fellow, it seems Ezra Riley is an interesting man."

"Oh yeah, but Lynne and Ezra weren't that much alike except for their love of horses and cowboying."

"What was their differences?" Landau asked. "If you don't mind me inquiring."

"Shoot, you're a reporter. You have to ask questions."

"And?" Landau asked.

"The differences? I guess it's Ezra being a writer and minister. Lynne was all cowboy. A cowboy's cowboy." Barney turned and stared out the window at the distant badlands of the Riley ranch as if to pluck words from the grass.

"Maybe Mr. Riley won't be a good subject for my article," Landau said.

"Oh, he'd be good. He knows horse history and how to put things into words."

"But he's not very typical."

"Shoot. Who is? Just stay out of the deep pool with Ezra. He attracts sharks."

"How about if I used you?"

"Me?"

"Yes. You have the background."

"No. You should use Ezra." Barney stood up and examined his empty tea glass. "If you use Ezra you might end up in a novel some day," he said. He jiggled the glass and listened to the ice tinkling. "Use me," he said. "And you'll end up in a cartoon."

CHAPTER FIVE

Garcia Jones was in cowboy heaven.

He had a bag of popcorn, large Coke, hot dog, and the Sunday matched bronc riding performance of the World Famous Miles City Bucking Horse Sale before him. The first two days' events -- bull riding, wild horse races, and amateur cowboys on untested broncs -- had amused him but he'd waited feverishly for the match.

Top bronc riders on top horses. Pure art.

He'd been obsessed with bronc riders since finding a reel of 16mm movie film after his grandfather's death. He'd had it converted to a DVD and the result was a grainy, shaky chronicle of his grandparents and father, then 14, vacationing in Montana in 1965. Clips of Beartooth Highway, Glacier Park, and Virginia City were mixed in with fuzzy portrayals of roadside picnic tables, trout streams, and tame elk on pavement.

His father's behavior in the scenes was shameful. He was a skinny, bushy-haired, sullen punk who took every chance to flip the cameraman the bird.

Dad, obviously, had not enjoyed the vacation.

The highlight of the movie reel was scenes from a rodeo. The camera captured a charismatic young cowboy behind a set of old, weathered bronc chutes. The young man looked directly at the camera before climbing up on the chutes and settling down on his horse.

To Garcia the cowboy's face showed honesty, courage, and friendliness.

Then the camera's view rushed in bounces to the fence where the cameraman squeezed next to a skinny little boy in a big cowboy hat. The chute gate appeared through blurred black squares of woven wire. It swung open and a bay saddle bronc soared high in the air and seemed suspended there, frozen in time. The cowboy balanced on its back gracefully, his front feet above the horse's shoulders with his toes turned out and sunlight reflecting off the saddle swells and the rowels of his spurs.

It was as if the cowboy rode the wind.

Jones decided this is who he wanted to be. This was the opposite of the long-haired, overweight, dope-smoking father who'd named him after a countercultural rock star.

Garcia was jammed into the grandstands next to a vacationing family from Wisconsin. In his new felt hat -- replacing the straw one Big Jack had ruined -- he was certain he blended in as a working cowboy.

The loudspeakers crackled above his head. The match was finally beginning. One-by-one contestants were announced and their accomplishments listed as they walked to the center of the arena, waved to the crowd, and waited in a line of presentation. Horseback, the rodeo queen and her court circumscribed the arena with the U.S. and Montana flags and the people stood for the national anthem. At its end a cheer erupted and the bronc riders filed back to the chutes.

"And let's not forget today's judges," the announcer's voice boomed. Garcia paid no attention to the first three names, but the fourth caught his ear. "And our head judge, hailing from here in Miles City, Montana, a two-time qualifier for the National Finals

Rodeo in saddle bronc riding, and the creator of the popular cartoon strip, *Graffiti on a Barn Wall*, Mr. Barney Wallace."

Garcia straightened on the hard bench and strained to see better. Barney had been a bronc rider? No one had said anything to him. His day became bathed in a fine glow. He turned to the tourists. "The head judge is a friend of mine," he said. "He and I have been working cattle together the last few weeks."

The wife seemed impressed. "Are you a rodeo cowboy, too?" she asked.

"No," Garcia said, affecting modesty. "I'm more of a ranch cowboy."

The woman looked at him thoughtfully, nodded, then turned back to the arena action.

When the event was over Garcia made a point of meeting Barney at his pickup. "Hey there," Garcia yelled as Barney folded himself into the truck.

Wallace was so tired even his mustache drooped. "Hey, Garcia," he answered. "How are ya, pard?"

"You never told me you'd been to the Finals."

"Oh, shoot, that was a long time ago. Hardly worth mentioning."

"What years were you there?"

"Seventy-four and seventy-five."

"A guy in the stands said you quit young. That you might have gone on and won the World."

"Oh, I doubt that, but yeah, I did quit young."

"What happened. Did you get hurt?"

"No, just got tired of traveling. Mrs. Wallace and I had two little ones and I wasn't seeing them much."

"That's was it. You just quit?"

"Well, actually, I did have an epiphany."

Garcia waited breathlessly.

"Second trip to the NFR I was leading the World through five rounds then they threw the eliminator pen at us. I drew Desolation of the Cervi string. A chute-fighter. They had a neck rope on him but he slipped it, reared up and came over backward on me."

Garcia's blue eyes lit with anticipation.

"There I was, doubled-up at the bottom of the chute with 1300 pounds of bronc atop me. About then I got to thinking that there had to be an easier way of making a living."

"That must of made you claustrophobic," Garcia said.

"No, no. It made me *broncophobic.*"

"So you started drawing cartoons?"

"No, that came later. Well, shoot, I gotta get home and feed White Crow and Kitty. Kitty's sure to have missed me."

Garcia watched his truck until it disappeared into the flow of traffic. Barney Wallace. More than just a cartoonist.

Peter Landau's rented SUV was packed with files, books, notebooks, magazines and newspapers. He'd had a busy week with visits to the Billings Livestock Commission, tours of the Pryor Mountain wild horse herd, and a stop at the large Padlock Ranch on his way back to Miles City and its Bucking Horse Sale. Covering the sale meant wading through crowds of drunks on streets graveled with beer cans and paper cups. He saw why Ezra Riley-- whom he'd tried calling several times -- stayed home that weekend.

Finally Landau reached him. "Can we meet after Sunday's bronc riding?" he asked.

"Sounds okay," Ezra said.

"Is there any chance we can get horseback together?"

There was a long pause before Ezra grunted an affirmative.

As he pulled up to the Riley corrals Landau reminded himself not to shake Ezra's hand too hard. Firm but not painful.

Ezra stepped from the corrals leading Simon and Big Jack. "We have less than two hours of light," Ezra said. "So I suppose we should get going."

Landau swung easily onto the big sorrel. Anne's saddle fit him perfectly and Ezra noticed he wasn't carrying a camera or notebook.

"We're heading east," Ezra said. "I have something to show you."

They lined out at a stiff trot with Casey bouncing happily behind them.

"What did you think of the sale?" Ezra asked.

"I don't know what to think. I'm not sure if it is a legitimate western event or simply an excuse for people to party."

"Good observation." Ezra broke Simon into a soft lope. "Where did you go on your little trip?"

Landau listed his itinerary.

"Pryor Mountains," Ezra said. "My late friend Lynne managed the wild horses there for twenty years until he quit."

"Why did he quit?"

Ezra sat easily on Simon's rocking-chair lope. "Have you heard of Dr. Adrienne Doyle?"

"Yes, I have." He did not mention he'd met her several times.

"Lynne quit because of Doyle."

He pulled Simon up on a high ridge overlooking the subdivision and swept the view with his hand. "This is what I wanted to show you. What do you see?"

"I see a subdivision with houses, barns, cars."

"And horses. Every lot has five to ten horses."

Landau looked at him curiously.

"This scene is repeated all over the nation. What are the horses doing?"

"Nothing. Just standing."

"And that's all many of them ever do. They're simply ornaments."

"We don't see anyone riding right now, but certainly the horses must get rode."

"Some do. But many of them just stand around, bored to death."

"And your point is..?"

"There are ten million horses in America. How many do you suppose live like this?"

"I don't know, but I suspect you are going to say it's the majority."

"Possibly, I don't know. I do know many of those horses are well-bred. Well-bred horses need a job. A horse with a thousand years of service in its blood was never meant to be a pasture ornament."

"You're saying these horses are dying of boredom?"

"At the least, they are not fulfilling their purpose."

Landau pointed to a grove of large cottonwoods where a massive indoor arena could be seen rising above the trees. "What's that large building?" he asked. "I can see some activity down there."

"That's the Boothe place. I don't know much about it. Barney says some rich kid lives there. He had a falling out with his sister so his grandfather bought four tracts, bulldozed the houses down, and built that new house and indoor arena."

"Corey Boothe," Landau said.

"You know him?"

"I know of him. His grandfather, Harlan Boothe, is an eccentric billionaire who made his fortune in space technology. He bought his two grandkids a horse ranch near Missoula to keep them out of trouble while their father's in prison."

"How is he eccentric?"

"He often travels alone taking scenic photos. No bodyguards."

"He sounds normal except for the money. Barn Wall says its all first class down there. Anything the boy wants he gets."

"Barn Wall?" Landau asked.

"A term of endearment for Barney Wallace. I hear you visited his magpie nest?"

"Yes," Landau said. He didn't mention that he was staying there. "Very nice fellow."

"Did you see the paintings on his walls?"

"The western art? Yes, he's put together a very nice collection."

"He didn't collect them. He painted them. Those are his."

40

Landau whistled softly. "It seems Barn Wall knows more than barn walls."

"Have you seen his cartoons?"

"He gave me a couple of his little books."

"Have you ever seen cleaner lines or a better use of shadowing?"

"No, I haven't. He's very professional."

"Yes, he is. You should interview him. You're probably looking for a pivotal subject, an archetypal character to build your story around. Barney Wallace would be your guy."

"Why him?"

"Because he has a true sense of humor. He makes fun of himself, not other people."

"I can see he doesn't seem to let things bother him much."

"Humor is his armor."

"I don't write comic pieces."

"He's more than comedy. He's a former NFR bronc rider and the son of a CBC cowboy." Ezra nudged Simon into a turn and pointed him home.

Landau reined Big Jack to follow. "But, you're the son of a CBC cowboy, too. I know that through your articles."

"Yes, I am."

"So what does it mean to be a son of a CBC cowboy?"

"It means knowing how to trot for miles and go without food or water."

"Barney loaned me his copies of your books. I've only glanced at them. You've had a non-fiction published by a literary house and a novel published by a religious publisher."

"A *Christian* publisher. I don't like the word *religious*."

Landau noted the undertone. "Were your publishing experiences difficult?"

Ezra shrugged. "The secular houses want political correctness and cynicism and the Christian houses demand bland mediocrity and sentimentality. Other than that, no difficulties at all."

"After I've read your books I would like to talk to you about your writing."

"Why?" Ezra's eyes were straight ahead. The soreness in his neck kept him from turning to make eye contact.

"I know you can teach me much about horses and the West. Probably about writing, too."

"You Googled me. I Googled you," Ezra said. "I'm doubt there's much I can teach you about writing."

"You're very cautious of journalists."

"It's been years since I met an honest one."

"Then you won't help me on this article?"

"Mr. Landau, I don't know if I am going to help you or not. You come here from New York to do an article about the West. Why? The past 30 years I've seen one journalist after another do their token cowboy story then leave without considering its effects. You're an experienced foreign correspondent. What are you doing in Miles City, Montana? You should be in Tel Aviv, Jerusalem, or Kabul."

Landau stared into the distance. The setting sun painted his face golden and accented the red highlights in his beard.

"Fair enough," he said. "I'm burnt-out. I've seen too much. I need to clear my head. What better place than the American West?"

"But what are you looking for, Mr. Landau? Solace? Do you expect the vast landscapes to cleanse your view of the human condition?"

"Why do I have to be looking for something? I'm here to do a job."

"An article on horses from a Middle East war correspondent?"

"I know a little about horses, Mr. Riley. I rode considerably before I moved to Israel."

"But do you understand rural people?"

"I'm here to write about horses. Not people."

"For some of us that's a thin line."

Dusk settled in a sheet of cool dimness. Ezra zipped his jacket to his chin.

"You're not completely ruling out helping me, though, are you?" Landau asked.

"Are you a man of your word, Mr. Landau?"

"I am."

"Will you treat my friends with respect? I'm not worried about me, but I take care of my friends."

"Yes, I will."

The rancher nodded and offered a handshake. "Okay. It's a deal. But don't mention my hands."

"You know that I've noticed?"

"We're both writers," Ezra said. "We are supposed to notice things."

CHAPTER SIX

The Saturday of Memorial Day weekend Ezra sat on Simon in the summer corrals on Dead Man Creek watching the sun rise over the breaks while Anne and Garcia sipped coffee and visited in the pickup. To guarantee his punctuality, Garcia had spent the night at the Rileys'.

Ezra was anxious because Barney had assembled the branding crew but no one had arrived. Not even Barney.

Ezra smiled as two broods of sage grouse chicks, fuzzy as tennis balls, scurried through the cover of the corral's tall grass. Sage hens regularly hatched their eggs in his pens because the woven wire offered protection from coyotes.

The summer corrals were eight miles north of the house and sat on a high, grassy flat from which one could see much of the pasture's 7680 acres. A flicker of movement on the ridge two miles to the south caught Ezra's eye. The Oswald mares were tasting the breeze. "You can relax, girls," Ezra whispered to himself. "We're not after you." Even from a distance Ezra imagined their distinctiveness: tall, stretchy mares, clean and trim of head, neck and limb, and carrying the awareness and presence old-timers called "the look of eagles." He needed to gather them for worming but hadn't decided how. All were halter-broke and gentle, but range mares left to themselves quickly resorted to feral instincts. They wouldn't trot into the corrals willingly.

"Are you watching the mares?" Anne called from the truck.

Ezra nodded.

Anne turned to Garcia. "He needs to gather those mares," she explained. "But I don't think he really wants to."

"How come?" Garcia asked.

"Because it means facing the question of what to do with them," Anne said. "The horse market is terrible, especially for ranch-type broodmares. Through a sales ring they'd sell by the pound and go to slaughter. I don't think Ezra's ready to send the last of the Oswald line to a slaughterhouse."

"I don't know anything about bloodlines," Garcia said.

Anne smiled. "Me, either."

Dust rose from the county road. Ezra guessed Barn Wall was making his appearance and moments later his silver pickup and gooseneck trailer crested a hill and came into view. The truck rattled to a stop by the loading chute and Ezra was surprised when Peter Landau stepped from the passenger side. He thought the New Yorker was on an excursion. Ezra also hoped this wasn't the sum total of Barney's crew. Barney unloaded White Crow and Anne and Garcia got out of the Riley truck to welcome them.

"Beautiful morning," Barney said.

Ezra nodded at them. "Mr. Landau, I thought you'd left our fair country."

"I was gone and I'm back. I still have many questions for you, Ezra."

"Well, you must be a heck of a hand if you're all the help Barney brought me," Ezra said.

"More comin'," Barney said. "Should be here any minute."

"You didn't bring a horse for our journalist?" Ezra asked.

"Shoot," Barney said. "I forgot."

"Well, let's get the cattle corralled," Ezra said. "When your mystery crew shows up we'll brand."

The four riders mounted up and lined-out toward the creek.

Landau stayed at the corrals and killed time by examining their construction and imagining their stories. The posts were old railroad ties. When had that track been laid? When was it tore up? A piece of wood tacked to a corner post caught his eye. It was a small surveyor's stake with something scribbled on it in red ink. The lettering was faded and unreadable. He made a mental note to ask Ezra about it sometime.

There was a deep peace about the corrals. It had the flavor, somehow, of Israel? He wondered why that would be? A similar atmosphere between two such disparate regions of the world? He'd have to ask Ezra about that, too. Sometime.

An hour later the cacophony of bellowing cows surrounded Ezra as he put another cedar fencepost on the branding fire. "The irons are hot," he said to Barney. "Where's the crew?"

Wallace, who had the advantage of four inches in height, looked over Ezra's head. "Here they come now," he said. Two dually pickups pulling aluminum horse trailers came into view. One truck and trailer had "Boothe Performance Horses" painted on the sides. Ezra stared at Wallace incredulously.

Wallace shrugged. "They're young," he said. "We old guys need young help."

"Are they going to be any help?"

"Shoot, the two guys with Boothe are cutting horse trainers," Barney explained. "The other three are students from Kansas. They should all know cattle."

Ezra watched six young men unload three horses from each trailer. Not one horse was over 14 hands and 1000 pounds. Boothe's trailer, a 24-foot aluminum gooseneck, had other horses in the front stall.

"Aim low," Ezra said. "Because they're riding Shetlands."

"Shoot, they ain't Shetlands," Barney said. "They're cuttin' horses."

The students tied their horses to the side of their trailer. The trainers, led by a wiry, athletic-looking cowboy with a diamond stud in his left ear, led their horses into the branding pen.

"Corey," Barney shouted over the crackling of the fire and bellowing of the cattle. "Come on over."

Corey Boothe, with curly blond hair creeping out from under an expensive custom hat, walked with an insolence that immediately put Ezra on edge. Introductions were made. Boothe's eyes were bloodshot, his nostrils were red and irritated, and his eyes rolled in his head like marbles in a cardboard box. Ezra knew the look. The two trainers looked even more stoned. "We're here to rope cattle," Boothe declared, looking through Ezra and Barney like they were clothes flapping in the breeze.

Ezra's mind hardened. Barney had brought him three coke-heads and their student victims. He looked at the three students as they stepped into the pen. They had a solid, weathered look, appeared sober, and seemed embarrassed to be with Boothe's bunch. Their names were Howie, Harold and Wilbur Miller -- two brothers and a cousin, 18 to 21 years old -- from a large ranch in Kansas. "You boys know how to wrestle calves?" Ezra asked.

"We can wrestle," said Howie, the oldest.

Ezra appraised his crew. "Where's Henrietta?" he asked Barney. "Your wife always vaccinates."

Wallace slapped himself on his forehead. "Shoot, I forgot her," he said.

"You forgot your wife?"

"I was so busy getting these guys squared-away that I forgot Henrietta."

Ezra shook his head in wonder. Barney forgetting his dog was nothing new, but forgetting his wife? "How could you forget her?" he said. "I thought she dressed you in the morning so you wouldn't leave the house without clothes."

"I can call her. I think I have my cell phone."

"You'll need to gallop up on that ridge to get service."

Barney hustled toward his horse.

Ezra looked at Anne. "You'll have to brand and vaccinate until Henrietta get's here," he said. "Landau, Garcia, I'll need you guys to wrestle. These three Kansas boys will teach you how. Barney will have to wrestle, too. That'll give us three teams. I'll castrate and help Anne brand." They all nodded. Secretly, Ezra wondered if he'd be able to castrate, a skill that required strength and feeling in his hands, something he didn't have.

It only took minutes for Ezra to realize Boothe and his buddies were not experienced ropers. Boothe flung a 60-foot rawhide reata and cast loops he'd probably only seen on videos. The other two used long poly ropes. One, probably too stoned to dally well, was tied on hard-and-fast. Their horses were confused. Trained for cutting, they wanted to work cows not position riders to rope calves. One horse reared over backward spilling its rider in the dirt. The boy cussed as he got up.

Ezra gave him a hand up. "You okay?" he asked.

The trainer cursed a blue streak.

"I'd rather you didn't talk like that," Ezra said.

The stoned horse trainer looked at Ezra like he were a museum display.

For as worthless as Boothe and his two sycophants were, the Kansas boys, were hands. They taught Garcia and Landau to efficiently handle the calves that got dragged to them. In a lull in the action Howie walked up beside Ezra. "Those guys are idiots," he said softly, staring at the ropers. "We came a thousand miles because we heard about this new cutting school, but the whole thing's a joke. Those guys can cut, but it's all the horses. That little roan Boothe is on cost $200,000."

Just then Boothe came in dragging a calf roped high above one hock on forty feet of line. After the Kansas boys got the calf on the ground Ezra approached him. "Don't drag them in on so much rope,"

Ezra said politely. "It makes them too hard to handle and all that rope is dangerous for the crew. Dally-up short." Boothe stared down at Ezra disdainfully then nudged the roan back to the herd.

Henrietta arrived. She was a slender woman whose compassionate face was ringed with red curls. She picked up a vaccine gun and went to work.

"Good to see you, girl," Ezra yelled over the noise of the cattle.

"Good to see you, too," she yelled back. "I would have been here sooner but someone left me and took my car keys with him. I had to find an extra set."

The crew passed on Ezra's offer for a mid-morning break and worked through to lunch. Anne's famous branding beans simmered in a Dutch Oven in the coals of the branding fire. When the beans were ready Ezra gave the ropers the signal to tie their horses.

Boothe strolled toward the fire, his two sidekicks trailing in his wake. Anne handed out bottles of water, soft drinks and tea. Boothe looked in the cooler. "Where's the beer?" he demanded.

"Sorry, we never have beer at our branding," Ezra said.

"No beer," Boothe growled. "What kind of branding is this?"

"It's best to be sober around livestock and fire," Ezra said.

Boothe swore to himself and kicked the cooler. The commotion caught everyone's attention.

Barney, frantic for a diversion, rushed over and pointed to the horizon where the Oswald mares danced. "There's your mares," he announced.

Ezra played along. "Yeah, I need to gather them but they're not easy to corral."

"Hell," Boothe said while whirling around and trying to find the mares in the landscape. "We'll go get 'em."

"Its time for lunch," Ezra said.

"Hell. Who eats? We'll have those mares for lunch." He looked at his two trainers. They agreed numbly. Corey was their meal ticket and they saddled any idea he suggested.

"It's not that easy," Ezra said.

"Hell, they're just range mares."

"Your horses are tired--" Ezra began.

"We got fresh horses in the trailer. They need some exercise." He reached into a shirt pocket and pulled out a roll of bills. "Five hundred bucks says we pen those mares before you finish your beans."

Ezra looked sideways at Anne. Her eyes cautioned him not to take the bet. Barney's eyes said he regretted bringing Boothe to the branding. The others watched expectantly.

"I don't think--" Ezra began.

"What's wrong, old-timer. No sportin' blood?"

Ezra couldn't resist the challenge. "Okay, done deal," he said. "You have one hour."

Boothe turned to his sidekicks. "Let's go, boys. Easy money." They led their tired ponies to the trailer and unloaded three fresh horses.

"Your money's safe," Howie whispered. "They couldn't gather balls off a billiards table."

"And they've never seen an Oswald," Ezra said.

"Oswald?" Howie said. "I've heard my grandfather talk about a horse named Oswald. He was a match race horse in Kansas years ago."

Ezra smiled. "That's the one. He was bred in Oklahoma, almost disappeared in Kansas, then came to Montana in the Fifties and a whole line of horses was built around him."

The kid shook his head. "I've only heard about 'em. I thought they'd all disappeared years ago. From what I've been told, I'm sure those stoners have never seen anything like an Oswald."

"And they're not going to get a very close look at these," Ezra said.

From the corner of his eye the Kansas boy saw Mrs. Riley approaching. There was something in her step that suggested he step away.

"Ezra," Anne said. "What are you doing?"

"There's no risk," he said. "There's one chance in ten they can gather those mares."

"I'm not worried about the money."

Ezra looked at her curiously. "Then what are you worried about?"

"What if he gets hurt? Ezra, that's a billionaire's grandson."

"Well, he shouldn't have to worry about medical bills then."

"You know what I mean."

"Anne, I don't think his grandpa is going to sue us if something happens to little Corey. Besides, he might be a jerk, and stoned out of his gourd, but Boothe can ride."

"Ezra, it's more than that. You know it wasn't the right thing to do. Especially here where we've done so much work, so much cleansing."

"What was I supposed to do?"

"You should have just ignored him. You can never walk away."

He sighed. "Well, maybe. But it's done now and there's only one thing we can do."

"And what's that?" Anne asked.

"Have lunch and watch the show," he said.

CHAPTER SEVEN

"Shoot, this is great," Barney said through a mouthful of brownie. "Dinner with a show. Better than Vegas."

The crew had moved plastic lawn chairs to a knoll just west of the corrals for a better view of the event. Balancing paper plates filled with beans, sandwiches and brownies in their laps, they watched Boothe and his two cohorts trot south.

"Do they have a chance of succeeding?" Landau asked.

"Not the way they're approaching the mares," Ezra explained. "He's just alerting them. If he put one guy to each side, then got around behind the mares without being seen, they might have a slight chance. As it is the mares are going to turn and run to the back fence. From there it's a three mile race this way. Those little cutting horses can't run with an Oswald."

The mares disappeared from the skyline.

"Twenty minutes from now they'll come this way," Ezra said. "There won't be a rider within a quarter-mile of them. Hopefully, Boothe will call it quits and not keep pursuing them."

"What'll happen if he tries?" Garcia asked.

"He'll kill that expensive horse he's riding," Ezra said. His own words sobered him. Boothe was idiot enough to do exactly that. He glanced to the corrals where Simon was tied and considered trying to stop the madness. "How ripped are those guys?" he asked Howie Miller. "Is it just coke or they do meth, too?"

"Coke and whiskey," Howie said. "Boothe thinks he's above meth."

They finished their meal in silence. What had seemed entertaining in the beginning now had a sad, tragic air about it.

"Mares coming," Barney said. The horses boiled from a tangle of roughs to the south, striding easily with a fence line at their left shoulders. There were no pursuers in sight.

"This is like the CBCs," Barney said. "A wild horse stampede across the sagebrush plains."

"It's not even close," Ezra muttered.

Landau looked at him wanting an explanation.

"My dad and Barney's dad rode for different wagons, but both rode in stampedes," Ezra explained. "My father's was at night and covered 60 miles."

"And the end result?" asked Landau.

"He turned the herd but rode his horse to death."

"How did your father feel about that?"

"He never said. He just said he got the herd turned."

"Here they come," Garcia exclaimed.

The mares rose onto the grassy plateau like a brown and bay tidal wave, an older, lanky mare in the lead. A slight smile creased the corners of Ezra's lips. It was Simon's dam. They ran like a collective myth on hooves, their strides in perfect unison, the long legs reaching, stretching, collecting, pushing like polished pistons in a single well-oiled machine. They passed within 100 yards of the audience, their shiny coats barely sprinkled with sweat.

"Shoot, look at 'em," Barney said. "They're drinking wind and farting fire. They're not even lathered-up yet."

The mares disappeared in a cacophony of hoofbeats.

A lone rider appeared a half-mile back, his horse laboring in a forced lope. Ezra shook his head. *Boothe's not going to quit.* He put his plate down and walked quickly to the corrals. He removed Simon's halter, bridled him and tightened the cinch.

Boothe neared, whipping his horse with his reata, his eyes, wide and wild, looking for horses that couldn't be seen. His dun was soaked in lather and nearly staggering.

Ezra trotted out to him, reached down and grabbed the dun's bridle near the bit and pulled the horse to a stop. The little horse's sides were heaving like bellows.

"Let me go," Boothe shouted, striking at Ezra with his reata.

Ezra stepped off his bay, keeping the reins in his left hand. With his right hand he unbuckled the dun's bridle and let the horse spit the bit.

Boothe slapped at Ezra again with the reata coils. "You sonuvabitch," Boothe said. "I'll step off and kick your ass."

Ezra reached up and grabbed the rawhide rope. "Listen to me," he said calmly. "I am not too old to fight, but I am too old to *lose* a fight. So step off only if you have to."

Boothe's manic eyes jolted as they hit Ezra's calm determination. As Boothe tried to recollect his resolve, Ezra pulled the reata from his hand, then deftly, as if his hands had no pain or stiffness, unclipped a pocketknife, cut the reata in four pieces, and let the pieces fall.

Boothe looked down at rawhide coiled like a nest of baby snakes. "That was a $500 reata."

"Then I guess we're even on our bet." Ezra coiled a loose rein around the dun's neck, patted the horse affectionately, and handed the rein to Boothe. He nodded toward the trailers. "You can go now."

Boothe's trainers arrived, their horses white with lather. The riders, too, were spent, their fantasies as dried and transparent as shed snake skins.

The three rode slowly to the corrals, loaded their horses, and rumbled off in a cloud of dust.

Ezra led Simon to the knoll where the crew was still seated.

"What are we going to do now?" Anne asked.

"We still have calves to brand," Ezra said. He looked at the Miller boys. "You guys in for the long haul?" he asked.

They nodded. "Be glad to help you, Mr. Riley," Howie said.

Barney nodded toward the north horizon where the pasture road led from the corrals and crested a ridge before reaching the county road. "Someone's coming," he said.

Ezra sighed so softly it was noticed only by Landau. If Boothe was returning he'd have to finish it.

"Who is it?" Anne asked. "Are they coming back?"

Barney grinned. "No, I don't think so." A smile broke across his face. "Ez, I think it's our favorite Indian."

Ezra glanced north in surprise. "Ropesaplenty?" he said.

"Yup," Barney said. "It's Joey Ropesaplenty."

An older cowboy stepped from his truck wearing shotgun chaps and a battered felt hat. He unloaded two Oswald geldings -- a mahogany bay and a bay roan -- from his trailer.

"What are you girls doing?" he teased Ezra and Barney. "I don't see much branding going on."

"A third of our crew just left," Ezra said.

"Yeah," the cowboy said. "I met them on the county road."

Garcia looked at the newcomer curiously. "Your name is Ropesaplenty?" he asked.

"That's what Ezra calls me."

"What tribe is that?" Jones asked.

Ezra did not give Joe time to answer. "Where have you been, Ropes?" he asked. "Working down in that Nevada desert again?"

"Been there some." He gestured to the corrals. "Are we going to visit or are we going to rope cattle?"

"I'm short on crew," Ezra said.

"I have three stakes with me," Ropesaplenty said, referring to a branding method where calves were dragged to an iron stake driven in the ground. Attached to the stake was a length of rubber and a rope. A ground crew member put the rope around the calf's front legs as it was dragged by and the rider then turned his horse to face the rope and hold the calf's hind legs.

"You three older guys can rope," Howie said. "Me, Harold and Wilbur can brand and cut. We've done thousands at home."

"Okay," Ezra said. "You boys pound in the stakes, we *older* guys will get our horses ready. Garcia, you and Peter will be putting the stake ropes on the calves. The Kansas boys will show you how."

Once Ezra, Barney, and Ropesaplenty had their arms limbered, the branding proceeded with a calm efficiency.

Ezra pulled a worn 35mm SLR from a tattered camera bag and offered it to Landau. "I can't shoot when I'm roping," he said. "And photos are a tradition here. I pay my crew in prints."

"I have cameras in Barney's truck," Landau told him.

"Go get them," Ezra said, putting his camera away. "I'm sure yours are digital. I'll shoot a few with this later, though I don't know if any place even develops print film anymore."

Landau came back with two digital Canons and shot when he wasn't helping. Through the lens he noticed the demeanor of the crew had changed now that the Boothe gang was gone. Everyone was relaxed and having fun.

After an hour of hard work Ezra called for a water and coffee break. There weren't many calves left but Ezra's hands were hurting, and he noticed Barney was rubbing his shoulder. Ropesaplenty roped a lot so he was in shape for it.

Over coffee Garcia kept looking at Mr. Ropesaplenty. "What tribe is he?" He whispered to Barney.

"Southern branch of the Forked Tongue Horse Eaters," Barney said quietly. "Twice removed from the northern branch of the Big Bellied Bull Shippers."

Garcia's anthropological textbooks flashed through his mind. He couldn't place those tribes.

Ropesaplenty rose off his haunches and approached Ezra. "The real reason I'm here is I have a proposition for you and Barney."

"This ought to be good." Barney laughed.

"The Skinner Brothers have a thousand calves to brand," Joe said. "But with this wet, late spring they have field work to do, too, so they're looking for a crew to brand their calves."

"The Skinners," Ezra said. "That's a big place."

"A thousand cows," Ropesaplenty said. "They'll pay us $10 a calf. Brand, vaccinate, and castrate. No ear tags or implants. They have a cow camp we can stay in and they'll supply the grub."

"The three of us brand 1000 calves?" Ezra said. "That could take us three weeks."

Ropesaplenty shrugged. "So think of it as a long vacation."

"The Skinner place is two hours up the road. I can't be gone from here that long. We'd have to have a bigger crew."

"I can come," Garcia chipped in excitedly. "The boss told us yesterday all July vacations are cancelled. No one's getting vacation this summer unless they take it immediately."

Landau stepped forward. "I would like to come, too. I can help a little and I can cook."

"See?" Ropesaplenty said happily. "The really good plans just fall together on their own. With five guys we can get them done in five days."

"Five days?" Ezra cautioned. "We're not that good."

"Maybe six," Joe conceded.

"If the weather holds and absolutely nothing goes wrong. Besides, Barney hasn't signed on yet."

All heads turned toward the cartoonist.

"A thousand head?" Barney said. "I don't know if Mrs. Wallace will let her boy out for recess that long." He looked at his wife.

"If its only a week," Henrietta said. "And I need the money for remodeling the kitchen."

"The ropers will need two horses apiece," Ropesaplenty said. "You still have that old Clydesdale mare, Barney?"

"Shoot, yeah," Barney said.

"I don't know about leaving Anne alone," Ezra said. "The oil boom has brought a lot of strangers in."

"Oh, go ahead and go," Anne said. "I'll be careful. I have the pepper spray you bought me for Valentine's Day."

"You bought her pepper spray for Valentine's Day?" Barney laughed.

When we first met he wrote me poetry," Anne said. "Now I get pepper spray."

"Then we all agree," Joe said. "Good, because I already took the job. That's $2000 each for all the roping we can handle. You can't beat it with a stick, boys."

Ezra felt his thumbs cramping in pain. He wasn't so sure.

Garcia's eyes widened. He wondered if he would get to rope.

They finished the remaining calves and turned the cattle out. The Kansas boys helped Anne and Henrietta load coolers and groceries. Barney and Garcia jumped horses into the trailer, Ropesplenty pulled stakes, and Ezra and Landau picked up the branding irons, knives, and vaccine guns.

Landau waited until he and Ezra were alone.

"Ezra," he said. "There's a couple of things I need to mention. First, Mr. Ropesaplenty, that isn't his real name is it?"

"No, his name is Joe Pagliano. You'll learn about the nickname in time."

Landau took a step closer and spoke more softly. "One more thing, while we are at this place we're going to, this--"

"Cow camp."

"Yes, this cow camp. I'd appreciate it if no one asked me any war stories. No stories about the Middle East at all."

"That sounds reasonable."

"Thank you." Landau headed for the truck his arms burdened with branding irons, a shovel, and an ax.

Ezra watched him walk away.

Peter Landau. International man of mystery, he thought.

And what could those mysteries be?

CHAPTER EIGHT

A jacket of dusk settled on the hills beneath a slash of scarlet and apricot-colored clouds.

Montana sunsets inspired music in Anne because they reminded her of God's glory. Her joy was singing and playing to Him. This evening she couldn't play the piano because Ezra and Garcia were in bed, their alarm clocks set for 3:00, so they could arrive at the Skinner Ranch for a full day's work.

From her living room chair Anne watched her carefully-tended flowers bid daylight goodbye. She had a way with plants. The inside of the house was a small jungle, and the yard, though cursed by hardpan soil and saline water, was verdant with herbs, bushes, and flowers.

Anne had never imagined marrying a cowboy and living on a ranch. She met Ezra in Lawrence, Kansas, where she'd been a music major hoping to overcome stage fright. He was in jail following a riot at the University.

Her attraction to him was his poet's soul. His thoughts were deep, his diction nearly flawless, and his broody mysteriousness intriguing. In time she learned his mysteriousness was dark. Almost gothic.

A harsh childhood on the Montana plains, ridicule from six bachelor uncles, a father's detachment, and a mother's anxieties had ensnared him in a web of complexities.

Anne's own background was hardly idyllic. Her father had flown 32 World War II combat missions over Germany and her mother had been raised on a Great Depression farm. They'd settled for a secure and shallow existence raising a daughter whose uncommon musical ability was surpassed only by shyness. Music was thrust upon Anne as an experiment, then became a duty, and when she finally rebelled and cast it aside, it wasn't counted as a loss by her parents. Music had been a phase, they reasoned, a frivolity subdued by common sense. If their daughter wouldn't fight for it it hadn't any real value.

She made one last attempt to regain her musical soul by going to college, but academics and practice could not defeat her fears so she quit again.

It had been Ezra, with his unflinching loyalty to art, who demanded she return to it. She resisted but he persevered. She had minor successes in public -- singing duets, leading worship in church, or singing solo in rest homes -- but she was more relaxed and inspired singing to creation. Rocks, trees, streams, hills, and valleys became her audience.

Ezra had also stirred Anne to physical activity. Passive by nature, she found contentment in the embrace of sunbeams, the warmth of cups of tea, and meditations on the Word of God. She wasn't driven like her husband, the warrior poet. Extreme physicality was his nature. He had run competitively, lifted weights vigorously, and had been a student of the martial arts. Ranch work, as strenuous as it was, was never enough. Until recently.

Anne's physical outlet was walking. She walked the hills and sang.

Together Ezra amd Anne found completion. He was the tempest, she the safe harbor.

Anne understood Ezra. Some knew him as a cowboy, some as a writer, but few grasped his spiritual side, especially his gift of dream interpretation. Dreams, Ezra said, were little different than poetry. You simply needed to know their dark language.

Anne smiled thinking about the men's coming week. They would have fun. Ezra was in physical pain, but drought, blizzards, family disputes, church politics, and broken promises from movie producers and publishers had not defeated him yet. Once he was horseback he'd forget much of his pain.

Her world was bordered by a protective hedge of hope. She refused to believe or consider anything except the best, the most positive, as if life were a piano and she had the power to play it beautifully as long as no one watched.

She smiled, too, thinking of the crew and its interesting chemistry. Ezra would enjoy reuniting with Joe who was solid, dependable, and, when not roping, cautious. He was an anchor.

Peter was a hard one for Anne to understand. Ezra related to his professionalism and competence -- he was, in a way, what Ezra could have been, had not the ranch called him home -- yet, Anne suspected Peter wasn't all he pretended to be. Or, perhaps, he was more than he let on.

Garcia was the wild card. He was a sweet young man, but could he endure the physical and mental challenges of branding a thousand calves in a week and Ezra's testiness when Ezra was exhausted or in pain?

And then, Barney. Barney was frosting. A good cowboy, his real value was keeping the atmosphere light. If Barney remained strong, he could pull the others through. If he got sick or injured he'd sink the boat. As festive as Barney was, the smallest ache or a simple sneeze could slide him downhill in a frenzy of panicked self-indulgence.

Darkness was settling in. Anne regretted not going for a walk. She'd stayed home in case someone called. She didn't want a ringing phone to awaken Ezra or Garcia.

The phone rang.

Anne grabbed it quickly. The caller ID said it was her daughter-in-law, Kristen. "Hi, how are you?" she whispered, moving from the living room outside to the deck. Anne loved hearing from Kristen.

"Hi, Anne. I hope I'm not calling too late." Ezra and Anne were known for going to bed early.

"No, not at all. Ezra's asleep because he's getting up really early tomorrow."

Kristen was a gentle-spirited young woman whose honey-colored hair and scattering of freckles bespoke a country freshness. "I just needed to ask you something," she said.

"Sure."

"It's not for certain, but I was wondering if you guys could take care of Gabby for about ten days?"

Anne's heart jumped. "Sure. We'd love to. What's up?"

"It's not settled yet, but Dylan and I have been offered a trip to Brazil…"

"Brazil?"

"Yes. It's exciting, but we think it would be too much for Gabby."

"We'd love to have her."

"It may be sudden if it happens," Kristin explained apologetically. "You would need to go to Billings to pick her up off the plane."

"That's no problem. What's this trip all about?"

There was a long pause. "It's about Dylan's business," Kristen explained. "There's a chance we will be moving to Brazil."

Moving to Brazil? Anne's heart sank. They were too far away from their only grandchild now. *Brazil?*

"It's a big step," Kristen admitted. "We both have mixed feelings. Especially me. But it could be a huge opportunity for Dylan, and it wouldn't have to be forever. Five or six years, probably."

Anne let the information digest. "We would be glad to take Gabby if the trip happens," she said.

"Thank you, Anne," Kristen said softly. "I love you."

Anne decided it was best not to tell Ezra. He had enough on his mind and this wasn't certain. She'd wait until he returned from the Skinner job.

Brazil?

PART II

Why do they ride for their money?
Why do they rope for short pay?
They ain't getting nowhere,
and they're losing their share.
Son, they all must be crazy out there.

Night Rider's Lament
Michael Burton

CHAPTER NINE

Ezra was worried, and Garcia was nervous as they traveled north to the Skinner Ranch. Joe was ahead of them, leading the way, and Peter and Barney followed in the reporter's rented SUV. Daybreak was still an hour away.

Ezra was concerned about leaving Anne alone for a week. He also wondered if he was physically up to a week of roping, branding, and castrating. He'd have to be. He needed the money for doctor bills.

Garcia was nervous because his cowboy dreams were about to be tested. It was one thing to wear a hat, go to rodeos, and imagine yourself a top hand. It was something else to be marooned in a cow camp with three older cowboys and an observing reporter. His nervousness had him peppering Ezra with questions which Ezra answered mostly with grunts.

"Who's the best bronc rider you ever saw?" Garcia blurted.

"Guess I've never thought about it," Ezra said.

"I saw Billy Etbauer at Pendleton."

Ezra didn't respond.

"How many times did you see Barney ride?"

Ezra scowled thoughtfully. He'd never considered this before. "None," he said.

"You never saw him ride broncs?" Garcia asked incredulously.

"Nope. When Barney was cracking out I wasn't much into rodeo. I was traveling a lot back then."

"Well, he must have been good," Garcia said.

"You don't get to the Finals if you're not good."

"He's big for a bronc rider. He doesn't fit the mold."

"He was skinnier then," Ezra said.

Garcia gazed out the window, trying to get landscape to materialize from the darkness. "He must have been fearless," he said, more to himself than to Ezra.

Ezra chuckled. "Barney fearless? He's afraid of elevators, spiders, and water."

"Water?"

"He can't swim."

Jones paused thoughtfully. "What do you think Peter Landau is going to write about?"

"I don't know," Ezra said. "But I hope it includes Barney and makes him famous."

"Famous for what?"

Ezra frowned. "For his art."

"Oh," Garcia said. He never thought much about art and he wondered how famous a cartoonist could become?

"Garcia, while we're up here at Skinners' I need a couple of promises from you."

Jones sensed the seriousness in Ezra's tone. "What?"

"No mentioning of the EEEP program to anyone. I don't want anyone to know I'm even considering it."

"No problem. I don't even want to think about work."

"And don't ask Landau any questions about his work overseas. No war stories."

"No war stories?"

"None. And that's a request straight from Peter. He's out here to forget what he's seen and we're going to help him. So, no mention of wars or politics."

No war stories? thought Garcia. Darn. He had a thousand questions for Landau. He wanted to know about firefights and IEDs and...

...and facing death.

That thought sobered him. That's what he really wondered about. *What was it like to stare death in the face?*

Landau was amazed. Minutes before, Barney had been telling stories, then as sudden as a wind gust, the cartoonist flopped his head against the passenger window and let loose a cacophony of yips, whistles, snorts, and growls that sounded like a pack of coyotes on a carcass. The reporter kept his eyes on the headlight beams cutting into the morning darkness. Ahead of him, but visible only when he crested hills, were the taillights of the trucks and trailers of Ezra Riley and Joe Pagliano. Behind him the eastern sky was paling, suggesting dawn's imminence. He glanced at the snoozing artist. Since graduating from the Columbia University Graduate School of Journalism in 2001, Landau had traveled and worked in extreme environments, but he'd never met anyone who could snore like Barney Wallace.

A frost heave in the black top sent the SUV air borne and its landing shook Wallace awake. He opened his eyes not knowing where he was, or where he was going. "Shoot," he said. "I must have dozed off for a minute."

"I didn't notice," Landau quipped.

"We were talking about something. What were we talking about?"

"We were talking about Lynne."

"What about him?"

"You mentioned the bronc riding contest at the Bucking Horse Sale."

"Oh, yeah." Barney chuckled. "My mind must of pulled into a rest stop. I was saying how some bronc riders are mechanical, and some ride with style and flair. Lynne had style. He was an artist. His spurs were his brushes."

"So he rode like a painter?"

"Well, no. More like a poet. A little cadence. A zing here, a ding there. He and the horse in rhyme."

"You mean in rhythm?"

"That, too."

"So, there are different styles to riding broncs?"

"Oh, yeah. Some guys try to overpower 'em. Some guys try to out hustle 'em. But the best learn to dance with 'em."

"Which style were you?"

"I tried to reason with 'em. Never worked."

"Did you know Lynne well?"

"Pretty well, but by the time I cracked out his career was about over. He was working in the Pryors then."

"It's a strange name for a man, isn't it? Let alone a cowboy?"

"What?"

"Lynne."

"Oh." Barney pondered the subject thoughtfully. "Guess I never thought about it. Lynne was just Lynne. But, now that you mention it, I've known cowboys named Shirley, Deb, Cotton, and Joyce."

"That seems odd to me."

"Oh, shoot. If you're a good enough cowboy, you can wear any brand."

The prairie blossomed with light as night rolled up like a series of retreating curtains. Wallace nodded to the west. "Out there a-ways is the old Kramer ranch where Lynne worked. They ran cattle, sheep and up to 3000 horses. Guess I told you that. Now I hear a lot of it has been plowed up." Wallace let the light soak into his eyes. "What country did you like most in all your travels?" he asked. His mind jumped to new subjects like a skipping needle on a phonograph.

Landau looked at him curiously -- he was still considering herds of thousands of horses.

"I'd like to see Argentina," Wallace said. "You know, the Pampas, the gauchos, and the way they throw those balls at cows instead of ropes."

"Boleadoras," Landau said.

"Golly, you've seen 'em?"

"I passed through the Pampas once."

Wallace shook his head thoughtfully as he tried to imagine how boleadoras -- or bolas, as they were commonly called -- were used.

"Israel," Landau said.

Wallace looked at him, wonderment tangling his eyebrows in a knot.

"You asked me what country I like. Israel, I guess. All the history, the tension. And of course, I'm Jewish."

"Turn," Wallace said. The taillights ahead were harder to see in the paling light. Pagliano and Riley were now half-a-mile down a county road that slanted westward.

"Some of the Riley ranch looks like places I've seen in Israel," Landau commented.

A soft red and white glow shone on the eastern horizon. "Oil rig," Barney explained. "The big boom is moving this way."

"Ropesaplenty," Landau said. "Ezra told me that's not his real name."

Barney guffawed. "Nope. Ezra hung that on him years ago. We just trot it out for greenhorns."

"So, this is for Garcia's benefit?"

"Garcia all the way. Ole Ez loves torturing the kid."

"I think he likes him."

"Yup. That's why he tortures him."

Minutes later, they pulled into a ranch yard that seemed larger and more populated than some western towns. Houses were scattered, as if dropped by twisters, and each was sheltered by a belt of trees on the north and west; rows of grain bins pointed to the sky like lines of silver rockets; trucks, trailers, tractors, combines, and other pieces of machinery created a rural traffic jam. The number of towering machine sheds made Landau think he'd entered the industrial park of a major city. Long-haired dogs ran and barked, four-wheelers zoomed and roared, and men in coveralls hustled about as if all the work in the world had to be done in the next ten minutes. One heavy-set man in an oil-stained jacket looked up as they passed. Wallace gave him a friendly wave which wasn't returned. "Skinner place," Barney said. They went through the yard then passed miles of dry-land farm ground before crossing a cattle guard and reentering prairie. Eight miles and two cattle guards later they pulled up to an old set of pens, a weathered shack, and a windmill. "Our happy home for the next week," Barney said. Joe, Ezra and Garcia were already unloading horses. Quickly, with little conversation, the men packed duffle bags and gear into a building with a peeling linoleum floor, dirty walls of chipping pale green paint, obsolete refrigerator, rickety card table, and three tiny bedrooms with folding cots.

"Let me you know if you find a lot of mice turds in one spot," Joe said. "I brought a gallon of Clorox for Hantavirus."

Barney pulled a Playboy calendar from the wall, tossed it in the woodbox, and hung a "Barn Wall" calendar in its place.

"Who sleeps alone?" Ezra asked rhetorically. Ezra would have preferred a room to himself but everyone knew Barney's snoring gave him rank. Ezra and Joe tossed their bags in one room, Landau and Garcia tossed there's in another.

"A shame," Wallace said, throwing his bags on his cot. "I'm the most social guy here and a slight breathing impediment makes me an outcast."

"And lepers have a slight rash," Joe countered.

Garcia pulled his cell phone from his pocket. "I don't have a signal," he said.

"Praise God for that," Ezra quipped.

"There's a knoll to the north," Joe said. "The Skinners said you can sometimes get a signal from the top of it."

"No Wi-Fi, either," Garcia noted.

"No what?" Barney asked.

"He misses his Twitter," Ezra said.

Barney scowled. "Where did he put it?" he asked seriously.

"And Garcia," Ezra said. "You didn't bring your XBox, did you?"

Jones shook his head.

"Good. We're here to be cowboys."

"That's right," Barney said. "And I'm going to give it the best shot I've got."

Their gear in place they moved outside to inspect the corrals. "We'll set a bench over here," Ezra pointed. "And one stake on each side of it." The bench would hold supplies like vaccine, vaccine guns, castrating knives and disinfectant.

The Skinner operation was set up with a calf-table -- which was no more than a small cattle chute that rotated onto its side -- coming off an alley. A branding oven on legs held the irons and a torch that was connected to a 100-gallon propane tank. Ezra had vetoed propane as being too noisy. Instead, they'd filled both pickups with old fence posts as fuel to heat the irons. They dug a fire pit near the bench and unloaded a day's worth of posts.

Joe drew in the dirt with a stick to explain the branding plan. "The Skinners have six cell pastures they use for calving," he said. "The cells are like the spokes on a wheel. They open to the one-section trap that sits outside these pens. Every evening the farm hands are going to empty one cell into the trap so that's all we have to gather in the mornings. When we're done at night we kick the cows and calves out north into 15 sections of summer fallow."

Ezra picked up the issuance of instructions. "To make this work and work right, we have to go slow and steady. Two of us -- me, Joe or Barney -- will be roping while one of us is training you guys --"

he nodded at the range conservationist and the reporter. "You two will start by putting ropes on the feet, branding and vaccinating. But we'll teach you to castrate, too. That way, if things get going good we can run three ropers."

"The farmers will be chousin' those cattle in with four-wheelers and dogs," Joe said. "Hopefully, the ole girls will settle down during the night, but these cattle aren't used to being worked horseback. The ropers will have to work as quietly as we can."

"And we have to double-hock everything," Ezra added. "Nothing pulled to the fire by one leg. If we can't rope well we'll have to unsaddle and use that tool of Satan." He nodded over his shoulder to the calf table. "We have six horses to rope on and we can't afford to get one of them sore. We'll change horses at lunch to let the first horses rest. If needed, we'll have to use those horses again."

"I've never branded anything before," Landau said. Garcia nodded. He hadn't either.

"It's easy," Barney explained. "They have a one-iron brand, a Monogram S on the left ribs. If the irons are hot and the hides are clean it'll just take a second. Just hold it down till you get a buckskin color."

"Well, it's already seven," Ezra said. "You guys get a fire started. Me, Joe and Barn Wall will gather the cows."

They worked hard but had fun. They laughed when they could, took several breaks, and the older men instructed and answered questions.

Garcia and Landau put ropes on the calves' front legs as they were dragged in, and in addition, Garcia vaccinated and Landau branded.

Joe and Barney began as ropers and Ezra castrated. After approximately a third of the calves were done, Joe and Ezra switched. Later, Joe and Barney switched. In this way each of the older men spent a third of the time on the ground crew.

After twelve hours the bunch was branded and Garcia was counting scrotum tips the castrators had tossed in a bucket. Each tip represented one steer calf so by counting the calves out the gate and subtracting the number of scrotum tips the crew had a tally of both heifers and steers.

"One-hundred-and-sixty-six head," Ezra announced as the horses were unsaddled and grained. "Eighty-four steers and eighty-two heifers." He had the day's total written down in a tally book.

"Let's ease the cattle out the gate horseback and check for bleeders," Joe said. *Bleeders* were castrated calves whose wounds hadn't coagulated.

Garcia and Landau walked wearily to the shack. The reporter had to start supper.

When the three older men walked in later Ezra could hear shower water running. "How long has he been in there?" he asked, nodding toward the bathroom.

"I don't know. Ten, fifteen minutes," Landau said.

Ezra went to the kitchen sink and turned on the hot water tap. It ran cool. "Hey, Jones," Ezra yelled. "Get your butt out of the shower." There wasn't a response so Ezra banged on the bathroom door. "Jones! Get out of the shower."

The shower shut off and moments later Garcia emerged from the room, a blue towel around his waist and his red hair plastering his head. "What's wrong?" he said.

Barney and Jose looked at each other and they both raised their eyebrows. They knew what was coming.

"First of all," Ezra said. "You don't leave a crew until everyone's done. It's different for Landau, because he has to start supper. Second of all, you used all the hot water. This isn't a college dorm, Garcia. The hot water here is for getting clean, not for therapy."

Garcia hung his head. "Sorry," he said.

"No big deal," Ezra said. "You worked hard, but there are rules in a cow camp."

Joe looked at Barney and smiled. "This is it, isn't it?" he said. "This is where ole Ez hangs a nickname on the redhead."

Barney nodded gleefully. He could hardly wait.

Ezra went outside to blow off steam. He liked the kid, and if he signed the EEEP contract he'd have to work with him, but Ezra disliked the younger generation's demand for instant gratification. He looked around for busy work while supper cooked and saw a stack of old corral posts that could be used in tomorrow's fire.

"Hey, Hot Water Jones," he yelled back at the house. "Come give me a hand."

Joe and Barney smiled.

Garcia came running from his room, buttoning his shirt as he went, a faint smile pooling on his lips. *Hot Water!* He finally had a nickname. Ezra liked him after all.

Barney stroked his mustache thoughtfully. "They say a nickname is the worst stone the devil can throw at you," he said. "But dang if that kid don't seem to love his."

CHAPTER TEN

J oe rolled over on his cot and whispered into the darkness. "Ez. You asleep?"

"Asleep? With Barney leading a troop of gut-shot bagpipers in the next room?"

"We gotta do something or we won't get any sleep."

"How's your faith?" Ezra asked.

"What do want to do, pray?"

"No. I've been praying. I thought maybe we could kill him then raise him from the dead in the morning."

"I don't have that much faith." Joe rose and padded from the room in stocking feet. Moments later, the screen door whined open, then closed.

I hope he's not going for a gun, Ezra thought. No, he decided, he probably just had to pee. That was the good thing about two older cowboys bunking together. They understood the middle-of-the-night trips to stare at the stars.

Soon a little ball of light was dancing on the walls as Joe came back with a flashlight. "I'm going to need some help," he said. "I got a theory all that noise is actually a big rodent caught in that brush pile he calls a mustache."

"You can't set it on fire. You'll burn the house down."

"No, no. We can't kill him or hurt him. He's got too many fans. Just follow me in and hold the flashlight."

The two cowboys, wearing only underwear and socks, tiptoed quietly into Barney's room. The cartoonist was lying flat on his back, as still as a corpse, his long nose pointed into the air like a missile. Ezra held the flashlight. Joe had a can in his hands.

"Pine tar," Joe said. "I got it off the vet bench this morning and let it warm near the fire. Should be cooled down just right by now." He pried the lid off with a screwdriver and stuck a toothbrush into the can.

"You're gonna ruin that toothbrush," Ezra whispered. The snoring rising from the cot was so loud neither was afraid of being heard.

"It's not my toothbrush," Joe said.

Deftly, Joe painted Barney's huge mustache black with warm tar. Immediately the snoring lessened to the purring of a big cat.

"See," Joe said. "He likes it."

They tiptoed back to their room and crawled into their sleeping bags.

"Hey Joe," Ezra whispered. "Whose toothbrush was that?"

"Yours," Joe said.

Joe and Ezra got up especially early and roused Landau and Garcia, too, telling them nothing of their nighttime escapade. The four were sipping coffee around the table when they heard Barney stirring. They listened as big feet shuffled down the hall to the bathroom. The light clicked on and there was a moment of silence, then Barney exclaimed, "It's a miracle!"

Ezra and Joe gave each other quizzical looks.

"Saints be praised," they heard.

"What's going on?" Garcia said.

Joe held a finger to his lips. "Quiet. A miracle is happening."

"Hey, guys," Barney yelled. "What's that shrine in France where the Catholics go?"

"Lourdes," Landau said.

"Well, they're going to be coming here now. When I went to bed my mustache was gray. Now its jet black and fuller than ever." He stepped into the kitchen and displayed his pine-tarred handlebars.

Joe and Ezra broke with laughter. Garcia and Landau were speechless.

"Nope, I can't do it," Barney said, pivoting on his big feet. "Thousands of people will flock here and the Skinners will get richer than they are now." He returned to the little bathroom.

"What are you gonna do?" Joe called out.

"Drastic times require drastic action," Barney said. Moments of silence followed before the bathroom door opened again and Wallace stepped back into the kitchen. The forest of a mustache was gone, replaced by a line of white skin barer than a baby's bottom.

"Got milk?" he asked, his grin spreading across the room.

Moments after the cattle were penned the skies clouded up and a light rain began falling. The ropers covered their saddles with slickers and took cover in the shack.

"This is God getting back at you guys," the freshly-shaved Barney said.

"It's clearing to the south, we should be able to brand, shouldn't we?" Landau asked.

"Not right away," Ezra explained. "The hair is wet on the calves. If we try to brand we'll scald their hides."

"So what do we do?"

"We'll see if the sun comes out and a breeze blows," Joe said.

"I found a deck of cards in my room," Barney said.

They settled on five-card draw poker with pennies and match-sticks for chips.

"Six o'clock in the morning and I'm playing poker," Garcia said. "That's what my mother was afraid would happen to me."

"Women worry too much," Joe said, throwing two matchsticks into the pot.

"I saw you three climbing that knoll and calling home last night," Garcia noted. "You don't see me and Peter doing that."

"That's what I mean," Joe said. "Women worry too much. The older we get, the more they need to know that we haven't done something stupid and hurt ourselves."

"Some of us do require more adult supervision than others," Ezra admitted.

"You two are very lucky," Barney said to the two single men. "Here at this table there's close to 120 years of matrimonial experience for you to tap. A veritable gold mine of wisdom."

"So what would The Three Wise Men suggest?" Landau asked.

"Marry a woman with a sense of humor," Joe said, raising the bid by a matchstick.

Garcia called his matchstick and raised the pot by a penny. "Where do you find one of those?"

"Well, it's hard," Barney admitted. "It's a religious problem. In our culture they circumcise boys. With girls they remove the funny bone."

"They do it the day before they circumcise the boys so the boys won't be laughed at," Joe said.

Garcia scratched his thin goatee. "Women don't have much of a sense of humor, do they?" he said.

"A sense of humor requires spontaneity," Ezra said. "Not many women are spontaneous, especially as they get older. They get less spontaneous about a lot of things. Like spontaneous sex, for example. You have to schedule it three weeks in advance."

"I fold," Barney said, laying his cards down. "The way I see it, women live for one thing and that's to become grandmothers. If they could become grandmothers without us they'd probably do it."

"Ever think you would be sleeping with a grandmother?" Joe asked rhetorically.

Garcia wrinkled his nose.

"Now, Henrietta," Barney continued. "On our honeymoon she turned to me in bed and said, 'sweetheart, make me a grandmother.'"

"No, she didn't," Garcia said.

"Well, not in those exact words," Barney said. "But that was the intention. Women live for grandchildren. They want to hold them and let go of everything else. Just let it slide. All downhill and into their lap. If they can hold a grand-baby, all's right with the world."

Joe turned to the young redhead. "So, Hot Water," he said. "Is there anyone you're boiling for?"

The range conservationist shook his head. "I'm more interested in hunting and fishing. I'm looking for a woman who likes to camp out."

Barney and Ezra laughed out loud.

"What?" Garcia asked.

"No woman likes to camp out," Ezra said.

"I met one once who said she did," Garcia said.

"And where did you meet her?"

The redhead blushed. "In a chat room."

"Chat room?" asked Barney. "Is that a beauty parlor?"

"It's on the Web, Barn Wall," Ezra explained. "It's where strangers go to lie to one another."

"She said she loved camping," Garcia insisted.

Joe shook his head. "Never trust a woman who says she likes camping."

Garcia looked disappointed. "There must be women who like camping?"

"Maybe at first," Ezra said. "But the thrill wears off quickly. Remember, women were put on this planet to domesticate men, not to encourage their wilder instincts."

"Shoot, if Hot Water needs a wife the government will requisition him one," Barney said.

"You guys are a lot of help," Garcia said. "What other great wisdom you got?"

"Here's mine," Ezra said. "Men like work, food, sports, and sex, though not necessarily in that order. Women like emotions, relationships, intimacy, and chocolate."

"I like chocolate," Barney said.

"That's because you're in touch with your feminine side," Ezra said.

"How about you, Peter?" Joe asked. "Is there a woman in your life?"

Landau looked down at the table thoughtfully and Ezra noted a change in the aura about him. "I was almost engaged once," he said.

"Almost?" Joe said. "What happened? Did you get a pardon from the governor?"

Landau paused. He knew he was going to alter the room's playful mood. "I met my girlfriend for brunch on 9-11 with a ring in my pocket. I was about to propose when the first plane hit The World Trade Center."

As he expected, a somber tone settled over the table.

"My father was a senior partner in a law firm. His office was in the North Tower."

"Oh shoot," Barney said. "We're sorry--"

Landau raised his hand. "It's okay, but thank you. I was supposed to leave that afternoon on my first assignment to Israel. Needless to say, I didn't fly any time soon."

"And the girl?" Ezra asked.

"She became a 9-11 Truther, someone who believes Israel staged the attack with the CIA. We broke up over that."

"We're very sorry for your loss," Ezra said. "It must have been terrible for your family, especially your mother."

"It was. For my sister, too. They were both in deep depression for several years. My sister's marriage ended because of it. But she eventually remarried and got on with life."

"And your mother?" Barney asked.

"After grief ran its course she looked for old friends and threw herself into charity work. She's come through it all well, though she worries about me and the places my work takes me."

"Bring her to Montana," Joe said. "The wide open spaces and fresh air will do her good."

A slight smile bent the corners of the reporter's mouth. "There's more truth to that than you know. She's always had a romantic obsession with the West and its cowboys."

Ezra looked out the window. "The sun's out, and a breeze is blowing. Let's see if the calves are dry."

The crew rose wordlessly from the table and pointed themselves toward the corral as one unit, feeling a new, unspoken, cohesion.

CHAPTER ELEVEN

"Garcia, time to get up," Barney said, shaking the redhead's shoulder. The young man continued sleeping.

"Hot Water!" Barney said more forcefully. One pale blue eye, almost reptilian in its coldness, half opened and stared up at Wallace. "What time is it?" Garcia mumbled.

"Quarter-to-four," Barney said. "Breakfast is on the table."

Jones crawled out of his sleeping bag, sat on the edge of his cot and tried to force both eyelids open. "Oh," he groaned, pulling on pants and socks. His lower back was sore. He couldn't remember ever being sore in his life. He stumbled to the kitchen expecting to see the rest of the crew looking as sad and weary as he, but Peter, standing over a griddle and a bowl of pancake batter, was the only person there.

"Where's everyone?" Garcia said. He figured they were all still asleep, including Barney. It must have been an apparition in his room.

"Outside saddling up," the reporter said. "You better pour yourself a big cup of coffee."

Ezra Riley bit his lower lip in pain as he flung his saddle up on Big Jack. He'd done everything he could to make the saddle lighter -- removed his cantle pack, fencing pliers, and hobbles -- but with his hands cramping into the shape of fish hooks he'd even had trouble with the saddle blanket. Big Jack wasn't an Oswald, he was a Hancock-bred horse from a line known for size and good dispositions.

"You're not riding Simon?" Joe asked.

"Too early in the morning for me to ride an Oswald. Even a good Oswald."

"I'm riding an Oswald," Joe said lightly.

"Yeah, but you're a better hand than I am," Ezra joked.

The three men gathered the section trap and ushered the cattle into the corral where the branding fire was lit and the irons glowing. Ezra knew Garcia was upset about not being asked to help gather -- he had, after all, brought his new saddle along -- but Ezra was not going to let him ride until he could get out of the sack by himself. Ezra knew the youngster wanted to rope, too, but they were here to do a job, not train dudes.

Ezra volunteered to start the morning on the ground. Roping hurt his hands. What he could do with the least pain was brand. He called Hot Water and the scribe to the fire.

"I'm going to teach you both to castrate today," he said. "You have to pay attention and do it right. These aren't our cattle, but we're responsible for them. We can't have a calf die because someone got sloppy or careless."

Joe dragged the first calf in. It was a bull so Ezra took time to explain castration. He cut the tip of the scrotum off and tossed it in the bucket, then pulled on one testicle. "When you feel it give you've pulled enough," he said. He sliced the cord and pulled the other testicle and did the same. "Now this is important," he said, pointing the knife blade at the fat in the scrotum. "You clean out enough fat to let blood drain." He put the knife back into a dish filled with disinfectant. "Got that?" he asked.

They nodded, each looking at the task through the lens of his own training. Landau as a reporter, Garcia, as a scientist.

They had a good day. The crew settled into a routine, the horses worked well, and the loops sailed straight and true. By five o'clock, 169 cows and their freshly-branded calves were turned out and the horses unsaddled and grained. For supper, they barbecued hamburgers on an oven rack over the branding coals.

In the distance killdeers cried, and a plaintive bawl could be heard from a confused calf.

Landau went to the house for paper plates and came back with a twelve-pack of Budweiser. "The farmers must have put this in the refrigerator while we were busy branding," he said, handing each of them a can.

"Golly, I'm not much of a beer man," Barney said. "But its been a warm day and a cold beer looks pretty good."

Their first beer went down quickly. Landau passed around the cardboard carton and each took another.

"We'll have two left over," Landau said.

"Give them to me," Ezra said. He put the two beers on the ground. "Those are for Lynne."

"To Lynne," Joe said, lifting his beer.

"To Lynne," said the others.

Landau toasted with the others, but when they weren't looking, he poured his beer out.

"Shoot, I miss Lynne," Barney said.

"He was always pregnant with laughter," Ezra remembered. "It was like his water was going to burst any second."

"And the way he laughed," Barney said. "He'd settle into a stance like he was sitting a horse, hook his thumbs in his belt loops, throw his head back and let it rip."

"Like a stud horse nickering into the wind," Ezra noted.

Garcia's eyes danced with excitement. He hoped someday people would talk about him this way.

"He was a cowboy's cowboy," Joe said. "Twenty years riding broncs. Thirty-eight years as a pickup man."

"I'm not sure I know what pickup men are," Landau said.

"Those are the mounted guys who pull the cowboy off the horse after the whistle's blown," Garcia volunteered.

Barney popped open one of Lynne's beers and poured it out on the ground as an offering.

The men were tired; the day had been warm, and the beer was carving a warm trail to their heads.

"Remember that wreck he was in at your Dead Man corrals?" Joe asked.

"Lynne was on a colt, a full brother to Simon," Ezra explained. "He was pushing cows down the alley when a heifer turned, went under the colt and tipped them over into a wall of bridge plank. Lynne was bent like a horseshoe with the horse and heifer on top of him."

"I was on the catwalk above it," Barney said. "I was sure he'd be all broke-up."

"He was 68 years old at the time," Ezra said.

"Shoot," Barney said. "He got up like it was nothing. Just limped a little."

"Lynne's the one guy Ezra never hung a nickname on," Joe said.

"I couldn't have," Ezra said. "Lynne was bigger than nicknames."

"Lynne sure did enjoy my nickname," Joe said. "I think he called me Ropesaplenty more than he called me by my real name."

"You're not an Indian!" Garcia blurted out. "I didn't think so. I went on the Web trying to find a tribe that had a Ropesaplenty and I couldn't find one."

Barney cracked his crooked grin. He'd been waiting for the big confession.

"No, I'm not an Indian," Joe said. "I'm Sicilian."

"You guys have been messing with me," Garcia said. He looked at the reporter. "Did you know it was a nickname?"

Landau smiled. "I deduced as much."

"Okay," Garcia said. "What's the story behind Joe's nickname?"

"Ropes," Ezra said. "Let's do this right. Did you bring your guitar?"

"It's in my truck," he said and he went to get it.

Ezra looked at Garcia. "Ropesaplenty's real name is Joe Pagliano. He was a long-haul trucker for 20 years. The past six years he's been wandering in search of his youth. A while back he showed up in the fall to help me ship."

Joe came back, sat down and began tuning his Gibson 12-string.

Ezra continued: "Anne had been wanting a cow of her own, so as a joke I bought her a spotted longhorn with a seven-foot horn spread. Joe didn't know about this cow or that I'd gotten Anne her own brand, so when he saw her he thought she was a stray. I'll let Joe take it from here."

Joe looked at his audience. "The tune is from *Windy Bill*. Or something close to that." He cleared his throat and sang a few scales. His baritone was smoother than bourbon over ice. He started the ballad:

"This is a song about ole Joe, a true and valuable hand,
All he ever wanted was to ride and rope and brand.
He was helping his friend Ez one bright and sunny day
when he spotted a Longhorn cow, she had to be a stray.
So he built a big loop and dabbed it around her horns
then spurred his Oswald horse and busted her forlorn.
"The cow got up and shook her head so he busted her again,
He laid a trip, didn't slip, and rolled her end o'er end.
Then suddenly he heard a voice a callin' out his name,
'Joe Pags, what you doin', just what is your game?'
Then Anne Riley, wife of Ez, rode up and into view.
'That Longhorn cow is mine,' she said, 'now what you gonna do?'
Now ole Joe, he hadn't blushed since he'd turned twenty.
'My name ain't Joe,' he said, 'I am Mister Ropesaplenty'."

Exaggerated cheers and applause broke out.

"Y'know, it's not that great," Garcia said. "But it is funny."

"What do you mean it isn't great?" Joe asked, feigning offense.

"Oh, you sing good." The youngster blushed three shades of crimson and shrugged his slight shoulders.

Landau mentally photographed the scene, detailing its sights, sounds and textures for later description in his story. He noted when the laughter stopped, Ezra was looking at the sky, following a jet contrail as it traced a white path across the twilight.

"So what do we call you?" Garcia asked. "Are you Ropesaplenty or Joe Pagliano?"

"When my loops are catching, I'm Ropesaplenty. When I'm missing, you can call me Barney Wallace." He laughed and slapped Barn Wall on his shoulder.

"Tell him what your boys call you," Ezra said.

"They call me J-Peg." He shrugged. "They think its funny but I don't get it."

"It's a computer term--" Garcia began but Barney cut him off.

"Speaking of great ropers like me --" Barney swished what little beer was left in his can. "I propose a toast: To older women, slower horses and watered whiskey."

Garcia finished his beer and wiped his mouth on his shirt cuff. "I don't think that's the way the saying goes," he said.

"Hot Water," Barney said. "That's the way the saying goes when you reach our age."

Landau kept a subtle eye on Ezra. He could not read the rancher's mind but he could speculate. Ezra was weighing the merriment and finding it a touch short of perfect. What was missing was Lynne and his laughter. Landau felt a pang of guilt. He'd not been totally honest with the crew, and knew, at some point, he'd have to be. Life somehow seemed pure on this prairie, under this sky. Almost sacred. And sacredness intrigued Peter Landau. He needed to understand it. He broke away from his thoughts and saw the tables had been turned.

Ezra Riley was now studying him.

CHAPTER TWELVE

I am in the company of men. They work hard and play hard. They strive desperately to hold time between their fingers, knowing it is sifting like sand, drifting like dust, blowing away on the gusts of prairie breezes...

Landau considered his thoughts. They were terribly over-written, he thought. Too melodramatic. But on this fourth morning he realized the daily routine -- its sights, sounds, smells, touches, aches and pains -- had worked itself into the marrow of his bones. He knew when it was over he'd miss this. He treasured the milling, noisy cattle, the sweaty work, and the smell of burning hair, but mostly he enjoyed the fellowship of easy smiles, fresh air, endless skies, and the camp's utter remoteness. Airport terminals, hotel rooms, city traffic -- even the beautiful tragedy of war in foreign lands -- would seem different to him.

He watched Barney, Joe, and Ezra reset their saddles and tighten their cinches. They were men he'd not forget.

Garcia was fiddling with the fire, pushing a cedar post closer to the center with his toe. At first Landau found the redhead bothersome, like a pup nipping at the heels of big dogs, but by simply receiving the nickname 'Hot Water,' a change had occurred. Garcia had been branded as belonging.

This made Landau wonder, did Ezra have a nickname for him? When this crew gathered again, perhaps in the fall to wean Ezra's calves, would they joke about the Jewish reporter from New York and recall him with simple, almost affectionate, pejoratives?

"Let's try three ropers today," Ezra said, leading Big Jack toward the fire. "We old guys are getting tired. Three of us roping at once will lessen the load. Peter and Hot Water are the ground crew. Peter, you cut and vaccinate. Hot Water, you brand and handle the stake ropes."

"You guys up for that?" Joe asked.

The two nodded. Nobody said it, but they were all getting tired. The camaraderie remained robust but the work was edging toward drudgery. Without complaining, Barney, Ezra and Joe were showing their age. Landau noted the subtle adjustments in Ezra -- how he held and tossed his loops, the way he managed the irons -- and knew his hand pain was increasing. He suspected Barney and Joe also had aches they didn't mention.

Garcia was disappointed that Ezra hadn't called on him to rope. He'd beat the green off his lawn all Spring tossing loops at a plastic steer head.

The new set-up worked. Garcia was precise and deliberate with the irons and Landau was deft with a knife. Three ropers relieved enough pressure that each roped better. When they stopped for lunch 97 calves had been branded.

Ezra squatted on his haunches, spur rowels pressing against his butt, and balancing a paper plate of beans with his left hand.

Landau walked over and squatted beside him. "Ezra, how are your hands doing?" he asked.

Ezra looked at him out of the corner of his eye. "I'm probably not going to take up fiddle-playing anytime soon," he said.

"What are you going to do about it?" Landau asked.

Ezra shrugged. "I took this job to pay for my last bunch of medical bills. When those bills are paid I'll consider the next step."

"This isn't any of my business, but I haven't seen you taking any medication."

"The nerve medicine screws up my sleep and the pain pills screw up my stomach." Ezra gestured toward Barney and Joe. "Those guys are hurting, too. Barney's had back surgery. Joe's had both knees replaced. You don't reach our age without being held together with baling wire and fence staples." He took a slow, careful bite of beans. "One thing I can say. I understand why some men end up with drinking problems. Whiskey would be a strong temptation if I were built that way."

Landau let his gaze wander. He knew Ezra had said all he was going to say about his condition. Finally he pointed at the black cattle. "Are they good stock?" he asked.

"Good enough. The Skinners are capable operators, in a sterile, modern sense. I bet they pick their bulls simply by reading EPDs and never look at the animal."

"EPDs?"

"Expected Progeny Differences. A pile of computer-generated statistics. Ranching has become technical, and the Skinners fit that mold. It makes for good, but boring, businessmen. They own six fat saddle horses that haven't been ridden in years."

Landau then nodded to where the three Oswald geldings were tied together. "Those horses have their own look, don't they?"

Ezra smiled. "You have an eye for horses, Peter."

"I was raised around some very good jumpers and dressage mounts. If you removed the western tack and put English saddles on those three they'd fit in with horses I rode in Westchester."

"Be careful, Mr. Landau," Ezra warned. "Or I will sell you eight head of Oswald mares. Range delivery."

"Be careful, Mr. Riley," Landau countered. "Or I might buy them."

Ezra broke the brevity. "So, Peter, how are you doing?"

Landau looked at him suspiciously. "What do you mean?"

"The noise, sweat, the smell of blood and burning hair--"

"You know?"

"About your PTSD? No, just a guess. We all know where you've been and that you don't want to talk about it. And, I saw you pour those two beers out on the ground."

"I've been through rehab," Landau said.

Ezra didn't say anything.

"But, to answer your question, I'm okay. I have my moments but it helps if I stay busy."

"Then I suppose we better get busy," Ezra said, and he rose stiffly to his feet.

That evening they dined on a stew that had cooked all day in a Dutch Oven. When they were finished they tossed their paper bowls onto the fire's embers and watched them ignite in blue and orange flames. As the others leaned back in their chairs, Landau reached in a cooler and pulled out two bottles of chilled wine. He turned, held them in front of the guys and bowed dramatically. "Gentleman, for your after-dining pleasure, two fine Merlots from the boutique vineyards of Kfira and Mayshar."

"What's a bo-teek?" asked Barney.

Landau handed out tall plastic cups and poured everyone a drink.

"Should we let it breath awhile?" Ezra asked.

"What's a bo-teek" Barney asked again, but everyone ignored him.

"A toast," Joe said. "To our Jewish journalist. The king of cow camp cuisine."

They raised the plastic cups and took a drink. Landau raised an empty cup.

"Pretty good stuff for a bo-teek," Barney said. "Though I'm not much of a wine man."

"I bet this is the first time kosher wine's been served in a cow camp," Ezra said.

"A toast," Barney said. "To Hot Water Jones, who has learned to take two-minute showers."

"Cheers."

Landau raised his empty cup. "A toast to Barney, Ezra, and Joe. To the artist, the writer, and the singer. The Renaissance wranglers of the prairie."

"Cheers."

"Have any of you been to Elko?" Garcia asked.

"You mean the big cowboy poetry gathering?" Barney said.

"That'd be slumming for Renaissance men," Joe joked.

"Slumming?" Garcia. "You don't like cowboy poetry?"

"Barn Wall's got nothing against cowboy poets," Ezra said. "Except that half of them aren't cowboys and fewer are poets."

"What?" Garcia said. "I don't believe this. I love cowboy poetry."

"Nothing wrong with it," Joe said. "Except they need to cull the herd. They've been reproducing too quickly and overstocking the country."

"What's Elko?" Landau asked. "Besides a town in Nevada."

"You don't know about cowboy poetry?" Garcia asked.

"I've never heard of it."

"Elko hosts a big cowboy folklore and western culture event every year," Ezra said. "It's the biggest cowboy poetry show in the country. It's a good deal and there's some great writers and musicians involved, but cowboy poetry is the rural version of Rap music. Too many imitators running around."

"Like Elmer Havig," Barney said.

"Who's that?" Joe asked.

"He's my neighbor. A former pig farmer from North Dakota. They struck oil on his place and he got rich. He bought a place below me, right next to Corey Boothe."

"Havig's a wannabe cowboy poet who sells his mimeographed poetry books in feed stores," Ezra said.

"I want to go to Elko," Garcia stated.

"Shoot, Elko's here," Barney said. "Ezra can make up a cowboy poem off the top of his head. What's the word I'm looking for?"

"Spontaneous," Joe said. "Like spontaneous sex."

"I think you mean, *extemporaneous*," Landau said.

"That's it," Barney said. "Ex-temp-or-rainy-whatever. Show 'em, Ez."

"I don't work cheap," Ezra said.

"Pancakes in the morning," Landau offered.

"Okay." Ezra nodded at Joe. "Maestro, a little accompaniment, if you please."

Joe reached for his 12-string and picked a few bars.

Ezra sang:

"As I walked out in the streets of ole Elko, as I walked out in ole Elko one day,

I spied a cowboy poet using poor simile, abusing weak metaphor, cold as the clay.

I see by your outfit, that you are a poet, these words he did say as I boldly stepped by.

Come sit down beside me and hear my bad poetry

For I'm shot in the syntax and know I must die."

Barney chuckled and snorted until Merlot shot out his nose.

Ezra resumed:

"Twas once in the reciting I used to go dashing,

In the memorizing I used to proclaim.

The first led to affecting, the second to pretending

I'm shot in the syntax and I'm dying for fame."

Ezra held up his hand to catch his breath, sip a drink, and collect his thoughts. Then he continued:

"Let six cowboy poets come carry my golf clubs,

Let six pretty gals shine my seventeen-inch boots,

Throw bunches of bad grammar all over my prosing

and dress sentimentality in cheap cowboy suits.

Oh, blow your nose wildly and stomp your verse blindly,

and step in poor rhythm as you bear me along
Take me to poetry meetings and pretend you adore me
for I'm a cowboy poet and know I write wrong."

Barney and Hot Water hooted and cheered.

Ezra held his hand up again. "The grand finis," he said. "A new tune, maestro."

Joe strummed *Leaving Cheyenne.*

Ezra sang:

"Whoopie-ti-yi-yo, get along, little doggerel,
its our misfortune and none of your own.
Whoopie-ti-yi-yo, get along little doggerel,
You know that poor meter will be your new home."

With that, Joe and Ezra removed their hats and bowed.

Barney raised his glass. "For your sakes, gentlemen, I hope you never go to Elko."

"I don't think there's much danger of that," Joe said.

"I still want to go to Elko," Hot Water said. "It's on my list of things to see."

"So, Ezra, what poets do you read?" Landau asked.

"Wendell Berry, William Stafford, Paul Zarzyski, Emily Dickinson."

"A cowboy who reads Emily Dickinson?" Landau said.

"I love Emily Dickinson."

"I'm still wondering what a bo-teek is," Barney said. "Isn't that a beauty shop?"

"It's a small, exclusive shop within a larger business," Landau explained.

"Like us," Joe said. "We're a small, exclusive group within the cowboy world."

"Shoot," Barney said. "I'm part of a bo-teek and didn't even know it."

"Stay humble or Havig will write a poem about you," Ezra said.

"Do another poem, Ezra," Garcia challenged.

"Do I look like an Automatic Poetry Machine?"

"Do one about Barney."

Ezra pursed his lips. "Okay, here goes:

There once was a cowboy named Barn Wall
whose memory was simply so darn small,
he'd leave the house in the morning,
giving the public no warning,
that the door was open to his barn stall."

Barney squealed with delight. "Shoot, Ole Ez is going to make me famous yet."

Landau had been watching quietly. He was going to write about them all, of course, but mostly about Ezra and Barney. They were the polarizing forces. Everything and everybody else spun in the orbit their interchanges created.

If he did write about them would they become famous? And if so, was that fair? Would attention destroy their charm?

Was it fair to expose the world to them? he wondered.

And was it fair to expose *them* to the world?

CHAPTER THIRTEEN

Landau got up and put what was left of the second bottle of wine back in the refrigerator. He'd produced the wine with the design of loosening tongues.

"Well, so far, we're getting through this job without any major wrecks," Barney said.

"Don't jinx us now," Joe said.

This subject gave Landau an open door. "So what's the worst wreck you've ever been in?" he asked, looking at Barney.

"Oh, I dunno--"

"The National Finals on Desolation," Hot Water chipped in.

All eyes turned to him.

"Not me," Garcia said. "I wasn't on Desolation. Barney was."

"That *was* a mite uncomfortable," Barney said.

"Did you get hurt often riding broncs?" the reporter asked.

"Shoot, no. You're in a bronc saddle, the arena is soft and level, you got two pickup men and a pretty good idea of what the horse is going to do. Lynne told me the worst injury he'd ever had riding broncs was a sprained ankle."

"What about you, Joe?" Landau asked. He was taking the round-about way to get to Ezra.

"I broke a guitar pick once," Joe said.

"I got bucked off Big Jack," Hot Water contributed.

"Hot Water, you fell off Big Jack," Ezra said. "Into the mud."

"What about your wrecks, Ezra?" Landau asked. "I still haven't heard what happened with that Oswald horse."

Ezra looked down into his cup and swirled the wine, making a small whirlpool in the center. "I don't know," he said thoughtfully. "I don't tell those kind of stories to white guys."

"But I'm an Indian," Joe joked.

"And I'm Jewish, if that counts," Landau added.

"What do you mean you don't you tell stories to white guys?" Garcia asked.

"White people are too cynical," Ezra said. "That's why I don't preach in white churches anymore."

"You preach?" Hot Water asked. No one had told him Ezra was a preacher.

"He's preached all over the country," Joe said.

"Used to. Now it's just once in awhile on a Rez," Ezra explained.

"Why won't you preach to white guys?" Garcia asked.

"Because The Trinity for white guys is Plato, Aristotle and Socrates," Ezra said. "White people are bound by rationalism."

"So what does preaching have to do with horse wrecks?" Garcia asked. "I don't get the connection."

"That's because you're white, Hot Water. You're a linear thinker."

"The Jewish world isn't linear," Landau said.

"What's linear?" Barney asked. "Isn't that going in a straight line or something?"

"You're the story-teller, Ezra," Joe said. "It's your duty to tell us. There's gotta be a storyteller code or something."

"Okay, I'll tell you the story," Ezra said. "But you better pour me two fingers of Merlot."

Landau brought out the wine again, poured everyone a few sips, then settled back for the story.

"For Hot Water and the reporter I'll have to start at the beginning," Ezra said. "Lynne and I bred a big Appendix mare and got a fancy bay colt I named Pedro. I started him as a two and rode him quite a bit as a three and four. He never offered to buck.

"Last November, on a really nice day, I was logging him. That's dragging logs to get him used to a rope. We were pulling a big log when he got sour and quit, so I gave him a little nudge with my spurs.

"He went off like a sack of grenades. I tossed my dally loose so as not to get tangled in the rope. He bucked like a bull, jumping and spinning in one motion. I was out of shape right away, but was bearing down to pull his head up when I felt a tight rope against my right thigh. I knew my lariat had hung up on something and it was time to find an exit. On the next spin I eased out over the cantle and let his hips launch me free."

He paused and appraised his audience.

"Now this is where it gets interesting, gentlemen," he continued. "I was in the air at an angle, my legs a little higher than my head and shoulders, when I saw my rope come sailing out of nowhere and two coils wrapped around my right leg." He put his cup down.

"Right then, a peace descended like a cloud and seemed to hold me in the air. Time stopped. I was suspended midair, and had all the time in the world to pull my right leg through those coils. And that's what I did. The moment I cleared the second coil, time caught up with itself. I crashed to the ground, that big bay horse bucked all over the top of me, and then took off full speed through the trees, still dragging that big log.

"He dragged that log over a quarter-mile before the rope came free. I could've been entangled between the log and the saddle, right under his back hooves."

"You would have been killed," Landau said.

"Maybe," Ezra said. "Or badly injured."

"Time suspension isn't too uncommon," Landau said. "You hear about it in life-and-death situations, like combat or serious car accidents."

"Well, it happened just like I told it. Time suspension doesn't mystify me. I just believe it was an encounter with grace."

"But there's more to the story?" Landau suggested.

"Yeah. I got on him again. I waited a week to heal up, then I got chapped-up to take him on a big circle and really ride the silliness out of him. I untracked him good, then tightened my cinch and eased aboard. I figured this time I'd be ready. Well, there is no being ready for a bad Oswald."

"Least-wise not in the hills in a stock saddle," Barney said.

Ezra continued. "He took one step and blew up again. This time he meant business. I rode him through the first two spins; then his ears came back, and I felt his eyes find me. He knew right where I was and threw such a hard lick at me that he lost his feet. He came down on his side on the edge of a frozen creek bank and we slid onto the ice. The ice broke beneath us and my head went under water. I was whammed, jammed, and water-boarded, just like that. The wind was knocked out of me, and, when I gasped, I sucked down icy water. He thrashed about and kicked me a couple times, then got to his feet and ran off.

"My body didn't want to move but I had to in order to breathe. I got my head up out of the water and lay there for a moment or two until the rest of my body responded. Then I crawled up the bank and used a tree to get to my feet."

"I bet you took inventory then," Barney said.

"I checked body parts. Nothing broken. I was numb, both from the cold water and shock, I suppose."

"Did you go to the hospital?" Landau asked.

"No. I just soaked in a hot bath."

"Pretty gutsy getting on him a second time," Hot Water said.

"No, not gutsy. Just stupid."

"And now your hands are suffering," Landau said.

Garcia looked at Ezra curiously. He didn't know anything about Ezra's hands hurting.

"Yeah, bruised spinal cord. Or spinal contusion, they say. And I wouldn't have this condition if I hadn't got on him that second time."

"Maybe you were hurt in the first wreck," Barney said.

The room had become noticeably more somber.

"No," Ezra said. "Grace intervened the first time, but I cancelled grace with my own stubbornness."

"But you still ride," Landau stated.

"Guys like us -- me, Joe, Barney -- we live to ride. We count Lynne lucky because he rode up until the end. He day-worked one day. Had a sudden heart attack the next. He never knew he'd saddled his last horse."

"Back to your first incident," Landau said. "That's the one that really bothers you. You wonder why you were spared. It's like God stopped time for you."

"Wouldn't you wonder?" Ezra asked.

"I suppose I would."

"It's like my life is an unfinished poem," Ezra said. "There's still a last line or stanza to be written."

"Shoot," Barney said. "This is giving me the willies."

"Well, here is the good news," Ezra said. "I know I'll never have to worry about being badly hurt in a horse accident again."

"Why is that?" Landau asked.

"Because if I ever feel a horse coil under me again, like he's about to blow, I'm going to die of fright before he can start his first jump."

Barney, Joe, and Garcia chuckled, but Landau knew Ezra was using humor to deflect a deeper issue. There was more to the story. With Ezra, it seemed there was always more to the story.

Garcia became quiet. Getting bucked off was his greatest fear, yet he fantasized about being a bronc rider.

"Getting busted-up some isn't the scary part," Joe said. "It's the idea of getting paralyzed. It could happen to any of us at any time. In an instant."

"Shoot, now I've gone from getting the chills to getting depressed," Barney said. "I love being horseback, but the idea of rocking on the porch watching the grandkids ride ain't all that bad, either."

"You know what you don't hear mentioned much these days?" Ezra said, changing the subject. "Is anyone talking about the satisfaction of riding a bronc to a standstill."

"What do you mean?" Landau asked.

"When me, Joe, and Barney were kids, there were a lot of bad horses in the country. My dad was a trader, and I rode some sour horses. When a horse bucked, you were expected to ride it until it quit. Ride it to a complete standstill."

"All this talk about broncs is making my back hurt," Barney said.

"How many, huh, *horse wrecks* have you been in?" Landau asked Ezra.

"All told?" Ezra said. "You mean buck-offs, fall-offs, getting kicked, being dragged, and having them buck but getting them rode?"

"Don't forget having them fall on you and roll over you," Joe added.

"Counting everything, I suppose about 30," Ezra said. "Maybe more."

"And how many times did you ride a bucking horse to a standstill?" Landau asked.

"Two or three times."

"You said people never mention this anymore," Landau said. "Why is that?"

"They train 'em differently these days," Barney said. "People are slower, more patient."

"And the horses are different, too," Joe offered. "They've bred the buck out of most of them."

"How many bucking horses do you suppose Lynne rode to a stand-still?" Landau asked.

Barney whispered softly. "Oh, shoot. Scores of them, I bet."

"And he wasn't the only one," Joe said. "For years all the horses were broke that way. That's all rough string riders did."

"Until they got stove-up," Barney said.

"Stove-up?" Landau asked.

"In the old days when you were crippled-up, you had to stay inside near the stove," Ezra explained. "So, you were stove-up."

"And if you were with a wagon and got hurt, then you rode in the groaning cart," Barney added.

"The what?" Landau asked.

"The wagon that carried the bedrolls," Ezra explained. "Men who were crippled lay in there and groaned."

"Wow," Garcia said, his blue eyes bright with excitement. "This is really good stuff. Someone should write a book about it."

Barney and Joe smiled and looked at Ezra.

Ezra looked at Peter Landau. "Yeah," Ezra said. "Someone should."

CHAPTER FOURTEEN

Ezra's hands seemed a combination of sparking electrical wires and ice cubes. What wasn't numb, hurt. He couldn't dally effectively, so he tied on hard-and-fast. Throwing a normal loop was impossible so he improvised, creating a loop he held in three fingers. When he released it he maintained the slack with his little finger so the loop traveled by itself, closing as it went. To rope this way his horse had to be positioned perfectly for each toss, but the advantage was not having slack to handle. Barney and Joe noticed Ezra's change to being tied to the horn but didn't say anything. They were tired and their shoulders ached but roping was still a pleasant chore.

By mid-morning Ezra tied his horse, hustled to the shack, dug through his war bag and found his medications. He gulped down some nerve medicine and two of the codeine pain pills -- knowing it was a risk -- then rushed back to the branding pen.

By noon he was in his own little world. The others wolfed down food, but Ezra leaned against a corral plank, sipped coffee, and stared into the distance. Landau watched him carefully.

If Ezra's roping improved or worsened that afternoon, he didn't notice. Everything he did was by muscle memory: twirl, toss, turn, drag, face the stake, watch the crew, then slacken the rope and let the calf kick free. By the time they'd finished, Ezra had returned to half his senses. He'd never been so happy to see a herd of cows and calves file out a gate.

After supper Hot Water suggested another game of poker. Ezra joined them at the table, but declined to play. Nothing was harder for his hands than peeling a flat card off a tabletop. Through the clouds of fatigue and drugs he heard someone mention old hippies and knew Hot Water was discussing his parents again.

Something was being said about dopey dopers and longhaired losers. Ezra tuned it out. When Garcia belittled his parents he reminded Ezra of a chained dog barking at the moon: no matter how much noise he made, the moon was still there.

"Ezra," Landau said.

Ezra didn't answer.

"Ezra," Landau repeated.

Barney elbowed his friend in the ribs.

Ezra looked up, startled. "What?" he asked.

"Peter's asking you a question," Barney said.

"Ezra, you were a hippy, weren't you?"

Hot Water was dumbfounded. No one had told him Ezra had been a hippy.

"Tie-dyed and fried," Ezra said.

"And you did the hitchhiking thing?" Landau added, trying to coax a story from him.

"About 12,000 miles," Ezra said slowly. Talking took energy.

"Ah, I don't believe it," Garcia protested. "You guys are playing another joke on me. Ezra was never a hippy."

"Hair below his shoulders," Barney said.

"No way," Garcia insisted.

Ezra got up. "I need a little air," he said. He went outside, picking his way carefully through the growing darkness, and stood by the corrals. He could hear the horses munching their feed. Nighthawks dived and darted, and, in the distance, an owl hooted. Stars were beginning to peek out from a turquoise sky.

Landau suddenly appeared beside him. "I hope I didn't say anything to upset you," he said.

"No. It's okay. Garcia can just get on my nerves when he starts ripping into his folks."

"He has some pretty serious parent issues."

"He'll grow out of it. But it might take having his own kids to do it." In the dim starlight, Landau could tell Ezra was rubbing his hands.

"I'm sorry about your hands, the pain--"

"We'll be done tomorrow," Ezra said. "We'll get the last of these Skinner calves branded and leave our halcyon world."

"I've enjoyed it," Landau said. "One forgets the value of physical work."

"It was nice to forget the pressures of the real world for a few days."

"Pressures?" Landau asked.

"Remember me mentioning Adrienne Doyle? She'll be at my place in a few days."

"Doyle? How come?"

"Anne wants us to sign up for a government program. I swore Garcia to silence about it because I don't want Barney and Joe to know. None of us like government programs."

"And Doyle?"

"She's the civilian contractor assigned to appraise our application."

Landau whistled softly. "You know her reputation?"

"I've seen her in action. And I've heard stuff, too, but whether it's all true or not--"

"It's true," Landau said. "I assume this program is something you need?"

"It could help."

"But your hands."

"People work in pain. It's nothing new."

"What if it gets worse, and you have to choose between ranching and writing?"

"I'm not writing much anyway."

"But you will. You have to. You *are* a writer."

"Right now, I just want to stay horseback as long as I can. Before that wreck on Pedro I was as fit as a guy could be for my age. In an instant that all changed."

"What about your son? Isn't he interested in coming back to help?"

"No, it's not in his blood. You can't be what you're not meant to be. Every generation has its mountain to climb. My dad was born in 1909 and was still part of the horse era. Anne's dad was born in '24 and was part of the internal combustion engine revolution. He loved mechanics. Dylan is an innovative software designer and entrepreneur. Technology is the new frontier, and he's a pioneer."

"In your example, you left out your generation."

"Mine? The Aquarius Generation? I can't say I'm very proud of us. We did some good things -- racial equality, gender equality, environmental awareness -- but we are a self-centered lot. Peter Pans in paisley."

"What was your generation's frontier?"

"Drugs. Quite the legacy, isn't it?"

"You've no hope for your generation?"

"Are you familiar with the story of Samson?" Ezra asked. "He was blinded and chained before he was truly a servant. My generation has been blinded by cynicism and chained to self-indulgence."

"But, you and Anne found something."

"No, we didn't find anything. We were found by someone."

Ezra turned and looked at the young reporter. Under the light of a rising moon, and in the stillness of the Montana prairie, Peter Landau had a timeless Jewishness to his face.

"We best get back in," Ezra said. "Barney and Joe probably need rescuing."

Joe first noticed the squall line of charcoal-colored clouds as he closed the gate on the cattle. He also felt something in the air; a calm, foreboding heaviness. They'd been blessed with five days of fair weather, and Joe hoped for one more, but the southwestern sky hinted at change coming.

Barney didn't notice the distant clouds. He sat on White Crow observing Landau and wondering how he'd draw him in a cartoon. The problem was, the reporter had done nothing hilarious or careless -- he just worked with a calm professionalism as if Columbia University gave doctorates in range branding -- and Barney's cartoons were inspired by drama, disaster, and dilemmas.

Garcia Jones, Barney noticed, was another matter. He'd fleshed-out with both color and muscle, but a restlessness rode him, like he had an unreachable itch he couldn't ask anyone to scratch. Barney was fond of the lad, sort of like he was fond of his dog, Kitty. Thinking of Kitty made him homesick. They'd agreed on no dogs, so Kitty had missed some fine days of bachelor food and socialization. Fortunately, Kitty would be able to smell the entire week on Barney's jeans as the cartoonist had remembered only the pair he was wearing.

Ezra tightened Simon's cinch and breast collar. He'd taken one nerve pill and one codeine pill at breakfast chased by four cups of stout coffee. Roping, like shooting a basketball, was a combination of mechanics, confidence and touch, and Ezra was hopeful for a good day. The fewer the misses, the less stress on his hands.

Ezra roped well in the beginning.

Joe seemed hurried and rushed his shots.

Barney roped as if he'd ridden into one of his cartoon panels. Finally, Ezra rode over to him. "Barn Wall, are you with us, or are you painting graffiti on the barn wall of your mind?"

Barney snapped from his thoughts and looked at Ezra as if he were a stranger.

"Just what I thought," Ezra said. "You're vandalizing your inner sanctums again."

Barney shook his head to clear it, then grinned. "Inner sanctums? Shoot, Ezra, I didn't even know I had any of those."

Ezra then rode over to Joe.

Joe wore disgust like a mask. He was tired of missing.

"Joseph," Ezra said.

"What?"

"See? That's the problem. You're answering to Joseph. You're not Joseph. You are Joey Ropesaplenty, magician of the long line."

Joe smiled. Within moments he was roping better.

They ate a hurried lunch as everyone watched the darkening southern sky. The storm was nearing.

"Think we can beat it?" Barney asked.

"We beat it or it beats us," Joe said.

At that moment a dust devil swirled in the pen, danced through the cows, then dissipated. Hot Water began a monologue on the science of air turbulence but was ignored. The ropers changed horses.

As the afternoon progressed the storm clouds stayed on a southerly course and the crew was only affected by the backside winds.

With twenty calves left Joe offered to make a quick run to the Skinner place to pick up their checks. "I don't think that storm's gonna hit us," he said. "But I think we should have our checks in hand when we leave."

Ezra stood in the saddle and pulled his watch from a front pocket -- he never wore a watch on his wrist. "It's only five," he said. "We can finish up here. Hot Water is going to boil over if he doesn't get to rope a calf or two."

"I should stay to watch that, but I won't," Joe said.

"Hey, Hot Water," Ezra yelled. "You can rope now."

Garcia tossed a branding iron into the fire and sprinted toward the truck. He came rushing back with his saddle and every rope he owned.

"Think he wants to rope?" Barney said.

"Yeah, I think he wants to rope," Ezra said. "But you better stay in there with him. Those last few calves will be wild and hard to find."

Ezra joined Landau.

After thirteen misses Hot Water's enthusiasm had drained. Barney, meanwhile, had dragged four calves to the stakes. Finally, Barney rode over to the youngster.

"Did you file a Government Form 114 on that lariat?" he asked.

Hot Water shook his head nervously.

"Well, that's your problem. Just imagine you did hours of paper-work to requisition one black calf on the end of a forty-foot poly."

Wallace rode off.

Garcia caught a calf with his next loop.

With one calf remaining Ezra told Barney and Landau they could begin packing to go. Ezra was already packed -- he and Joe had done it long before sunrise -- all he needed was to load his horses and point his truck south. "One calf left," Ezra yelled at Garcia. "Catch it any way you can."

Hot Water stalked the last calf for fifteen minutes before crowding it in a corner and dropping a loop over its head. He dragged it to Ezra who flanked it as Barney and Landau returned.

"That's it," Barney announced as let the branded calf up. "We're done! The great adventure is over."

As they let the cows out Joe came back with their checks.

"Let's load horses and go," Barney said. He was thinking of his pal, Kitty, and how glad the dog would be to see him.

"I'm staying," Joe said.

They looked at him curiously.

"I've hired on to A.I. two hundred heifers. I guess that shack will be my home a little longer."

"A.I.?" Landau asked.

"Artificially inseminate," Garcia explained.

"Does Mrs. Ropesaplenty know about this?" Barney asked.

John L. Moore

Joe grinned sheepishly. "No, but I guess I can send her roses." He pulled his cell phone from his pocket. "That reminds me, Ezra. It looks like Anne's been trying to call my number."

Ezra took the phone. "Anne? That seems odd."

"You better call her," Joe said. "Ride up to the knoll. You might get a signal."

Ezra mounted Simon and rode to the small swelling of prairie that had become their phone booth. His home phone rang five times before Anne picked up. "Anne?"

"Ezra? Is that you? The reception is bad."

"It's me. Is everything okay?"

There was a short pause. "No," she said.

"What" I can't hear you."

"Ezra, can you come home?"

"Home? We're coming home now. What's going on?"

"What? I can't hear you, Ezra."

"I said, what's going on? Are you okay?

"Ezra. If you can hear me, just come home. We had a funnel cloud go through the yard."

CHAPTER FIFTEEN

"A funnel cloud?" Barney asked.

"Yes, a funnel cloud."

"Is everything okay?" Joe asked.

"I don't know. The connection dropped." Ezra rushed to load his horses. Simon and Big Jack jumped into the trailer eagerly. They wanted to go home. Ezra slammed the partition gate then loaded White Crow and Barney's old mare.

Landau watched him with concern -- his journalistic detachment yielding to friendship. He handed the keys to his rental to Garcia. "Take my SUV," he said. "I'm riding with Ezra."

Barney looked relieved. He knew someone, besides Garcia, whose immaturity often made him oblivious to other people's hardship, should ride with Ezra. But Barney didn't want to do it. He preferred humorous situations.

Ezra slammed the trailer gate shut and latched it. "Let's go," he shouted. When he got behind the wheel he was surprised to see the reporter get in.

"I'm riding with you," Landau said, meeting Ezra's dark, turbulent stare.

"Fine." Ezra shifted his one-ton dually into gear and roared away from the cow camp.

They rode in silence down miles of graveled roads. When they hit the blacktop Landau reached for his cell phone. "I need to make a call."

Ezra assumed he was calling an editor or business associate back East, but he was wrong.

"Hello? Anne? This is Peter Landau. I'm with Ezra. We're on our way. How are you doing?"

Ezra couldn't believe it. The reporter had called his wife.

"Okay. Yes."

Ezra heard intermittent responses.

"Yes. Okay, I'll tell him. We've just reached the highway. Okay. No, the storm never reached here. Okay. Bye." Landau put the phone away and looked at Ezra. "I thought you might need a situation report."

"And?" Ezra said.

"Anne just came in from inspecting everything. Things are good, all things considered. The roof of the house is damaged, but the insurance will cover that. There's some water in your basement but hardest hit were the corrals and the old boxcar. The boxcar is kindling. Part of your corrals were laid flat and the stack of hay bales is gone."

Ezra swallowed hard. Thirty ton of hay missing? Plus, six tons of horse cake in the box car. He tried to be thankful Anne hadn't been hurt, or even killed, but the idea of rebuilding the corrals was staggering. At his age, with his hands...

"She said it was a downpour of rain and some hail, along with the funnel cloud."

They drove in silence for several miles. Landau knew Ezra needed time to digest the news.

"Thanks for calling her," Ezra said finally.

"You're welcome. Excuse me, I need to make one more call while I can get a signal."

After a short pause Ezra heard him say: "Henrietta? This is Peter Landau. Are you okay? Is your house okay?" Ezra realized to his shame he'd not considered the Wallace home which was only three miles from his.

Landau talked for a minute and put his phone away. "The funnel cloud didn't touch down there," he said. "They just got a lot of rain."

Ezra shook his head. "I can't believe I didn't even think about Barney's place."

"You're not yourself, Ezra. You're in pain, you're exhausted, and you're worried about Anne and your home."

"And I'm stoned out of my gourd, and you came along to keep me from killing myself on the way home?"

"And I will drive if you want me to."

"No, that's okay, I can drive. But I do appreciate what you're doing." They traveled a couple miles in silence, and Ezra slowly accepted Landau as a calming influence, a role Anne usually played.

"Okay," Ezra said abruptly. "You're here to keep my mind off things, so tell me about your article. How's it going? Is it taking the direction you thought it would?"

"It's coming together, but it's early. You know how it is. There are many different directions one can go."

"But the important direction is the direction in which one is pulled. And your pull is…?"

"It's still the same. The current role and status of the horse in America."

"Are you still going to report on the horse slaughter issue?"

"Sure. That can't be any more dangerous than the Gaza Strip."

"Don't bet on it. So where do you go from here?"

"Nevada. There's someone there I need to interview. Then I think I'll come back here."

"Here? Why?"

"You and Barney. Unless I find a couple of characters who are more interesting."

"This project seems bigger than an article. It sounds like a book."

"It could be. What do you think?"

Ezra laughed. "You don't want advice from me. It's been 12 years since I wrote a book."

"Are you going to start writing again soon?"

"I don't know. Technology has changed everything. Writing is no longer a meritocracy. First-time writers are publishing their own ebooks cheaply, then getting their friends to give them great reviews online. Being a *published* writer doesn't mean what it used to."

"It's the same with journalism. When everyone has a blog does that make everyone a journalist?"

"You sound like an old fart like me, Peter."

Landau shook his head. "Sometimes I think I am."

Dusk turned to darkness and Ezra noticed the blacktop glistening with wetness. A mile later they splashed through their first little puddle. They were on the edge of the storm track.

Ezra worried about the ranch. Had pastures been hailed out? Were reservoirs washed-out? It was a terrible having to wait until dawn to discover the damages.

"You're worrying," Landau said.

"So, distract me. Do you have a working title for your project?"

"I've had several, but nothing that's stuck."

"Don't do a *last of the cowboys* article," Ezra warned. "It's been done to death. That theme has been used since the 1890s. Besides, *Monte Walsh* has already been written."

"Monte who?"

"Google Lee Marvin. He didn't write it, but he starred in the movie."

"I've never seen it."

"How about *Lonely are the Brave?*"

"Never heard of it."

"Kirk Douglas. It was based on an Edward Abbey novel called *The Brave Cowboy*."

"Edward Abbey?" Landau asked. "The author of *The Monkey Wrench Gang*? Abbey is Doyle's favorite author."

"You know that for sure?" Ezra asked.

"Yeah, I do."

The road pulled them quietly as each was lost in his thoughts, then Landau said, "If I can't do a last-of-the-cowboys theme, how about a character study of the crew at a remote cow camp?"

"That might work. How would you would paint us? Start with Joe."

"A character portrait of Joe? We're talking about two people, aren't we? Pagliano and Ropesaplenty? The latter is a nostalgic romanticist who's convinced his life is real and everyone else's is imaginary. But Joe Pagliano is cautious and introverted. He's the nice guy who sings well."

"And Garcia?" Ezra offered.

"Hot Water Jones." Landau chuckled softly. "He's a difficult portrait to draw," Landau said. "He's too young to have defined himself yet."

"He's an enigma," Ezra admitted. "He lives in a fantasy world of bronc riders, but he doesn't have any recklessness in him. He's measured and scientific."

"I know you're concerned he'll become a bureaucrat, but I don't think you have to worry. He won't sell out."

"He could. Any of us could. But so far rebellion has been his salvation. If he were a conformist he'd be living with his parents, smoking dope, and charting horoscopes. And that leads us finally to the indescribable."

"Barney Wallace. He's Shakespearean," Landau said. But is he comedy or tragedy? He's deeper and more serious than he lets on. And he's certainly devoid of affectation."

"Well, it's hard to swagger when you're looking for your lost dog... lost glasses... lost wallet.. lost phone..."

"He does misplace things, doesn't he?"

"Everything except his heart. It's too big to lose."

"And then there's you," Landau said.

Ezra stiffened.

"I can't leave you out. You're the hard one and you know it."

"Okay, let's have it. How do you view me?"

"I've learned more about you by reading your articles than by being around you. You're a natural observer and chronicler. You're a romantic, like the others, but they have a noticeable warmth. You are..."

"Cold?"

"No, not cold. If anything, you're hot. Smoldering hot. Like a branding iron. You want to leave a mark."

"And the others don't?"

"Not like you. You fight life harder than they do. They're content with landscape but you dig for meaning."

"Motivation," Ezra said. "It is the root of every good character, and we're all just characters in a big story."

"So, what motivates Ezra Riley?"

"Ezra sighed softly and fixed his gaze on the highway's intermittent striping. "I want to please God," he said.

"I would not have thought that."

"Then I must be doing a poor job."

Silence became a soft wedge between them. Ezra sought to breech it. "How about you, Peter? You're a part of this crew. Define yourself."

This took Landau aback. "I'm not part of the story."

"Yes, you're definitely part of the story."

"Okay, let's say I am. You define me. Be my co-writer."

Ezra smiled. His opinions were more often given than solicited. "You're all of us in a cosmopolitan package. Like Hot Water, you're a mixture of zeal and academics. Like Joe you're a vagabond chasing a dream, but your adventures are larger, more complicated, and better-funded. Like Barney, you struggle with a balance between depth and superficiality. Barney's armor is humor. Your's is analytical detachment."

"And how am I like you?"

"You're a seeker. You tend toward intensity. And you want to leave your mark."

"So, what am I seeking?"

"You tell me. It's your quest."

The journalist stared thoughtfully into the night. He noticed the barrow pits at the side of the highway were filled with water. They'd entered the heart of the storm's track. "I don't know if it is *what* I am seeking," he said. "But rather *who* I'm seeking."

Ezra tapped on his brakes. They were approaching his mailbox. "And who is that?" he asked.

Before Landau could answer the Riley yard was before them and both men fell silent. Ezra's question became forgotten.

The scene was surreal. Ezra felt as if he were driving into a Salvador Dali painting. Broken tree limbs reached up from a small lake where moonlight danced and shimmered. The lake was his yard. It stretched from his house to the corrals. The truck and trailer splashed its way to the barn. Ezra parked and got out. The storm had passed, the night was still, stars twinkled, and the air was humid and fresh. Sunday Creek, swollen and fast, was a roar in the darkness and little streams rippled toward it. The corrals were a jumbled patchwork of shadows. Some poles and posts stood tall and straight like good soldiers while others were down, casualties of a sweeping hand of wind. His good dog, Casey, leaned against Ezra's leg, his body trembling with happy exertion. Ezra's hand dropped reflexively to the dog's head, and the trembling ceased.

Barney and Garcia pulled in. Ezra heard the splash of their feet as they stepped from the SUV.

"We'll take care of the horses," Barney said.

Ezra's mind was transfixed by water and shadows. "Throw 'em in the pasture behind the barn," he said. "There's no corrals to hold them." He turned slowly toward the house.

"I'll be by tomorrow to get mine," Barney said.

"I can stay around for a few days and help you clean up," Landau offered.

Ezra shook his head. "Too muddy. But, thanks."

He walked toward the house, his boots soaked above his spur straps. Faint light flickered through the windows. The electricity was out, but Anne had candles burning. She met him at the door and melted into his arms. He couldn't see her face, but he could imagine: Anne Riley, tall, strong, principled. Deep-set blue eyes bridged by a narrow, distinctive nose. He felt her cheek against his. She allowed him to comfort her and she gave comfort in return. They'd been through so much, and now, this blow of water and wind.

He felt his arms strengthen in holding her, felt her head arch back and knew her eyes were searching his as she was prone to do. She strained to see his face, but couldn't in the darkness. She sighed softly. He felt her breath leave her and felt his own stay contained within him, filling his lungs, buoying a heart that was adrift in rough water.

She was his music, and he was her words. She, afraid to sing and play in front of people, and he, gifted to write for those who seemed wordless.

They rocked softly in each other's arms. Two streams pooling in the moonlight.

PART III

"Its not what you look at that matters,
it's what you see."
-- Henry David Thoreau

"Horse and poets should be fed, not overfed."
-- Charles IX

CHAPTER SIXTEEN

D r. Adrienne Doyle's past month had been terrible and she couldn't imagine it getting worse. Then she looked in her rearview mirror and saw Peter Landau.

She trembled.

At forty-three years of age, with hundreds of thousands of miles of travel, several hundred thousand words in print, and scores of angry confrontations with farmers, ranchers, government officials, lobbyists, and politicians she'd rarely shown weakness of any kind, let alone fear. But now she was afraid. She pulled her cap brim lower hoping he wouldn't recognize her. Doyle had chosen this remote truck stop in Nevada solely to avoid seeing anyone she knew or anyone who might recognize her from recent newspaper articles. Landau was a newshound. The fact he was on her tail couldn't be a coincidence. He had to have picked up a blood trail. His vehicle was a few feet behind hers at a pump island and neither of them had filled their tanks yet.

She considered her options. Desperately low on gas, she could pull away and park by the big rigs, hoping he'd leave. Pulling away without fueling might draw his attention so she decided to wait and pretended to be busy with something in her purse. Women did that all the time, didn't they? Doyle snuck a peek. Landau was going around his SUV with a squeegee cleaning the dust and dead bugs from the windows. He paused for a second and looked toward her, and she quickly dropped her eyes.

God! Was he psychic, too? she wondered.

Another concern hit her. Landau wasn't known to be opportunistic. It wasn't his pattern to read the news, see controversy, and follow an existing story. If he were on her tail, it meant he'd been researching her for weeks. Maybe months. He was good enough to have suspected something a long time ago.

But why her? Why here? Landau's speciality was combat zones, and, particularly, Middle East conflicts.

Landau did not cover small stories.

A huge fear gripped her. How much could he know? Could he know about--

No. Doyle was being paranoid and knew it. The best thing she could do, she told herself, was get out of her SUV like everything was normal, begin gassing up, keep her back to him as much as possible, and hope for the best.

That might work if he wasn't actually tailing her. If he were tailing her what difference did it make sitting like a scared rabbit? It only showed a vulnerability he could exploit. She moved her hand to the door handle but her hips and legs wouldn't follow. Her right foot told her to tromp on the gas pedal and roar away. Outrun him. But that was silly. She didn't have enough fuel. He'd only find her stranded a few miles down the road.

This, she thought, was as bad as her father's funeral and she'd thought that was as bad as things could get.

It had begun with her father being diagnosed with pancreatic cancer.

Some survive months with the disease, maybe a year, so she'd hesitated in getting home to see him. She had work to do, after all.

Important work. But her father died in 17 days. It wasn't cancer that killed him. He was found in his office at Rutgers with his head on a desk littered with papers. His heart, never strong, had torn apart like pages ripped from a notebook.

Sorry, professor, your story is over.

She couldn't help but be macabre. It helped her accept reality. At the funeral she realized she was alone. Her mother had committed suicide when she was four, leaving her an only child to be raised by an academic who doted on her on weekends and neglected her during the week. She'd loved her dad but had grown tired of him and his repeated stories.

Adrienne, did I ever tell you how I met your mother at a Weather Underground meeting?

His funeral had seemed cold, dry and dark. It was held in a small chapel with a Unitarian minister. The mourners were colleagues and a few foot soldiers from the Sixties; old men now, with pot bellies, short gray ponytails, watery eyes and sagging faces. They gave her sad, desultory stares.

You are the future. You are the hope of the Revolution.

Leaving the service she'd received a text from her lover, Lars. She'd been dumped. A text? What could she expect from a lawyer, she decided, even if he were an environmental attorney? The loss of her father and lover were left jabs, irritating and painful, but nothing that could knock her down. Then, six days ago, came the haymaker. The *Washington Post* -- the *Post* of all things; she could have understood it if it had been *The Washington Times* -- linked a young Idaho rancher's suicide to Doyle having *discovered*, three years ago, an endangered insect, *Nicrophorus Americanus* -- American burying beetle -- on his property.

The rancher had insisted the insect had been planted, if not by Doyle, then by her cronies. He sued. His lower court victory was overturned by the Ninth District judges, he lost his land, was bankrupted by legal costs, and recently ate the barrel of his .357 Magnum.

Was Doyle complicit? the article had asked, and supported its suspicions with a list of other questionable incidents, though all were allegations without substantiation. Still, she knew the article was the reason her boyfriend, Lars, had dumped her.

Where had the Post gotten the information? Had it been her blog? Lars had warned her not to create a blog -- *Stay below the radar. You lose value if you draw attention* -- but she had, and she'd promoted it vigorously. Getting favorable attention hadn't been hard. Half the journalists in the country owed her something, didn't they?

Even those bastards at the *Post.*

Lose value? If you wanted to be someone, you had to have a blog.

Doyle was still struggling to get out of her vehicle. *Dammit, just do it,* she told herself. She pulled on the door handle and swung out of her SUV and looked straight at Landau, who was taking the hose from his tank.

"Dr. Doyle?" he asked.

She sensed he was genuinely surprised. "Hi, Peter." She removed her gas cap, inserted the nozzle, swiped her debit card and let the machine begin its work.

Landau hung his nozzle on the pump and approached her. "What a coincidence to see you."

She extended her hand and said icily, "Yes, isn't it?"

He was confused by her tone. "I bet I know where you're going."

"Do you?"

"Yes, but… say, have you had lunch? I understand the food here is good."

She looked at him cynically, almost ready to arch her back and hiss, then reason softened her. Was it possible, she thought, that he was unaware of her status? Who knew where Landau had been the past week? Libya? Syria? Yet, he claimed to know where she was going.

"Sure," she said. "Lunch would be fine. I'll meet you inside."

He pulled from the pump island and parked next to a Kenworth bull rack.

Keep your enemies close, she told herself. But then again, maybe he wasn't an enemy. She'd first met him at a summit in Geneva six years ago, had calculated the risk of fostering a relationship with him, but chose not to. He wasn't the typical journalist. She couldn't hook, twist, and bend him for her purposes, so she'd stayed cordial but aloof. But that didn't mean she couldn't play him. As far as Adrienne Doyle was concerned she could play anybody.

Landau looked across the table and realized he'd never have recognized Doyle if she hadn't looked directly at him. Her hair, once long and auburn, was a dirty brown, cut short, and showed streaks of gray at the temples. Her face had lost its healthy, outdoor glow and was weathered and wrinkled. The real surprise was her weight, not fat but muscle. Her shoulders were bulky -- from years of carrying heavy backpacks in wildernesses, he guessed -- and her legs seemed thick and stubby. Too many mountain trails? It was ironic, he thought, but she looked like an overworked western ranch wife -- the very type of woman he knew she loathed -- only less centered. Less fulfilled.

"So, Dr. Doyle --"

"Adrienne."

"Adrienne. So, how have you been?"

She paused, her right hand holding her fork with the tines pointed down. "I'm sure you know my father passed away recently."

"No, I'm sorry. I didn't know. I've been busy."

Landau was still flush with the freshness of the past week, of being with men who said what they meant, meant what they said, and took you at your word. Normally, he would have sensed Doyle's duplicity. Today, he missed it.

"And you? Where have you been that you would think you know where I am going?"

"I've been in eastern Montana. In fact, I spent a week in a remote cow camp. I got to know Ezra Riley. That's where you're going, isn't it? The Riley ranch."

Doyle put on a pensive look. "I don't know. I suppose it could be. I have a couple of EEEP applications to screen."

Landau nodded. "Oh, of course, confidentiality. I don't spend a lot of time in the States, so I sometimes miss the little cultural changes. In any case, you're going to find Ezra Riley interesting. If that's where you're going, of course."

"And, if that is where I am going, why would I find him interesting?"

Landau took a drink from the water glass. "For one thing, he's a writer."

"A writer?" Doyle said sarcastically. "Another cowboy poet?"

Landau laughed out loud remembering the cow camp song of Ezra's and Joe's. "No, I wouldn't say that."

"It doesn't make any difference. I'm not going there to socialize, Peter," she said, slightly scolding him. "I'm going there to appraise rangeland conditions in regard to sage grouse habitat. Besides, if this Riley guy was any sort of writer I would have heard about him."

Her rebuking undertone awakened Landau, and he realized Doyle was playing him. Instantly, he shed a cloak of prairie air and cowboy humor and became the seasoned, traveled journalist. His long, hard look made her jaw clench and her lower lip quiver. He was now the chronicler of Iraq and Afghanistan, of Tripoli and Ben Ghazi.

She tried glaring back, but her eyes lacked fire.

"The Rileys are good people," he said. "And they've just lately suffered a terrible loss when a funnel cloud went through their ranch."

His warning was implicit: *Ezra is a friend of mine.*

"I don't get involved in personal matters," she countered.

Landau smiled wryly. "Don't you?"

She held his eyes though ghosts were beating against the backs of her eyelids; ghosts of people used, manipulated, lied to, and the few who were destroyed.

"A good scientist," she said, with a slight uplift of her chin. "Is as objective as a good reporter."

He smiled. "Yes, and both must remain objective, mustn't they?"

Landau got up and took the check. "This one's on me. By the way, I'll probably see you in Montana. The story I'm working on will take me back to Miles City."

She tried to stare at him with the cold, calculating confidence that had been her forte, but her glare lacked foundation. She felt herself quivering within and knew he noticed it. Peter Landau always noticed things.

Dr. Doyle left the truck stop so angry she could barely see straight.

She'd destroy this Ezra Riley. No matter what it took, she'd ruin him to get back at Landau for his cuteness, for his little rebuke and warning. When she was done with Ezra Riley, whoever he was, he'd be ashes and dust.

Then she caught herself. *The Post* article flashed in her mind and she knew she couldn't be threatening anyone, especially not a friend of Landau's. God! Why did it have to be Landau? He was published repeatedly in papers and magazines she'd only hoped to get into: *Outside* (she had been mentioned there once), *Rolling Stone* (they had done a small sidebar on her), *Men's Journal* (she didn't care about them), but others, like *Time, Newsweek, Esquire,* and *National Geographic.* Good lord, she'd love to be published in *National Geographic.* Frigging Landau! How he'd risen so fast she didn't know, but she couldn't mess with him now. If anything, she needed him on her side. Maybe she'd better be nice to this… Ezra… Ezra Riley.

Be nice to a cowboy? The idea nearly made her sick. She thought of the young rancher in Idaho but could barely remember his face. It had been lean and angular, an aquiline nose holding wire-rimmed classes. His wife was a redhead and they had three children. No. Two. A boy and a girl. She knew his name only because of the *Post* article. Ralph Wilson.

Naming him loosed the ghosts: a farm couple in Colorado, a rancher in Arizona, an orchard grower in Washington. They rolled backward through her mind like a slide show, stopping finally with the first one.

The slender cowboy from the Pryor Mountains.

What was his name?

Len.

No.

Lynne.

Lynne with an "e."

She suddenly saw him clearly, his face lit by the sun, his crew behind him smiling, East Pryor Mountain in the distance. His men had respected him, but so what? They were all just barbarians. Beasts. Worse than beasts. They weren't human. They didn't matter. Suddenly she pulled her truck over and stopped. She was trembling, then shaking, then convulsing, and finally Dr. Adrienne Doyle did what she hadn't done since she was four years old. She cried.

As her guttural sobs faded to whimpers her cell phone vibrated. She didn't want to answer it -- she'd neglected 27 calls in the past two days -- but knew she'd better see who it was.

The NRCS office in Miles City.

"Arrgghh," she moaned. She had to answer it

CHAPTER SEVENTEEN

J oe Pagliano didn't think of himself as a dreamer, because he didn't
consider himself an artist. Artists dream.

Others spoke of his smooth baritone, reminiscent of Ian Tyson in
his prime, but embarrassed, Joe would shake his head and ease com-
fortably into the background.

This evening, as he penned three wild heifers, Joe was dreaming,
but he thought he was planning. Joe's plan was to find a large ranch
to lease and run steers on, enabling his two boys to move home. The
ranch wouldn't be too far from his wife's job in Sheridan because she
had four more years before retirement.

Finding ranches to lease was difficult. A high cattle market and
soaring energy development were pushing land prices and leases out
of reach, but that didn't stop Joe from dreaming. Or, *planning*.

He was also lonely and a little bitter. Lonely because Ezra, Barney,
Garcia, and Landau were suddenly gone and he was left with a job
meant for two men -- the artificial insemination of 200 yearling heifers
-- and bitter because the Skinners had made a small fortune through

sod-busting and government programs. Joe believed the prairie was meant to stay in native grass and farm programs were welfare.

Joe knew livestock well enough to dream while he worked. In this he was similar to Ezra and Barney. Ezra plotted stories, and Barney contemplated cartoons while going about their daily tasks. But Joe avoided most of the mistakes made by his friends, because he lived on the periphery of imagination while they homesteaded in its center. But left alone, Joe dreamt more, and he was lost in thought when he finally noticed a strange pickup sitting by the shack. He swung off his bay roan, closed a gate on the alley, and glanced about for the truck's occupants. Probably one of the Skinners, he thought. The pickup was an '84 Ford Crew Cab, the sort of truck farmers kept around for field work in the summers.

The screen door screeched and Joe saw a large, bald-headed, tattooed man step from the house and onto the porch.

"Hey! What are you doing up there?" Joe shouted.

The man turned and said something to someone in the house.

Joe felt vulnerable. Normally he had his dog with him, a McNab that could handle most creatures, four-footed or two-legged. But his dog was home in Sheridan. He'd been meaning to bring a handgun but hadn't. And even if he had one, it would've been left in his pickup or the house.

The screen door screeched again and a skinny, dark-haired guy stepped out. The strangers started toward the corrals.

Joe needed a weapon or a reasonable facsimile. Stepping quickly to the cattle chute he opened the veterinary kit, grabbed a 50-cc stainless steel vaccine gun, made sure no needle was on its tip, and thrust it under his shirt and into his pants. He then swung back up on the bay roan and met the men at the gate. The big man had tiny blue eyes squeezed into a pallid face. A ragged scar began at the bottom of his left eyebrow and carved a trail down his cheek before disappearing into a dirty orange goatee. The smaller man had stringy dark hair and droopy eyes. His smile showed bad teeth. Both wore enough ink to look like walking cartoon strips.

"What do you guys want?" Joe asked.

"We're lookin' for the rig," the big man said.

"No rigs around here," Joe said.

"The people in Sidney says there's oil rigs up here."

The skinny guy was strangely silent.

Joe guessed the two hadn't worked in years. He nodded east. "The closest rig is 20 miles that way."

"Maybe if you drew a map?"

Joe wasn't about to dismount. He pressed his right hand against his shirt so the men would see the imprint of the vaccine gun. He hoped their imaginations were fertile. "What were you doing in the house?" he said.

"We knocked," the big man said. "When no one answered we got worried. Thought maybe someone sick or hurt."

"Well, as you can see, I am neither sick nor hurt," Joe said calmly. "Now I think you guys better get going." He lightly padded the bulge under his shirt. "Drive east. When it gets dark, you'll see the lights of the rig."

The skinny man stared up at the big man for a cue. Big man's blue eyes turned cold. "See you around," he said and spun toward his truck. Skinny man followed.

Joe stayed horseback until they had driven down the lane, crested a hill, and had disappeared from sight; then he collapsed forward, pushing the vaccine gun into his groin. "Whew," he sighed.

He dismounted slowly, tied the roan, pulled the vaccine gun from his pants and hurried to the house to see if anything had been stolen. He found his 12-string moved from the bedroom to the front door. Nothing else seemed touched. He rushed to his pickup. It had been ransacked. A box of tools was missing from the back. He reached for his cell phone and punched 9-1-1. No service. He remembered he had to climb the knoll to get a signal.

He thought of rushing to the Skinner place to call the sheriff, but he had three heifers to inseminate and daylight was fading fast.

The job at hand was more important than a box of worn-out tools. But what if the two men came back?

Joe made a plan. He'd inseminate the heifers, then go to the Skinners', report the strangers, and borrow a gun. Maybe he'd also borrow a dog if they had one that would stay with him.

He moved briskly back to the corrals and started the heifers down the alley on foot. The automatic catch on the head gate would stop the first one. As he harassed them forward, he kept glancing up to look for bad guys. The last heifer stalled and he bumped into her. She kicked, catching him in the shin hard. He doubled-over and hopped backward on one leg as the heifer swapped ends. Joe saw her coming, but it was too late to move. Her chest struck his head and knocked him down. He heard the other two heifers backing from the alley. They turned where the alley widened and exploded toward him, wild-eyed and desperate. The heifers hit him just as he was getting to his feet. The first knocked him against the corral planking. The second knocked him down and ran over him.

He struggled to his feet with his shirt in tatters and blood streaming from his mouth. He looked for his horse.

"That's it," he said under his breath. "I'll rope and tie all three of you down and inseminate you on your sides."

No more Mr. Nice Guy. It was time to be Joey Ropesaplenty.

The first afternoon home from the cow camp Barney went to get his horses and check on Ezra. He found him plodding through the mud, water, manure and wreckage of his corrals. "How ya doing, buddy?" he asked.

"It could have been worse," Ezra said. "It could have been much worse." Taking two halters from a post, he went to the one pen still standing and caught Barney's horses.

Barney nodded toward the bunkhouse that stood unscathed amid the destruction. "God must have wanted you to keep writing because He sure protected your bunkhouse."

Ezra wasn't thinking about writing. "I hired a plane this morning," he said. "Had a pilot fly me over Dead Man and Crooked Creek. We checked all the pastures, reservoirs, and what stock we could find." He led the horses to Barney's trailer.

"And?"

"The storm went right through the center of the ranch. We were just on the edge of it here and the corrals on Dead Man were on the other edge. No damage at all up there. But in the direct storm path I lost two reservoirs. One washed a cut in the spillway, the other burst through the middle of the dam. From the air it looks like we got a bunch of wind and hail followed by a downpour of five, six inches of rain."

Barney didn't say anything. He knew repairing two reservoirs was a huge expense. One that could surpass six figures. "Livestock okay?" he asked.

"Cattle are scattered. Some are in the neighbor's wheat. The water boiling out of the gumbos took out a hundred yards of fence."

"Did you see the mares?"

"They're fine. Hard to kill an Oswald. How's your place?"

"Shoot, it's good. I only got about an inch of rain." Barney opened the trailer gate and White Crow and the old mare stepped in willingly.

"Freak storm," Ezra said. "Just a really freak storm."

"Well, I know its too muddy to do anything right now, but when you need help riding give me a call."

"Thanks. Waiting is hard. I want to get out in the hills, check things out, get the cows back in."

Barney got in the truck and slammed the door. "Don't rush it. Remember, its always easier to plow around the stumps, especially when the fields are muddy."

Returning home, Barney decided to relax and create a cartoon, so he stretched out in his recliner with a drawing board and sketch pad in his lap. His cartoons were drawn first in pencil then outlined in ink, so he kept a mug of pencils and pens at hand. Another mug sat beside him filled with sweet tea. He had been known to confuse the two. He wore a pair of eyeglasses and another set rested on his head. The home was a spectacle of spectacles. Reading glasses dotted the rooms like agates on a hillside. His dog, Kitty, lay at his feet. Unlike Ezra, Barney let dogs in the house. Kitty was old and suffered from flatulence. On those rare occasions when Barney thought company had stayed too long, he'd open the sliding door, let Kitty in, and usually, within minutes, the guests found excuses to leave.

This time Barney decided it was he who needed air. "Good gosh, Kitty," he said, putting his sketch pad aside. "You're dead and don't know it." As he opened the door, the phone rang. Barney always answered the phone with a cheerful, hopeful tune as if someone was calling to announce he'd won a lottery he'd never purchased tickets for.

This time he was right.

"Hello," he sang happily.

"Is this Mr. Wallace?" the voice asked.

"Yes, it is!"

"Mr. Wallace, this is Mr. Lewinski. I'm with National Public Radio…"

"With what?" Barney chirped.

"National Public Radio…"

"National Public Rodeo?" He'd never heard of National Public Rodeo. It had to be a new organization. Rodeo groups were calling all the time wanting something. Sometimes they needed a judge. Sometimes they wanted a cartoon drawn.

"No, no. Radio. National Public Radio. NPR."

"Radio?"

"Yes, National Public Radio. You do listen to NPR don't you?"

"No."

"Well, you do listen to radio…"

"No. I never listen to the radio. When I'm in the house I listen to the television. When I'm driving I think about cartoons."

"You don't listen to radio at all?"

"Nope."

The NPR man sighed. This was not going as he expected. "Well, Mr. Wallace, we have heard about you and your cartoons and radio commercials. NPR is starting a new segment featuring voices from our rural constituency."

Rural constituency? wondered Barney.

The man continued. "We are looking for someone like yourself to provide radio installments of two-to-three minutes in length."

"What do I have to do?" Barney asked.

"Just give us a few minutes of rural life, glimpses from the farm, you know. A little humor, a little poetry. Some cowboy philosophy."

"But I'm a cartoonist," Barney said. He couldn't imagine how cartoons could appear on the radio.

"Just put your pictures into words," the man said. "Maybe draw something first then describe it to our listeners. Your cartoon has a name, doesn't it? A title or heading?"

"Yes. I call it *Graffiti on a Barn Wall.*"

"Oh! That's very good," Mr. Lewinski said. "We can work with that. It has broad appeal. Urban and rural."

"Gee, thanks," Barney said. He wondered if he should mention it was his friend Ezra who'd thought of the title.

"So, will you do it? We are in a bit of a jam. We need your first installment right away."

"How much does it pay?" Barney asked.

"You will be paid $300 a segment providing you can produce something we can use."

Kitty had never left the room. At that moment the old dog stood, passed gas, then lay down again.

"Shoot," Barney Wallace said. He was thinking of $300 for two minutes of work. He never smelled a thing.

"Then you'll do it?"

"Do ducks fly?" Barney asked.

His first morning back Garcia Jones awakened at 4:30. It took him several moments to realize he was not in a remote cow camp in Garfield County. And he missed it. He got up, ate a big bowl of cereal and drank three cups of stout coffee. The crew moved in his memories like ghosts. Barney cutting jokes. Ezra scowling and laughing through pain. Joe thoughtful and smiling. Peter observing and analyzing. He had two hours before work so he dropped to the floor, knocked out 30 pushups, rested, and did another set. Then he did the dishes, made his bed, and wrote his mother a long email about his week in the cow camp. Finally, he decided to go to work early. He was scheduled for a week in the field. Getting his hands dirty while helping farmers and ranchers better utilize soil, water, grasses, and crops was his passion. He hated office work. Besides, he could now tell ranchers how he'd helped brand 1000 calves. Garcia Jones walked a little taller and carried himself lighter as he approached the truck. The cow camp had given him an identity. He was Hot Water Jones, someone with stories to tell.

He bounced into the office with a smile and swagger, but stopped cold when he saw the office whiteboard. His field schedule had been wiped clean. Then he saw his desk. It was buried under a pile of manila folders.

Garcia's supervisor stepped from his office. "Jones," he said. "Glad you're in early." He pointed at the desk. "State sent that back last week. They want it all done over. Plus, there's a slew of new initiatives and program reports."

"But I was scheduled to go to the field…"

"Won't happen." The boss gestured for him to come closer. "One more thing," he said quietly. "The district supervisor went out on a limb for Adrienne Doyle and said he'd make motel reservations for her. He forgot. She's due any day. All the motels are filled with oil field workers." He handed Garcia a note. "Here's Dr. Doyle's cell number. You need to find her a place to stay, then you need to call her and tell her where. Got it?"

Garcia stood numbly holding the note.

He'd been startled from a great dream by a drenching of cold water.

He missed the shack.

He missed the guys.

He missed being Hot Water.

CHAPTER EIGHTEEN

The following morning found Ezra stuck in the east fork of Dead Man Creek, because he'd ventured out in his 2001 Chevy instead of his '78 Ford. Newer trucks -- even those 13 years old -- didn't have the ground clearance for the badlands. They were designed for Interstates.

Barney's warning had been right. He should have plowed around stumps and stayed home.

Ezra fought his predicament for two hours. Using old fenceposts for a foundation, he labored on a Hi-Lift jack until the rear tires broke from the suction of mud and water. Then he crammed flat rocks under the tires while his dog, Casey, lay in the brush watching patiently. Ezra repeated the process in the front. He was tired, wet, muddy, and sore when he climbed in the truck, said a quick prayer, and tried driving forward. His heart sank as the tires spun and settled deeper into the mire.

He wasn't going anywhere. Fortunately, he and Anne had a standing agreement on days like this: if he were not home by one o'clock she'd come looking for him. He pulled his wristwatch from a front pocket. Ten-thirty. It was either a long wait or a long walk to the county road.

Spasms began contracting his hands into the shape of sickles, so he got out of the truck, knelt at the edge of the creek and thrust them into the cool water and mud. Therapy.

Then, on a hill to the north -- toward the corrals -- he saw something. First he dismissed it as an old post, then it moved. It was a person bent over something. He got up, wiped his hands under the armpits of his shirt and pulled his 8x42 Leupold binoculars from the truck. It was a man and he was looking through a long-lensed camera on a tripod.

Adrienne Doyle was stuck in a quandary. She'd driven angrily from Elko to West Yellowstone, got a room about midnight and slept fitfully. Morning found her reluctant to get on the road. Why drive on? Why continue with this life? Her father was dead, the press -- which she'd coddled as a lapdog for years -- had turned on her, and her lover had not only dumped her, he'd dropped her for a 28-year-old Manhattan socialite. Arm candy. She'd discovered this with a Google search in her motel room. She'd tried phoning him until midnight, but he wouldn't pick up. Now, sitting in her SUV in the parking lot, she tried again.

He answered.

"Lars, you bastard," she said. "You not only text me at my father's funeral to end our relationship, but you hook-up with a slut who can't fill a training bra."

"Adrienne, listen. I'm sorry about the call at the funeral. I didn't know your dad had passed--"

"Call? It was a text and of course you didn't know. You were too busy escorting the little society bitch to black-tail-and-tie affairs. My god, Lars, she's a petri dish for STDs."

"Adrienne--"

"A match made in heaven, Lars. You, the king of torts, and her, the queen of tarts."

"Adrienne. Your hostility doesn't serve any purpose."

"My hostility doesn't serve any purpose? You used my hostility quite effectively for many years. I won many battles for you and your deep-pocketed buddies."

"Adrienne, you were a good foot soldier. Those days are over. With the present administration we don't need infantry anymore. We're poised to win at the highest levels."

"Oh, so now you're the warrior elite, is that it? And I'm the unwanted grunt? No room on the ladder for the one who sweated and bled in the trenches? How many tactics did I devise? Letter-writing campaigns from school children? That was my idea. Mustangs, wolves, white-tailed prairie dogs. I did the dirty work on all of those and more. And the Pagosa skyrocket, Parachute beartongue and fifty others. I laid the groundwork on all of them."

"Yes. And you did an excellent job."

"Free-ranging bison, Lars. I want to work on the bison projects."

"No, Adrienne. You have become too polarizing for that."

"Let me continue with the sage grouse, then. I'm already deeply invested and this could be huge. We can make great strides with sage grouse."

"The sage grouse isn't important, Adrienne."

"Not important?"

"Not in the big picture. It's already taken care of. The sage grouse will be listed in time, and yes, the ramifications will be large, but it's just a detail now. Strictly a past tense situation."

"And me? What type of *past tense situation* am I?"

"Adrienne, you were good at what you did, but you never should have started that blog. You drew too much attention to yourself. I told you not to do it. I told you to stay behind the scenes, but you thought you had to be the second coming of Rachel Carson."

Doyle wanted to scream. She'd never really wanted a blog, she'd wanted to publish a book because books were substantial and permanent. Blogs were transient, insubstantial, wispy. But her manuscript -- that she'd worked on for seven years without Lars knowing -- had been rejected sixteen times.

"I deserved to be heard," she said angrily. "I deserved some attention."

"Well, now you have it. I must have seen you mentioned in a half dozen east coast dailies this week and that's nothing compared to the blogs and web sites. You're toxic, Adrienne. None of us can be close to you now."

"So, for me its off to the leper colony in Miles City, Montana?"

"Adrienne, darling. You have no political instincts. You're a pit bull. We need poodles that only bite on command."

"I didn't say anything in my blog that I regret."

Lars released a heavy sigh. "You took too much credit. You practically confessed to a dirty tricks policy; of planting species, or at least, planting evidence of endangered species. Again, you don't see the big picture, Adrienne. You never have. You like your little wilderness hikes and all the bugs and grasses and furry animals. We're after more than that. We can finish coal and big oil in this decade. Destroy them. Then we can abolish property rights and establish wildlife corridors that stretch from the Pampas to the Arctic. World-wide, the death of capitalism is within reach. And with all that you want a pat on the back and a field full of prairie dogs."

"But I can help," Doyle insisted.

"No, you can't. We have other plans. Plans I am sure you would agree with, but you have attracted too much attention to yourself."

"But... Lars, what can I do?"

"You have an uncle in Canada, don't you? Go visit him. In fact, stay with him for a year or two."

"Stay with him?" Lars, what's coming down? What's about to happen?"

"You don't want to know, Adrienne. In fact, it's better if you don't. But get out of the country. Soon."

"That's it? Just disappear?"

"Yes. Disappear. And don't ever call me again." He hung up.

Doyle flamed hot for an instant, almost smashing the cell phone against the dashboard. Then she cooled, and the coolness became a chill that descended into her guts with fingers of ice. *Leave the country? While he stays with the blond in the training bra?*

She didn't know how, but she would hurt Lars Andersen, attorney-at-law.

She drove for an hour before she fully exhaled. She had to concentrate. She needed a plan. Secretly, she'd always hoped that one day she and Lars would attend a White House dinner together, arm-in-arm. She'd be featured in the *Society* section while her book won rave reviews in *Arts*.

Twenty-five years dedicated to the environmental cause and now kicked out to pasture like an old mare. The sage grouse issue still hung in the balance. And then there were wolverines, free-roaming bison, and more insects, birds, and rodents than she could shake her walking stick at. There was plenty to do. What did Lars know that made him think the battle was over?

What meetings hadn't she been included in? Many. She knew that. She'd been too busy tramping through fields with sunburnt farmers and pimply-faced range cons.

What could she do? How could she carry on the battle for her late father and those sad-eyed old friends of his? She needed a cause and an enforcer. She'd always had someone. Lars wasn't the first. He'd simply been the latest and the best.

The first was...

Doomay. That was his name. Atcheson Doomay. The BLM cop in the Pryors. What an idiot. She'd played him like a cheap harmonica. She wondered where he was now? Retired undoubtedly. Probably living in Yuma, Arizona and bragging to other old geezers how he'd been a lawman in the wild west.

She shook the thought of him out of her head.

She was wrong. She didn't need an enforcer. Whatever she decided to do she could do by herself.

She'd show Lars Anderssen that Dr. Adrienne Doyle was not to be trifled with,

When Ezra made it to the top of the hill he realized there was a fence post there. A twisted cedar post whitened by the rubbings of thousands of cowhides over scores of years. There was a person there, too, just a lariat-length away, and he resembled the post. He was slender and gnarly with thin grey hair and a white beard that edged his features like icing. His camera was a Nikon D4 wearing a 600 mm Nikkor lens mounted atop a Gitzo 1500 series carbon fiber tripod.

Ezra looked at the equipment wishfully. His 35mm Nikkormat film camera seemed less than worthless in comparison.

The man looked at him, smiled, and came forward with a slender, muscled hand. "You must be Ezra Riley," he said.

"I hope so," Ezra said. "Otherwise I'm trespassing, too."

"Oh, I don't mean to trespass, Mr. Riley. My name is Boothe. Harlan Boothe."

Ezra's eyebrows raised. "Corey Boothe's grandfather?"

"Yes, I understand you met my sometimes-wayward grandson."

"Yes, I have. Back there at the corrals. Is this about that little meeting?"

"No, not at all." He unscrewed the D4 from the Really Right Stuff ball head on the tripod and laid the camera carefully in a padded gear bag. "I stopped to see you at your house. Your wife told me how to find you."

Ezra glanced a few yards behind him where a silver Range Rover sat. "I suppose I should be glad you're here. I'm stuck in the creek down there."

"Oh? Are you? I was wondering what you were doing. When I pulled up on this knoll I saw the horses on the skyline over there--" he gestured to the south where the Oswald mares were patrolling their ridge-- "and I couldn't resist taking some photos. I hope you don't mind. Photography is a passion of mine."

"Mr. Boothe, what do you want? You didn't travel through miles of mud to take a few photos."

"Okay. I will get to the point, Mr. Riley. I want to buy your ranch."

Ezra smiled. "You want to buy my ranch?"

"Yes."

"Or does your grandson want you to buy my ranch?"

A faint flush colored Boothe's weathered face. "It was Corey's suggestion. I'll admit that. I think you know he has some acreage in the subdivision that borders your place. Your ranch would be a natural addition to what he already has."

"I guess I didn't realize my ranch was for sale," Ezra said.

"Well, in the right time and season, everything is for sale, Mr. Riley. That doesn't mean you have to accept my offer, but I can assure you it is above market."

"Well, just for kicks and giggles, Mr. Boothe, what would that offer be?"

"Two-point-five million."

"Two-and-a-half million? You must not understand. I only own a third of this ranch. I lease the rest from my sisters."

"I understand completely and I know you love this place. But, you're getting older, you've suffered an injury, and this last storm has been a setback. It's going to take a lot of money just to get you back on your feet."

"How do you know so much about me and my situation?"

Boothe shrugged. "I'm a thorough man. I suspect you know a little about me, as well."

"I know its rumored you make almost a million dollars a week just off the royalties from your inventions."

"That was before I entered the horse business. It's much less now."

"Yes, there is that. You finance your granddaughter's horse operation in the Bitterroot. The biggest money sinkhole in Montana.

Two-thousand acres and 21 employees. Millions flow in. Nothing comes out."

"I think we're getting off on the wrong foot, Mr. Riley."

"No argument there."

"Listen," Boothe said. "If I had my way I would pay you a million dollars just to mentor my grandson. But you and I both know that's not going to happen."

"Your grandson has some serious problems, Mr. Boothe."

"Yes, but his mother died when he was nine and his father is serving a life term in prison. My two grandkids are all I have. Unfortunately, they can't get along. The girl has her place. The boy should have his."

"And it just happens to be mine?"

"Where Corey lives now I only have to buy two more lots for him to adjoin your property. I'll buy three or four, of course, to make sure the access is clear and simple."

"And if I don't want to sell?"

"You may not want to sell, but I must tell you, your sisters are showing some interest."

Ezra's look could have frozen a branding fire. "You've contacted my sisters?"

"Yes, though out of deference to you, I did not offer them the same amount."

"If you buy out my sisters you rip the guts right out of my operation."

"That's why I'm offering you a price that's well above the current market. I know this isn't an easy thing." The billionaire looked down at the Chevy mired in the creek. "What can we do about your truck, Mr. Riley? Will my Range Rover pull it out? If not, I would certainly be happy to give you a ride home."

Ezra shook his head. He wanted to ask to use Boothe's phone but wouldn't. He'd walk the 12 miles home if he had to. Then he saw a motion on the ridge north of the corrals. Another truck was coming. Anne?

No. He knew this truck.

It was Barn Wall to the rescue.

CHAPTER NINETEEN

Barney's truck, plastered end-to-end with grey gumbo, came to a stop by the Range Rover and Barney fought his way out of the cab. His boots had accumulated enough mud to resemble manhole covers; his reborn mustache, looking like a strip of steel wool, stretched above an upper lip bulbous with hippy chew. On his head was a black hat Kitty had fetched from the trash and suspenders sagged from his shoulders like bridge cables. He was not dressed to make the cover of *American Cowboy*, which was possible as Harlan Boothe's handiwork occasionally graced national magazines.

"Shoot, Ezra," he chirped as he lugged his heavy feet forward. "I have some news." Then he noticed the stranger and felt embarrassed. "Dang, I didn't know you had company." Somehow Barney had not noticed the large luxury SUV.

"Mr. Boothe," Ezra said. "I want you to meet the one-and-only Barney Wallace. Barney, this is--"

"Shoot. You must be Corey's grandpa," Barney thrust a welcoming hand and pumped Boothe's like he'd struck oil. "That Corey sure is a pistol."

Boothe eyed the newcomer curiously. "Good to meet you, Mr. Wallace. I understand you and my grandson are neighbors."

"Yup, he's just down the hill."

"Barney," Ezra interrupted. "You said you had news."

"Boy howdy, do I?" He leaned to look down the hill. "Say, is that your truck down there? Looks like you're buried axle-deep on a Ferris wheel."

"Barney, some of us anxiously await your breaking news."

Barney's face lit like dawn breaking against steel siding. "Shoot, Ez. I'm going to be on the radio."

"Barn. You're already on the radio."

"No, I mean real radio. NPR."

"NPR? National Public Radio?"

"Yeah, that one. A guy called me last night."

"Wait, wait, don't tell me," Ezra said. "In this morning edition, all things considered and to the point, in this moment in time, in this fresh air, you are going to be on the commie radio network?"

"Yeah! Uh, I guess. What do you mean, commie?"

"Barn Wall, they lean a little to the left, you know."

"They do?"

"Just a wee tad. Say about about ninety degrees from center. But they play good music. I even send them money once in awhile."

"You do?"

"Not much. Not often. Now what's this all about?"

"A guy called me last night. I didn't know what National Public Radio was. I thought he said *Rodeo.* Anyway, they may want to give me a regular two-minute show. Three minutes if I'm good."

"Barney, you draw cartoons."

"I know. I told him that. But it pays $300 a shot. That's $150-per-minute. If it's two minutes."

"Yeah..." Ezra said, opening his hands in exasperation.

"Well, that's $9000 an hour. Imagine. I don't know anyone that makes $9000 an hour."

Ezra looked at Boothe. "I can think of one," he said. *Or even more.*

"Nine-thousand-dollars-an-hour is $216,000 a day."

"That's for a twenty-four-hour day."

"Well, shoot. It'd still be..."

"Seventy-two thousand dollars for eight hours," Boothe contributed.

"Shoot!"

Ezra shook his head. "I don't think it works like that, Barney. When you rode broncs you rode for eight seconds. Say you won Cheyenne for $8,000. Were you making $1000 a second?"

Barney's eyebrows tangled in thought. "Well, yeah, I guess I was."

"Then go back to riding broncs. It pays better."

"I can't." Barney stiffened. "I'm too old."

"Then you better sign on with the commie radio network."

"But, Ez, that's why I'm here. I need your help."

"My help? Barn, my truck is stuck in the creek. I have reservoirs washed-out, fences to fix, and my cattle are in my neighbor's wheat."

"But you're the writer. I draw cartoons. You can't see cartoons on a radio."

Ezra shrugged. "So, what do you want?"

"Let me use that song you sung up at Skinners'. The one you and Joe did."

"Barney, your singing would scare the brown off a paper bag."

"No, no. I'll just recite it. I'll try to give you credit at the end. I just need a start. Something to prime the pump."

"The ditty that poked fun at cowboy poets?"

"Yeah, that one."

"Barney, that could kill your career before it starts."

"Or it could make me famous."

"You're going to get hate mail. The cowboy poets will be really mad."

"Henrietta reads all the mail, not me. And if the cowboy poets don't have a sense of humor they shouldn't be cowboy poets."

"Fine," Ezra said. "It's all yours."

Wallace sagged with relief and a crooked grin broke across his face. Then his eyebrows raised with revelation. "Oh, I have other news."

"What now? PBS? Carnegie Hall? You're going on Letterman?"

"No, Joe's hurt. He's in the hospital. I need to run up to the Skinner place and bring his horses home. Can he keep them at your place?"

"Joe's hurt? How bad? What happened?"

"As I understand it, some heifers ran over him in the alley. But that's not what hurt him. That just made him mad. So he went to rope 'em. He got the first two and got 'em A.I.'ed, and he caught the last one but she ran around his horse and something bad happened. Not sure what. He was knocked cold for awhile. When he came to, he drove himself to the highway before he passed out. The mail truck picked him up."

"How bad is he?"

"Concussion. Broke six ribs. One lung collapsed or something. They're keeping him in the hospital for awhile."

"But he's going to be okay?"

"Far as I know. You have room for his geldings?"

"Yeah, sure. I wish I could go with you, but--"

"No, no. That's fine. I have to run to town and record my program. Then I'll scoot up to Skinners tomorrow and get his Oswalds."

"Okay. Do you have time to pull me out first? Or if you have your phone you can call Anne for me--"

"Anne's not home," Barney said. "She's in Billings."

"What?"

"Yeah. That's more news. I'm a regular news reporter. Guess that comes with working for NPR."

"What's she doing in Billings?"

"Don't you know?"

"No. That's why I asked."

"She went to pick up your granddaughter at the airport. She left a note for you on the kitchen table. I knocked and the door was unlocked so I went in. I had to find you."

"Why is she picking up Gabby?"

Barney shrugged, and the suspenders slipped off his shoulders and dangled below his waist. "I don't know," he said. "It's your family."

Boothe nudged Ezra's shoulder then pointed north. Another vehicle was coming down the ridge.

"Dang," Ezra said. "Now what? You'd think this was a freeway."

"Bet it's more breaking news," Barney offered. "It's just one of those days."

Soon Garcia's pickup coasted to a stop, and the lanky redhead jumped out, his freckles flaring like tiny Christmas lights. "Ezra, I've been trying to find you all morning," he exclaimed.

"You and the rest of the world."

Garcia looked down at the creek. "Is that your truck down there?"

"No. Actually, I was digging for worms and found that thing. What do you need, Garcia?"

"I need a favor. A big favor." His pale blue eyes ached with need.

"How big?"

Jones grimaced. "Ah, I need you to let Dr. Doyle stay in your bunkhouse while she's here."

"Doyle? In my bunkhouse?"

Garcia leaned forward imploringly. "Please, please. My boss dumped it on me. I have to find her a place to stay and all the motels are filled."

"It's pretty Spartan."

"Then you'll do it? She's Spartan. She's a Spartan warrior queen."

"Isn't there a conflict of interest?" Ezra asked. "She's here to review my place."

The mention of this piqued Boothe's attention.

Barney looked nervously at his watch. He needed to be in town.

"She'll have to pay you. It's strictly business."

"Does she know about this?"

Garcia shook his head fearfully. "No. I'm going to have to tell her."

"Whatever. Other than getting hit by a drone strike, not much new can happen today."

Barney was fidgeting the mud off his boots. "Ez, I need to get to town."

"Go ahead. Hot Water can pull me out."

Boothe looked at the skinny, urgent redhead. *Hot Water?*

Ezra directed Garcia's attention to the stranger. "Garcia Jones, this is Mr. Harlan Boothe."

Garcia's eyes widened as the two shook hands. "Harlan Boothe? You developed the technology in spy satellites. You were mentioned in *Wired* magazine last month," he gushed.

"Just their tribute to an old dinosaur," Boothe said. "Nothing important."

Jones took a tentative step back. In the middle of nowhere he was standing next to one of the nation's richest men.

"Garcia," Ezra said, breaking the spell. "How is it that everyone knows where I am."

"Oh. Anne left a note. She wanted someone to know where you were in case you didn't make it home."

Well, fine, Ezra thought. He had a billionaire wanting to buy his ranch; Anne was in Billings getting their granddaughter and he hadn't the slightest idea why; Barney was going on NPR and now the infamous Dr. Doyle would be staying in his bunkhouse. What next? "So when will Doyle be here?" he asked.

"This evening," Jones said sheepishly.

"This evening. And Anne doesn't know? The bunkhouse hasn't been cleaned for months."

"I'll sweep it," Jones blurted. "Vacuum it. Dust it. I'll wipe the walls down."

"And why is my granddaughter even coming? Was that on Anne's note? Are Dylan and Kristen okay?"

Jones shook his head. "The note didn't say."

"Dylan Riley?" Boothe asked. "From the Seattle area?"

Ezra looked at the billionaire incredulously. "You know him?"

"No, but I've heard of him. He's a bright young talent in innovative software technology and he's on his way to Brazil."

"Brazil?"

"Yes. I follow him on Twitter. He's been contracted to design software for Rio's Olympic Games."

"Okay," Ezra said, throwing his hands up. "Is there anything else I don't know? Did they find Jimmy Hoffa? Did Ted Turner take a vow of poverty?"

"Who's Jimmy Hoffa?" Hot Water asked.

In spite of the activity around him, Ezra had to deal with the immediate. "Okay," he said. "Both you guys. Let's get you hooked up to my truck and get me pulled out of there. I've got things to do."

As Boothe and Jones jumped for their vehicles, Ezra had to pause and smile.

In one sentence he'd given orders to a billionaire and a government employee.

Maybe things were looking up.

CHAPTER TWENTY

Jeremy Pratt was speechless. In fact, he had not uttered a word in 10 years. Not since the day the casino owner took his uncle, Cletus, beat and bloodied beyond recognition, and tossed him from an airplane two thousand feet above the desert while Jeremy and his cousin, Nicholas, watched. Cletus had been Nicholas's father.

The shock of that event and the dire warning from the killer -- "That, boys, is what happens when you steal from the boss" -- had taken every word from Jeremy's soul but doubled the inventory in Nicholas's. Nickie talked and talked and talked. Always brash, constantly bragging, occasionally threatening. Jeremy knew Nickie would get them both killed someday, but he didn't care, just as long as he could talk again first.

The way Jeremy saw it, the rent had run out on his life a long time ago. His soul was like an old house with mice chewing the wiring. He could feel them gnawing now as he stood at the back door of a home in Glendive, Montana with a crowbar in his hand. Nickie was at the front door talking to the blue-haired old lady who'd answered his knock. The two of them had followed her home from a pharmacy.

Jeremy tried the door knob. It was open. He wouldn't need the crowbar. He couldn't believe how trusting small town people were. Even with the oil boom they couldn't quit trusting people. He slipped up three steps into a sparkling kitchen. He could see into the living room where an oval rug hugged the floor and photos of grandchildren smiled from the walls. He wished he'd grown up in a home like this, but he and Nicholas hadn't. They grew up in a Las Vegas casino.

And in rundown motels used as whorehouses.

Or, sometimes, cheap apartments when their mothers tried to quit turning tricks and selling dope. But they always went back to turning tricks and selling dope.

The casino was their real home. Jeremy had felt safe there until Uncle Cletus got tossed from the plane.

He could hear Nickie visiting with the old lady. He was doing his best to act cordial which isn't easy when you're a behemoth with an orange goatee and earrings. He assured her he was a professional from the oil fields looking for a friend. His sleeves were rolled down to conceal some tattoos but only a body bag could have concealed them all.

The white pharmacy sack sat on the kitchen table. They'd followed it the way a kitten would chase a ball. The old lady had fallen and hurt her hip. The doctor's script was for Hydrocodone. Jeremy loved Hydro. He grabbed the bag and eased quietly down the steps and out the door. He couldn't help but look right away. The Hydro was there along with Cumadin and Lasix.

Following old people home from pharmacies was Jeremy's favorite gig. So far they'd only been caught at it once, but the old fellow couldn't do anything. He just stood sad-eyed as they walked out with his medications.

Ten years after Cletus went flying without wings, the boys decided they had to get out of Vegas or they'd test gravity, too. There wasn't any future in sweeping floors, taking out the trash, and cleaning toilet bowls, anyway.

They wanted more. Nicholas wanted to be a personal bodyguard like his daddy, but knew he was tainted. No casino owner was going to trust the son of a thief even if Nicholas was big, obedient, and stupidly ruthless. Nicholas didn't know he was stupid. Stupid people seldom see their own stupidity unless they're humble. Nicholas wasn't humble. He knew it was intelligence that separated him from the rest of the world but he thought it was everyone else that wasn't smart.

Jeremy was smart, but he was also dumb in the true sense of the word. Because he couldn't talk, he couldn't explain to his cousin how dim he was. It was just as well. Nickie probably would have beat him to death.

The boys knew they had to leave Vegas. But where could they go? Jeremy was 24 and Nicholas, 23. They'd made drug runs to L.A. and Reno, but had no other education or job experience. Neither had made it past middle school.

Then one day Jeremy's face brightened, he grabbed a napkin and scrawled MONTANA in big red letters with a felt pen.

Montana. Sounded cold to Nickie.

It was the whores who changed Nickie's mind. They hauled trailers north, stayed in the oil patch until they got run out, then came back rich. Simple. The gang-bangers did the same thing. Haul the drugs up. Sell. Get rich. Come back. There was money in Montana and North Dakota. Everyone knew that. The boys just had to get their share.

But Jeremy wanted to go to Montana because of the cowboy who stopped in the casino every December during the National Finals Rodeo. He had hazel eyes and a quick laugh. Slender fellow. He knew the casino owner. The cowboy played a little blackjack and had a drink or two. He was never loud or mean. He was good to the cousins. Sometimes he'd tip them five bucks for doing nothing at all.

What Jeremy remembered most was his belt. It was leather and worn and had his name carved on the back. LYNNE in pretty letters. Jeremy had wondered what it was like to live where people wore their names on their belts.

When Jeremy went dumb the cowboy never asked questions. Jeremy knew he understood. The cowboy could tell he'd seen something deep, dark, and damaging.

The last time Jeremy had seen him Jeremy had almost talked. The words were pulled up by the cowboy's dancing eyes, but wouldn't come out. He had to try it again. He had to find the cowboy from Montana. He'd mentioned Miles City. Lynne from Miles City. That's all he knew. All he needed to know. But he couldn't let Nickie know. The only reason Nickie found people was to beat them up and rob them. Jeremy didn't want that to happen to the cowboy.

Nicholas finally decided Montana was a good idea.

People in Montana couldn't be too smart. Or too tough. They could build a reputation in Montana. People would talk about them. Soon Nicholas could return to Vegas and get on as a personal bodyguard. He would wear a nice suit. When he snapped his fingers people would jump. Even pit bosses.

The pickings in Montana would be easy. They were Vegas boys. When they got to those hick towns the other criminals would throw money at them. His main concern was keeping Jeremy in product until they got established. It was sad how hooked his cousin was. That came from not being as smart as he was, Nickie thought.

But nothing went as planned.

Jeremy didn't know how to find the cowboy, so he resorted to staring at the backs of belts, a practice that made people uneasy.

Nicholas's boast of gangsters whimpering like puppies wasn't so. He hadn't counted on the Mexican Mafia or Laotian gangs from Yakima.

The spics and slopes weren't worried about a side of beef like Nicholas Pratt. They could carve him up like any other.

And they almost did. The Laotians caught Nicholas and Jeremy on the banks of the Missouri and beat them within an eyelash of eternity all because of Nicholas's tattoos. What seemed harmless in Vegas read differently in Laotian. Worst of all, the Laotians had stolen their tent, sleeping bags, PlayStation and collection of video games. Nickie was foul about losing *Custer's Revenge*, *Ghetto Blaster*, and *Ethnic Cleansing*.

Restoring their electronic library was a priority behind drugs, food, fuel, and an occasional motel room.

But how to get the money? The oil patch itself wasn't safe, so they moved to the outskirts; close enough to be near money, but a long way from gang-bangers who didn't respect their Vegas heritage.

The easiest pickings, they soon learned, were down the hundreds of miles of graveled county roads that transversed the open country.

It was like this: They'd pull up on a hill, watch a ranch yard through binoculars until they were sure no one was home, then they'd slip in, kill a dog if they had to, steal what they could, and move on. A number of area pawn shops accepted guns, guitars and chain saws without questions, and the boys soon developed a circuit.

They learned to pay special attention to older ranchers. Their bathroom medicine cabinets, especially in the homes of bachelors and widowers, were a treasure box of painkillers.

Ranchers had to work hard to be so beat-up, Jeremy thought, or be uncommonly unlucky.

Sometimes Jeremy would steal a book, but only one because they traveled light. Reading kept an inner flow of words going. If he didn't read he thought he'd turn to stone. The problem was the addiction. It made reading hard.

Nicholas got mad if Jeremy took cowboy magazines because he hated cowboys. He constantly told Jeremy he'd kill one before they left Montana.

Jeremy hoped that that one wouldn't be Lynne.

If Nicholas killed Lynne, Jeremy would never talk again.

Then Jeremy would have to kill Nicholas.

He didn't want to kill his big cousin, but he knew enough to know a man sometimes had to do things he didn't want to do.

CHAPTER TWENTY ONE

After leaving Elko, Landau drove 35 miles south to the tiny community of Jiggs. The scenery -- sagebrush flats, prairie and badlands -- reminded him of eastern Montana with the exception of the majestic Ruby Mountains to the east. Just past Jiggs, he turned left and followed the directions he'd scrawled on the back of an envelope.

He'd arranged to meet Jerry Cherry, a retired BLM cowboy, who'd herded mustangs and burros in Montana, Wyoming, Nevada and California. In Montana, he'd worked in the Pryors with Lynne.

He found the mailbox, pulled through an open woven-wire fence and stopped in front of a small, clean-looking cabin. A mottled Australian Shepherd barked from the porch but made no effort to move. Old. And retired.

A lanky man clad in blue denim, stitched through his middle by a plain leather belt, and topped by a weathered black hat, stepped from the cabin, a toothpick protruding from thin lips. His face was burnished like oiled saddle leather, creases ran like arroyos from cheekbones to jaws past ridges of gray stubble. Crows-feet flared from the corners of pale blue eyes. A man who'd spent his life in the saddle.

"You the reporter who called me?" he asked.

"Peter Landau." Landau extended his hand, and it disappeared in Cherry's calloused mitt.

"Come on in, I guess," the old cowboy said. "If you're a phony I can shoot ya just as well inside as I can out here."

They took chairs at a chrome-legged table that sat on a clean linoleum floor. The kitchen's white cupboards were speckled yellow where chipping paint revealed an earlier coat. Bouncing in on three legs, the Aussie curled up and settled on a tattered rug.

"Now what was it you wanted to talk to me about?" Cherry asked.

"I'm doing an article on horses in America--"

"You from back east?"

"Yes, I was raised in New York."

"Young man--" Cherry leaned forward and his eyes sparkled devilishly. "The last eastern reporter I talked to almost got gut-shot and left to die in the desert. Should have shot 'em. One of the bigger regrets of my life that I didn't."

"I understand your concern," Landau said. "I've spent the last two weeks in eastern Montana."

"Where at?"

"Miles City, mostly. And Garfield County."

"Garfield County? Well, I guess if the Freemen up there didn't kill ya then I might give ya a minute or two."

"I appreciate it, Mr. Cherry."

"Call me Jerry." He leaned back in his chair and pulled a tin of tobacco and makings from his shirt pocket. "Hope you don't mind if I smoke cuz I'm going to anyway. My house." He held a paper deftly in his left hand and sprinkled a line of Bugle tobacco down its center. Then he rolled his smoke, lit it, and exhaled toward the ceiling. "Now why the hell you doin' an article about horses anyway?"

"Have you ever heard the term *husband horse?*"

"Hell, no. What's that?"

"In the West, as I understand it, you have *kid's horses* and *ladies' horses*. East of the Mississippi they call a gentle horse a *husband horse*."

"Husband horse? Damn world's gettin' upside down."

"I found it a curious juxtaposition," Landau said. "I was also intrigued by the horse slaughter issue--"

"Ha."

"You have thoughts about horse slaughter."

"This country thinks every animal's a pet. A horse ain't no parakeet. What are you gonna do with old or crippled horses? Most people can't bury one in their backyard. Horses are a prey animal. They were born to be eaten. They understand that."

"My friends back east would stone you for that answer."

"Let 'em try. Damn fools. We got two places ruinin' this country. Hollywood and Harvard."

"It seems many people in the West favor horse slaughter as long as it's humane."

"Course we do. We ain't lost our common sense. No one wants to kill a horse, but sometimes it has to be done. Do it fast, do it clean, and don't waste the protein. Are you an organ donor?"

"Yes."

"Then why can't a horse be a protein donor?"

"But doesn't horse slaughter run contrary to the revolution in horse training I keep hearing about?"

"You mean the horse whisperin' stuff? Hell, I ignored that world once they cast Robert Redford in the movie. Listen, youngster. There's been gentle horse handlers forever. Now these new guys, they've made it more popular, and that's good. But they sure as hell never invented it. Ever hear of Xenophon? He was doin' it 2300 years ago. He just didn't have a TV show and a catalog full of pricey gadgets."

"Anyway, getting back to the present," Landau said. "I understand you worked with the mustangs in the Pryors."

"That I did. For three years."

"You worked with Lynne--"

"Yes, I did," Cherry said. A glow of warmth softened his rugged face. "Good man. Helluva a horse hand. Good as there ever was. He could ride a rank one and make him look good. He treated a horse like he would a kid. Mostly kind and gentle, but if they needed a spankin', he wasn't afraid to do it."

Then Cherry stiffened and he became suspicious again. "Why do ya wanna know about Lynne? He's dead, y'know. Ain't no good to speak ill of the dead. Not that there was anything bad to say about Lynne."

"No, I'm not here to dig up anything bad on Lynne."

"If you were to print anything foul about my friend Lynne I would hunt you down. Me and about a hundred others."

"I can assure you, Mr. Cherry -- Jerry -- I have gained nothing but respect for the man from all I've heard."

The old cowboy cocked his head. "Okay, I'll give you the benefit of the doubt. But I seen people go after Lynne before. Back in the Pryors. Nothing like that should happen again."

"Who went after him then?"

"A man named Doo-may," he said, spitting the name out. "Atcheson Doomay. We called him Asshole Dummy. Retired cop from the midwest. The first law enforcement ranger to work for the BLM. Why the hell they hired him I'll never know. Typical government deal. Thicknecked, short-legged little pot-licker. Came west to be John Wayne, I guess. He should of stuck to checkin' campgrounds and patrollin' speed zones, but he fancied himself the boss marshal of the mustangs.

"Ya gotta realize that was a controversial time. Wild Horse Annie and all those folk. Country was overrun with mustangs. Still is. Doomay was convinced Lynne was stealin' horses."

"Stealing mustangs?"

"Yeah, and who would wanna steal a mustang? They say we have 37,000 mustangs in the wild, but there's a lot more than that, and over 50,000 in what they call *containment facilities*. How wild is a wild horse in a containment facility?"

"What did Doomay think Lynne was doing with the horses he was supposed to be stealing? Sending them to slaughter plants?"

Cherry laughed. "No, no. It was crazier than that. Lynne had connections in upstate New York with dude ranches. He dealt in saddle horses a little. We all did. When he got horses that didn't work for chasin' mustangs or got a little too old and slow, he'd haul 'em back to New York and sell 'em to a dude ranch. He did that during his vacation time."

"And Mr. Doomay was convinced he was taking mustangs back east?"

"Yup. Even tapped his phone."

"Why would someone think he was doing something like that?"

"Well, because we was movin' horses, sort of."

"Moving horses?"

"Look, Lynne was all about the horse. He didn't give a damn about the government and bureaucrats, let alone, those mustang zealots that didn't know a broom-tail from a broom closet." He leaned closer. "The herds were gettin' in-bred-- do you understand in-breedin'?"

Landau nodded.

"It's not the same as line-breedin'. The Oswalds that Lynne raised are line-bred. That's a science. Inbreeding is just poor management."

"The mustangs?" Landau steered him.

"Color and confirmation was being bred out of the mustangs. The Adopt-A-Mustang program was getting started and the public doesn't want an ugly horse. So Lynne castrated the plain-colored studs, and when a herd needed new blood he'd go get it."

"Go get it?"

Cherry looked at Landau as if he were denser than a knot on a cedar post.

"Lynne and I hauled studs around," he said. "If Wyoming needed a good-looking dun stallion and we had one, we'd haul it down. If someplace had a good stud we needed, we'd go get it. Did it all at night. Illegal as all get-out, but it made the horses better. As I said, Lynne was all about the horse. Now these days those high-paid experts point to the colors in the Pryor herd and claim that's proof they trace back to Coronado. Hell, they trace back to Lynne, his castrating knife, and our long, nighttime drives."

"But Doomay knew something was going on?"

"And guessed wrong. But it wasn't really Doomay. He was an ambitious little rooster, that's for sure, but he wasn't the brains behind it all."

Landau waited. "Who was?" he asked.

"A-dri-enne-Doy-le." Cherry said the name long and slow as if it had to leave his mouth like a snake.

"Dr. Adrienne Doyle?"

"Weren't no doctor, then. Just plain ole Adrienne Doyle, royal pain-in-the-ass. Especially Lynne's. You see, this Doomay had the hots for her. She played that up. Got him all bothered then sicced him on Lynne."

"Why?"

He waved a dismissive hand. "She hated cowboys. Hell, she hated men. She was a left-wing commie. Everyone could see that."

"And did she actually get Lynne fired?"

"Wasn't quite like that. Lynne got fed-up and finally quit. Took an early retirement. That was just after I nearly killed Doomay."

"You nearly killed Doomay?"

"I did two tours in Nam. Sixty-five and sixty-six. Marine Corps. When I came back I never thought I'd kill a man again, but I would of killed Doomay that day."

"What day?"

"We were shippin' horses for a big adoption deal. Took us days to gather 'em, work 'em and get 'em loaded on trucks, then Doomay showed up and ordered em unloaded. He wanted to read brands. Hell, they were already brand inspected. The day was hot, the men were tired and Doomay couldn't read a brand anyway. Besides, you get horses hurt by unloading 'em and loading 'em again. But Doomay didn't care about horses."

"I assume you lost it for a moment?"

"I was crawlin' over the rails and about to kill 'im when Lynne grabbed me by the legs. He knew I'd do it. I woulda beat that sonuvabitch to death, or close to it."

"Lynne pulled you back?"

"Yeah. Not by himself, though. That writer was there and he helped him."

"Writer?"

"Yeah, the guy with the odd first name. Comes from over Miles City way. He just came and helped us that one time. Mostly he took pictures."

"Riley? Ezra Riley?"

"Yeah, that was it. Ezra Riley. Slender fella. He and Lynne got me by the legs and pulled me down. Lynne sat on me like I was a colt fixin' to be branded."

"And what did Riley do?"

"He headed up the hill to where the reflection was comin' from."

"Reflection?"

"I saw it first. Even in my rage. Marine trainin'. It was the glint off glass. Binoculars up in the junipers. Doyle. She was watchin' everything from up on a hill. Riley went right up the hill after her."

"What did he do?"

"Well, as Lynne told me later, he politely identified himself as a freelance journalist who had questions for her."

"And?"

"She got in her fancy government rig and drove off."

"What happened then?"

"Nuthin'. We unloaded the horses and let Doomay take a look. Lynne kept me outa the way. I knew then I had to get outa there or I would kill him sooner or later. A job came up down here in Nevada, so here I am."

"You've been retired for awhile?"

"Fourteen years. Worked for the government longer than I should have. Now I do a little day work for neighborin' ranches. Brand inspect a little. Mostly ole Roscoe and I" -- he nodded at the old dog -- "have a wonderful partnership going on. He attracts flies and I kill 'em." He paused. "Maybe it's the other way around."

"When Lynne retired he started raising horses."

"Yeah. Those Oswalds I mentioned. Heard a lot about 'em. A real cowboy's horse, they say. Not many cowboys left that can ride an Oswald all day."

"He ran his horses on Ezra Riley's place."

"I guess so. I don't really know this Riley, but before he got to breeding Oswalds with Lynne he was sort of a one-man horse rescue guy."

"Horse rescue?"

"Lynne said he'd find well-bred horses wastin' away in somebody's backyard, buy 'em, ride 'em, then sell 'em to a good home. Lynne respected him for that. Course, once they started breedin' Oswalds he didn't have time for that no more."

"That's much different than the horse rescues you hear about today."

"There's a lot of people with good intentions who can't do math. There's simply a few million too many horses in the country."

"When was the last time you saw Lynne?"

"Until he passed away, I saw him every December when he'd drive to Vegas for the Finals. He'd always stop by for an hour or two. Or maybe spend the night, dependin' on whether the wife was with him. She usually was."

"But you didn't go with him? To the Finals?"

"No. I don't care for cities and crowds. Elko's too big for me. When they have that big poetry gatherin' me and Roscoe head into the Rubies and make camp till its over."

"What do you do up there?"

Cherry's eyes glazed like he was taking a long ride into twilight. "I just think," he said dreamily. "Like any old fart, I just sit and think about the old days; the good horses I rode; the bad ones; the good friends. I think about Lynne some, I suppose. Those were some good times." He crushed his smoke out. The dog whined.

Nostalgia was thicker than the cigarette smoke in the small kitchen.

"You miss Lynne, I'm sure."

"Well, I wish he was here now," Cherry said dryly. "To see Doyle get what's comin' to her."

"What do you mean?"

"You ain't heard? I got a friend who's retired in Virginia. He called yesterday and read me a story from the *Washington Post*. Seems some people are blamin' Doyle for the suicide of a young rancher in Idaho."

So that's why she seemed so on edge in the restaurant, Landau realized.

"She's a scalded cat on the run now," the old cowboy said. "I'd sure as hell hate to be the first person who crosses her path."

Landau looked through the screen door at his SUV sitting baking in the Nevada sun.

He had to get back north.

The first person to cross Doyle's path was likely to be Ezra Riley.

CHAPTER TWENTY TWO

Garcia Jones knew the Riley home well; had slept there twice, but he'd never been in the bunkhouse. It had always loomed mysteriously, an old railroad building roofed in red steel and supported by a porch braced by twisted cedar posts. The place where Ezra wrote. Not that Garcia cared much about writing. He imagined the building more as a rustic cowboy heaven decorated with antique spurs, Charley Russell prints, dusty chaps, lever-action rifles, saddlery catalogs, bullwhips, quirts, and yellowed and tattered stacks of *Western Horseman* magazines.

He was close. There were a few old spurs and chaps. There were plenty of old magazines -- *Western Horseman, America's Horse, Quarter Horse Journal, Persimmon Hill, Range Magazine* -- but they were stored neatly in Rubbermaid containers. The prints on the walls were not C.M. Russell or Will James. He examined one closer: a pen-and-ink of a bronc and rider going off a cut bank. It looked like an early Charley Russell but was signed *Barney Wallace, 1986.*

Barney? No one had told him that Barney did serious art.

But the dominant force in the bunkhouse was the books. Hundreds of them, standing like soldiers in formation on solid shelves built from corral plank. The Riley house was filled with books and Garcia never imagined more could exist. How many could one person read? Or two people? Anne, he knew, was a reader, too. And why didn't they just buy a Kindle or Nook and save space? And trees?

Garcia was not a book person. His days were usually spent on government paperwork so he relaxed in the evenings browsing hunting and rodeo websites and playing combat video games. He'd ordered Ezra's two books, *The Land* and *Days of Big Circles*, from Amazon but they remained unopened but prominently displayed on a shelf for visitors to see. But, since moving to Miles City, his only visitors had been Jehovah's Witnesses and Mormons.

His arms were filled with clean sheets, blankets, a vacuum cleaner, wash bucket, dust rags and brooms, He watched through an east window as Ezra left the corrals -- or what remained of them -- on Simon with Casey following happily. Ezra was going to get his cows out of his neighbor's wheat, and, for a second, Garcia wished he were riding too. But as the big bay plunged into the murky, swollen waters of Sunday Creek, Garcia was satisfied to be a glorified maid.

He had a job to do.

And he did it briskly. He swept the wooden floor, ran the vacuum over the rugs, and was wiping down the walls when he realized the weight of silence. Wanting noise for company, he noticed an appliance that resembled a CD player, plugged it in and was amazed to discover it was an eight-track tape player. He'd heard of them but had never seen one. He looked around for tapes, found none, so he moved a selector knob to FM radio and fingered the tuning dial.

A deep, gravelly voice jumped out at him: *"Thank you, pard. Shoot, it's a doggone pleasure to be here."*

Barney Wallace. Again.

Jones looked at the dial. Was this another ad for weed-killers or wagon tongues?

Another voice came on. Smoother, slicker, citified. (Even patronizing?)

Jones studied the dial. This was the public radio station. NPR. And the host was introducing Barney. He turned the volume up.

"Folks," Barney announced. *"The little ditty I am about to recite was birthed in a cow camp in Eastern Montana..."*

Cow Camp. That meant him: Hot Water Jones.

Garcia's cell phone chimed. He checked it in case it was his boss. It wasn't. It was his mother -- the fourth call from her that day he'd ignored. He didn't have time for her prattle on the alignment of the stars, PETA issues, or the dangers of white bread.

He had a bunkhouse to clean and a celebrity to listen to.

Maybe the poem included him, he thought. Hot Water Jones. Young legend of the prairies and plains.

From the moment five-year-old Gabriella Jo Riley stepped from the plane she was talking. "Come on, Gramma Anne," she said, taking her grandmother's hand. "We must get to your car right away. I have something to tell you, but mommy said I have to wait until we are in your car."

Anne smiled. There were no words to describe her granddaughter. *Precocious* came close, but didn't capture the little girl's extensive vocabulary.

"Oh! And I have to give you a note first," Gabby remembered.

A shudder of apprehension ran through Ann. Was Dylan and his family moving to Brazil for good? Was that the news? Certainly they wouldn't let Gabby break news as important as that? No, it was probably something simple. Maybe a favorite meal she enjoyed.

Anne pulled the luggage from the terminal, and Gabby, in turn, pulled Gramma Anne.

"Come on, Gramma," she urged. "Don't be so slow." Her peaches-and-cream face, framed by strawberry blond air, lit by blue eyes and accented by faint freckles was carved in earnestness. "This is very important news," she insisted.

Once they were both belted into their seats, Gabby began rummaging in her pockets for the note. "I know it's here somewhere. I don't know why I just can't tell you but mommy made me promise I'd give you the note first." She lit up with joy. "Here it is." She handed Gramma the crumpled card.

Anne opened it and read:

Dear Anne and Ezra, we wanted to call and give you the news but Gabby insisted she be the one to tell you. So, this note is our way of giving Gabby permission. Love, Kristen and Dylan.

"Did you read it?" Gabby asked.

Anne nodded.

"Okay," Gabby said, folding her hands in her lap. "This is the important news. I am going to have a baby brother."

Anne nearly ran into the car in front of her. "Your mommy's pregnant?"

"Yes. She wanted to tell you herself, but then what would I have to talk to you about?"

"And you know it's a boy?"

"Yes, mommy and daddy went to the doctor and got pictures. He's not very cute. Mommy says he'll look better when he's outside her tummy. I think I should name him. I want to name him Roger, because I want a puppy named Roger, but daddy won't let me have a puppy. He says our yard is too small. But Roger would be a good name for a puppy because then I could say ruff-ruff-Roger." She giggled, and her plump cheeks jiggled like peach Jello.

Ann was lost in thought.

"Ruff-ruff. That's how a dog barks, Gramma."

"Yes, sweetheart, but I think your mommy and daddy will want to name the baby."

Gabby frowned. "I suppose. Adults have all the fun. They'll probably give him a Rio name. Something I can't pronounce."

"A Rio name?"

"Yes, Rio. That means river in Span-ish. It's where we're going to live, but I can't say the whole name. I keep forgetting it. It's long."

"Rio de Janeiro?"

"That's it." She laughed. "I always want to say Rio doe-January."

"Do you think you're moving there? Have your parents said so?"

"No. That's where they're going now. Right now they are over Mexico. Mommy showed me on a map. It's a long way to Rio..."

"de Janeiro."

"Yes. It's a long ways. I'm glad we don't have to walk."

"How do you know you will be moving there?"

Gabby Jo shrugged. "I just know," she said. "I know things."

After two hours of constant chattering on subjects ranging from Preschool to Facebook, Gabriella slumped into the seat and drifted to sleep.

They were still 20 minutes from home so Ann let Gabby nap. She cautiously turned the radio on -- the dial was usually set to NPR -- thinking soft classical music would help the little girl sleep.

For a score of miles Chopin was Anne's companion, just as he'd been in her youth when she felt chained to classical piano.

But it changed as they neared the ranch. A gruff voice broke the air. *"As I stepped out on the streets of old Elko..."*

No! It was Barney. On NPR. And worse, it was Barney reciting the silly song Ezra had written.

She carefully turned it up a nudge.

"As I stepped out in ole Elko one day..."

No, Barney, she thought. Don't do it. You're committing professional suicide.

Gabriella stirred. Barney's deep voice had awakened her.

Ann slowed to make the turn to the ranch. At the back of their yard she saw Garcia's pickup parked next to the bunkhouse. The building's door was open and a soft glow shone through the evening's dusk.

Garcia? What was he doing in the bunkhouse?

"I spied a cowboy poet all wrapped in poor simile, wrapped up in bad metaphor as cold as the clay..."

Gabby woke up and looked around. "Gramma," she said. "Where's Casey? And who's that funny man on the radio?"

Simon, the good Oswald, slugged through mud like a steam engine on pistons. With each step the earth burped but the bay purposed on, his little fox ears pricked toward the east like pointed fingers.

Ezra posted the trot and held the butter-smooth rains loosely because his hands ached. He was thankful for mud for it kept Simon slow and deliberate, allowing Ezra not to grip the reins tightly. Behind them, Casey was tiring, but Ezra knew that would change once they found cattle.

Ezra's mind was a stampede of thoughts.

How do you stop a stampede?

You turn the lead steer gradually and bend the herd into itself.

But which was the lead steer?

The offer from Boothe?

Boothe's offer to his sisters?

Adrienne Doyle staying in his bunkhouse?

Gabby coming?

His son moving to Brazil?

The EEEP program?

Getting reservoirs repaired and fences fixed?

Joe lying injured in the hospital?

Too many lead steers in this runaway herd, he decided. It would be easier to ride drag. Stay in the back and go with the flow.

What was in the back? What dwelt in the rear of his mind?

Barney Wallace on NPR, he decided.

At least that was something that couldn't get him in trouble.

He glanced at the sun's position in the sky. Any time now -- as he reckoned it -- ole Barn Wall would be on his way to fame and fortune.

He chuckled to himself and Simon's ears pricked at the sound.

Barney on NPR. How crazy.

At the steep gumbo divide, Ezra dismounted and carefully led Simon down the greasy grade. On level ground he mounted again. The main creek draining the gumbos was where he found the ruined fence. The deluge had washed the creek 60 feet out of its banks. Fence posts lay on the ground and entanglements of wire were rolled into a long tortilla of cacti, sagebrush, yucca, and mud.

Ezra needed the fence up enough to turn stock, so he dismounted, mucked debris, pulled on wires, and swore when his gloved hands argued against the labor. Finally two strings of spliced wire and half-a-dozen posts propped-up a poor man's bluff. It would have to do until he returned in the pickup and repaired it correctly.

Once in the wheat field he saw his cattle couldn't do any more damage than the storm had already done. Only a scattering of stalks stood headless in wide swaths of rubble. Most of the wheat was pounded into the dirt. There'd be no harvest for this field. But being a good neighbor was in Ezra's blood. His cattle belonged on his side of the fence.

The cattle saw him, and as if clairvoyant, lined homeward. They didn't fear the cowboy, horse, and dog, but they respected them. Casey, propelled by generations of breeding, came alive with obedient energy. Cows and calves plodded on, but the bulls -- farmer-raised and accustomed only to four-wheelers-- panicked. One ran north and Ezra sent Casey after it. The other went south.

Simon, like Casey, was up to the chase. Generations of great race horses boiled in his bloodline: the patriarch Peter McCue, Johnny Barnes, Quick M Silver, Miss Chubby, Three Bars, Leo and old Oswald himself; plasma phantasms and goblins of hemoglobin pulsing with the hooves and hearts of a hundred horses. Simon refused to gallop a wide circle around the bull, instead, he insisted on a laser-like path. The bay was a haired Hellfire missile, directed straight at the bull's head. Huge divots of mud, dug by his size two shoes, flew up behind him.

"Dammit, Simon," Ezra whispered as he tried to pull Simon in.

Simon shook his head angrily and took the bit. He would not be denied.

The bull was not a *mudder.* After two hundred yards the beast was drenched in sweat, slinging snot, and its eyes rolled crazily in its head.

Simon threw a shoulder into the bull while reaching with open jaws to rip a mouthful of hair and skin from the animal's neck. Seventeen-hundred pounds of Polled Hereford turned violently to the right and Simon pivoted with it.

But all four of the horse's feet slid in wet clay. In an instant, horse and rider were parallel to the ground, then the field rushed at Ezra before he could even consider fear. It struck him like a dirty fist, the ground pummeling him as Simon slid sideways, his hooves thrashing for footing. For a scant second, Ezra remembered the bad Oswald, Pedro, and the fall through the ice. But then Simon was on his feet shaking nervously. Ezra spit mud, rose to hands and knees and looked up. The sky was awash in unnatural ambers and blues and little black spots flew about like crows. He shook his head to clear it and got slowly to his feet. With his right had he picked up his hat. He was coated with caramel-colored mud. Ezra hobbled toward the horse on a pained knee, stabbed the reins, collected himself, and labored into the saddle.

"Damn you, Simon," he whispered. "You just had to go and be an Oswald, didn't you?"

The big horse grunted an excuse.

Ezra exhaled and looked for the bull. It had conceded and was following the retreating cattle.

To the north, Casey was coming down the fence with the other escapee.

Ezra gave Simon a nudge. All in all, he thought, not so bad. The job was getting done, no bones broken, and Simon seemed content to move at a brisk walk.

Still, his neck hurt, and an absence of pain in his hands was due to numbness from the wrists down.

He lifted his left hand to adjust his hat and a rip of pain split his shoulder.

Rotator. He'd torn the rotator cuff.

His knee was sprained, too.

Oh well, just a couple more cloths to hang on his clothesline of pain.

Doggone you, Simon. You sure picked the wrong time to be the Oswald that you are.

CHAPTER TWENTY THREE

Adrienne Doyle was laughing so hard she almost couldn't pee.
The reason was the crazy guy on National Public Radio making fun of cowboy poets. Doyle hated cowboys and cowboy poetry and couldn't tell if the speaker was serious or not, but he was hysterical. It wasn't the quality of the poem. It was his contagious dead-pan, tongue-in-cheek delivery.

She was parked on a farmhouse approach on a frontage road beneath a blanket of stars. The Interstate rest stop was closed, so she'd taken a quiet two-lane blacktop and stopped where she wouldn't be bothered.

She relieved herself with the radio blaring and never noticed the approaching vehicle until the headlights shone on her SUV's open door. She zipped quickly and rose.

A truck stopped beside her and the passenger window rolled down.

"You havin' trouble?" a man asked.

Doyle nearly crumpled with fear. She glanced inside her SUV where the pepper spray was stashed under the front seat.

Out of reach.

"No, everything's fine," she said. "I just stopped for a minute."

The man looked through her like she was made of paper and rags.

Doyle tried to muster resolve, but couldn't meet his eyes. He was a massive young man in a wife-beater shirt. The sheen on his pupils was pure savagery, and he fed on her fear like a wolf licking blood.

The driver was thin, silent, and barely visible in the shadows. Doyle sensed a weakness from him, as if he seldom drove and didn't like this disturbance. Nervous tension fluttered from his side of the truck.

For a moment her fate balanced in the intentions of the tattooed monster. He was deciding what, if anything, to do with her. Doyle felt reduced and helpless. It was night. There was no one around. A glimmer from a farm porch light was as distant as the stars.

Could she jump in her car before he grabbed her? Would motion provoke him?

He looked at her with contempt then turned his head, grunted at his nervous driver and the old pickup rattled away.

Doyle collapsed against her SUV as the truck retreated.

"Ah, ah, ah, ah." She could neither cry nor scream. She could only released gasping, wordless breaths.

She knew she'd never been closer to death.

Ezra unsaddled Simon in slow deliberation, the pain stinging his shoulder like an army of biting ants. Casey followed him to the house then collapsed on the steps.

"I'll be back out to feed you," Ezra told the dog.

Gabby met him at the door.

"Granddad," she said, reaching to be picked up.

"Hey, sweetheart. I can't pick you up right now. I'm too muddy. Let me get get some of these clothes off."

"Mud won't hurt me."

He bent over and gave her hug. Lifting her would hurt him. It was a sad situation when a man could not pick up his granddaughter.

Anne came from downstairs where she'd been preparing Gabby's room.

"Ezra, what happened to you?" she asked.

"Took a little mud bath beauty treatment," he said.

"Oh, Granddad, you did not."

"I think Gabby's right," Anne said. "Are you hungry?"

"Starving."

"Gramma. Can I go see my room?"

"Okay, sweetheart, but say *may I,* not *can I.*"

The little girl nodded and went happily but carefully down the stairs.

Anne turned back to Ezra. "So, what really happened?"

"Nothing. Simon slipped is all."

"Are you okay?"

"Yeah. It was the least-eventful part of my day." He kicked off his boots and strained to pull off his shirt.

Anne helped him, thinking the discomfort was only his hands.

"Tell me what else is going on," she said.

"You mean besides you suddenly going to Billings to get Gabby because Dylan and Kirsten are flying to Brazil?"

"It was a sudden thing," Anne said. "Kirsten had given me a heads-up but she didn't really expect the trip to come together." Anne paused and look at him curiously. "How did you know they were going to Brazil? Did Gabby tell you already?"

"Harlan Boothe told me."

"The billionaire?"

"Yup. Corey Boothe's granddaddy just offered to buy the ranch."

"What?"

"And he's already made offers to my sisters."

Ann exhaled. "Oh my."

181

"It's out of our hands in some ways."

"What about EEEP? Maybe the government--"

"No. I don't want to even think about government programs, but, the other news is Adrienne Doyle will be staying in our bunkhouse."

"I know. I talked to her."

"You talked to her?"

"She called for directions. She didn't sound too happy about staying here."

"I bet not."

"Actually, Garcia told me first. He was here when I got home; then he took a phone call and hurried off."

"What was that about?" Ezra asked.

"No idea. Anything else?"

"Joe's in the hospital and Barney's on NPR."

"I heard Barney when I was driving home," Anne said. "But, what happened to Joe?"

"Ropesaplenty roped one too many. Broke some ribs, punctured a lung."

"That could be serious."

"He's fine. I'll get in to see him when I can. Barney's going north tomorrow to get Joe's horses. We're going to have to find a way to keep them here."

Ann looked down at the floor. So much had happened. So much to assimilate. Especially the news about Boothe.

Ezra caught her downward gaze. "Don't worry about anything," he said. He smiled through the pain, mud, and turmoil of the day. "Except feeding your husband, that is."

"There's more news."

"What?"

"Didn't Gabby tell you?"

"No, she didn't tell me anything. She gave me a hug and ran to look at her room."

"Dylan and Kristen are expecting again," Anne said. "It's a boy."

"Well, that's great. We'll have a grandson."

"Yes, but--"

"But what?"

"They're going to be in Brazil, Ezra. Through the Olympics. Maybe longer. When will we see him?"

"Anne, the baby's not even born yet."

"I know, but what about Gabby? She might be half-grown before we see her again."

"Dylan hasn't gotten the job."

She folded her arms across her chest. "You know Dylan. He lives for this. He'll get the job." A tear rolled down her cheek. "Ezra, I don't want to be on the other side of the equator from my grandchildren."

Ezra sighed. One could reason with arrogant billionaires, immature soil scientists, and cowboy cartoonists; one might survive panicked bulls and runaway saddle horses; even Adrienne Doyle could probably be handled; but grandmothers were a world of their own. He eyed the medicine cabinet.

"Sweetheart," he said. "We need to take something and get a little sleep."

Adrienne Doyle pulled into the dark yard, her wandering headlights bouncing off pools of water, flashing on the ruins of corrals, and reflecting off the eyes of a Border Collie chained by a doghouse. She pulled up by the bunkhouse porch, grabbed her bags, and opened the door. A night light cast the room in a warm glow. The bunkhouse was nicer than she'd expected. Rustic, but there was a certain charm to it that she half-resented. Doyle was determined to be angry.

One night at this ranch was all she hoped to endure. She was an experienced camper and the back of her SUV was packed with gear. She had a tent, sleeping bag, and Coleman stove. The weather was nice. She'd move into the hills in the morning.

She dropped her bags heavily and her attention went to the bookshelves. The books were so prolific she'd not noticed them at first

-- they were like wallpaper. She ran a finger across the nearest ones, then stepped closer to see the titles and authors. Barry Lopez. Anne Dilliard. Wendell Berry. Aldo Leupold. Ernest Thompson Seton. And on and on. That was the section of nature writers. Next came history. Then literature. Hemingway, Steinbeck, Faulkner, Wolfe.

Someone here was a reader. Probably not the rancher, she thought. Maybe his wife or a child.

The next row of books were theology. Doyle shook her head in disgust. Christians, she should have known. She hated Christians. If there was one class of people on earth--

She shook the thought off. Too late at night to get worked up.

On another shelf was a line of collegiate text books. *American Literature, Poetry and Prose, Fiction as a Model, The Short Story in History, Essays and Thought.* Her hand seemed pulled to one -- she thought it was just curiosity -- and she broke it open. Her eyes fell on an essay and its author.

On Land and Memory by Ezra Riley.

Ezra Riley? Landau had said he was a writer, hadn't he? Well, she'd never heard of him. She put the book back.

She then caught the glint of light on picture frames.

She stepped closer. Three black-and-white photos.

The first, a mounted cowboy on a high hill with a line of horses in the distance. Odd, she thought, it almost looked familiar.

Second, a group of men around a campfire with canvas tents in the background. A setting sun made the tents glow. It too, was a haunting scene.

The third photograph was of a cowboy; hat tipped back; stampede string loosed; chin up; two days of stubble; and his head tossed back with laughter.

It jolted her. She knew him.

It was Len. No, Lynne. Lynne with an 'e.'

She remembered it now. The mustang trap in the Pryors. These were the pens where she'd made Doomay harass Lynne and his crew.

Ezra Riley took these photos. He had to have been there. Ezra Riley was Lynne's friend.

She stepped back brusquely, and her thigh nudged a nightstand, knocking something to the floor. She shone the light down on snapshots spilling from an envelope.

She picked them up. Kodak prints. Who used print film anymore? Was it even available? There was a note with the prints. It didn't bother Doyle to read it. Being nosey was her craft.

Garcia,
Here are some prints to send your mom. Maybe next year I'll have a digital camera and you can email prints. Thanks for the branding help.
       Ezra.

She inspected them one my one. A dozen photos of branding scenes.

There was a tall fellow with a scruffy gray mustache. What a goofball, she thought, not knowing she'd recently peed to the sound of his voice.

A skinny kid with bright red hair. She guessed this was Garcia Jones, the kid she'd talked to on the phone. The young range con.

In another shot a pretty older woman was looking at the photographer with sweet contempt. She did not like having her photo taken. The rancher's wife, she guessed.

An on and on, and then, a final group scene. She wanted to see Ezra Riley and get a feel for the adversary.

From left to right: the tall guy with the mustache and a woman who had to be his wife; the blond lady; an older cowboy who looked to be bald; three young cowboys standing stiffly; and a hatless, bearded guy in khaki.

She guessed none were the ranch owner, Ezra Riley. He had to have taken all the photos.

Then her eyes went back to the last person in line. The hatless, bearded guy in khaki.

It was Peter Landau and this proved what he'd said. He was a friend of Ezra Riley.

And Ezra was a friend of Lynne's.

Doyle sheaved the photos and lay the envelope on a shelf.

The room seemed to hold her in a tight but comfortable grip. For a moment she even felt peaceful, not tormented, as she had been for weeks.

No, years.

But she shook that off.

Comfort made for complacency. She needed an edge. She needed to stay angry.

Doyle prepared for bed. She had a few busy days ahead of her, and she planned on starting early. Hopefully, before anyone else was up.

She'd escape to the hills as she always had. Flee to seclusion. To nature. To isolation.

Like the rancher in whose bunkhouse she slept, she'd always felt safest in the hills.

CHAPTER TWENTY FOUR

Ezra heard the scrunching of tires on gravel and forced himself to stir. What was it? Where was it? Where was he?

He was in bed with Anne. She was still asleep, and the house was bathed in sunlight. That couldn't be. He and Anne were always up early. Five, five-thirty.

His mind began to clear. The night before, they'd each taken a sleeping aid -- Excedrin PM. He, for his pain, Anne, for her anxiety about grandchildren.

He turned and looked at the clock. Six-forty-nine. They never slept that late.

He heard voices outside. The tires on gravel. Had someone driven in?

A sweet voice.

Gabby!

He swung from the bed, pulled on jeans and a shirt, and hobbled barefoot down the hall to the door. It was a beautiful morning. He could see Gabby outside by the corrals playing with Casey.

He couldn't see a vehicle.

Someone hadn't driven in. Someone had driven out.

He shuffled to the utility sink and splashed water on his face. Shoulder pain stabbed him awake.

Ezra called to Anne. She didn't stir.

"Anne, it's late," he called again. And Gabby is up and already outside." He heard her cast the sheets off.

He slipped on socks and boots, opened the door, and stepped into the day.

"Granddad," Gabby shouted from the corrals and came running.

He teetered down the landing steps and she gripped him around his sore leg. "Granddad, you guys are sleepyheads."

"What are you doing outside, sweetheart?"

"I got up early," Gabby said proudly. "I went outside real quiet. I turned Casey loose and talked to the angry lady."

"What angry lady?"

Gabby put her fists on her hips as if she were scolding. "Granddad, the angry lady who sleeps in your bunkhouse."

She meant Doyle. It was Doyle's vehicle he'd heard leaving.

"Was she mean to you?" he asked.

Gabby shrugged, and her strawberry blond tresses lifted like sunrise. "No. But I don't think she likes little kids. And she's not really angry."

"What do you mean?"

Gabby's eyes darted coyly to the left, then the right. "Can you keep a secret, Graddad?"

"Yes."

"I see colors."

"You see colors?"

"Yes, like when you color a coloring book. The colors tell me how people feel. I only see them on people. Not horses. Or cows. Or dogs. If the lady was angry I would see red, but I didn't see red."

"What color did you see?"

"Yellow. The lady is afraid. She's very afraid."

Casey's ears pricked up and the dog stared toward the highway. Ezra noticed a pickup pulling a small utility trailer pulling into his lane. Now what?

He bent down and gave Gabby a squeeze. "Sweetheart, would you do Granddad a big favor?"

"What, Granddad?"

"Would you go in the house and ask Gramma to make the biggest, stoutest cup of coffee she can make, then bring it out to me?"

"Okay." The little girl skipped happily away.

The visitor was in a beige-colored government truck pulling a Polaris Ranger UTV on a trailer. The vehicle swung by the corrals, parked, and Garcia Jones got out.

"Where's Doyle?" the redhead shouted.

"Good morning to you, too, Garcia."

Garcia's freckles were flaring like landing lights on a carrier. This was not a good sign.

"Did she leave already?" He looked at the bunkhouse. "Did she even stay here last night?"

"She pulled out early."

"Dang." Garcia slapped the hood of the truck with his palm.

"Garcia, what's going on?"

Whap. He slapped it again. This time it stung his hand. "I'm as qualified to do this EEEP inventory as she is," he said. "And what am I doing? When I'm not buried beneath paperwork I'm cleaning her room or running errands for her."

Ezra nodded at the Ranger.

"Yeah, she get's our new Ranger. Brand new stimulus-money Ranger. It's a piece of crap. But, it's our piece of crap. Dang. Have you talked to her?"

"No, and I thought she'd wait around to get some ranch maps from me."

"Maps? Ezra, she has the latest GPS. She can mark a section boundary down to less than a foot. Heck, she can probably call in a satellite and take pictures of you pissing behind the barn."

"So, now what are you going to do?"

"Now I have to run this Ranger up to your corrals on Dead Man."

"Nice morning for a drive," Ezra offered.

"Have you ever wondered why she's here in first place? She's got a doctorate, and she's running around the hills like some intern GS-5."

"Yeah, I have wondered--"

"You know what else I have to do today?"

"Well--"

"I have to go to a LGBT Sensitivity Training Session."

"LGBT?"

"Yes! Lesbian-Gay-Bisexual-Transgender. And do you know what we do? We sit around singing, 'Pilgrims were invaders and the Puritans were wrong, this is our message and this is our song.'"

"You sing that?"

"Yes. Over and over." His face puffed up, his eyes squinted shut and he seemed about to cry.

Casey crawled off and hid under the bunkhouse.

Ezra scowled. "Garcia, what's really wrong?"

"My dad got arrested yesterday," he blurted.

"Arrested?"

"Yeah. Five felony counts for growing marijuana with an intent to distribute."

"But I thought he was a legal grower."

"He is. In Montana, Colorado and Oregon. But these are federal charges."

"I'm sorry, Garcia. Is there anything I can do?"

"No. He's going to prison. I know that. Probably five-to-ten plus a big fine. What's my mom going to do, Ezra? Her PETA buddies aren't going to help support her and her astrology charts are a joke. She gives most of them away."

"Golly, Garcia, I --"

"No," he said, throwing up his hands. "Don't worry about it. I'll talk to you later. I have to get this machine up to devil doctor Doyle."

He roared off as if trying to shake the towed Ranger to pieces.

The front door opened and Gabby stepped out carefully holding a big mug of hot coffee.

"Be careful, sweetheart," Ezra said, and he moved quickly to meet her.

She handed him the mug and looked toward the highway. "Someone else is coming, Granddad."

Ezra looked. Now what?

A one-ton dually, its new-truck smell wafting before it, drove down the lane and parked halfway between the house and corrals. A plump man with an oversized flat hat and pants tucked into high, black-topped boots, stepped out.

He looked like a beach ball stuck into two stove pipes with a garbage can lid on his head.

He moved aggressively toward Ezra.

"Granddad," Gabby whispered. "Who's that?"

"I don't know, Gabby Jo," he said, while coaxing her up the steps. "Why don't you go in and have breakfast with Gramma?"

Her little feet tapped up the steps and through the door.

Ezra turned to face the stranger.

"Are you Ezra Riley?" the man shouted.

"Yes," Ezra said. He took a deep breath and lowered his center of gravity.

The man moved within an arm's reach. He was Ezra's age but four inches shorter and fifty pounds heavier.

"Well, I got a bone to pick with you," he said.

"Really?" Ezra said. "I don't think you have any bones at all. It appears to me that you're made of balloons, beach towels and bowling balls."

"Wha-wha-wha..." the man stammered.

Ezra took a long sip of coffee. God, it was good. It seemed he'd waited for that sip for weeks. "Now what can I do for you?" he asked.

"I heard that poem on the radio," the man barked. "The one Barney Wallace recited. The one making fun of cowboy poets. I called Barney's house and his wife said he wasn't there. She said he was over here. Besides, she said he didn't write it anyway. You wrote it."

Ezra took another long sip. The coffee was improving.

"Well, and what about it?" he asked the stranger.

"That poem was makin' fun of cowboy poets."

"*Some* cowboy poets," Ezra corrected him. "Just the bad ones."

"Do you know who I am?"

"I'm guessing you're a bad poet."

"My name is Elmer Havig--"

"Same thing."

"And what right you got to make fun of people, anyway?"

Ezra took another long sip and nodded at what remained of his corrals. "See over there, Mr. Havig? Those used to be my corrals? I had a round pen there with a snubbing post set up in the middle."

"Yeah, so?"

"Do you love horses?"

"Well, I, of course --"

"Now imagine you'd pulled in here and found me with a colt snubbed up and I was beating it half to death. Would you do something to stop me?"

Havig jutted his jaw and swelled with pride. "Yes, sir, I --"

"Well, Mr. Havig I love the English language and when I read poetry written by you its like seeing a colt being beaten to death."

Havig's lips pursed, his reddened eyes rolled together like tomatoes, and his right arm bounced spastically with a closed fist at it's end.

Ezra held one hand up. "Mr. Havig, I didn't invite you here, but I am inviting you to leave. If you unclench that fist you can grip the steering wheel better."

Havig leaned up on his heels, blew air, then wheeled and fumed away. There was a clatter as he climbed in the truck.

Then he, too, roared off.

But, Havig nearly hit another truck as he left. That truck was now coming down the Riley lane.

Ezra saw Barney's pickup and trailer approaching. Two people sat in the front seat. Now what?

Anne cracked the door and leaned out. "Ezra, what's going on? Are you coming in for breakfast?"

He shook his head but reached up and handed her the cup. "I have to direct traffic," he said. "But, I could use more coffee."

Barney Wallace pulled slowly around the lane and stopped next to Ezra with the pickup pointed back to the highway. Harlan Boothe was the passenger.

The window came down. "Hi, pard," Barney said cheerfully.

"Barney Wallace," Ezra said, the name sliding out like a sigh. "Poet Lariat of the communist set. I see you are heading north to get Joe's horses."

"That I am."

"And you've picked up a hitchhiker who's a little down on his luck."

Barney's lips and brow almost met in a scowl. Then the light came on. "Oh, you mean Mr. Boothe. He's riding along to keep me company."

"I bet he is," Ezra said. "Now, Barn Wall, I have some very good news for you."

Barney's face brightened. "What?" he asked.

"As you well know, I have been suffering from writer's block. It's been 12 years since I wrote a book."

"I know," Barney said emphatically.

"Well, today it's cured."

"It is? That is good news."

"Yes, and you did it, Barney."

"I did it?"

"That's right. You have inspired me. I am now going to write a novel and model the hero after you."

"After me?" Barney was both pleased and humbled.

"After you. And at the end of the book I am going to kill you off."

"Kill me off?"

"That's right."

"The hero?"

"The hero."

Barney brought a long finger to his lip and thought carefully. "Shoot, am I going to die a heroic death?"

"No, I am going to have you dragged to death by a team of runaway Shetlands."

"Shetlands?" Barney acted insulted.

"Through a cactus patch filled with baby skunks, porcupines, and half-grown rattlesnakes."

"Shoot. What did I do to deserve such a death?"

Ezra pointed toward the highway. "You saw the pickup that nearly sideswiped you?"

"Yeah. Looked like Elmer Havig. What was he doing here?"

"He wasn't here to start a local chapter of the Barney Wallace Fan Club."

Barney's blanket of eyebrows lifted. "No?"

"No," Ezra said. "He was mad about the poem you read on National Public Radio."

"Oh." Barney swallowed hard. "I'm sorry about that, Ez. You know, not giving you proper credit and all, but time just ran out."

Ezra shook his head. "Barney, I don't care about the credit. The glory is all yours."

"Really? Shoot. That's great. Then can I ask you a favor?"

Ezra looked at him suspiciously.

"Can you write me another one?"

"What?"

194

"Yeah. It doesn't have to be right now. I can pick it up when I drop Joe's horses off. I have to be on air live tonight at six."

"You? Live on NPR? When did NPR get so brave?"

"I dunno. But they liked me last night. They want four more live broadcasts this week, and Ez, I don't know what to say."

"Barney, you always have something to say."

"But not something that makes sense."

"Yeah, well, there is that."

"Shoot, Ezra, please. Just one more. I'll be your main cow boss for the rest of your ranching life."

Ezra looked passed him and aimed his response at Boothe. "Yeah, well, who knows how long that'll be?"

"Please." Barney folded his big hands together and begged pathetically.

"Barney, you can write."

"No, I'm a cartoonist."

"You write the captions under the cartoons."

"It takes five seconds to read a caption. I have to fill three minutes."

"Okay, one more. Got a pen?"

Barney pulled a ready one from his pocket and lifted up a pad of paper. "I'm locked-and-loaded, boss."

Ezra leaned back, thought for a second, then lapsed into rhyme:

"Gents, don't let them fool ya
theres darn few cowboys in Missoula,
mostly old hippies with stringy gray hair."
So don't let them school ya,
they haven't a clue, yeah,
their wheels are just spinning in air."
They're still tokin' and smokin'
though their moonbeams lie broken
and they've no dirty tie-dye to wear..."

195

"That's it, that's it," Barney yelled, breaking Ezra's focus.

"What do you mean, that's it?"

Barney turned the key and his truck roared to life. "That's it. You've primed the pump. That's all I need. I can take the rest."

"Think so?"

"I got it."

"So, now that you've angered all the cowboy poets you want to anger old hippies, too?"

"It's a great country, Ezra. And I have a sign-off line too. Want to hear it?

"Have I a choice?"

Barn Wall affected his radio voice: "This is Barn Wall Wallace reminding you, 'Never use money to measure wealth.' What do you think?"

Ezra looked past the cartoonist to the billionaire. "I think you should consider the company you keep."

"You talking to me or to him?" Barney asked.

"Both," Ezra said. "And I need more coffee."

PART IV

"To make a prairie it takes a
clover and a bee. One clover, and a bee.
And revery.
The revery alone will do, if bees
are few."

-- Emily Dickinson

CHAPTER TWENTY FIVE

So peaceful.

Blue sky, pale at the apex, azure at the edges. Cumulus clouds drifting slowly like old white-haired women walking home from church.

Little kisses of sunlight warming the face.

Soil and grass against the back of the head. The smell of moisture in the earth. Life. Growing things. Humus.

She slept.

There were changes coming. Moving. Wondering, what was to be?

She wanted to stay here. She wanted a pony. A dappled pony with cumulus clouds painted on its sides and streams of mane and tail colored like dandelion fuzz.

And a puppy. She'd always wanted a puppy.

One that would lick her face and make her laugh. And wouldn't grow. It would stay eight weeks old forever. Roly-poly, dark eyes dancing; pouncing on stubby legs, it's belly almost bouncing on the ground.

Every girl should have a puppy and a pony.

And a mommy to kiss the boo-boos and bless her hair with pink and blue ribbons.

She wanted her mommy.

Not just a daddy with a big office and books everywhere and adult men talking and planning late into the night. Nor long empty hallways leading to more big offices with dusty books and more dust in the air, floating like tiny fireflies circling shafts of light from half-draped windows.

She'd no one to play with.

Cookies. Who would bake cookies?

"Mommy."

The sound of her own voice awakened her.

Adrienne Doyle opened her eyes and was confused when she saw the sky. Sleeping? She'd been sleeping? Someone stood by her head. No, some *thing*. An old cedar fence post. Weathered, twisted, rubbed smooth and shiny. Tacked to it was a small surveyor's stake. She remembered now. She'd wondered about the stake. It was modern. Why was it nailed to a fencepost from the homesteading era? Faint color was barely legible on the stake's grainy surface. She'd lain down to inspect it closer and had fallen asleep.

Doyle got to her feet.

She was on a high prairie bench thick with Big Sage. A lek, she thought. A dancing ground for sage grouse. Their droppings were everywhere.

And tussocks. Little islands of grass, heads above other grasses. And off this plateau, ran fingered coulees; mesic funnels draining to a deeply-cut creek forested with Silver Sage. She was in sage grouse heaven.

Why had she slept? She had work to do.

In the distance the railroad ties and bridge planked corrals stood like a black and silver forest. Two vehicles sat there and this startled her. She recognized hers. What was the other one? As her eyes focused she realized it was a UTV. The young range con had brought the Ranger and she hadn't even heard him.

Doyle lifted a blue-and-silver backpack, heavy with inventory tools, field glasses, and water, from the ground and headed toward the utility vehicle. Through a notch in the western skyline a glint caught her eye. Sunshine off glass. About a mile away a truck was parked on the county road.

Until now she'd seen no sign of human life on Dead Man. There were no power poles, and even fence lines were scarce and far apart.

What were the people in the truck doing?

She pulled her binoculars from the pack and focused on the road.

They were just sitting there. It was too far away to be sure, but she thought there were two men in the cab.

Two men in an old pickup? That made her remember the men on the frontage road.

Was this them? Had they followed her?

She couldn't tell. In last night's darkness she'd not really noticed the color of their truck, and now, from this distance, she wasn't sure of the color of this one.

But one thing she was sure of: sleeping alone in the hills had lost its appeal.

You are toxic to us.

Doyle stopped in her tracks. His words. Isn't that what Lars had said? *You are toxic to us.*

What had he meant? They couldn't be seen together at functions and dinners?

Did he mean more?

Dread clutched her. She knew the inner workings of the world's most radical environmental groups and had done much to further their agendas. But she didn't know everything. The groups Lars represented were years beyond Agenda 21 and other milquetoast remedies for restoring the earth. Did they assume she knew more than she did?

There had been times when Lars had taken calls and left the room. Was he worried about pillow talk; her access to his laptop;

her conclusions about long trips to distant countries and visits with assorted leaders in politics and science?

Did he think she knew so much she had to be silenced?

It seemed so ridiculous -- Lars putting a hit out on her -- that she tried to laugh it off.

But it wasn't that ridiculous.

They'd fought side-by-side in a war for the future of the planet. What was one person's life in exchange for a healthy Earth?

Nothing.

They'd often talked about the greater good, and she'd said she was willing to sacrifice herself for the cause if necessary.

Was that time now?

She looked back toward the county road. The truck was gone.

Killing her would not be his decision. Lars was simply a mercenary. A man under orders.

But would they use trailer trash to do it? Would they hire a couple of hillbillies when they could afford to hire the best?

Yes, hillbillies made sense. A random act of violence by crazed drug addicts. It would create sympathy. She'd be the victim. *The Post* and others -- including Landau? -- would back off.

Stop, Adrienne. Think. What are the actual chances they want to kill you?

Logically?

Fifty-fifty. Odds that would keep a thinking person on edge.

Barney's pickup and trailer scooted north, but his thoughts were miles past the farthest horizon. He had another radio program to prepare for.

"Barney, are you sure you want me traveling with you?" Harlan Boothe asked.

Barn Wall snapped from his fog. "Shoot, yeah. I like the company. I'm just thinking. Gotta get a dally on this Old Hippy thing. No, I better get tied hard-and fast."

Boothe stared at him wordlessly. He hadn't a clue what the cartoonist meant.

"I know. I should listen to NPR. Where do you find it on the radio dial?"

"FM. In the low 90s I think. That would be on the far left side of the dial."

"Far left? Shoot, Ezra was right. They are commies."

Boothe stifled a laugh. He didn't know if Barney was playing with him or not.

"Shoot, there's nothing on but music without words."

"They play a lot of classical music in the mornings."

Barney clicked the radio off. "Well, that doesn't do me any good."

"Are you sure you want to do a program that provokes old hippies?"

"Sure. I've already provoked the cowboy poets. Maybe them and the old hippies will show up and wail the tar out of each other."

"But what if they show up at Ezra's house?"

Barney stared at the yellow dashes on the highway. He gave this scenario serious thought. "Shoot, Ezra would love it," he said.

Boothe shook his head. "This certainly is an entertaining country. Not all like where I grew up."

"Where did you grow up?"

"Cape Canaveral. As a kid I used to watch the first space shots. That's what inspired me to design technology for satellites. I started out with NASA, then branched out on my own."

"What made you buy a place near Miles City for your grandson?"

"That's an odd story. When I bought my granddaughter's place by Missoula she found some mares she wanted in Wisconsin. I thought it would be good if I delivered those mares myself."

"You hauled mares cross-country not knowing anything about horses?"

"Yes, and I had tire trouble on the Interstate outside Miles City. I blew two tires on the trailer. I didn't know what to do. I have AAA, of course, but this involved horses. What do you do with horses in a situation like that?

"While I was deciding, a pickup pulling a trailer stopped and a cowboy about my age got out. Do you call them *cowboys* when they're in their seventies?"

"Yup."

"This cowboy was real pleasant. He knew I was out of my orbit and he did everything to get me going again. Even gave me his spare tire."

"Nice guy."

"Very nice gentleman. I tried to pay him but he wouldn't take any money. He said the spare wasn't that good and he had a pile of them at home."

"Sounds like a local."

"Yes, I'm sure he was. I decided then that I'd invest in this region if the opportunity came up. It came up when it became obvious Corey needed his own place. I've wanted to find that cowboy ever since, but I never got his name."

"Shoot. I know everybody. What kind of rig did he have?"

"Rig?"

"Yeah, what was he driving?"

"Oh, just a truck. I think it was fairly new but the trailer was in bad shape."

"What did he look like?"

"My age. About my build, too."

"That doesn't help me much."

"He wore a leather belt with his name on the back."

"What was the name?"

"I couldn't read it. Belt loops covered a couple of the letters and the edges were worn smooth. "The name started with an *L*, I'm sure of that, and I think it ended with an *E*."

"Larrie?"

"No, I don't think so. Larry ends with a *Y*."

"Lassie? No, that's a dog's name."

"There were two *N*s or one *M* in the middle. I'm not sure which."

They were quiet as each considered possible names.

Then Barney slapped the steering wheel.

"Lonnie," he declared. "It has to be someone named Lonnie."

Adrienne Doyle left the Riley pasture that evening on full alert, looking for two men in an older pickup truck. She didn't hear her radio at first because she had the volume low.

"...so cut a wide swath around Missoul-lee
where old hippies smell of patchouli..."

It was him. That funny guy. She turned up the volume but the reception was cutting in and out.

"...old hippies with stringy gray hair
with nothing but bell-bottoms to wear..."

He was making fun of old hippies. She thought of her dad's friends. She could relate to this.

"...moonbeams lay broken
like the roaches they've been tokin'..."

So true, so true. Who was this guy? He had to be a cast member from *Saturday Night Live*. Who else could get away with lampooning cowboy poets one night and old hippies the next?

She had good friends at NPR. She would call them and find out who he was.

No. She couldn't do that. She didn't dare call any members of the media.

She was cut off from the world.

Two tractors and a dozen young people were busy in the corrals when Doyle eased into the Riley yard. One tractor was pushing debris into piles while another dug holes for new posts. Teenagers were pulling nails, cutting debris into firewood, and nailing up new planks. By the amount accomplished they'd been busy all day and were hurrying to finish before dark.

Doyle still didn't know what Ezra Riley looked like. Maybe he was on one of the tractors. Everyone seemed industrious and happy. She'd never seen anything quite like this. Somehow, she knew they were volunteers. The rural community, to Doyle, was nothing more than a voting bloc of peasants who resisted social progress. They were hicks who took pigs to the county fair, won ribbons, and then had pork for supper.

As she got out of her SUV, both Casey and the little girl came running to her.

"Hi," Gabby said. "Where have you been?"

"I've been in the hills working," Doyle answered flatly.

"My Gramma took my Granddad to the hospital."

Doyle looked down at her. "To the hospital? How come?"

Gabby shrugged. "I dunno. He's hurt."

"Who are all the people in the corrals?"

Gabby turned to give her official report. "The man in the red tractor is Barney. He's funny. I don't know the other man. The kids are 4F."

"4F?"

"Yes, ah, maybe not."

"Do you mean 4H?"

"Yes, that's it." Gabby looked up at Doyle intently. "Are you a doctor?"

"Yes, in a way, I am."

"Could you have helped Granddad?"

"No, I'm not that kind of doctor."

"What kind of doctor are you if you don't help people?"

The question made Doyle pause. Why was she even standing here talking to this urchin? But, she wasn't an urchin. She was actually quite cute. And very smart.

"Well?" Gabby waited.

"I am a doctor who takes care of the planet."

"Oh, my Gramma and Granddad do that, too."

Doyle bent down. "What's your name?"

"Gab-bri-ella-Jo. I am five years old."

"And your Gramma and Granddad left you here alone?"

"I'm not alone. Can't you see all the people?"

"But those are strangers."

"No, those are friends. Besides, Gramma said Doctor Doyle would be back soon, and if no one else was here, Doctor Doyle would be. But I think she knew that funny Barney would stay. Barney got here late. Just before you came. He was doing something in town. Something about a radio. Did you know that when I grow up I am going to live here?"

"No, I didn't know that."

"Yes, I am. And I am going to have a puppy. His name will be Roger."

"That's good. Well, if you'll excuse me--"

"And I will have a pony, too. A pony with dimples."

"Dimples?"

"Yes, dimples."

Doyle gently poked a finger into one of Gabby's cheeks. The action surprised her. She couldn't remember when she'd last touched a child. "You mean a dimple like that?" she asked.

"No, don't be silly. I mean horse dimples. You know. The white spots on the side of the pony that look like little white clouds."

The imagery raised scenes still floating in Doyle's mind.

"You mean, dappled?" she asked. "You are going to have a dappled pony."

"Yes, dimpled. With a white mane and tail."

Doyle took a step back as if pushed by subconscious images. "I have to go in my house now," she said. "Will you be okay with your friends?"

"Yes, of course," Gabby Jo said. "Because I'm not afraid of anything. Nothing at all."

CHAPTER TWENTY SIX

Nicholas and Jeremy were running their hospital scam. Nickie put a sharp rock in his shoe and hobbled into the Emergency Room almost crying in pain. He told the ward clerk he'd aggravated a back injury. He hoped for a young nurse he could bluff for painkillers. Preferably Hydro or Oxy.

Meanwhile, Jeremy was sprawled in the walk-in clinic waiting room. No one bothered him because he looked sick. He was actually listening carefully, hoping to hear patients say what drugs they'd been prescribed.

Jeremy was slumped into a chair like a thrown-away jacket and had neither bathed nor eaten for several days. People didn't sit near him. They wouldn't even look at him. There was a stack of old magazines by his chair so he grabbed one. He hadn't seen a book, newspaper, or magazine for a long time.

As he thumbed through a horse magazine, a tall, blond woman in her early 60s took a seat two chairs from him. Ranch woman, he thought. There was something about her he liked. She seemed kind without being weak. If he could find Lynne and get his tongue back she was someone he'd like to talk to. Someone who might talk to him.

At one point the woman got up and went to the receptionist. They seemed to know each other. The receptionist let her use a phone. The tall lady talked for a minute then came and sat back down.

That was odd, Jeremy thought. Everyone had cell phones these days. He'd had one since he was 13. Of course, you needed a cell phone when you worked the streets.

The woman stood up again and looked at the glass entrance doors. "Peter?" she said.

A young man with curly black hair and a trimmed beard walked in. Jeremy eyed him carefully over the pages of the magazine. He had an energetic, confident manner. Experienced, but not dangerous.

"I just got back in town," Peter said. "I called the Wallace home and Henrietta told me both Ezra and Joe were in the hospital."

"Ezra's just getting X-rays," the woman said. "It's just a formality. He needs a different painkiller. The one he was prescribed makes him sick."

Bingo, Jeremy thought. *Painkillers.*

"Joe's room is on the other side of the hospital. I went to see him but he was asleep. I was hoping Ezra could see him, but we left our granddaughter at home."

"Barney's there. I got ahold of him."

The woman sighed. "Oh, I'm so glad. I tried just a minute ago but he didn't pick up. Barney's so sweet. He brought some 4H kids to work on the corrals."

"Yes, that sounds like Barney. Listen, Anne. Go to your granddaughter. I can wait and take Ezra home."

"You don't mind?"

"No, of course not. But what happened to Ezra?"

"Simon fell with him. I think it aggravated his injury. This morning I saw him working in the corrals with our granddaughter and went to see how they were doing. Ezra had his hands duct-taped around a tamping bar so he could grip it. Gabby had done the taping."

"His hands have been hurting him since I met him."

"I know, but I think they're worse. Or something is. He just isn't being himself."

"Anne, is Adrienne Doyle around?"

"Yes. She's staying in our bunkhouse."

"Why?" Landau asked. The concern was obvious in his voice, even to the eavesdropping Jeremy.

"There are no motel rooms and we're under a deadline to do the EEEP application," Anne said. "Oh, I don't suppose you know what that is."

"Yes, I do. Ezra mentioned it to me at the cow camp, but he didn't want Joe or Barney to know about it."

"I don't understand."

"He said his back was against the wall and this program was something he might have to do, but he hated the idea of it."

Landau watched this information settle on Anne's face.

"That's not all of it, you know," he said. "He knows Doyle. And I know Doyle. She's not someone you want to do business with."

"But, we're not doing business with her. She's just a civilian contractor."

"She's more than that. But, you get home, Anne. I'll bring Ezra out when he's done."

"You'll need to stop and get his prescription filled."

"That's no problem. You get home to your granddaughter."

The tall ranch woman hurried off. The young bearded man took a seat on the other side of the room.

This situation looked promising, but Jeremy didn't know if he and Nickie should move on it or not.

Then his eyes dropped to a small photo in the magazine he was holding.

It looked like *him*. He couldn't believe it.

It was the nice cowboy. Lynne.

He looked closer. It was him.

But the article was an obituary.

Jeremy Pratt's hopes sank to the floor. He glanced quickly at the magazine's cover. It was over three years old.

He turned back to the photo. It was him. No doubt it. Lynne was dead. And now Jeremy knew he'd never talk again, so nothing else mattered.

He checked to see who had written the article. Someone named Ezra Riley.

Ezra?

He'd get Nickie. They'd follow the bearded fellow and the cowboy -- this *Ezra* --and get his drugs. Maybe they'd get more than that because nothing mattered now.

Adrienne Doyle had heard the vehicles leave the yard one-by-one, until only a single pickup remained. It belonged to a tall, older cowboy who went in the house with Gabby Jo. It had to be a neighbor or close friend. Someone the Rileys trusted.

Soon another vehicle pulled into the yard. This had to be Mrs. Riley. She was alone and walked quickly.

A few minutes later, the tall cowboy got into his pickup and drove away.

Though the bunkhouse had a small microwave and a hot plate, Doyle considered going to town for a restaurant meal, but knew she shouldn't. She still didn't know about the two men in the truck. Were they targeting her?

She jumped when the knock sounded on the door.

"Who is it?" she said. She regretted leaving her pepper spray in her vehicle.

"Dr. Doyle. It's Anne Riley."

She opened the door to a tall woman with piecing blue eyes and hair so blond it fell like whitewater to her shoulders.

"We haven't met," Anne said. "I just wanted to welcome you. Do you need anything?"

"No, I'm fine." *This woman makes me feel short and fat.*

"I have to fix something for Gabby. I understand you've already met her. You are welcome to come eat with us."

"No, no thank you. That wouldn't be allowable. I need to keep a certain professional distance."

"Okay. Well, if you need anything at all--"

"Mrs. Riley."

"Yes. And call me Anne."

"How's your husband? I saw that you came home alone. Is he in the hospital?"

"No. Our friend Peter is bringing him out."

"Peter?" She paused not knowing if she should pursue this.

"Peter Landau," Anne said. "He's a writer."

"I know Peter. I bumped into him in Nevada. He mentioned he'd been up here."

Anne smiled. "It really is a small world, isn't it."

"Yes," Doyle said, closing the door slowly. "It certainly is."

An hour later the house's porch light came on. Doyle looked out her window. A car pulled in and stopped beneath the light. Landau got out. Then a man got out of the passenger side. The two of them went up the steps and through the door Anne held open.

So that was Ezra Riley. She really couldn't see him, but he appeared to be Peter's height, and from a distance, he looked trim for an older rancher. Most of the old cowboys she knew had two spare tires crushing a belt buckle they'd won forty years ago.

Doyle stepped out to the SUV, grabbed the pepper spray, and put it in the zippered pocket of her windbreaker.

The night was pleasant. Above her stars stretched forever. She sensed a motion beside her and looked down to see the Riley dog. If he were supposed to be tied someone forgot. Doyle found most dogs annoying, but this one seemed different. He was polite. What had the little girl called him?

Roger? No, that was the puppy Gabby wanted.

Casey?

"Casey." The smooth-coated, brown-and-white Border Collie came forward and obediently sat at her left side.

"My, you have had some training, haven't you?"

He wagged his tail but didn't offer to lick.

"Do you want to go for a moonlight walk?"

His eyes said yes.

"Okay, heel." She moved off and Casey fell in behind her.

They walked past the corrals, moving carefully around piles of boards and poles, and toward the highway, but stayed far enough from the house so not to be seen. She wasn't being secretive in a bad way, she told herself, she just didn't want to alarm anyone.

A four-wire barbed-wire fence slowed her, but she went through it without ripping her jacket. Behind her, light glowed through the house windows, but she couldn't see anyone.

She imagined the Riley's were introducing Peter to Gabby. That could take a while. Talkative little urchin.

A dim light appeared in front of her by the highway.

What was that?

A pickup. There was a truck sitting on the approach opposite from the Riley mailbox.

The pickup.

It was easier for her to recognize the truck in the dark. She crouched behind a sagebrush. Casey cuddled in beside her and she was thankful for his warmth.

The light she'd seen was probably a cigarette lighter flashing on. She heard voices. No. *A* voice.

The voice.

It was the big man. She was sure of it. It had to be. This was the pickup.

So it was true. They were targeting her.

She wanted to call Lars and confront him. *Call it off, or I will go to the press. You think you have problems now, you...*

No. He would deny everything; call her insane. Then he'd hang up and make another call and a cell phone would ring in the pickup in front of her.

Do it. Do it tonight, he would say.

Then what?

The killers would drive into the yard. They'd go to the bunk-house, but she wouldn't be there, so they'd go to the house.

The Rileys would be friendly. Anne would open the door. Or Gabby.

She couldn't let that happen.

She took her cell phone out, cupped her hands around it to shield its light, and checked her bars. Not many. Maybe not enough.

She punched in 9-1-1.

She could hear a dim ring. "This is ... County...Dispatch... your... emergency?"

"Hello," she whispered as load as she dared.

"Please....up.....what....emergency?"

"North of town. Near the Riley Ranch. A suspicious truck on the highway." She said it slowly, clearly, with emphasis.

"M'am... speak...is....emergency?"

"Send-a-patrol-car."

The line went dead. Did they hang up? What should she do now?

She should go to the house and tell the Rileys about the truck. They had a land line. They could call the authorities.

Yes, she had to tell them.

But that would only be helpful tonight. What could the authorities do? Maybe the two had outstanding warrants? Or maybe the pickup would smell of dope?

Too many maybes. What if the authorities only warned them away. Then what?

She heard a door close. Landau was leaving the house. He disappeared around his SUV and she heard its door close. The lights came on. He drove up the lane toward the highway.

The old truck rumbled and it's lights came on.

Then the old truck moved north.

Landau came to the highway, stopped, signaled, and turned south.

She didn't move for five minutes and became chilled and cramped. Casey became restless. He whined, lay flat on the ground and put his head on his paws.

A light appeared in the north. She watched it tensely. It sped by. Not them. The truck was too new.

Why didn't they kill me last night on the frontage road? she wondered. *Were they needing a positive identification? Did they have a certain time and place in mind? Just like Lars. Make it dramatic. Send a signal to others like her. That was silly. There wasn't anyone else like her. Was there?*

Ten more minutes. More chill. More cramps. Two more vehicles. Not them.

Maybe he was just trying to scare her. Terrify her into silence.

He was doing a good job.

Behind her one light went off in the house. Then another. The Rileys had gone to bed.

Is that what the men were waiting for?

Another ten minutes went by, then headlights appeared.

It was them. She knew it. Her flesh crawled.

The lights came slowly. She heard the old truck's rumble.

What to do? What to do? Could she race to the house and warn the Rileys? She'd have a fence to get through. Would their doors be locked? Were they cautious? Certainly Ezra Riley was the type of man who had guns in the house. Piles of guns. All ranchers did.

The pickup slowed at the Riley approach. She tensed.

But, then it accelerated and drove off. She watched, even rising stiffly to better see the retreating taillights. The lights kept going. Toward town.

Tonight was not the night.

They know the Riley's have a dog, she thought. They're worried about the dog. He'd bark. There would be no surprise.

She looked down at Casey. Friendly, workaholic Casey.

"Like you're any sort of watchdog," she said.

Casey wagged his tail.

CHAPTER TWENTY SEVEN

Jeremy stared at fire ants busily building a mound. They scurried this way and that, humping many times their body weight. Ferocious stings. Bites like fire. His brain felt like an ant pile. The ants were busy there, too. Scurrying little things with bites of fire.

Some Hydrocodone would put his fire out.

He and Nicholas were parked on an approach a half-mile north of the Riley house. Nickie watched the house through binoculars, while Jeremy watched the ants.

The night before, they'd followed the cowboy home but hadn't acted. Too many vehicles and no assessment of the dogs. The Pratt boys weren't stupid. Most ranchers had stock dogs, but a few had regular guard dogs like German Shepherds, Dobermans, or Rottweilers. Better to wait.

They were still wide-eyed from uppers they'd stolen from a Peterbilt at a truck stop. Amphetamines were useful when they had no place to sleep.

Nickie was speed-rapping about getting paid, needing the works, a Q or Zip soon, maybe DMT.

DMT? Doubtful, thought Jeremy. It was the most powerful hal-
lucinogen in the world. It had more fire ants than Nickie had brain
cells. He'd talk some sense into his cousin if he could talk, but he'd
never talk now that Lynne was dead.

Nicholas was teetering on a dangerous edge. He needed something. Anything. Maybe bath salts. Maybe they could knock off a
meth lab or stick up a pharmacy at gun point, if he had a gun,
which he didn't. Amphetamines made Nickie think more, and
faster, than he was accustomed to. Speed made him feel slick, sleek,
and smart.

But, Jeremy hated amphetamines. His mind was fast enough.
He didn't need to be pedaling downhill with a breeze at his back.
Rubbing some Hydro against a hose clamp and smoking it in a light
bulb was his thing. Numbness. Sweet sleep.

Nicholas watched an expensive vehicle pull into the Riley yard.
He'd seen this kind before on the Vegas Strip. A Range Rover. A
skinny guy with white hair and beard got out. He talked for a few
minutes to the cowboy, Ezra, then he drove away.

"Jeremy. Gotta go," Nickie said. "Been here too long. They'll see
us. Let's go get some dogs."

By dogs, Nicholas meant hot dogs micro-waved at a Quick Stop
and washed down with cans of Red Bull. Breakfast.

Jeremy shuffled to the truck holding his side as if his guts were
spilling out. He didn't know why he did it -- sometimes he felt to see
if he'd been shot, but there was never any blood. It was like he was
holding something in or holding himself together.

At the Riley mailbox, they met another truck slowing down to
pull in.

"Get down," Nickie snapped. Jeremy folded up like a wrapper.
Nickie pulled the eye-visor down. He thought he recognized the
driver and didn't want the driver to recognize him.

The man in the truck gave a casual wave.

Nicholas remembered the guy. It was the big cowboy with the crooked grin who'd given them gas near here. The bearded guy from the hospital was with him.

Too many comings and goings, Nickie thought.

Ezra awakened that morning sensing a change. Circumstances were the same -- his hands, shoulder, knee, and neck hurt; Doyle was in his bunkhouse; Boothe was offering to buy the ranch -- but the atmosphere around him seemed different.

He felt better and it certainly wasn't the single Hydrocodone he'd taken before bed. Maybe it was the new pillow he'd purchased when he got the prescription.

Heck of a deal, he thought. Thirty years ago, his priorities were handmade boots and custom saddles. Now, they were pillows and painkillers.

As he made coffee, he heard Dr. Doyle leave and he wondered about her early start. It was not yet five-thirty.

He took his coffee to his chair, read a chapter from Proverbs, then switched on Fox News low, so not to awaken Anne.

She was up a little after six, late for her, and they had breakfast about seven.

Gabby was still in bed when Ezra went outside at 7:20 to feed the horses. He had his own, plus Joe's, to care for. Halfway across the yard he saw the silver Range Rover pull in. Harlan Boothe. Now what?

Ezra waited in the yard until the luxury SUV stopped and Boothe got out.

"Good morning," the billionaire said. "I hope I'm not disturbing you folks."

"We're up," Ezra said.

"I'm on my way to the airport. I'll be gone for a couple days and I just wanted to check in. I feel like I approached you the wrong way, Mr. Riley, and I want to apologize for that."

"Apology accepted," Ezra said. To the north, Ezra noticed a pickup sitting on an approach to his western pasture. That wasn't too unusual. People often stopped on that hill to get cell phone service.

"And I would like to increase my offer to 2.7 million," Boothe added.

"Duly noted."

Boothe waited for more reaction. He didn't get it.

"You seem to be in a hurry this morning," Ezra said.

"It's my granddaughter. She got hurt yesterday. I've chartered a plane to fly to her. Nothing too serious. A broken arm and plenty of bruises."

"I'm glad she's okay."

"Thank you. She was, uh--"

"She was messing with a horse she had no business messing with."

"How did you know that?"

"I've been to her web site, Mr. Boothe. She breeds the hottest barrel horses in the country, stables them as colts, gins them up on hot feed and supplements, then fries their brains on an accelerated training program."

"Well, I don't know much about training horses, but--"

"Mr. Boothe, you know nothing about horses and neither does she. I don't mean to be unkind, but she's going to get herself, or somebody else, badly injured or killed."

"Right now she's determined to raise barrel horses. In a year or two it could be something else. How would you do it differently?"

Ezra grinned. "I don't want to give you another reason to buy my ranch, but she needs to run the mares and colts in the hills where they'll develop bone and muscle the way God intended. Start them slow and easy, but ride them in big, rough country. Give them more to look at than barn stalls and a tiny, indoor arena. Your granddaughter is raising hand grenades with hair, then she wonders why they blow up."

"I would like her to meet you, Mr. Riley. Perhaps you could explain this to her. But, I have to get going. Consider my offer. I should be back tomorrow night or the next morning. I still have matters with Corey to sort out."

Minutes after Boothe left, Barney drove in with Landau riding shotgun. They found Ezra feeding Joe's horses.

"Top of the morning to you," Barney said.

"Morning, gentlemen. Thanks for all the work you guys got done yesterday, Barn. I appreciate it."

"I have another crew coming out today. I talked the college rodeo team into lending a hand."

"Well, that's mighty good of them. How did last evening's NPR session go?"

"Fantastic. Couldn't have been better. They're calling me a new Will Rogers. Shoot, I grew up wanting to be Will James, not Will Rogers."

"I suppose you're wanting another poem."

Barney grinned sheepishly. "If you wouldn't mind."

Ezra sighed. His friend was basically rebuilding his corrals for him. What could he do?

"What's your subject?" Ezra asked.

"Government bureaucrats."

"Barn Wall, you are an equal-opportunity offender," Ezra said, shaking his head. "Okay, here's your primer:

When government is tight and lean
'We the people' run the machine,
when government is big and fat,
we're at the mercy of the bureaucrat.
And what is a bureaucrat? you say,
but a soulless wonder made of clay.
With selfish ambitions most fervent
he's no longer a public servant.
When the servant spirit is the rule
the common man is given tools.

When politicians take the reins,
common sense goes down the drain.
So if you want to cut the fat
lay the knife on a bureaucrat.
And for added exhibition
slice and dice a politician."

"Ooh-ooh," Barney said, waving his hands as if they were on fire. "That's a bit hot to handle. I'll need some ice tea and sugar to help this go down."

"Well, it's yours," Ezra said. "You make your own sweet tea out of it."

"Shoot, it's radio, Ez. How are they going to see that I'm saying this with a smile?"

"Just get in character. Remember, you're Barn Wall Wallace, the bane of broadleaf weeds and the orator from odoriferous outhouses."

"Shoot. It's getting dangerous to be famous."

"So, who are you going to take on tomorrow night?"

"I was thinking the news media."

"That should go over great. Why don't you just go to Mecca and insult the Prophet Mohammed?"

"Shoot--"

"Don't even think about it. I hate to leave this assembly of literary brilliance, gentlemen, but--"

"What's on your schedule today, Ezra?" Landau asked.

"Well, if Barney can handle managing a rodeo team, I have fence to fix."

"I could help," Landau said.

"Sure," Ezra said. "Glad for the company."

He led the way to the '78 Ford. No way was he taking the low-slung Chevy.

Adrienne Doyle blamed it on having too much on her mind. She made it to the corrals on Dead Man before realizing she'd left her iPad charging in the bunkhouse. She could do without it, but it was better to go back twelve miles to get it. If she hurried, she could make the roundtrip in 40 minutes.

Having slept well, Doyle had almost convinced herself the men in the truck were not after her. It was a coincidence that she'd seen them twice. They were only drifters pulled in by the oil boom. Criminals, probably, but not hired killers.

She laughed at the idea of Lars hiring hillbillies to kill her. He was so proper and urbane. He'd never employ trailer trash.

How *would* Lars do it? He was a legal assassin, not a literal one. He'd hire a professional. Probably a slender, dapper man in a tailored suit, who knew about rare, untraceable toxins derived from endangered equatorial blowfish. He'd dry the poison to a powder and place it in a cayenne container. A little sprinkle on her salad, and...

But there they were again. The two men in the old truck were parked on an approach above the Riley place. She braked hard, then wished she hadn't? Had they heard the tires squeal?

No. She backed onto an approach a quarter-mile behind them. Doyle pulled out a pair of 12x40 Swarovskis binoculars. She recognized the big guy. He was looking through binoculars, too, only he was watching the Riley ranch.

His skinny partner was shuffling around, head down, and holding his side. Was he injured or doing a junkie two-step?

There was no doubt now, was there? They were looking for her, but what could she do? Make a run for it? Drive north to Jordan, then turn west and go to Grass Range? Turn left again and drive to Billings? Stay there overnight?

That was a long way to go just to get to Billings.

Maybe Canada was a better idea.

But what good would fleeing do? She had a federal contract to fulfill. Disappearing would bring more attention.

She had to stay.

She needed the proverbial ace up her sleeve.

And she had one. She'd seen him last night.

Peter Landau.

She grabbed her cell phone and looked at its screen. Maybe enough bars for a call. She hit memory dial and heard a tone from the other end.

He won't pick up.

But his answering machine did.

"Lars, listen to me," she said. "I know your game. You call these two goons off or I'm giving everything I know to Peter Landau. He's right here in Miles City. Call them off, Lars, or Landau gets it all."

She hung up.

So there.

But how long would it take for those two imbeciles to get the word from Lars? What if their phone was lost or they'd hocked it to buy dope?

No, worse yet, Lars knew better than to contact hired killers himself. He would contact someone who would contact someone else. This could take time.

It didn't matter. She'd stay in the hills all day. She'd use a back road to return to the Riley place at dark in the Polaris Ranger, and in the evenings she'd put everything she had on Lars on two flash drives. She'd take one with her when she left and mail the other to Landau's mother in Westchester.

But, she needed a gun. Pepper spray wasn't enough. That big guy probably used pepper spray on his eggs.

Where would she get a gun?

She didn't dare go to town. She didn't even know what the process was for buying a firearm in Montana.

Landau wouldn't have a gun. He probably didn't even have pepper spray.

But, Ezra Riley, *he* would have a gun.

And he would understand that a girl like her, alone in the hills, might feel the need for protection.

Ezra Riley would be her protector. The only problem was, she hadn't even met him.

225

CHAPTER TWENTY EIGHT

Old Yeller, the '78 Ford, rolled onto the blacktop like a war horse released from the barn. Casey balanced precariously on its flatbed.

"I think there's been a rip in the space/time continuum," Landau said.

"Because we're in a truck as old as you are?" Ezra asked.

"That, too. But, I was thinking, a week ago we were branding calves in Garfield County. Since then, Joe's been hospitalized, Barney's on NPR, Garcia's father has been arrested, and you have Adrienne Doyle staying in your bunkhouse."

"General misfortune for everyone," Ezra said dryly. "Especially Barney."

"So much has happened to everyone so quickly."

"What about you? You made a quick trip to Nevada, barely got there, and turned around and came back. There must be a story in that."

"Yes, there is. A fairly big story that I'm sitting on, and I will probably continue to sit on it."

"Can you tell me?"

"It's Doyle. Half the print journalists on the east coast are trying to locate her. I saw her, you know."

"I suppose. She's in my bunkhouse."

"No, I mean in Nevada. I bumped into her at a truck stop. I thought she was acting peculiarly then, but I didn't know what had gone down."

"And what's gone down?"

"She wrote a blog post suggesting she might be responsible for a young rancher's suicide. A media watchdog group caught it and passed it on to a friend of mine at the *Post*."

"Have you read the blog post?"

"Yes. My friend forwarded me the text. Of course Doyle took the post down but not before it had widely circulated."

"Do you think it's true?"

"It could be. She's suspected of doing dirty tricks, including planting false evidence of threatened or endangered species."

"So, what are you going to do? Are you going to try and interview her?"

Landau turned his head and stared out the passenger door window for several moments. "No," he said finally. "Not while she's here on your ranch. She has a job to do, and I have a separate story I'm working on. I'm going to give her some space and see what happens."

"But you're not going to tell your friend at the *Post* where she is?"

"No, I'm not sharing."

"Good." Ezra said, and he took a turn onto a two-track pasture road.

"Let me ask you about something else," Landau said. "Barney and I passed a new Range Rover on the highway this morning, the *Autobiography* model. That's a $140,000 vehicle. It looked like it might have come from your place."

"Yup. Harlan Boothe stopped in for a little visit."

"And?"

"A couple days ago he offered me $2.5 million for my share of the ranch. This morning he increased that by 200K."

"Are you tempted?"

Ezra gripped the steering wheel tightly as Old Yeller splashed through a mud puddle larger than a wading pool. "At my age I would be foolish not to consider it, but basically--" he turned to Landau and smiled -- "hell, no."

"But, you and Anne are in your sixties. You can't run a ranch by yourselves forever. Not without help of some kind."

"What's worse, getting in bed with the government, or selling out to someone like Boothe?"

"Squeezed between capitalism and socialism?"

Ezra changed the subject. "Peter, I get the feeling you know something else you're not telling me."

Landau was no longer surprised by Ezra's questions. "It's probably nothing," he said. But there's a rumor circulating that there's a hit out on Doyle."

"A contract hit?" Ezra stopped at a gate.

Landau got out, opened it, and waited as Ezra drove through. Then he closed the gate and got back in the truck.

"You don't think that's really true, do you?" Ezra asked.

"No, but it's not without some merit. Doyle has been involved with some very dangerous people, and they might be afraid she's losing it. They've used her boyfriend as her handler, but he's been sidetracked by a young socialite."

"Boyfriend?"

"Lars Anderssen. An environmental attorney."

"*Bad Day at Black Rock* for Adrienne," Ezra quipped.

"What's that?"

"A western movie. Lee Marvin, again."

"What if *Black Rock* happens to be your bunkhouse?"

"I never took you to be a conspiracy nut, Peter."

"My homes are in New York and Tel Aviv. As conspiracies go, this would be a small one."

"So you're serious? You think there could be a hit out on Doyle?"

"I'm saying it's possible."

"Who started the rumor?"

"My *Post* source says Anderssen got drunk at a party and spouted off."

"Then I would think the hit would be on Anderssen, not Doyle."

Landau stared through Old Yeller's dirty windshield. "There's probably nothing to it," he said. "But, I can't rule out the possibility."

Ezra pulled up to the stretch of fence he'd jerry-rigged two days before and stopped. Old Yeller's bed was filled with steel posts, coils of barbed wire, post pounder, wire stretcher and a plastic bucket filled with post clips and staples. Casey jumped out and looked around for something to do.

Ezra never had to look to find things to do, nor did he have to look to see everything. The badlands were as familiar to him as a child's face to its mother. He knew every bush, rock, outcropping, gully, tree, hill, and swale. And he'd noticed something out of place on a far north ridge; a small shape that didn't belong; not horse nor cow, nor deer or antelope. He took note.

"What would you like me to do?" Landau asked.

"Toss out twenty steel posts."

The journalist jumped up on the flatbed, and the posts, bundled in sets of five, clanged to the ground.

Ezra pulled on his worn leather gloves and appraised the job before them.

Landau looked down at him. "You know, Ezra, one way or the other it isn't safe having Doyle in your bunkhouse."

"I'm not worried."

"Not at all?"

"No."

"Why not?"

"I don't know. I'm just not."

Landau wiped his brow with the back of his hand. The day was warming quickly. "This is about time standing still again, isn't it?" he asked. "You think there's something bigger in play, something you can't control? Some predestination?"

Ezra pulled fencing pliers from the plastic bucket and stuck them in a back pocket. "Time froze for me in the air," he reminded Landau. "What would you think?"

Adrienne Doyle almost panicked when she saw two men and an old pickup. They were almost a mile away, but she held the high ground. There was no way they could get to her, yet, she was tempted to run.

But the truck didn't seem right. A little too old. Wrong color. She decided to sneak closer for a better look.

Half-a-mile later she parked the Ranger in a coulee and crawled stealthily to a rock outcropping on the ridge's crest. She pulled her binoculars from her pack and focused on the two men.

She felt a huge relief when she saw Riley and Landau. Her protectors. She rolled onto her back, propped herself against the rock and glassed her back trail. Miles of broken prairie, buttes, and ridges washed through the lenses.

No sign of anyone.

A tiny voice still argued it was a coincidence she'd seen the men in the pickup three times, but that was silly. Once or twice, maybe; but she'd not only seen them she'd caught them spying on the Riley house. Who else but her could they be after? Ezra Riley? Not likely. He was just an aging rancher with an undistinguished writing career. Landau? No, they'd had their chance with him when he'd left the Riley house by himself in the dark.

As far as Doyle could tell, she was the only person around worth killing.

Ezra and Peter took a water break in the shade of the truck. The work was slow, dirty, and hot. Ezra had let Landau pound the posts as shoulder pain kept him from raising his left arm. Landau leaned against Old Yeller's rear tire with Casey beside him.

"We're being watched," Ezra said.

"What?"

"I noticed something earlier. A little bump on the skyline that didn't belong. It's been gone for over an hour. But, now someone is watching us."

"Can you see them?"

"No, I can feel them?"

"How?"

"If you're in the hills alone enough you know when eyes are on you. Usually it's just a coyote."

"And this time?"

"Has to be Doyle. There's no one else around for miles. She's probably taking a break like we are and entertaining herself by watching us."

"What if it's not her. You know--"

"Hit men?"

"Just saying."

"No, it's Doyle. I'm sure of that."

Landau shook his head. "You sense more than you see, don't you?"

"I'm a writer, remember? You're the same way. We're constantly observing."

"But the things I observe are capable of being seen."

Ezra broke off a stalk of bluestem wheatgrass and sucked on it. "What are you suggesting, Peter?"

"Those little ditties you make up, the ones Barney is using on the radio, how do you do that so spontaneously?"

"They're just silly little verses that rhyme. The meter isn't even good. I have thousands of words spilling through my mind all the time. It's not too hard to dip a few out with a net."

"No, it's more than that. Are you psychic?"

"Psychic powers are soul powers. I'm not interested in soul power."

"Do you plan on keeping me confused?"

"No, I'm just waiting for the right questions."

"Okay, so, what do you see about me that--" he paused, wondering how to say it -- "that, uh, can't be seen?"

Ezra gave him a leveling look. "For one thing, you're not everything you say you are. Your intentions are okay, but there is duplicity around you."

"Okay, let me tell you something that even my mother doesn't know. My career is propped-up. When my father passed away, I was left with a considerable inheritance. I've used it up bankrolling my own journalism assignments."

"That's not duplicitous. That's professional expediency. But mentioning it is obfuscation."

"So, my clairvoyant cowboy, what do you see?"

"There's a simple rule in horse breeding," Ezra said. "Good stallions make good mares and good mares make good geldings."

"I don't get it."

"Males produce good females. Females produce good males. That's why my Oswald mares are important."

"So the daughters carry the power of their sire which they transmit to their sons?"

"Precisely. It works with humans, too. But, our culture doesn't understand this, so it sets up a conflict within the genders. Especially with males."

"You're suggesting fathers are not the main influence on their sons."

"They're not. Society sets up sons to compete against their dads. In actuality, sons are almost always more like their mothers."

"You think I'm competing against my dead father?"

"No, I think you are expressing traits you inherited from your mother."

Landau laughed. "She would be happy here, that's true."

Ezra glanced at the sun. "That fence isn't going to fix itself."

"Before we get back to work, I have a question," Landau said. "Can I stay with you, Anne, and Gabby"?

"You're offering another set of eyes in case the conspiracy theory is true?"

"What can it hurt?"

"Sure, you can stay. Anne and Gabby will be tickled."

"But, what about Barney?" Landau asked. "I just moved back in with him. Will he be offended if I move out?"

"That's no problem," Ezra said. "Tell him it's too risky to be around him because of his radio shows." He pulled his gloves back on. "Barn Wall will be thrilled to know he's the source of such considerable danger. He will probably apologize for putting you in harm's way."

CHAPTER TWENTY NINE

Doyle sped down a pasture road, racing a platoon of yearling antelope bucks that emitted a musky, goat-smelling fog.

She tromped on the Ranger's gas pedal.

The acceleration brought her into an orbit of large, black eyes and shiny hooves that sliced the wind into litter.

Legally, she was harassing wildlife, a crime she'd never normally consider, but this was play, and the antelope knew it. The antelope could dismiss her at any time.

Which they did. As Doyle reached a risky 35 miles-per-hour, the bucks simply shifted smoothly and left her instantly distant.

Doyle laughed loudly, then realizing her speed, she lifted her foot from the gas pedal, and braked carefully.

She couldn't explain herself. It was as if this land influenced her like no other place she'd been. She was peaceful while inventorying the Riley Ranch -- sometimes nearly joyous -- except when she allowed herself to dwell on the men in the pickup.

Then she became morbidly afraid.

Still no call-back from Lars.

It had to be his guilt. What could he say if he did call? *"Yes, Adrienne, we put a contract out on you, and for poetic justice, we picked two of the lowest life forms we could find. You are going to be wiped by white trash, peppered by peckerwoods, crushed by crackers, and ruined by rednecks."*

Bastard. Why couldn't he just do the job himself?

She laughed at that. Lars Anderssen a killer? He was an assassin in courtrooms, boardrooms, and bedrooms, but in the dirty, gritty, real world he was a wimp. The proverbial pussy. That's why she'd done his dirty work for years.

She motored slowly back to the Dead Man corrals to gather a few items from her SUV and inspect her perimeter. Just to the north of the corrals, on the egress to the county road, she scratched a line across the pasture road. If anyone accessed the corrals she'd know. She also inspected the undercarriage of her SUV. A bomb was unlikely, but anything was possible. Even hillbillies could get bomb-making plans off the Internet.

She was quitting early to travel the length of the ranch cross-country in the Ranger. No more county roads and highways for her. Her SUV would stay at the corrals.

In spite of everything, Doyle was enjoying this job. The ranch's condition was a pleasant surprise. The majority of ranches she inspected were overgrazed, but, if anything, the Riley Ranch was suffering from the opposite. It was under-grazed. Insufficient stocking rates, and a lack of watering sources to distribute cattle, had caused ground litter -- accumulated dead grass that blocked the sun, soaked-up moisture, and spawned grass-killing fungi. Ezra Riley was the rare rancher who was literally loving his land to death.

And the ranch's wildlife status was excellent. The corrals sat on a sagebrush steppe -- rolling plains and high ridges with a sagebrush canopy and an understory of native grasses and forbs. There were isolated pockets of invaders, like cheatgrass, but the prairie was generally healthy. There were no encroaching conifers or power poles from which raptors could launch aerial assaults on sage grouse.

That day alone, she'd spied three broods of the birds, and the area around the pens was thick with their droppings.

Doyle hated to admit it, but the only factor working against the grouse here was predators. She'd seen coyotes, Red-Tailed Hawks, Golden Eagles, badgers, rattlesnakes, bull snakes, skunks and fox. In one mesic area she'd even noticed raccoon tracks. She'd no idea raccoons could be this far from rivers or farm fields.

Content that her SUV and the belongings were secure, she got back in the Ranger and pointed it south. By pasture travel it was 10 miles to the Riley bunkhouse. She looked forward to being near their home -- she'd abandoned the idea of camping alone in the hills.

The solace of company in the face of a threat?

She'd never been lonely before her mother died. Mommy had spent every moment with her.

"Let's play dress-up," Mommy would say, and Mommy dressed-up in polka dot dresses, white high heels, strings of costume necklaces and purple hats. She'd dress Adrienne similarly if clean clothes could be found.

In their wild clothes they danced and sang to exhaustion, then Mommy made bowls of popcorn and they watched old movies on television. Adrienne saw *The Wizard of Oz* so many times she knew the lines by heart, and she could still hear Mommy singing *Over the Rainbow* with Judy Garland.

Mommy was always happy except in the evenings, after her father came home, when she'd lock herself in her room and cry for hours. It was many years before Adrienne understood manic depression.

She was the one who found Mommy.

Mommy said she was going upstairs for more jewelry. When she didn't return Adrienne went to look for her. Mommy had strapped many different colored belts together and fastened them to the railing on the second floor landing. Then she'd put the loop around her neck.

Adrienne found her hanging.

People said later her mommy had jumped, but Adrienne believed she'd been a kite that flew until the string tangled.

There were no dress-ups after that, just a long succession of grumpy nannies, until her father decided she could be alone in their large, Victorian home with its hardwood floors, tall bay windows, and heavy oak doors.

There was plenty of company, but no children. Her father had meetings almost every night. Some nights it was students or faculty, and he dreaded those, but other nights it was friends who came with a fierce energy, as if they lived on butane and fireworks.

Adrienne often sat outside the library door and listened to the gatherings. She heard her father say students had to enter science and journalism to save the world.

Her dad kept saying *Water Gate* -- she thought it was two words -- and talked about two people, Woodward and Bernstein. She didn't know who they were, but they must have done something wonderful.

"J-Schools," her dad said over and over. "The secret is to get our young people into the J-Schools." She had no idea what a J-School was.

When she could stand it no longer, she asked her father about J-schools.

He didn't rebuke her for eavesdropping. Instead, he sat her down and explained that he and his friends were in a type of war. Not a shooting war, but a secret war, and they were secret agents. J-School, he explained, was where college kids went to become journalists.

Journalists?

Reporters. Broadcasters. Newsmen. The people who wrote the newspapers.

He asked her if she wanted to be a newspaper writer.

She shook her head, no.

"Then, how about a scientist? A natural scientist."

"What's that?" she'd asked.

"Someone who works with trees and flowers and grasses and rivers and wild animals," he'd explained.

She nodded happily. Adrienne loved Nature. The garden -- always so sadly neglected -- was better than the house. Even the city parks were better. She loved flowers, especially tall, brightly-colored flowers, because when they swayed in the wind they reminded her of Mommy dancing.

So she chose to be a scientist. Someone who had flowers and trees for friends.

She'd had few human friends. One or two girls talked to her, but most thought her odd. She was the kid whose mother hanged herself; the kid who talked to flowers. So she became serious and determined to get past childhood and accomplish her goals. She graduated high school at 16, had dual bachelors in Rangeland Resources and Climate Change and Energy at 20 from Utah State University, and, at 22, a Master's in Environmental Studies from the University of Oregon. With the incidentals out of the way, she concentrated on the causes her father's friends found important. By 30, she'd burned through two federal agencies -- Bureau of Land Management in the Pryor Mountains and Forestry Service in Missoula -- but had managed to earn a Ph.D. in Environmental Science, Policy, and Management from UC Berkeley, and was hired with United States Fish and Wildlife Service.

There she met Lars Anderssen. He eventually brokered a deal between her and several large environmental groups. If she became a civilian contractor, they'd equal her salary in exchange for information, advice on tactics, and sabotage. But, they didn't want to know about the sabotage.

She, the good soldier, had agreed.

Her dirty tricks included arranging photo shoots in prairie dog towns or old burns as *evidence* of overgrazing; first seducing, then making sexual harassment claims against peers who presented obstacles; flooding lawmakers with letters from schoolchildren through a network of sympathetic teachers; spying on farmers, ranchers, sportsmen, or anyone, who stretched the rules on federal land; and always, leaking tidbits of information -- or in most cases, *misinformation* -- to the press.

She was rewarded with travel and limited prestige. At first she resisted the travel, thinking it too costly.

Don't worry, Lars had told her. The people supporting us are choking on money.

Gradually, having tasted some privilege, she wanted more. She wanted to be appreciated. She wanted recognition and honor. She wanted to write a book and receive rave reviews.

In due time, he'd said.

In due time? Well, the hell with Lars Anderssen.

Her anger was back. She'd smoke him. She'd find a way -- she always had -- to come out on top. The rednecks in the old truck could be taken care of. She'd talk to the local sheriff. No. She would have Ezra Riley talk to the sheriff. He needed to please her, didn't he? She'd seen the two washed-out reservoirs, and had even found a drowned bull he probably didn't know about, yet. He needed this EEEP contract. But she had to be careful. Peter Landau was still around and he was Ezra's friend. And Ezra Riley knew that cowboy, Len.

No, Lynne.

She'd be subtle. She'd say she'd seen the hillbillies trespassing. They were probably meth heads looking for an isolated place to set up a mobile lab. And yes, they seemed threatening, and could she borrow a gun? You know, just in case.

The gun thing scared her. She'd never touched one in her life.

She roared through the hills on the Ranger thinking she was alone.

Then suddenly there was a wave of earth-toned motion beside her. Brown, bay, black.

A herd of horses raced beside the Ranger. The mares. She'd seen them earlier in the day from a distance. Now they ran playfully beside her, tossing their heads and tails, and kicking for fun. She was on their turf, and they wanted her to know it.

Beautiful mares; the quality she remembered as a child watching dressage riders at the stable; mares with long, clean legs; straight heads; and an arched wither descending to a short back and long hip. Good blood.

But, bad news for Ezra Riley.

Under the new EEEP criteria, brood mares were considered unnecessary livestock. They denuded wildlife habitat. Ezra Riley, if he wanted a federal contract, would have to get rid of them.

Tired of their game, the mares bent to the west and galloped off, moving like a single unit, a flash of bay and brown lightning, with trailing black manes and tails.

Beautiful, she thought. *Too bad they had to go.*

She motored on, following a rough jeep trail that scratched across a spine of badlands. This wasn't grouse country now. Too rough, too little water, not enough grass. This was mule deer, coyote, and bobcat country. The worst sort of badlands.

Then the land leveled some as she neared Sunday Creek and the Riley Ranch. Stands of old cottonwoods, their tops glowing green in the setting light, came into view.

The pasture road bent off a hill, curved to the south and there, beneath a sandstone cliff and in an arbor of trees, sat an old truck.

A little further away was a man with a gun.

CHAPTER THIRTY

Garcia Jones had had a rough day.

It had been all he could do to keep his mouth shut while his supervisor piled paperwork on him. No one in the office knew his father was in jail -- his dad had been unable to make a $200,000 bond -- so he'd no one to share his burden. Not that he'd wanted his co-workers to know, but a pat on the back would have been comforting.

At day's end, he realized he still hadn't cashed his check from the branding work. He had $2000 to deposit or spend.

"Did you hear about that ranch lady at Brockway?" the office manager asked.

She was beaten terribly. She's in a coma. They flew her to Billings."

"Who did it?"

"They don't know. Her husband says a pickup with two men fled when he came home. It's that darn Bakken attracting too many low-lifes. This area just isn't safe anymore."

That's right, Garcia had thought. It's not safe anymore. The clock struck 4:30, the end of his work day, and he rushed from the office to the local sporting goods store.

The store was busy. Men and women crowded the handgun display, others inspected black rifles, and more surrounded the reloading supplies.

A clerk who hurried by with boxed rifles in his arms.

"What's going on?" Jones asked him.

"It's that beating in Brockway," the clerk explained.

In his turn at the handgun display, Garcia decided to buy just about anything still available. He spent $1600 in minutes, filled out the paperwork, and left the store no longer feeling like a pencil-pushing desk jockey. He felt confident, competent and empowered. It didn't matter that his father was a convict, just for a moment, walking to the truck with three cased handguns, he was again Hot Water Jones; someone worthy of a moniker, a handle; the bearer of a name that surpassed his parents' countercultural predilections.

Wanting to shoot the guns immediately, he drove to the Riley Ranch. No one was home, but the door was unlocked and a note lay on the table.

> *Ezra,*
> *Gabby and I went to the hospital to see Joe.*
> *Love, Anne.*

Joe? Garcia had forgotten all about Joe.

He drove past the corrals to where Sunday Creek curved beneath a sandstone cliff. It was the perfect backdrop for shooting and the creek was low enough to be passable. There were no cattle in the pasture, so Ezra wouldn't mind. He parked, set the three pistol cases on the lowered tailgate, set up a target, put on his earmuffs, loaded the Smith Model 500 and touched off the first round.

Kaboom.

The recoil knocked him back a step and the revolver almost flew from his hands.

He hadn't expected that.

He gripped the massive wheel gun with both hands, centered the front sight on the target, and reluctantly began squeezing the trigger.

Then he saw something out of the corner of his eye.

He'd never met Dr. Doyle so he didn't recognize her, but he did recognize *his* Polaris Ranger. It was twenty yards away with a surprised-looking woman sitting behind the wheel. He lowered the Smith, turned, placed it in the case, removed his ear muffs, and approached her.

"You must be Dr. Doyle," he said.

She was too scared to speak. Then she looked at his pale blue eyes, the sprouting of carrot-colored hair, and the wispy blonde goatee and knew this couldn't possibly be an assassin.

"Yes," she answered tentatively.

"I'm Garcia Jones, area range con for the NRCS." He extended a thin hand.

Doyle took it. Her grip was stronger than his.

"I didn't mean to scare you."

"Uh, that's okay. I wasn't scared. You just surprised me, that's all."

"I bet I did. That's a .50 caliber Smith & Wesson. That gunshot must have been loud even above the Ranger's motor."

"Yes. What are you doing?"

"I just bought three handguns," he said proudly.

"Three?"

Jones turned sheepish. "Well, I made some extra money, so--"

"Can I see them?"

"What?"

"The guns."

"Oh, yeah, sure." He nearly skipped to the truck in happiness. He wanted to show the guns to someone but never imagined it would be Doctor Doyle.

The three cases were open. Doyle leaned over them.

"What are they?" she asked.

Garcia was elated to answer. He picked up the largest.

"This is the Smith 500," he said. "It will kill anything on the planet."

"It's huge," she said.

"It weighs five pounds. I plan on carrying it when I go fishing in Alaska. Brown bears, you know."

For a brief second, Garcia was tempted to ask her if she wanted to shoot it. The image of the revolver's recoil blowing back and knocking her between the eyes with five pounds of chromed steel was an amusing consideration. *Borrow my Polaris, will you?*

But he didn't dare.

He put the behemoth back in its case and picked up gun number two. It was a plain black, toy-like object.

"This is a Glock 35. It holds 15 rounds of .40 caliber ammo."

Doyle scowled. "Its an automatic."

"No. Semi-automatic. There are no automatic handguns."

Doyle frowned. She didn't know the difference. "What's it for?"

"Its mostly self-defense, but it would stop a black bear."

Or a very big man, Doyle thought. But it looked complicated.

Garcia put it down. "The only problem is, I don't have any ammunition for the it. The clerk said they'd been sold out for two weeks and he didn't know when they'd be getting more."

"What's that last one?" Doyle asked.

Garcia picked up a chromed revolver. "This is a Taurus Tracker in .22 Mag. It actually weighs more than the Glock, though the bullets are only half as big." He tipped the cylinder open. "It holds eight rounds. Good little snake gun if you use shot shells. I didn't really want to buy it, but the store had almost nothing left."

"Shot shells?"

"Yeah. Like a shotgun. TIny little BBs."

"And that's all it shoots?"

Garcia looked at her like she was the second coming of stupid-on-a-stick, then remembered she could have his head on a stick.

"No, it shoots these." He held up a brass cartridge with a small pointed bullet.

Doyle took it from him. "This? I take vitamins bigger than this. What good is it?"

"Well, you could shoot rabbits--" He saw instantly that she was horrified at that idea.

"I don't shoot rabbits," she said with an edge.

"Well, actually, with the right ammo you could use it for self-defense."

"Against a big man?"

"Sure. They make self-defense ammunition for .22 Mag now. In fact, that's what you're holding. That's a Speer Gold Dot."

"This little thing is going to stop a big man? I mean, *big*."

"It could. They penetrate the chest, then ricochet all over the place."

She looked at the revolver thoughtfully.

"But, maybe not in winter," Jones added.

"What do you mean?"

"If it was a really heavy man wearing an insulated vest covered by a canvas coat, it would probably still penetrate, but it might not have enough energy left to ricochet."

It's not winter, Doyle thought.

"I want to buy it," she said.

"What?"

Doyle pulled her wallet from her backpack. "What did you pay for it?"

"Four-hundred-dollars."

"I'll give you five but I need the bullets."

"But--"

"You said you really didn't want it."

"Yeah, but--"

"Listen," she said, arching one eyebrow. "You know who I am, right?"

Garcia nodded.

"I can make things happen, right? Good and bad?"

"Yeah."

"Sell me the stupid gun. I'll see that good things happen for you."

Garcia's mouth dropped and his pale eyes glazed.

"Early promotion? That transfer you'd been hoping for?" She could tell he was tempted but not wavering. "Look, you do me a favor now and I return the favor later. You can imagine what it's like for me. A woman alone in the hills. Especially around here. There are a lot of strangers drifting around the country these days."

"Yeah," he said, thinking of the woman who'd been beaten.

She had him.

"Okay," he said. "You're right. I really didn't want it anyway." He began to hand the revolver to her but Doyle recoiled.

"I..I.." she stuttered.

"Don't you want it?"

"Yes, but." She realized she'd thrown her hands up near her face in terror. She quickly brought them down. "I've never...touched...a gun before."

"Never even *touched* one?"

"No." She'd always been proud of that fact but now it made her feel stupid.

"How are you going to shoot it?"

"You'll have to show me."

Garcia smiled. "Sure, it's easy. This is a small caliber. It doesn't hardly recoil at all and you wear muffs when you practice." He nodded at the target. "Come on."

Doyle stepped hesitantly forward.

Garcia showed her where the cylinder release lever was, popped the cylinder open and loaded it with seven rounds of Gold Dots.

"Why not all of them?" she asked. "Why not eight?"

"If you want to be safe you leave the hammer on an empty chamber." He showed her how.

"You must have been in the military."

Garcia laughed. "No, but I watch a lot of YouTube."

He taught her how to stand in the Weaver Stance and the difference between single-action and double-action. He did all of this without firing.

She watched carefully. If nothing else, Dr. Adrienne Doyle was a quick study.

"Now you take it," he said.

"But--"

He handed it to her and she took it as if it were a snake.

He moved behind her and put his muffs over her ears. "Square your shoulders and bring the weapon up," he said.

She brought it up.

"Breathe and relax."

Her body softened noticeably.

"Focus on the front sight."

Resolve darkened her eyes.

"Squeeze slowly."

The shot popped off. A little round hole appeared just above the bulls-eye.

"Wow," Garcia said. "That was good."

"I want to do it again." She brought the revolver up and methodically fired three times single-action, then twice double-action." The three single-action shots grouped just high and to the right of the bull. The double-action shots were low and to the left.

"Boy, you could be good with practice," Garcia said.

"It's not so bad. I almost like it." She emptied the cylinder and handed him the money. "Thank you. I appreciate this." She turned toward the UTV with the cased revolver and two boxes of ammunition.

"Ah, wait," Jones said.

She turned around. "What?"

"Thats not a POV," he said, nodding at the Polaris. "You can't carry a firearm in a government vehicle. Not even as a contractor."

"My POV is up at the Riley corrals," she said, meaning her SUV.

"You know the rules. You can carry in a Privately Owned Vehicle but not in a government vehicle."

"Are you going to turn me in?"

"Well--"

"Oh," she said disgustedly. "What a Boy Scout." She handed him the pistol case. "Okay, here's what we do. You carry this up to the Riley bunkhouse for me and give it to me there. Tomorrow morning none of this will be your responsibility, okay?"

"Well..."

"Fine. I'll meet you up there."

She got in *his* Ranger and sped off.

"Gee whiz," Garcia said softly to himself. "I just sold Dr. Adrienne Doyle a gun."

I hope nothing bad comes of this, he thought.

CHAPTER THIRTY ONE

At twilight, Ezra turned Old Yeller into the subdivision so Landau could pick up his gear and SUV. Moments later a pickup carrying two men followed them in.

Ezra knocked. Barney's booming voice bid them to enter. He and Henrietta were in the kitchen making supper. Landau went to the spare bedroom to gather his things.

"Greetings, gents," Barney said. "You wanna stay for supper, Ezra?"

"Thanks, but I need to get home. Peter's getting his stuff. He's going to stay with us a couple days."

"He's probably mined-out my vast supply of knowledge. By the way, did you know there was no such word as *deportance*?"

"It never occurred to me that there might be."

"Shoot, I thought it was a word. I used it this evening on NPR. I was adding to the poem you gave me: *Bureaucrats of self-importance, should face fast and furious deportance.*"

"National Public Radio will never be the same after you, Barney."

"Two more shows before they decide if they keep me," Barney said. "But I need something for tomorrow, Ez."

"Sorry, Barn. Can't help you. It's your show. Just go on it and be yourself."

"Shoot."

"Ezra," Henrietta turned from the kitchen counter with a paring knife in her hand. "Neither you nor Barney have been up to see Joe."

"Yeah, I know," Ezra said.

"He doesn't want us to see him lying in a hospital bed," Barney said. "He's Joey Ropesaplenty, not Joey Bedpan."

"Well, I just came from there," Henrietta said. "Anne and Gabby were there, Joe's wife is on her way from Sheridan, and his two boys are coming from California."

"His boys are coming home?" Ezra asked.

"They're coming to go to work for him," Henrietta said.

"What?" Ezra and Barney asked in unison.

"Joe's doctor is an Iranian who just bought a big ranch by Lame Deer. He's hired Joe and his boys to run it. It's a big operation."

"I wonder if Joe will learn to speak Iranian?" Barney said.

"Farsi," Landau said. He'd reentered the room with his bag. "The language is probably Farsi."

"Well, Ropesaplenty will get to rope aplenty," Ezra said. "That'll keep him happy."

He moved to a sliding glass door. Below, much of the subdivision, with its many homes, barns, yard lights, cars, horses and dogs, was visible.

"Forty years ago my dad could have bought all this," he noted. "Our neighbor gave him first crack at it before a developer bought it."

"Shoot. Why didn't he buy it?"

"He was in his 60s and his only son was drifting around the country. He saw no reason to expand."

"If he'd bought it I wouldn't have a home up in these cedars," Barney said.

"Corey Boothe wouldn't be down there in his big fancy house, either," Ezra said.

"Or, our friend Mr. Havig," Barney added. "That's his place next to Corey's."

Headlights came up a graveled road and parked in front of Havig's. There was just enough light for Ezra to see the vehicle was a crew-cab truck. Two men got out of it.

"Speaking of Corey Boothe," Barney said. "His grandpa ran his two buddies off. They pulled out early this morning. And I bet young Mr. Boothe ain't real happy about it."

Ezra stared down at the scattering of lights as night erased the last streaks of daylight. "So, Barn Wall," he said absently. "You've chastised cowboy poets, harangued old hippies, bedeviled the bureaucrats, and plan on messing with the media. What's next on the menu?"

"Shoot, seeing as you're not going to help me, I've decided to be spon-taney and ex-temp-oh-rainy."

"What?" Henrietta exclaimed.

"He's going to wing it," Ezra explained.

"Oh, I almost forgot," Henrietta said. "Joe heard they struck oil up on the Skinner place."

"To those who have, more will be given," Ezra said.

Elmer Havig met the Pratts at his door. "Come in, boys, come in. Grab your gear. I have two extra bedrooms down the hall. My Lena passed in '09, so it's just me here with lots of extra room. Sure glad I ran into you boys in town. I could use a little help around here the next few days. Mostly some heavy liftin'." He winked at Nicholas. "Bet you can handle that, can't you?"

Nicholas grunted.

Havig watched the two young men choose their rooms. Too bad the skinny one was a mute, he thought, because he looked fairly intelligent; someone to have an intellectual conversation with. The big guy was scary with a bullet-shaped head and a neck as wide as his shoulders. Havig reminded himself not to make him mad.

They both had plenty of tattoos. The big one had more ink than a road map. Havig wondered if the two were gang-related. The more he thought about it, the more he regretted offering them a job. Oh well, he had a Smith & Wesson .357 Magnum under his pillow, loaded with 158-grain hollow points. That was probably enough to even put a hurt on the big fellow.

Jeremy came out of his room in his underwear. His physique reminded Havig of pool cues glued to a bird cage -- that was an image he could use in a poem. Thinking of poetry made him mad again. Dang, that Ezra Riley. He'd like to sic big Nicholas on him. *See how quick he is on the rhyme after that.*

Jeremy pointed at the washing machine in the laundry room.

"Yeah, yeah," Havig said. "Wash your clothes. Then take showers. Both of you. Get cleaned up. There's a guest bathroom and one of you can use mine. Take showers and I'll get supper on the table."

Jeremy took Havig's bathroom, locked the door, and rifled the medicine chest. All he found was an old prescription bottle with a label too faded to read. He swallowed two of the pills, just in case.

Havig slipped into the master bedroom, got his Smith .357 and moved it to a drawer in the kitchen to have it handy. Then he sliced up a roll of venison salami and a dozen red potatoes and fried them in a deep-dish skillet.

The Pratts came to the kitchen looking halfway human and took seats at the table. Havig shoveled heaps of dinner on their plates. Nicholas wolfed his down but Jeremy only picked at his portion, spearing the smaller pieces of potato, but avoiding the meat. Years of drug abuse had wasted his system and he ate selectively.

"You some sort of vegetarian?" Havig asked him.

Jeremy shook his head, but patted his stomach and mimicked pain.

"Oh. Got a bad gut. Well, you better eat up on the taters cuz we got a big day tomorrow. We gonna build some pens. I'm fixin' to raise horses. Not many good horses in these parts. I'll let you in on a little secret," he said, leaning forward. "There ain't many real cowboys around here."

Havig waited expectantly. Neither responded.

Well, how could they? Havig thought. One's dumb and the other one's dumber.

"Some of them think they're cowboys," he continued. He motioned with his fork. "Like up there in the cedars. Up high on the hill. Barney Wallace lives up there. A cowboy cartoonist. I thought he was a pretty good guy, but he ain't." He pointed the fork over his shoulder to a kitchen window. "And you know what I got next to me? A snotty rich horse trainer. And I mean, rich. Name's Corey Boothe. Little hothead with a billionaire granddaddy. Can't train horses worth a lick if you ask me, 'course how can ya when you spend all your time shovelin' snow up your nose."

Again he waited for a reaction. Jeremy stared at him vacantly. Nicholas dumped a second helping of potatoes and salami on his plate.

Havig brought an index finger to his nose. "Nose candy," he said. Neither flinched.

These boys must not know drug language, he thought, and he found solace in that. Maybe the tattoos and overall appearance was strictly a style thing. They probably went to church on Sundays.

"He's a drug dealer. Cocaine, marijuana. Don't know what else," Havig concluded.

Nicholas looked up with interest. Jeremy's eyes widened minutely.

"He had two buddies hanging around, but old man Boothe ran them off this morning. Then the old man left. He'll be gone a couple days from what I hear."

"Old man's gone?" Nicholas asked.

"Yeah. Flew to Missoula. Another grandkid up there. A girl."

"But he's comin' back?"

"He better. Someone's got to drag little Corey off to rehab while there's still braincell one between his ears."

Nicholas pushed his girth from the table, stood up and went to the sink. He looked through the window at the huge house and indoor arena only a few hundred yards away.

"Oh, you're lookin' at my photos," Havig said. He walked up to Nicholas. Above the sink were shelves lined with picture frames. Havig reached on tiptoes and grabbed his favorite. "This one here," he said, pointing to a photograph of him standing next to a skinny cowboy in a big hat and red scarf. "That's me in Elko with Baxter Black. You know who Baxter Black is, don'tcha?

Nicholas grunted.

"Why, he's the most famous cowboy poet of them all. Mor'n a poet, actually. Philosopher. Comedienne. And a veterinarian, too. A real one."

Nicholas kept staring at the Boothe house.

"And these others," Havig motioned at the other photos. "Those are all me with other big-name cowboy poets. I guess you wouldn't know who they are though, seein' as you don't know who Baxter is. Now me, I wasn't down at Elko performin' or anything. I mean, that's the big leagues. I'm not there, yet. Will be, though. Just a matter of time."

Nicholas whirled around, took the photo from Havig and held it close to his face to stare at it. He saw a fat guy in a cowboy hat. That was Havig. And a skinny guy with a hat, big scarf, and mustache. He turned his head and looked down at Havig like he was another roll of salami. He always wanted to kill a cowboy. He took a closer look at his host. Western shirt. Big shiny buckle barely poking out from a landslide of tummy. Pants tucked into high-topped boots.

Nope, he decided. He didn't know what this guy was, but he weren't no cowboy. Nicholas had a certain cowboy image in mind, one engrained in his brain from when he was rolling drunks in the alley behind the casino during the big rodeo. He was a kid, but a monster one for his age. He'd poleaxed an old tourist with a blow that sent him flying back against a Dodge Ram pickup truck. Nicholas brought his fist back, ready to deliver the nightcap, when a steel trap grabbed his wrist.

He turned around and looked into the dancing hazel eyes of the cowboy his cousin liked; the guy from Montana with his name on his belt.

The cowboy just shook his head -- his way of saying enough was enough -- and there was disappointment in his eyes. Because he'd never known shame, the dirty carpet that settled over Nickie's heart was nameless to him. But, it made him feel small. He backed off a step and the cowboy let him go. Nickie tried to decide what to do.

The cowboy stood there waiting.

Nickie turned and ran. He didn't know why. Even as his big feet slapped asphalt and concrete, he told himself the cowboy was smaller than him and old, but something in the cowboy's eyes was big and bold, like the vast expanse of desert and sky that was Nevada. Nickie feared he could fall into those eyes and never come out.

The next day he hated himself for running. When the cowboy was back a year later Nicholas avoided him. And the year after that, and the year after that. When the cowboy quit coming to Vegas, Nicholas was glad because he was determined to kill him, and if he did, things would never be the same with his cousin. Jeremy might run away and how would he survive? He was skinny and couldn't talk. Jeremy needed him, so Nickie had done a good thing by not killing the cowboy. That's how he figured.

But, just the same, he wanted to kill one. The trouble was, Havig wasn't a real cowboy. Even Nicholas could see that.

Havig knew he was being measured and it terrified him to the bottom of his three-inch heels.

"Well, you boys are probably all tuckered and want to get to bed," he said. "Don't worry about the dishes. I'll take care of those."

"Yeah. Okay." Nicholas said.

The two moved down the hall.

Havig sighed deeply. Then he pulled the revolver out of the drawer, stuck it in his waistband and put on an apron. As he did the dishes he kept glancing over his shoulder, expecting the big one to appear, so large as to block out all light. When the dishes were done he tiptoed down the hall with his hand on the Smith.

He heard snoring coming from each room. The boys were asleep. Or pretending to be.

Havig went to his room, turned on the light, and closed the door. The door didn't have a lock. He looked around the room. The only thing he had to block the door was Lena's heavy dresser, so he muscled it into place.

There. At least that would give him ample warning. He stripped to his underwear, turned off the light, and climbed into bed with the revolver in his hand. He lay there looking up into the darkness.

Lord, what had he done?

He'd stepped into that dingy bar for only a minute. It was where daylight drunks fueled-up. Feeling deflated since his run-in with Ezra Riley, he needed company lower than himself. But, two young strangers were the only patrons, and one thing led to another, one beer to more beers still, and now look at the mess he was in.

He wished Lena was there beside him. Not that he wanted her in danger, but if she were still alive he'd never had gone to the bar in the first place, and two dangerous drifters wouldn't be sleeping just down the hall.

They weren't workers. He realized that now. Neither would take to building pens. So why had they come?

To kill and steal, he decided.

Hadn't he heard something about a woman at Brockway getting beat up and two men in an old truck spotted leaving the scene?

Oh, God.

He'd never missed Lena more in his life. And he missed their little farm outside Williston where they'd had a big garden, a milk cow named Molly, and raised chickens, sheep and a passel of hogs. The Havigs were known for miles around for their hogs.

Havig was ashamed of himself and disgusted. He wasn't a cowboy -- he never had been -- but he'd always dreamed it. When Lena died and the oil people came in and offered him a fortune for his half-section, he thought providence had found him.

He'd move to a cowtown. A famous one like Elko or Miles City.

Miles City was closer. He bought forty acres in the subdivision, as many high-topped boots and custom hats as one man could store, and he began writing poems. He'd dabbled at poetry before, but instead of love poems to Lena, he wrote about bronc rides, dallies that slipped, bulls that broke bones, and a hundred other subjects he knew nothing personally about. He got himself invited to area poetry readings and convinced himself he was the person he wrote rhymes about.

What was he doing?

He was, he knew, just a sad, old man looking for his late wife.

He was looking for Lena.

And he went finally to sleep with hopes of waking up alive.

When Jeremy heard snores from Havig's room he got up and rapped softly on Nickie's door. Nickie answered, fully-clothed, and the two of them crept down the hallway. At the kitchen, Nicholas detoured to the sink and grabbed Havig's favorite photo and thrust it in a pocket as a trophy.

The boys went to their truck, got in, and closed the doors quietly. They backed out slowly, turned, and drove to the Boothe mansion. They parked in the driveway, got out, and banged on the door.

When no one answered, they banged louder.

Finally, the door opened and standing before them was a slender guy, about their age or younger, whose eyes looked like saucers filled with iodine.

"We hear there's a party here," Nicholas said.

Corey Boothe rocked on his heels. "Party? Well, hell yeah, there is," he said. "Come on in."

PART V

"A cowboy is a man with guts and a horse."
-- Will James

CHAPTER THIRTY TWO

Ezra moved silently from the bed to the recliner in the living room. Pain in his hands hadn't kept him from sleeping, nor the pain in his shoulder.

It was worry. He hated it when he worried, especially in the middle of the night, but it helped him remember his mother. Pearl Riley had been a world-class worrier. She could fret the feathers off a flying duck.

The Irish in Ezra gave him a passion to own land and a willingness to fight for what he owned. It seemed he fought often. Barney said his friend was hardwired for hardship, and that seemed true. Nothing came easily for him.

Except writing. Writing came easily. But writing, and making a living as a writer, were not the same thing. Producing art was not the same as producing a market.

Ezra sighed and shifted in the chair to take pressure off his shoulder.

Conflict.

Conflict made for good stories. The Bible said God was the author and finisher of one's faith. God was a storyteller, and, in crafting Ezra's story, He seemed determined to weave in ample conflict.

"It builds character," Anne was fond of saying.

Ezra smiled. He was married to a woman of strong principles.

But Ezra blamed neither God nor Anne for his troubles. Most of his stress came through his decisions. He was the one who hitchhiked thousands of miles rather than go to college. He was the one who returned to the ranch after his father died, knowing he was entering a familial hornet's nest where grievances, both present and past, surfaced daily. Family business tended to be that way, especially businesses that involved land.

Ezra didn't know what Boothe had offered his sisters, but what he'd offered Ezra for his share of the ranch was absurd. It certainly wasn't a business decision. It was personal. Punish Ezra -- with money! -- and reward Corey. If he took Boothe's offer, what would he have left after taxes? Not enough to buy another ranch -- maybe enough for a few hundred acres with a house and corrals. He could look into an IRS Section 1031 Exchange, but those could be difficult, and the family ranch would still be gone forever. And that was land they'd prayed for and prayed over. Could he sell it to someone who'd abuse, neglect, and defile it?

What did the Lord want him to do? This was the main question and the irony was Ezra received impressions and interpreted dreams for others, often with baffling ease, but directions for his own life seemed always out of reach. Decisions for him were matters of blind faith. Get out of the boat and walk on the water.

Splash.

He heard soft steps on the basement stairs.

Gabriella came padding on little bunny feet, her hair disheveled and smelling of Baby Shampoo. The warmth of sleep still coated her skin. She crawled up in his lap and laid her head against his chest. Her little weight pained his shoulder. "What's you doin', Granddad?" she said through a yawn.

"Just thinking, Gabriella. Why are you up so early? Did I wake you?"

"No." She squirmed in trying to stretch. "I got up because I want to ride with you."

"You want to ride?"

"Yes. You ride Simon and I'll ride Big Jack."

"We can probably do that later," Ezra said.

"No. This morning. When big people say later it never happens."

"You're a wise young woman, Gabriella Jo, but you're not dressed for riding."

"I can get dressed."

"It's five o'clock, Gabby. You don't want to ride before breakfast, do you?"

"Yes. Right now. Can we?"

"I suppose we can, if the horses have come in."

"They have. I already checked."

"Why do you want to ride so bad?"

"That's why I come here, Granddad. I come here to ride horses."

"You ride in Seattle, sweetheart. Your mother takes you to the stables."

"That's not riding, Granddad. Those are riding lessons. It's riding here with Big Jack and Casey."

He gave her a little squeeze.

She looked up at him. The sleep was gone from her eyes. "Granddad, I wasn't going to tell you because Gramma says you have a lot of things on your mind, but I had a bad dream last night. Not a bad dream, really. But a scary one. What does it mean to have a lot of things on your mind?"

"It means you think too much. Now what was your dream?"

"I dreamed that a big black bird was sitting on a tall pole and it was going to swoop down and get Gramma, and me, and you, but, then another bird came and knocked it off the pole."

She rested quietly for a few moments.

Ezra shifted to ease the pain in his shoulder.

"Granddad, Mommy says you can tell people what their dreams mean."

"Yes, sometimes."

"So, what does my dream mean?"

"I think it means a good angel is going to save us from the bad angel."

"Oh. Granddad, can you make me a promise?"

"I will if it's a promise I can keep," Ezra said.

"Can you make sure the good angel is here with us, and not some-place else?" she said, then she crawled down and scampered away to get dressed.

Doyle came awake at the noise outside the bunkhouse. She grabbed the .22 Magnum revolver from the nightstand, stood in the center of the room, and pointed the gun at the door.

If the door opens, shoot, she told herself. *Then shoot again and again.*

She realized her eyes were closed and her head turned to the side.

That won't work, she thought. *I may miss him entirely even though he'll fill the entire door when he comes in.* She straightened her head, but kept her eyes closed.

She didn't think she could kill someone while looking at him. She was trembling, and the revolver shook in her grip. *Hurry up*, she thought. *Let's get this over with.*

Then she heard a child's giggle. She strained to make sure. She heard it again, so she opened her eyes and stepped to the window.

Just past the bunkhouse porch, at the gate that opened to the creek, was Ezra, his granddaughter, and two horses.

Ezra had his back to her, but he turned to the side as he bent down, picked up Gabby, and put her in the saddle on Big Jack. Doyle could not see his face, but she could see his pain. It was all he could do to lift his granddaughter onto the horse.

Ezra turned toward the gate leading Simon by the reins. Gabby followed. On the big sorrel's back she looked no larger than a bird. She nudged the horse with her little boot heels, and as Big Jack stepped forward, Gabby turned, and looked right at Doyle in the window.

And smiled.

Doyle looked at the door.

It was locked.

What had she been thinking?

Nicholas nearly filled one bench seat in the truck stop cafe. Jeremy slouched in the seat across from him.

A waitress brought menus. She was a slender, hard-bodied woman with a face defined by make-up. She poured their coffees and left.

"Man, I'm going to eat everything in here," Nickie said.

Jeremy's head rested on the window pane. The sun was beginning to rise. He moved his head away because his eyes avoided sunshine.

"I got rich boy's wallet," Nickie said, holding it up for his cousin to see. "Let's see what's in it." As he counted out greenbacks, Jeremy glanced around, hoping other customers weren't paying attention. Two retired ranchers sat at the counter. A truck driver was sipping coffee and reading a paper in a booth. Two other truck drivers sat kitty-corner to them. They were engaged in conversation.

"Look at this, Jeremy," Nickie said, clutching a wad of bills. "There's over $800 just in his wallet."

Jeremy frowned and motioned with his hands for Nickie to put the money away.

"I think I'll leave a big tip," Nickie said. "Just like the high-rollers do. This is just practice for us, Jeremy. Practice bein' rich people." He stuffed the bills back in the wallet and returned to studying the menu.

Being speechless had sharpened Jeremy's hearing. He could hear the two truckers easily.

"She's in the hospital in Billings in critical condition," one said.

"Did they catch the guys who did it?" the other asked.

"No, but the husband says it was two men in an older pickup. There's been some talk of a couple drifters preying on isolated ranches."

Jeremy's eyes widened. That was *them*. He and Nickie. He searched his memory. Had Nickie beaten anyone? He didn't think so.

They hadn't done it. But the law would be looking for someone just like them. Good thing they didn't have the old pickup anymore. They had Corey's. And they had Corey, too.

A cold sadness fell on Jeremy.

He'd come to Montana hoping for a miracle, but it would be the devil's miracle if they were caught and charged with something they didn't do.

There's no way out of this, he thought. He wasn't the type to survive prison, even if Nickie went with him. And that probably wouldn't happen, would it?

He wished he had someone to talk to.

Landau awakened to the metallic sound of a gate closing. The clock on the nightstand read 5:35. He heard hoofbeats and soft voices. He dressed and went upstairs.

Anne sat in her chair by the window in a heavy white bathrobe, an open Bible in her lap, and her coffee cup held in both hands.

"Excuse me," Peter said as he entered the kitchen. "I didn't mean to disturb you."

Anne smiled. "That's okay. There's fresh coffee on. Come join me."

"What are Ezra and Gabby doing?" he asked, as he found a cup.

"Gabby's been dying to ride with her granddad, but I didn't think she'd be up this early."

Landau took a seat. He was still embarrassed for invading Anne's privacy.

"Ezra told me you don't want to talk about Israel, but that's been hard for me to do," Anne said. "I've always wanted to go there."

"I would make a poor tour guide. The places I spend my time are not very pretty."

"Still, it has to be a special country."

"Parts of your ranch remind me of Israel," Landau said. "And not just the topography. It has a *feel* to it, a spirituality, that reminds of my homeland."

"That's good to hear," Anne said. "We work at it."

"That's what the stakes are about?" Landau asked.

Anne smiled. "The stakes?"

"Yes, the little wooden surveyor stakes with faded ink, as if they'd been written on. I've seen them all over, but mostly up around the corrals on Dead Man Creek."

"We believe in the healing of land," Anne said. "The stakes are dedications. They mark areas that've been prayed over and dedicated to the Kingdom."

"Is this something your denomination believes in?"

"We don't belong to a denomination."

"A local church?"

"No, it's mostly just us."

Landau shook his head. "I know little about my own faith, let alone Christianity. What does healing the land involve?"

"Redemption," Anne said. "The breaking of curses and the establishment of blessing."

"How do you do this?"

"Many ways. Mostly I sing. I worship God and proclaim His blessings."

"And the faded ink on the stakes?"

"Bible verses. If they are faded we need to refresh them. Blessings require maintenance."

"And the corrals on Dead Man, they've been a focal point?"

"Yes," Anne said. "How did you know?"

"Just something I've felt. I feel it in this room, too, surrounded by these house plants."

"The atmosphere at the corrals was very dark at first. We're not sure why. It could have been homesteaders or Ezra's uncles. There may have been warfare or Native activities that included blood sacrifice. Sometimes you just don't know."

"It's terribly subjective, isn't it? And what's the practical result of this?"

"Cursed areas attract more curses," Anne said. "Blessed areas attract blessing."

"I don't know," Peter said. "I like landscapes, but to me, a land is about peoples and cultures. Otherwise land is just dirt."

"But what if the land is like a giant recorder?" Anne asked. "What if it were able to record and store all that's ever happened on it?"

They were interrupted by a knock on the front door.

Anne started to rise, but Landau raised his hand. "You better let me get it," he said.

Anne noted the concern in his voice. She glanced at the clock. It was 6:05.

Landau went to the front door and opened to an astonished Dr. Doyle.

"Peter?" she said. "I didn't know you were here. Where is your vehicle?"

"It's parked behind the barn," he said.

For an awkward moment neither spoke.

"If you're looking for Ezra, he's not here," Landau said.

"I know. I saw him and his granddaughter ride off. I just wanted to leave a message with, well, someone."

"I can give him a message."

"Okay," she said reluctantly. "It's about EEEP. I really shouldn't do this, but I don't care. My work here will be finished today. Mr. Riley has a very good chance for an EEEP contract--"

"If he wants it."

"Yes, of course, but there is a problem. It's his mares. Under the EEEP guidelines they are NIPNEAUs. Non-Income Producing,

Non-Essential Animal Units. They count as a subtraction. If the mares are here when I sign off on his application, he hasn't a chance. If the mares are gone, he has a good chance."

"Are you saying he has to get rid of the mares today?"

"Yes. At the least, I have to see evidence that the process has begun."

Landau nodded. "I'll tell him, Adrienne. Where will you be if he needs to talk to you?"

"My SUV is parked at the corrals at the back of the ranch," she said.

She turned to leave but stopped. She turned back to Landau. "What do you think he'll do?" she asked.

"That's his business. He's mentioned getting rid of the mares, but that's a hard thing for him to do."

"Do you think he will corral them?"

"I suppose if he wants this contract he'll have to."

Doyle looked down. Her lips moved before words came out. "Tell him, that if he is going to corral the mares, I would like to help. I want to ride."

"You would like to help?"

"Yes. I know how to ride," Doyle said.

Landau took a deep breath. He hadn't considered this, but Ezra would need help. What was Doyle's angle? Why would she want to be horseback? Was she that desperate to certify the mares as removed?

"Yes, I'll tell him," he said. "And actually, I would like to help gather those mares, too."

Where you go, I go, he thought.

CHAPTER THIRTY THREE

Landau watched Ezra and Gabby lead their horses into the unsaddling stall.

The corrals were functional but not completed. Destroyed hay bales and tons of fermenting alfalfa pellets formed an unnatural hill to the north and added a tang to the morning air.

"Peter," Gabby called, skipping from the barn. "I rode Big Jack this morning, and I unsaddled him all by myself."

"All by yourself?" Landau asked.

"Well, almost all by myself. Granddad gave me a pail to stand on, and he helped me a little bit."

Ezra stepped out rubbing his sore hands. He noticed a seriousness in Landau's posture. "Gabby, sweetheart," he said to the little girl. "You better go in and get some breakfast. Tell Gramma I'll be in soon."

Gabby danced away, her blonde pigtails bounced golden in the early light, and Casey trotted beside her.

"What's up, Peter?" Ezra asked.

"Doyle came to the house this morning. She'll wrap up her work here today. Here's the situation: if your Oswald mares are gone when she leaves, you have a good chance at the EEEP contract. If they're still here, you have no chance at all."

Ezra felt his chest thicken.

"And," Landau continued. "If you do decide to wrangle the mares, she wants to help. She wants to ride."

"What? You can't be serious. She wants to ride?"

"That's what she said. I think the pressure is getting to her. She was acting really strange. She either needs to verify that you've gathered the mares, or she's simply gone nuts because of the contract out on her."

"The contract hit? You don't know that, do you? Or do you have more information?"

"No, I haven't heard anything new, but if Adrienne's heard rumors that'd be enough."

"Do you suppose she's making it up?" Ezra asked. "Could she be the one behind the rumors?"

"It's possible. There's some mental illness in her family."

"Everything is upside down," Ezra said. "Everything is crazy."

"What are you going to do?"

"I'm going to gather the mares."

"You are? What are you going to do with them?"

"The horse sale in Billings is this weekend. The loose horses sell Sunday. They'll sell by the pound and go to a slaughter plant in Canada."

"You're serious?"

"It's either that or I shoot them myself."

"You want that contract that bad?"

Ezra shook his head. "No, it has nothing to do with EEEP. The mares have to go. I've known that since Lynne passed. There's little market for ranch horses anymore, especially Oswalds. Most guys today ride motorcycles and four-wheelers."

"But, the Oswalds are special."

"They're also unknowns, Peter. Lynne could sell a few because of his name. I'm not Lynne."

"But it's the last of a line of horses. How about the rescue places?"

"There aren't any legitimate ones close by. Old saddle horses, I shoot myself. But, we're talking about eight mares. And, through the sales ring, there's a chance they'll sell as brood mares."

"Okay, then I want to help, too. I can ride. What's the plan?"

"I'd be crazy to put you and Doyle horseback."

"Can you do it without us?"

"I can get Barney. Anne won't ride. She told me a few years ago she'd never run horses with me again. It's a little more adventure than she wants at this point in her life."

"Can you and Barney do it by yourselves?"

"Possibly, but you know Barney."

"How about Garcia?"

"He works until 4:30, and he'd be about as much help as you and Doyle." Ezra looked down. His brow wrinkled with thought. "Unless..."

"What are you thinking?" Landau asked. "Do you have a plan?"

"Maybe. It might work if you, Doyle, and Garcia do as you're told. But there's a risk. One of you would be on Big Jack and he loves to run horses. The other two would be on Joe's Oswalds. There is a better chance for wrecks than there is for success."

"Garcia likes Big Jack. Doyle and I can ride Joe's horses."

"But we don't know if Garcia can come. If we wait until he's off work we may run out of daylight."

"We can get Garcia."

"How?"

Landau smiled and held up his cell phone. "If I can get a signal, I'll call Doyle. She'll get Garcia."

"You can go to the house and use our land line, but there's still the matter of you and Doyle being horseback."

"Adrienne and I grew up riding hunters and jumpers."

"That was a long time ago, Peter. You've never actually seen her ride and we're talking about chasing mares in the hills, not cantering around an indoor arena."

Landau glanced down to gather his thoughts, then looked back with a fierce resolve. "I think this is something I need to do," he said. "I can't speak for Adrienne, but I almost feel like I came this far for this reason."

Ezra nodded. "Okay, get in touch with Doyle and Jones. I'll get a hold of Barney." *This will be a crew for the ages,* he thought. *The best cowboy of the bunch is a cartoonist.*

Doyle sped north in the Ranger pondering why she'd volunteered to help Riley gather his mares. Was it because she'd often watched that cowboy, Lynne, gather mustangs in the Pryors, and had wondered what it was like to ride like that? She was bothered by more than her impulsiveness. Why had Landau parked his vehicle behind the barn? Was he hiding from someone? Was he hiding from her?

She knew many people had questions about Peter Landau. A year ago, he'd disappeared for six months, and her media friends had no idea where he was. Lars thought he was in a Mossad training camp. That was possible. Correspondents can crave combat and Landau was a fervent Jewish nationalist. He nay have crossed the line between the reporter and the story. But, why would he now be in the American West, and in particular, in eastern Montana?

Could Landau be the assassin? she wondered. *Maybe the two hillbillies were a smokescreen.*

But why Peter? It didn't make any sense. He was involved in MIddle East politics. Her cause was larger. It was the health of the planet. Lars and his friends had no stake in the Middle East, did they?

Maybe they did. Their tentacles were worldwide.

The phone in her breast pocket vibrated. *Lars? He'd finally called back?*

She fished it out and looked at the screen. It wasn't Lars. It was Peter Landau. How did he get her number?

As the Ranger crested a hill a big, brown object swooped down at her. Doyle dropped the phone. A second larger brown object was behind the first -- a sage grouse pursued by a golden eagle. Seeing the UTV, the eagle banked upward but the grouse collided with the Ranger's roof frame and its momentum whipped it forward into Doyle's face. She felt feathers and warmth, like a pillow pressed over her face. The Ranger spun left. Doyle stomped on the brake. The stunned grouse flopped onto the passenger floorboard. The stop threw Doyle into the steering wheel, bruising her ribs, and she spit feathers from her mouth.

Doyle screamed, stumbled from the UTV, and stood trembling for a moment. A trickle of blood came from her lips. She wiped it with a shirt cuff, took a deep breath, marched around the Ranger, grabbed the grouse, wrung it's neck and flung the body down a gumbo hill.

"Damn bird," she yelled.

Ezra haltered Simon and led him back into the barn. Stepping into the tack room was like falling into deep water as waves of memories rushed over him -- a lifetime of horses, tack, jobs, friends, challenges, laughs, cries, winters, droughts, newborn calves, foals, friends.

He looked down at his new saddle on the rack. Custom-made by Oregon horseman Charley Snell, it was worth thousands, but Snell had given it to him because he admired Ezra's books. It was the best book review Ezra had ever received. Beside it was his old saddle, the leather worn smooth by thousands of miles and twenty-five years of use. Then Dylan's saddle; and Anne's; and lastly, his father's CBC saddle. He ran his hand across the smooth seat of his father's, now nearly black with age and oil. It had been built in Miles City in 1934 by Al Furstnow on a Sid Special tree.

His father had been horseback up to his end. The same for Lynne.

That was all Ezra had ever hoped for, but he knew it was selfish. He had other gifts. He could write. He could minister. He was not fully a cowboy like Lynne and his father. But a part of his destiny was land. How could you explain that to someone who only saw land as dirt, or profit, or an expanse between one's self and others? You couldn't. Destinies transcended explanations.

As he threw the saddle pad on Simon, the horse looked at him with a big, questioning eye. "You're going to have fun today," Ezra said. "But I don't want you having too much fun." Hoisting the saddle onto Simon's back took all his will power and the shoulder pain made his eyes water.

But, as he pulled the cinch snug, his anxieties mysteriously withdrew, and Ezra instinctively looked about to see if someone, or something, had entered the stall.

Something had.

He felt steeled as if built from iron and forged in fire. Fortification flowed into his soul. This was the day. This is why time had stopped when the rope coils had wrapped around his leg.

Simon snorted and pricked his ears. The bay horse felt it, too.

There were energies around them. Good energies and bad energies. Angels and demons.

Simon looked back to him as if awaiting instructions. Ezra patted him on his massive rump. "Stay with me, ole boy," he whispered. "For today, I believe we ride into the valley of the shadow."

CHAPTER THIRTY FOUR

"You're going to do *what?*" Anne asked.

Ezra refilled his coffee cup. "I'm going to gather the Oswald mares," he said.

"Using Dr. Doyle, Peter, and Garcia?"

"Doyle and Peter insist on going. We have to try to get Garcia because he'd pout for a week if he wasn't asked."

"Can't just you and Barney do it? You and Lynne used to do it by yourselves."

"No. White Crow can't run with an Oswald for any distance."

"Barney could ride one of Joe's horses," Anne insisted.

"He could, but he won't. Barney's odd that way."

"I think this is crazy."

"Anne," Ezra said, putting his cup in the sink. "You're the one who first called NRCS about EEEP. If we want the contract, the mares have to go."

"Do you even want the contract?"

"It doesn't matter. This has to be be done anyway. I've known that since Lynne died. He was the heart behind these horses and his heart stopped."

"If I take a pickup with grain, and you and Barney rode, wouldn't the mares follow me to the corrals?"

"No. They've run loose too long. They treasure their freedom more than a mouthful of grain." He paused to consider a new thought. "Are you bothered by me selling the mares?"

"No," she said. "I know you have to do it. But, they're all you have left of Lynne and there won't ever be horses like those again."

"Times change, Anne. Time was catching up and passing Lynne before he died. Deep down I think he knew that. The Oswalds are yesterday's horses."

Anne folded her arms across her chest, then released them because she knew it was a defensive gesture. She was about to cry and didn't want to. "Where did Peter go?" she said, changing the subject. "He came in the house, made some phone calls, then got in his SUV and left."

"He's going to try to find Doyle because her phone's turned off. When Barney gets here we'll haul the saddle horses up to the corrals and meet everyone there."

"What about you, Ezra? You have bad hands and a sore shoulder. You know Simon gets hot when he runs horses. What makes you think you can do this?"

"I'll do it because it has to be done," Ezra said. "Besides, I have a plan. If the plan works this won't be too hard."

"And if your plan doesn't work?"

"If we can't get the mares gathered, we'll just have to take it as a sign that we're not meant to have the EEEP contract."

"But putting Doyle and Peter on Joe's Oswalds?" she asked. "Isn't that dangerous?"

Ezra stopped at the door and turned to her. "They both insist they can ride," he said. "I guess we'll find out if they can or not."

"Ezra, you're being cavalier," she scolded.

He smiled. A twinkle flashed in his eyes that reminded Anne of the sparkle that lit Lynne's. "Cavalier," he said. "Which means, *a cavalryman.* I can accept that."

"Get a grip on yourself, Adrienne. Get a grip." Doyle was wandering around the Riley corrals talking to herself. "There is no way Peter Landau is an assassin, and if he were, he wouldn't be after you. It's the two men in the truck. The hillbillies. But what if it isn't them?

What if there isn't a contract out? What if I'm imagining all of this?"

She hurried to the Ranger where she'd left her phone. "I have to call the Miles City office," she said. "I'll make that kid, whats-his-name, come out for the paperwork, then I'll go to Canada like Lars suggested."

Canada?

"Why did Lars suggest Canada?" she asked quietly.

The highways between Miles City and Canada were long and lonely. Was that the plan? Were the hillbillies waiting for her to make a run for the border?

She'd call Lars again, she decided. She pushed the directory button on her phone. No coverage. She returned the phone to her backpack and pulled out the revolver. She liked its heft and its smooth and shiny finish. She'd keep it with her. On her person.

But how? It had come with a case, not a holster. How could she carry it horseback? She couldn't.

"Why did I volunteer to help gather those mares?" she asked herself again. "That was stupid. Impulsive. That's not me."

She decided she wouldn't ride. The mares didn't matter. She could mention them or not mention them in the Riley application. No one questioned *her.* She'd find a place she could get a signal, call the redheaded kid, and have him come out for the Ranger and the paperwork. Then, she'd make a run for the border. If she used the backroads they'd never find her.

But is that what they expected her to do?

Her spinning mind braked when she saw the vehicle approaching. Her heart went to her throat, and she gripped the revolver tightly. A thin line of perspiration beaded beneath her hairline.

Thankfully, it was not an old truck. It was Peter's SUV.

Peter stepped from his vehicle smiling. "Adrienne," he said. "I didn't think it would be this easy to find you."

"I'm just wrapping things up," she said cooly. She returned the revolver to her backpack. Hidden, but reachable.

"I have a favor to ask. Can you call the NRCS office and get Garcia away from work to help gather the mares?"

"Actually, I was about to call him anyway. I want to give him my paperwork so I can get out of here."

"But, you're going to ride, aren't you?"

"I don't know," she said. "It's been awhile since I've ridden."

"I volunteered because of you," Landau said.

Doyle detected the challenge in his voice. She couldn't resist challenges, especially from men. "So we've both lost our minds?" she asked.

"I like to think of it as being adventurous."

She glanced down at her backpack. A sliver of gunmetal glowed softly between notebooks, binoculars, camera, gloves, and scarf. She looked quickly back to Landau. "Peter, you know about the *Washington Post* article, don't you?"

He was caught by surprise. "Yes," he said.

"Your being here, does it have anything to do with me?"

"No. Like I told you, I'm doing an article about horses."

"Horses," she huffed. "And since when did Peter Landau become an equine writer?"

"It's a diversion. I needed a break."

"So, it's a coincidence that we keep meeting?"

"Yes, it is."

"Okay, if you say so," she said. "I'd call Jones, but I can't get service."

"You can get a signal on the ridge back there," Landau said. "And tell Garcia to bring his saddle," he added.

Jones stared at the growing pile of paperwork on his desk. He'd been at work for two hours, but nothing was getting done. He kept thinking of his father sitting in a jail cell and his mother mortgaging their home to pay for a lawyer.

Some days he wondered why his dad couldn't just grow up and be like him. He was the one in the family with a secure job and future. The father should learn from the son.

Life wasn't fair. If life was fair, he'd be Ezra Riley's son and Ezra would leave the ranch to him so he could be a cowboy full-time. If he were Ezra's son, he wouldn't carry the name of an old rock star.

But that made him stop and think. What was Ezra's son's name? Dylan. He was named for an old folk singer. Better Dylan than Garcia, he thought.

"Jones, wake up," his supervisor snapped. "I need you to go see Doyle. But she wants to talk to you first. She's on line two."

Garcia picked up his phone. "Hello?"

"Hey," Doyle said. "I need you to come up to the Riley corrals. I'm ready to sign-off on the Riley app."

"Okay."

"Bring the trailer so you can take your Ranger back."

"Okay."

"And one more thing," Doyle said. "Bring your saddle. Now put your supervisor back on. I'll make sure you're covered for the day."

Anne was busying herself making a lunch for the crew. If Ezra was going to risk their lives with a wild run through the hills, the least she could do was feed the survivors. Being the son of a CBC cowboy, Ezra never thought about food. He considered it normal to be hungry and thirsty.

Being preoccupied, Anne didn't hear the Range Rover pull into the yard, and, Casey, being Casey, didn't bark to warn her.

"Gramma," Gabby said. "There's a man at the door."

Anne wiped her hands on a dish towel before opening the door to Harlan Boothe.

"Mr. Boothe," she said. "Please come in."

He followed her to the kitchen.

"I'm just making lunch for a crew," Anne said. "Can I get you something? A cup of coffee?"

"No, Mrs. Riley. I'm fine. Sorry to barge in. I assume your husband isn't around."

"Ezra and Barney left a few minutes ago. They're going to gather the mares on Dead Man."

"Really? Now, that would be a sight to see."

"You're welcome to come with us. Gabby and I will be going once I get a lunch thrown together."

"I have my cameras," Boothe said. "I would love to photograph the mares in action, but I don't want to be an imposition, and perhaps Mr. RIley wouldn't want me there."

"Ezra? He'd be fine with it. He's a photographer, too. Or used to be. He hasn't quite caught up with the digital age."

Gabby pulled a chair to the kitchen counter and volunteered to smear mayonnaise. Anne laid out slices of bread for her, then turned back to her guest. "Mr. Boothe, are you okay?"

He sighed and slumped into a chair. "I can't find Corey. The other night we had words and I ran off those two *trainers* of his. Now I come back from Missoula and find him gone and a strange truck sitting in his driveway."

"Have you gone to the sheriff?" Anne asked.

"No, I don't think I want to do that. Not yet."

"How's your granddaughter? Ezra mentioned she'd been hurt."

"She's fine, but things have changed there, too. I took Ezra's advice--"

"Ezra's?"

"Yes, he seems to think a cowboy approach would serve us better, so I hired a cowboy to manage my granddaughter's operation. Someone you probably know."

"Someone we know?"

"Yes, Elmer Havig. He's Corey's neighbor in the subdivision. I bought his place this morning and hired him to run my granddaughter's ranch. A bit of luck, I think. He seems to be a sure-enough cowboy, as they say."

"My, you did all of this this morning? You've been busy."

"I went to Havig's to see if he knew anything about Corey. He didn't, but we got to talking and he seemed open to selling. I offered him the job and he took it."

"Well, I'm sure your grandson will show up," Anne said. "He's probably just made a couple new friends."

Boothe shook his head sadly. "I think your husband considers me a failure as a grandparent, and honestly, I have to say he's right."

Anne put the sandwiches in a large Tupperware bowl. "Gabby, sweetheart," she said. "Can you pack this to the door, please."

"Yes, Gramma." She left the room proudly packing a burden almost as big as herself.

Boothe looked up with sad eyes. "I apologize. I'm bothering you with my problems when you have better things to do."

Anne smiled. "It's okay. I don't have better things to do."

"If I may, can I use your land-line? I want to leave a message with Corey and let him know where I'll be, but I can't seem to get cell service here."

Anne directed him to the phone. As she packed the sandwiches she heard him say: "Corey, this is Grandpa. I am going to be at the Riley corrals on Dead Man for awhile. I hope to see you when I get back." He hesitated. "Or, you can come up there if you get this message right away. You know the place. Just up Dead Man Road and through the red gates."

Anne was struck by the irony: she had a billionaire in her home, a man who made more money in a month than she and Ezra would see in a lifetime, yet, at this moment he was someone more important than that. He was a grandpa.

CHAPTER THIRTY FIVE

"Stop here, stop here," Barney exclaimed.

Ezra hit the brakes sending the five horses in his trailer slamming into each other. "What?" he asked. "What's wrong?"

"Nothing's wrong," Barney said. "I just have to check my cell phone before we get off this ridge."

Ezra sighed, set the parking brake, grabbed a pair of binoculars and stepped from the truck. While Barney transacted business, he scouted. A half-mile to the south were the corrals and several vehicles. Landau, Doyle and Jones were there. Two miles further he glimpsed the shadowy forms of the mares on their ridge. He sensed they were watching him.

They know something's up, he thought.

"Shoot," Barney said.

"What's wrong now?" Ezra asked.

"Nothing's wrong. I was just thinking this is my favorite place in the whole world."

"Barn Wall, you haven't seen the whole world."

"I've seen enough to know I like this place the best."

"What do you like about it?"

"No power poles, no traffic, nothing manmade in sight except your corrals."

"You had me stop here so you could wax eloquent on your affections for this locale?"

"Nope, I had you stop so I could call the NPR people, but they're not picking up. I wonder if they're blocking my calls? What does *waxing eloquent* mean, anyway?"

"It's what you need to do to your sprouting mustache if you're going to be an NPR celebrity."

"Celebrity? Shoot, I bet I'm fired, but they're afraid to tell me and hurt my feelings."

They pulled up to the corrals. Landau, Doyle, and Jones walked over as Barney and Ezra unloaded horses.

Doyle approached Ezra and extended her hand. "Mr. Riley," she said. "I'm Dr. Adrienne Doyle."

Ezra took her hand. Her grip was firm and her eyes were softer, more vulnerable, than he'd expected. He didn't mention that they'd met before. "Nice to meet you, Dr. Doyle," he said.

"Call me Adrienne."

"Okay." He handed her the reins to Joe's bay roan. "I appreciate the help," he said. "But are you sure you want to do this?"

"Am I in good hands?"

"I hope so."

Barney handed Landau the reins to Joe's bay.

"Adrienne, you're in my wife's saddle so you'll need to shorten the stirrups," Ezra explained. "Peter, you're in Dylan's. Those stirrups should be set about right."

Girths were tightened and the crew mounted and circled the boss for instructions.

"You all know this pasture," Ezra explained. "That rough divide serves as a border, but the east fence is actually below it. If the mares spill off the divide it could take hours to bring them back, so the east is our vulnerable side. The mares are on the ridge due south of us. Four of us are riding east as if we're going below the divide to gather cattle. Barney is staying on the west side.

"Stay relaxed and don't look in the mares' direction. We want them to think we're not interested in them. At certain points I'll drop you off one at a time, then I'll circle around and get behind them. When I bring them north, make yourself visible as they come in sight. Ride parallel to them. Think of the mares as a stream of water and direct the flow toward these corrals. Your horses will get excited. Give them enough rein to keep them from fighting you, but keep control. Don't give them their heads."

He pointed to where two arms of woven-wire fencing extended for sixty yards from the south side of the corrals. "We want to direct them into those wings and through that south gate. If, by chance, Barney or I can take the lead, the mares might follow a rider into the wings. But I can't guarantee that'll happen."

"What if they start running towards us?" Garcia asked.

"You have a lariat. Raise it in the air and talk to them."

"If they get past us and go under the divide, then what?" Peter asked.

"Nothing. You wait for me and Barney. The job for you three is containment. Watch the lead mare and try to read her intentions. She can run, so don't underestimate her.

"I'll be behind them, but I'll be able to see you and shout directions. Give the mares some space until we get close to the corrals, then move in gradually to squeeze them into the wings."

The three rookies nodded nervously.

"One more thing," Ezra said, turning to Barney. "Barn Wall, I don't think you noticed, but as we were leaving my yard, Kitty jumped in the back of my truck."

"Kitty's here?" Barney asked.

"Yeah, he's hiding, hoping no one will notice. You better take a moment and tie him up. We don't need your dog bailing into the middle of the mares just as we near the gate."

They rode cautiously eastward. Ezra dropped Jones off first and showed him where to wait without being seen. He positioned Doyle a quarter-mile on.

Ezra placed Landau behind a rock outcropping. "Stay even with the lead, but 100 yards to the side," he told him. "Be a deterrent, not a threat. As you come up on Doyle, let her get ahead of you by about fifty yards. Do you remember where the corrals are?"

Landau pointed to a large plateau to the north. "Up there somewhere," he said.

"Close enough," Ezra said and he trotted off.

Ezra considered himself the weak link in the crew. He had the sore hands and painful shoulder; would ride the farthest and fastest on an Oswald that loved the chase; and over a terrain that was brushy and rough -- there were gullies twenty feet wide and fifteen feet deep. He braced himself to get the job done. This was not a poem or short story. There was no room for romance, background, or sentiment. He didn't think about his father running horses with the CBCs, or recall the good horses he'd ridden, or the friends and family that had ridden beside him. This gather was a short article based on facts. He needed the mares in the corral on the first attempt, or at the worst, the second. Should the mares pass the corrals once, there was a chance he could turn them and bring them back. But, if they managed to run past the corrals twice, it was over. He didn't have the crew for a third run.

Ezra had two fears: Simon taking the bit and charging blindly in wild pursuit, or, one of the rookies getting hurt in a spill.

Cresting the ridge he had a strong sense of *deja vu*. This was the scene he had imagined in the MRI tube, only now, the grass was green and the weather warm.

The mares had moved south to water. Ezra spotted them, slipped down a grassy coulee behind them, then approached them at a walk. Simon's dam lifted her head -- water dripping from her muzzle caught sunlight. She pricked her ears toward him and snorted. Seven other heads raised. She spun from the reservoir in a measured gallop and the others assembled in her wake.

Ezra slowly released enough pressure on the reins for Simon to break into a canter.

It was on. The mares bucked and kicked in wild enjoyment. Simon pressed and lunged against the bit. Ezra fed him rein slowly, as if he were a shark on a fishing line. The first mile was sport and psychology. The mares enjoyed the challenge while testing Ezra's resolve and intentions.

The little herd boiled over the ridge, toward the trail that led off the divide. Just in time, Landau emerged from the rocks yelling and waving an arm. The mares bent back to the north, manes and tails streaming behind them like kites. Ezra gave Simon more rein and the bay erupted beneath him, his stride swallowing the prairie in long gulps.

They galloped on, leaping ravines and sliding down dry, brittle gumbo buttes on their hocks.

The lead mare bent east again, but Doyle was there on Joe's bay roan, and the mare slammed against a sister in turning back. Doyle bent over the saddle horn, took a handful of mane, and nudged her horse forward. In seconds, she'd settled into her position on the right flank.

So far, so good, Ezra thought. Now it was up to Garcia to do his job.

They came to the first gully, one so wide and deep it was crossable only by deeply-cut cow trails. The herd, jockeying to cross single-file, bottlenecked in a swarm of dust. Uphill, Doyle spotted another trail and reined her roan to it. Landau saw her action and followed.

Ezra smiled. Doyle was thinking on her feet, and Landau was wise enough to notice.

The mares popped out of the gully like pinballs and now Ezra was on their heels. The lead mare made one last desperate bid to race north. Her ears pinned back against her head, her nostrils flared red, her stride lengthened, and her hooves threw divots of sod backward.

The other mares joined the lead mare and they moved as one glossy bay-and-brown body. The fun was over. Seriousness rippled through them. They were prey running for their lives.

Ezra glanced at Doyle. She was riding fast, but controlled. Behind her, Landau looked steady, but Ezra noted a stiffness in his shoulders and back.

Ezra reined Simon slightly to the right, positioning himself to charge past Doyle and Landau, and turn the mares if Garcia failed to show.

Where was Garcia? Ezra rode in a mixture of mud, dust, sweat, and heavy breathing. Simon's hooves hit the ground with the cadence of heartbeats.

The lead mare's head came up, and her ears pricked forward.

Does she see escape ahead, Ezra wondered, or did she sense another rider?

The mares coiled for an uphill sprint. Their coats were sweat-soaked and shiny and slivers of slobber sailed from their lips.

Then Jones appeared on the hilltop, his mouth open in a voice-less shout, and his coiled lariat raised in the air. Big Jack seemed as massive as a mountain.

Ezra saw the lead mare's spirit deflate at the sight. She bent sharply west and purposed herself to a new goal: the hardpan and gumbo maze just west of the corrals.

Now it was up to Barney.

If Barney had been watching the chase, Ezra knew he'd had plenty of time to position White Crow to turn the herd to the corral wings.

But Barney could not always be counted on. For all Ezra knew, he could be at the truck patting Kitty, or on a hillside hunting agates and antler sheds.

But Barney was there.

The mares raced up a grassy coulee to find a black-and-white paint in their path. They had no choice but turn toward the corral wings.

Now! Ezra thought.

He gave Simon his head and nudged him with both spurs. The big bay seemed to break in half as his stride extended. From the corner of his eye -- wetted by rushing air -- Ezra saw Landau had noticed his move and was swinging tighter to the herd. Doyle pressed in easily ahead of him. Garcia was struggling to keep Big Jack under control but managed to plow-rein him into position.

The mares were pointed like an arrow toward the corrals. Sage, bunchgrass, and gravel flew by beneath them.

Ezra reined Simon to their west flank. He felt neither his hands nor his shoulder because he had become part of his horse.

White Crow wasn't fast, but he was fresh and excited. He ran steadily near the mares' lead.

Ezra tensed to make another move. Barney had to hurry or the mares would swing past the wings and the race would begin anew.

Barney made his move. His lariat rose in the air and slapped White Crow hard on the rump. The paint horse exploded in a burst of flatulence. Simon's dam saw the wings and the narrow opportunity to swing past them. She made a frantic lunge, but White Crow matched it. The mare slammed against Barney's chapped leg, then bounced away as the railroad tie split them. She and her sisters funneled through the wings and gate, while Barney raced on the other side of the fence beside them.

Still on their heels, Ezra pulled Simon up, swung from the saddle, and dragged the gate shut.

Landau, Doyle, and Garcia slid their horses to a stop beside him.

The Oswald mares were captured.

CHAPTER THIRTY SIX

As Landau stepped off his horse, time slowed, his vision blurred, his legs wobbled and he wondered if he were having a stroke. He became two people in two places. He was on a cowboy crew at a set of remote corrals in Montana, but he was also lying in the dust, his head to the side, in a West Bank village in Israel. He heard shouts in Arabic and Hebrew, heard sirens, screams, the roar of engines and the crackling of fire. An acrid smoke filled the air and blood rolled from his forehead, down the side of his face and onto his lips. His eyes cleared and focused on a girl's dismembered leg. He knew it was a girl's because of the painted toenails.

He was on the edge of unconsciousness, teetering back and forth on a thin bridge over darkness. There was a rush of footsteps, a goat bleated, a dog barked, more footsteps, shouts, and sirens. Something was placed beside him. A litter. Strong hands gripped him and he was lifted up, moved, placed down, lifted up again, jostled. He saw the roof of a building pass by and an expanse of bleached Israeli sky. He was thrust into a dark, metal cavern. Tires spun. Sirens wailed. A young man in a white shirt stood above him and said to the driver:

"Only concussed, I believe." Then Peter's eyes rolled up in his head and everything went dark.

"Peter!"

He opened his eyes to Ezra Riley and wondered why a Montana cowboy was in an Israeli hospital.

"Are you okay?" Riley held him by both shoulders.

Landau shook his head to clear it and stepped back. "Yes, yes, I just got a little dizzy," he said. "I must have got off my horse too fast." He pushed past Jones and Doyle and leaned against the woven-wire fence. Inside the pen, the eight mares were both nervous and trusting. Nervous, as they raised heads and looked past their captors to the ridge that had been theirs; trusting, because man had done them no great harm in the past. Stallions had been introduced, foals weaned, worming medication given, but the gates always reopened and they'd burst from the corrals at a run.

Ezra tossed his left stirrup leather over his saddle's seat and loosened Simon's girth. Doyle and Jones followed suit. When Landau didn't move, Ezra stepped to his horse and loosened the saddle's cinch.

Ezra turned to Jones and Doyle. "Good job, you guys," he said. "Very good job."

Jones blushed with pleasure. Doyle nodded a thank-you.

Ezra looked over Doyle's head. He could see a vehicle approaching. "That looks like Boothe's Rover coming," he said.

"Who's Boothe?" Doyle asked.

"Someone we know," Ezra said. "Let's tie our horses away from these mares."

Doyle quickened her steps to walk beside him. "You don't mean Harlan Boothe?" she asked. Ezra pretended not to hear her.

The Rover stopped in front of the corrals.

Ezra was surprised to see Anne and Gabby step from Boothe's Rover. Gabby came to him running. "Granddad," she said. "We brought lunch."

Ezra bent down and hugged her. Anne and Boothe set up a portable card table and covered it with Tupperware containers of food as the crew gathered.

"Mrs. Riley's famous date bars," Barney said. He reached for one, but pulled back. "Excuse me," he said. "I forgot we always say grace."

"You can say it if you can keep it shorter than your radio programs," Ezra said.

Doyle's ears perked. Radio program? Now she recognized his voice. "You're the satirist on NPR," she said.

"What's a satirist?" Barney asked.

"That's an inspired person descended from a satyr," Ezra quipped.

"What's a satyr?"

Ezra fibbed. "That's someone who's half-man and half-horse."

Barney beamed. "Thank you, m'am," he said to Doyle. "That's about the nicest compliment anyone's ever paid me."

Ezra quickly diverted Doyle's attention. "Adrienne," he said. "Have you met Mr. Boothe?"

The two were introduced as Landau came in late.

"We're all here," Barney said. "You can pray now, Ezra."

Ezra looked to his granddaughter. "Gabby, will you bless our meal?"

She nodded and squinted hard. "Lord Jesus, we thank you for our friends and we thank you for horses and we thank you for dogs and we thank you for Gramma's date bars and whatever else it is that we eat and we pray that you will keep us all safe and especially keep us safe today. Amen."

Amens sounded and a food line began with Barney in the lead. "Shoot, it's a beautiful day," Barney said, slapping his plate with beans, bacon, and salad. He piled date bars on the side.

"It is nice," Ezra said. "Not too hot and the rain greened things up a little. Reminds me of my halcyon days of youth."

"What halcyon?" Barney asked.

"A time in the past that was idyllically happy," Landau explained.

"Shoot, you mean the *hell-they're-gone* days," Barney said.

"That's NPR material," Garcia joked.

While everyone chuckled, Anne moved close to Ezra. "Were the mares any trouble?" she asked.

"Nothing we couldn't handle," he said. "I had a good crew."

Gabby pointed at the corrals. "Granddad, what are you going to do with the pretty horses?"

He bent down beside her. "Well, sweetheart, I'm afraid those horses will be going to a new home."

"Can't you keep one for me?" she asked.

"None of them are broke to ride, Gabby. They're just halter-broke."

"I could break one to ride," she said emphatically.

"We'll see," Ezra said. He noticed Landau walking off by himself with a paper plate filled with food. The reporter went to the corrals and leaned against a railroad tie. Ezra took his plate and walked over to him.

They stood silently for several moments, both staring at the mares.

"It's a shame," Landau said finally. "They're beautiful horses. They should stay in production."

Ezra nodded but he had other things on his mind. "What happened over there by the gate, Peter? You almost fainted."

Landau dipped his sandwich in Anne's branding beans and took a bite. "For a moment I was back in Israel," he said. "I was in a suicide bombing eight years ago. On the edge of it, actually. Fourteen people died, but I was only knocked unconscious."

"Have you ever re-experienced it liked this before?"

"No. Never."

"Well, I'm not surprised," Ezra said. "Things happen here at these corrals."

"What do you mean, *things happen?*"

"The sage grouse come here to hatch their chicks. One reason is the woven-wire keeps the coyotes out, but it's also because Anne comes here to pray and sing. Worship changes things."

"Anne and I discussed this a little."

"But, you're skeptical."

"A little."

"The land around corrals can absorb a lot of cursing," Ezra said.

"And Anne's singing cleanses that?"

"We think so. But it requires maintenance. This isn't magic. It's a stewardship methodology."

"The curses try to retake the ground?"

"They do."

"So, what happened with me?" Peter asked. "Was that a blessing or curse?"

"I think that's in your hands," Ezra said. He looked back at the crew. Doyle, Boothe and Jones were visiting. Anne was busy with food. Barney was sitting on a tailgate, his legs crossed, letting Gabby ride one of his big feet like it was a pony. Ezra turned back to Landau. "When I was a child I saw things," he said. "Colors around people, colors around places."

"Auras?"

Ezra shrugged. "I don't know. Probably not in the popular New Age sense. My mother told me it was all in my imagination and made me stop it. In fact, I quit all at once. I'd planted some morning glories, but my father ordered them destroyed because he didn't think little boys should grow flowers. One evening while everyone else was watching bucking horses, I pulled them up."

"So, were the colors imagined or not?"

"No, they weren't imagined," Ezra said. "Reality isn't always rational, logical and linear. There is a world around us that the natural eyes cannot see."

"Hey, Ezra." Barney was shouting and waving him over. Peter and Ezra rejoined the others.

Barney was laughing and Gabby's pants were dirty. "Gabby, just got bucked off," Barney said. "But she still claims she's the best bronc rider ever."

"Probably the best one in this crowd," Ezra said.

"Hey, Barney," Garcia said. "What's the best bronc ride you ever saw?"

"The best? You mean for scoring points, or for being memorable?"

"The most memorable."

"Well, it certainly wasn't the best, but the one I'll always remember was Lynne in the Matched Bronc Riding at the Bucking Horse Sale about '64 or '65. He drew Sage Hen, the bay mare of Harry Knight's. I was probably 12 or 13 and Lynne was one of my heroes. I was near the fence by the chutes when a fellow rushed over and started taking movie pictures just as Sage Hen came out. She made an unusually high leap and Lynne sat up there like he was on a big bird. That movie camera was whirrin' in my ear like an insect. Lynne and Sage Hen hung in the air so long, it was like time had stopped."

Garcia nearly dropped his drink as his grandfather's film scenes flashed through his mind. That was the scene that had made him worship bronc riders. His grandfather had stood next to a young Barney.

"I've always wondered who that guy with the camera was," Barney said. "I'd sure like to see the film of that ride."

"I have that --" Garcia started to say when Barney's cell phone buzzed.

"Shoot," Barney said. "It's NPR and I can't get a signal." He looked at the loading chute and it's tall poles and side boards. "Maybe up on the chute." He ran to the corral with surprising speed, bounded up onto a catwalk, then climbed the cottonwood planks to the top. He check his phone. "I got two bars," he announced.

"Climb up on the top of the poles," Ezra joked.

"Don't tell him that," Anne scolded. "He'll fall and break his neck."

Barney leaned as tall as possible and held the phone in the air. "Three bars."

"Answer it," Ezra yelled.

"Hello? What? Hello? Yes, this is Barney? Can you hear me? What's that? Hello. Okay, I can hear you now? What? Okay. I'm on my way." Barney climbed down from the chute. "The NPR people need to see me. One of them's in town. I need to get to Miles City." He looked about for his pickup. "Shoot," he said. "I didn't bring my truck."

"Take my SUV," Landau said. "I'll catch a ride back with Ezra."

"We'll haul White Crow home," Ezra said.

Landau handed Barney his keys.

"You're trusting a cartoonist with your SUV?" Garcia joked.

"It's just a rental," Landau said.

Barney got in the SUV and drove away.

"There goes Barn Wall, off to his destiny," Ezra said.

Boothe approached Ezra eagerly. "Ezra, I got some great shots of y'all gathering those mares."

"You did? I didn't even see you."

"I parked out of sight, then set up with camouflage. I caught the whole sequence of the horses coming in and you riders herding them."

"That's great," Ezra said. "I'd like to see them sometime."

"I'll see you get prints. Also, I want to shoot your badlands," he added. "Your lovely wife and granddaughter have offered to be my guides. Anne says there's a jeep trail that takes a person back to your place? Would it be safe to travel?"

"Maybe, if it's dried out from the rain."

"If not, we could turn around and come back. I won't take any risks, but I would love to shoot the badlands at sunset."

"If Anne is willing to take you, that's fine with me."

"Thank you. There's something else --" Boothe began.

Ezra noticed Doyle standing by her SUV. She was signaling him to come over. "Excuse me, Mr. Boothe, I don't mean to interrupt, but I think Dr. Doyle wants to speak to me." On his way to Doyle, he saw something move under the loading chute. It was Kitty tethered to a post. Barney had forgotten his dog again.

Doyle was moving her belongings from the Ranger to her vehicle. All that remained was her backpack on the Ranger's seat. She motioned Ezra to follow her behind the SUV.

"I'm about to leave," she said. "And there are a couple of things I want to say. First, thank you for letting me ride and help gather the mares."

"I should be thanking you," Ezra said. "You were good help and fun to have along."

"Now, on a more serious note," she said. "I know you're suspicious about this EEEP program, but I want to encourage you to take the contract."

"Why?"

"Look, I know you are a friend of Len's--"

"Lynne."

"I meant Lynne. Anyway, because you are a friend of his, you probably know a little about me."

"A little," Ezra agreed. "But Lynne's passed away."

"Oh. I'm sorry. I didn't know." She paused for a second, then continued. "Anyway, there are *people* who do not want this program to succeed. I know these people. They are very powerful and have big plans. This program would delay things for them. If enough landowners sign up for it, matters will go back into the courts. Don't worry, they won't be suing you. They'll be suing the U.S. government."

They were interrupted. "Granddad," Gabby came around the SUV and hugged Ezra's leg. "We are going to go take pictures now."

"That's nice, sweetheart. Can you say goodbye to Dr. Doyle? She'll be leaving us soon."

"Goodbye, Doctor Doyle," Gabby said.

Doyle reached down and laid a hand on her head. "Goodbye, Gabby," she said.

Gabby looked up at the woman and smiled. "Your colors are better," she said. Then she ran back and climbed in the Rover.

"What did she--"

Ezra interrupted. "You were saying this program can protect me?"

"Yes. At least it will buy you time."

"Time? Before what happens?"

"Ezra, you have to understand you are the new Indian. The best you can hope for is to keep your ranch as your reservation."

"Is Boothe one of *those people?*"

"Why do you ask that?"

"He's trying to buy me out," Ezra said. He heard the distinctive sound of the Range Rover's engine coming to life and the vehicle leaving.

"No, he's not one of them," Doyle said. "Frankly, I would rather you have this land than him. I've not met many ranchers like you, Mr. Riley. You really do care for the land and the wildlife, don't you?"

"Yes, but there are many like me."

"Too few, too late," Doyle said. "Global wheels are in motion."

"As far as these mares go, they won't technically be gone until morning. I'll leave them here tonight and haul them to Billings tomorrow."

"Your word is good with me, and I don't think I've ever said that to a rancher before."

Ezra looked north. He had caught the shine of a windshield reflecting sunlight. He was growing accustomed, here, and at home, of people driving into his life and thought he was beyond being surprised. He frowned.

"What's up?" Doyle asked.

"There's a vehicle coming," Ezra said. "And it's Corey Boothe's."

CHAPTER THIRTY SEVEN

Corey Boothe's one-ton dually slid to a stop, nose-to-nose to Doyle's SUV, and next to the government's Polaris Ranger. Nicholas Pratt lumbered out and saw Doyle's backpack sitting on the Ranger's seat.

"It's them," Doyle said, and she gripped Ezra's arm for support. Her clinch restrained Ezra, who had moved to confront the strangers.

Nickie fumbled through the pack, happier than a child with a Christmas stocking. "Lookee this," he called to Jeremy. He held up a Garmin GPS, TuffBook, and Canon digital SLR. "There's more." He held up Nikon binoculars. Then he saw the revolver. He set the binoculars down and grabbed the Taurus Tracker. "We got a little bang-bang," he laughed.

"That's my stuff," Doyle protested. She tried to sound firm, but her voice was thin and fragile.

Landau and Jones stepped forward, but stopped when the big man wielded the revolver in their direction.

Jeremy collapsed from the truck as if he'd been running a marathon since birth. Dark circles pooled beneath his eyes and his pale face sagged with fatigue.

Nickie pointed the revolver in the air. "Bang, bang, bang," he said, then he pirouetted and pointed the .22 Magnum at Doyle and Ezra. "Bang, bang," he said again. Life, at that moment was his stage, and everything and everyone else, were merely props.

Doyle gripped Ezra's arm tighter. "They're here to kill me," she whispered.

Jeremy leaned against the truck hood and moaned urgently.

His cousin understood and interpreted. "Where's old man Boothe?" Nicki demanded.

"He's not here," Ezra said. His voice was firm but cautious. The big man's arrival was like finding a grizzly bear going through your garbage. Ezra was still determining how to gain control of the situation.

Nickie waved the gun at Landau and Jones. "You two," he said. "Get over here." He gestured at Doyle and Ezra again. "Join 'em."

Ezra gently removed Doyle's arm from his while the gunman herded the four together. He weighed his options. A firearm was kept in all of his vehicles. Under the front seat of his Dodge was a .357 Magnum, but the truck was 30 yards away.

Nickie stuck the gun barrel against Ezra's forehead. "Where's Boothe, old-timer?" he asked.

The gunman's stink reminded Ezra again of a bear in garbage. His thick neck was stained with cheap tattoos and bits of breakfast encrusted his goat tee.

"He's not here," Ezra repeated.

Nickie cocked the trigger. "I said, where is he?"

"In the hills," Doyle blurted. "He's taking pictures in the hills."

Nickie turned to her. Doyle almost lost control of her bladder as his eyes pierced hers like a hot poker. "What hills?" he said, and he moved the gun to her head.

She pointed east. "Over there."

Nickie used the barrel to brush back a strand of her hair. "He comin' back?" he said.

"I don't know. I don't know," she cried. She felt urine flow warm and wet down her leg, and she wondered if she'd leave this earth with this as her last sensation.

"Mmm-grrrr-mmm-grrrr," Jeremy groaned and mimicked punching a cell phone.

"Come here," Nickie snapped. Jeremy wobbled over.

Nickie put the gun in his hands. "You cover them," he demanded. "If one of them moves you shoot 'em."

Jeremy held the weapon in both hands, stepped back, and pointed it at the four.

Nickie stormed to the back of Boothe's truck and the tailgate crashed down. There was a thud and grunt as he wrestled a heavy weight, then he came back, half-carrying, half-dragging a bloody, taped-up bundle which he dropped at their feet.

It was Corey Boothe, though he was barely recognizable. His hands were tied behind his back with cords, and his arms and legs were wrapped in duct tape. His head was swollen and bloody. Ezra could not tell if he were dead or alive.

"We want the grandpa," Nickie said.

"Mmm-grrr-mmm-grrr."

"What?" Nickie grabbed the revolver back from his cousin.

Jeremy again pantomimed making a phone call.

"Yeah, yeah," Nickie said. "I gotta do it all cause you're a damn dummy. Can you guard 'em?"

Jeremy shrugged.

Nickie looked at the corrals. "Over there," he said. "All of you get over there."

Ezra allowed the others to go ahead so he could stay close to the gun. Again, he considered his options. Disarming a much younger man who outweighed him by 100 pounds wasn't likely, but there was always a chance. He took a deep breath to settle his nerves and tried to dredge up his martial arts training.

No good, he thought. *If I have to think about what I'm going to do, whatever I do, won't work.*

Nickie pushed him hard in the back. "Get goin' old-timer. I wanna kill an old cowboy. Might as well be you."

Landau was in the lead. He stopped at the small gate that led into the main pen. Ahead of him, in a corner of the main pen, was an old squeeze chute that connected to a narrow alley that led back to a crowding pen behind the loading chute. Landau went through the gate followed by Jones, Doyle, and Ezra.

"Lookee that," Nickie said, gesturing at the squeeze chute. "A little jail. It got bars on the side and everything."

In the alleyway behind the chute was a small man-gate. The chute itself -- it's head-catch, tail-gate, and side-squeeze -- were closed-up.

Nickie put the revolver barrel against Doyle's mouth and looked at Ezra. "Old-timer, get this cow jail opened up or I blow this lady some new cavities."

With his good arm, Ezra pushed a lever that caused the sides to expand. He then eased behind the others and pulled the tail-gate open.

"Lead the way, old man," Nickie said.

Ezra opened the man gate, stepped into the alley, then passed through the tail-gate and into the squeeze chute. He shuffled ahead until his bad shoulder pressed against the head-catch. Out of the corner of his eye he saw Simon tied at a post. The big bay looked at him curiously. Behind him he heard the Oswald mares stirring in the pen.

"All of you," Nickie said.

Doyle went next. She moved down the chute and pressed against Ezra who could smell her fear. Jones followed. Landau was last.

Nickie pushed the tail-gate shut, then pulled the lever that caused the sides to squeeze. The bars barely touched them but the four were still tightly contained.

"Lookee that," Nickie said. "We got 'em all in a cow jail." He glanced around at the available supplies. "We should brand 'em," he said. A propane bottle sat on a work bench, and branding irons hung from nails in the corral planks. He picked up a stainless steel dehorning tool. "I could take their noses off with this," he said.

Jeremy stumbled forward, groaning and shaking his head. "Mmm-grrr..."

"Yeah, yeah," Nickie said. "Maybe later. You got baby boy's phone?"

Jeremy pulled Corey Booth's SmartPhone from a front pocket and handed it to him. Nickie looked at his four prisoners and smiled. "I'm gonna call Granddaddy," he said. "And see what he wants to pay to get baby boy back." He handed Jeremy the revolver. "You watch them while I make the call." He pushed his way through the gate and walked to the vehicles.

Jeremy leaned against a railroad tie and used both hands to support the little revolver.

Ezra knew the workings of the chute well. He'd put thousands of cattle through it. The lever that opened the head gate was impossible for him to reach. The side bars could be easily opened one at a time, but crawling out would be awkward. Landau was next to the end-gate. If Peter slid it open he was still confined to the alley.

"Listen to me," Ezra said to his captor. "You don't want to do this. This is not the way you want things to go."

Jeremy looked at him dully. He looked like death painted on a dirty sheet.

"You're not dumb," Ezra said. "You know this isn't right. You don't want to listen to your partner."

Jeremy pointed the gun at him shakily.

"You're not a killer," Ezra said. "I've known killers. You could kill us if you had to, but you don't want to."

"Mmmm-ggrrr."

Ezra tried to recall if the big man had used the little man's name. He hadn't. "You can talk," Ezra said. "What's your name?"

"Ja-ja-ja-ja."

"That's good," Ezra coaxed.

"Ja-ja-ja-ja."

"Jason? Is your name Jason?"

Jeremy shook his head.

"Jackson?"

"Jer-jer-jer-jer."

"Jerry?"

"Jer-jer-jer-jer."

"Jeremiah?"

The little gate clanged open. The big man was back. "Jeremy," he said. "What you doin'? You tryin' to talk?"

Jeremy shook his head.

Nickie held up the phone in disgust. It looked the size of a postage stamp in his meaty palm. "I can't get no damn bars," he said.

"We have poor reception here," Ezra said. He wasn't sure what to say next. Anne and Gabby were with Boothe and he couldn't bring them back to this. He'd gladly die to save them, but could he sacrifice Doyle, Garcia, and Landau?

Nickie stepped to the chute and stared at Ezra angrily. "How do I get reception?" he demanded.

His voice was clear, sharp and authoritative. This bothered Ezra. A stoned maniac was better than a cognitive one.

"Stand on one of the trucks," Ezra said. "The higher the better."

Nickie wheeled around. "Keep 'em covered," he told his cousin. "And don't be tryin' to talk."

Ezra waited until Nickie was out of earshot. "Jeremy," he said softly.

The skinny man's head was down, but at the sound of his name he looked up. The voice was familiar as if he'd heard the dead cowboy who wore his name on the back of his belt.

"Jeremy," Ezra repeated. "You are a better man than this." He nodded to his left. "Look at these three," he said. "They're good people. They've never hurt you. Are you going to let your big friend kill them?"

Jeremy's eyes widened.

"He is going to kill us," Ezra said. "He has to. We're witnesses. And he wants to do it. But you don't want to."

Jeremy's eyes darted left, then right.

"My name is Ezra Riley. If I am going to die, you should know my name."

Jeremy remembered the name on the magazine article and the scene in the hospital. The bearded man at the end of the chute had been talking to a tall blond woman. He liked that woman. She looked like someone he could talk to.

"If Boothe comes back he'll have my wife and five-year-old-grand-daughter with him. Your friend will kill them, too. Can you take that, Jeremy? Can you take that much killing?"

The skinny addict let his arms droop. The revolver was too heavy to hold up all the time. Decisions were too heavy. Nickie was too heavy. Life was too heavy. He wanted to lie down and become a feather and let a breeze blow him away.

The gate rattled again and Nickie came through it in a rush. He reached down, grabbed the revolver from Jeremy's limp hands, took a step forward, and aimed it at Garcia's head. He looked at Ezra. "Old man, you listen to me," he said. You quit jackin' with me or I blow this boy away. You want that? I stand on the truck and I only got two bars. I can hear Grandpappy Boothe but he can't hear me. You tell me what I gotta do or I blow this one away."

Ezra wished time would stop, and grace would descend from heaven again. He needed a miracle.

Nickie cocked the revolver.

But time didn't seem to be merely pausing. It seemed to be coming to an end.

CHAPTER THIRTY EIGHT

Anne sat on a rock ledge overlooking the trail that led off the divide and through the gumbo badlands. A quarter-mile to the north Boothe had set up his tripod, and below her in a wash of sandstone, Gabby was looking for round sandstone balls created thousands of years before by oceanic waves.

In his essays Ezra had written how a man could slowly resemble the land he loved and worked. Bodies became gnarled and bent like juniper trunks, hands worn and veined as creek beds, and faces lined and creased with erosion, like the badlands that now stretched in Anne's view.

Anne's own love for this land had caused a similar but more gentle resemblance. Her complexion was sandstone with enough lines to denote character. Her eyes were set like pools of spring water reflecting a canvas of blue sky. Her hair was the shade of cured bluestem grasses with the iridescence of sunlit foxtail. Her spirit was as nourished and nurturing as the spring-fed evergreen that, in the descending coulee, spread its boughs and carpeted the hardpan with juniper berries.

Of all the places on the ranch, this was her's and Ezra's favorite. She cherished her walks near their house on Sunday Creek, and he spoke and wrote about the corrals on Dead Man, but those were affections of convenience. Anne loved being able to leave her house and walk, sing, and pray on the creek bottoms at leisure, taking time to study plants, observe birds, and collect rocks. Ezra liked the remoteness of the corrals and the memories of working livestock with good friends on good horses.

But the sacred spot was here, on this divide, in this rugged land, where a sweet water spring flourished and grew wildflowers and grasses beside a towering cedar, and tipi rings lined the ridges as reminders of another peoples' affections.

In the evenings the badlands staged a presentation of colors washing into each other, then flaring, and growing distinct, before shadows darkened and draped the land's contours in blackness.

This spot had the sense of a well-used chapel.

Anne watched Boothe pick up his equipment, shoulder his tripod, and walk slowly toward her. He stopped once, took his cell phone from a pocket, listened, and put it away. In a few minutes he was beside her.

"This is a beautiful place," he said. "But for some reason, it's not willing to share its beauty with me."

"It's stubborn that way," Anne said. "This is one of our favorite places."

He watched the colors cast by lowering light settle into the clays, but the tripod and camera stayed shouldered. "I've not been completely honest with you and your husband," he said.

Anne turned her gaze from the hills to his eyes.

"I have talked to Ezra's sisters," Boothe said. "And they are willing to sell, but not particularly eager. They say they will sell if that's what Ezra wants to do."

Anne's eyebrows raised slightly. "That's good to know," she said.

"Mrs. Riley, outside of technology, I do few things well. When I offered Ezra a price above market value, I thought I was complimenting him, favoring him for his years of stewardship."

"He saw it more as if you were trying to buy his soul."

"I know. I see that now. It makes me sound like the devil, doesn't it?"

Anne didn't respond.

"Both you and he are getting older," Boothe said. "It will get harder and harder for Ezra to work a ranch like this, by himself, as he has done for years. If I may be so bold to ask, do either of you have health insurance?"

"We used to," Anne said. "I worked part-time at the hospital for years, mostly for the benefits, but then Ezra started needing more help, so I had to quit. I'm not a lot of help on the ranch but I do what I can."

"Wouldn't you like to retire to a smaller place in a less harsh environment?"

"Mr. Boothe, you have to understand that it's not simply about us."

He looked downhill where Gabby was busy in the sand. "She is a long way from adulthood and ranch management," he said.

"I'm not talking about Gabby," Anne said. "It's about our spiritual beliefs. I don't know what that means to you. To many people one's faith is just tradition or philosophy."

"You're religious people, I understand that."

"No, you don't. It's not about religion."

"Mrs. Riley, I'm a man of science. I'm not sure I follow you."

"No, you don't. You can't. And that's okay."

His phone vibrated. "Excuse me," he said and checked its screen. "Corey is trying to call me, but I can't get service."

"At least you know he's safe and is trying to reach you."

"Yes, that's a good thing. A little surprising, even."

"Mr. Boothe, may I ask you a question?"

"I hope it's not about religion," he said.

"No, it's about pain. How much physical pain have you known in your life?"

"Pain? I hate going to the dentist."

"You haven't known much, have you?"

"No, I guess I've been lucky."

"I see men all the time who work in pain. Some, in order to provide for their families. Others, because they love what they do. Ezra, and cowboys his age and older, work in pain every day."

"But that's what I'm saying," Boothe said. "He doesn't have to. He would never have to work again."

"And so you would buy his soul," Anne said.

Boothe shook his head. "No."

"It's not about relief or comfort, Mr. Boothe. It's about being who you are as long as you possibly can."

"But he's more than a rancher. People say he's a writer."

"He's been struggling lately."

"Writer's block? I've heard of it. Artists are a temperamental sort."

"No, emotionally, he's steady and disciplined," Anne said. "He has some physical issues and the market is changing, but mostly it's the technology. He starts a book, then gets busy with ranch work. When he finds time to get back to his work the technology has changed. It's a full-time job just keeping up technologically."

"Technology is stopping him? I could help him with that. He could be nicely set up somewhere and able to write as much as he wanted."

"But it's not over," Anne said. "He's not *done*, Mr. Boothe. Can't you understand?"

"No. What's not over?"

"When I worked in the Emergency Room I saw people come in for the silliest things. Paper cuts. Nosebleeds. A rash. But old cowboys would drive themselves to town with broken sternums, deep lacerations, fractured arms. One old guy walked in after losing three fingers and you know what he said? He said: *My hand hurts but I can't quite put my finger on it.* He had those fingers with him in a cup of ice."

She paused and sighed deeply. Anne was a shy person. This was not like her. She resumed but her voice softened. "I am talking about *men*," she said. "This land grew men once, and now men are hard to find. Money, comfort, and convenience does not make you a man. Your grandson will never become a man as long as you're willing to give him anything he wants. Ezra is not simply stubborn, Mr. Boothe. He's principled. In resisting you he is doing something you do not see."

"And what is that?" Boothe asked.

"He's trying to protect your grandson from you, Mr. Boothe."

Boothe took a half-step back as if punched in the chest.

"I'm sorry," Anne said. "I'm out of line."

"No, that's fine. I'm just not used to people speaking to me with such brutal honesty."

"This land does that to you, Mr. Boothe. It doesn't suffer fools gladly."

"May I change the subject and not have it appear as avoidance?"

"Certainly."

"The mares Ezra just gathered. What is to be done with them?"

"Tomorrow he's hauling them to the sale in Billings. One or two might get picked for a breeding program, but more likely they'll sell as canners and be shipped to slaughter plants in Canada."

"I could buy a few," Boothe offered. "Maybe all of them. And put them in my granddaughter's breeding program. Mr. Havig would manage them."

"Do you know anything about the Oswald line?"

"Only what I've learned the last few days. They're line-bred Quarter Horses. Descendants of an old horse named Peter McCue."

"I don't think Ezra would sell them to you, Mr. Boothe."

"Why? Would he consider it charity?"

"No. It's because Mr. Havig is not Lynne and you're not Lynne. It takes a certain type of person to handle those horses."

"But they don't seem that wild. A little spirited, maybe."

"Its not how they act. It's what they are. What's in their blood. I know because I've heard this speech from Ezra over and over. They are big country range horses. They're not meant for some girl's barrel racing program. It could be done. But it would take someone who understands them to do it."

"You're probably right," he said. "And my granddaughter would not approve, anyway. She already has her bloodlines picked out. The names just confuse me, but they're popular horses breed specifically for barrel racing." He paused, looked toward the east and chuckled. "The Interstate is over there somewhere, isn't it? That's how all this started. I was hauling mares to my granddaughter and had two flats. A guy stopped and helped me. I didn't even get his name and he had it carved on the back of his belt. So I know what you mean about this country and the type of men it produces. I bought Corey a place here hoping he'd grow to be like that man."

"Speaking of your grandson, we should probably drive to a ridge where you can get cell service so you can call him back."

"Yes, we should do that. Do you have any suggestions?"

Anne looked about. "We can try the jeep trail to the south. There's a high place halfway home that's covered with tipi rings. I bet you can get service there. Or we go back the way we came and call from the ridge above the corrals."

Before they could decide, Gabby came up from the sandstone wash. She stood and looked at her grandmother intently.

"Gabby," Anne said. "Didn't you find any sand balls?"

"I did," she said. "But I left them."

"Left them? Why?"

"Because we have to go to the corrals," she said. "The big, bad bird is on the pole."

CHAPTER THIRTY NINE

L andau pressed his left foot against a railing in the squeeze chute's tailgate and pushed. It moved slightly. The gate was designed to slide out, perpendicular to the chute. At its top a roller moved on a steel rod and at the bottom an iron frame served as a track. The roller hadn't been oiled recently and the track was impeded by dry manure. He could use his left arm to push the gate open, and then he'd be in an angled alleyway with thick-planked sides. By staying low he might avoid being shot and get to another pen, this one with two gates. One opened to a larger pen, the other opened to the loading chute. Neither was likely to lead to a quick escape and there would still be the matter of his three friends left in the chute.

The big man held a revolver to the boy's head and was demanding Ezra tell him where to get cell service. The hand holding the revolver was within Landau's reach, but in a tussle the gun could go off, killing Garcia.

Who were these guys? Landau wondered. Where had they come from?

There were no doubts about the gunman's intentions. He was leaving no witnesses. He would shoot until the revolver was empty.

If more killing had to be done he'd use his fists, a rock, a branding iron, anything that worked.

Just two hours ago Landau had been on an Oswald gathering the Oswald mares. In that short time -- how long had it taken? he wondered. An hour, maybe less? -- he'd fulfilled, as much as possible, his reason for coming west. He understood Ezra Riley, Barney Wallace, and Joe Pagliano. It was something he could go home with. Something he could tell his mother.

Now, he suspected he'd never go home, and if he did, all he wanted to do was hold his mother. He'd hold her until she mustered the strength to push him away. Where his soul would go if he died, he didn't know. It hadn't been a consideration for him -- even in the dangers of the Middle East -- until he'd met Ezra and Anne.

But, with death just inches away, Landau had no regret for having come. Still, after years in the war zones, he didn't plan on dying in a set of remote corrals in eastern Montana at the hands of a thug covered in Aryan tattoos.

He'd made his decision. He was not going to try to escape. He was going to attack.

The loudest noise Garcia Jones had heard in his life was the revolver being cocked; a revolver that, only hours ago, he'd purchased on a whim. Now its smooth muzzle was pressed against his head. All this because Dr. Doyle had insisted on buying the Taurus, then had left it carelessly on the seat of the Ranger.

The shock of the situation had him reeling. Today he'd reached a life highlight by helping corral the mares. It was something to write his mother about, though with his father in jail, she'd be too distracted to appreciate it. His father was still part of the problem.

Now he was at life's lowest point. Perhaps at life's end, and nothing in Garcia's training had prepared him for this. He wanted to trust Ezra to effect a rescue, but while Garcia had a gun to his head, Ezra was saying nothing. Ezra was stalling.

Garcia knew how to get cell service. They all did. One only had to drive up on the ridge. Why didn't Ezra explain this? Garcia would have, but the pressure of the muzzle made his jaws lock. He was too scared to talk. Almost too scared to breathe.

In his soul he screamed a high-pitched, desperate plea, as shrill and inaudible as a dog whistle, that soared skyward, beyond his parents and past his own plans and fantasies. It was a cry to an unknown eternal. It was desperate and sincere, and somehow, it touched *something.* For a second he saw his desk back at the office, piled high with paperwork, and his co-workers seated at their own desks. Life there was normal. The people were breathing and not thinking each breath was their last. And Garcia Jones knew he was neither abandoned nor alone.

He took a deep breath.

Doyle finally realized she was not the target. This made her angry. After all, wasn't she more important than Harlan Boothe? Evidently not. They didn't even seem to know who she was.

Still, it seemed she might die.

Death, in a cattle chute in eastern Montana, while Lars and his socialite dined in Manhattan? They celebrated, oblivious to her being held by drug addicts, the biggest of whom held her gun to the head of a kid she'd manipulated into being there.

Doyle's mind amazed her because these were not the only thoughts she was having. They were simply the ones in the slow lane. Other thoughts whizzed by like speeding cars with drivers tossing out streams of litter. Other thoughts, colored as browns and bays, thundered by on pounding hooves. She saw sunlight glistening on their sweat-soaked sides. She imagined she was still horseback on the bay roan, holding her side of the herd with swagger and skill, being part of a crew where her mastery was displayed and appreciated.

So many thoughts. Where were they going and would they arrive together? Where had her mother's mind gone when she pretended to be a kite and flew from the second-story landing? Doyle had always wondered about that impulsiveness. Was it genetic? Did she carry a crazy gene?

She found herself thinking about the funny man, Barney Wallace. Had he really missed the word prank Ezra had pulled on him about satyrs? Surely, he didn't think a satirist was an inspired half-horse lyricist? But then, he could have, and more importantly, why was she even thinking about this when a loaded and cocked revolver was a foot or two from her own head?

But, luckily, not pointed *at* her head.

I have the crazy gene, Doyle decided. *But, when I die, at least I won't be passing it on.*

But, she had no idea where *she* would pass to. Life after death had never been a consideration. Such thoughts complicated grand obsessions, but now, with those obsessions deflated, the unknown opened and enclosed her within a cold tomb of stillness. Her racing thoughts crashed into a pile-up, and she emerged from them dazed, confused, and stumbling. Her only shelter was a dark domicile within the state of catatonia. She entered it.

Ezra Riley's vision was limited. Most of the corral was fenced with woven-wire, but there were planks, too, and near the squeeze chutes planks also created a catwalk, work bench, and tool wall where various implements hung. Through the man-gate Ezra could see parts of certain vehicles and what appeared to be wrapped laundry lying on the ground. That was Corey Boothe and Ezra still couldn't tell if he was alive or not. Through a knot hole in the plank he could see Barney's dog, Kitty, chained beneath the loading chute and being oddly quiet.

Mostly he saw Nicholas Pratt's angry face, garish with tattoos that Ezra now noticed in detail: poorly-drawn Chinese characters, a lightning bolt, goat's head, two tear drops and several swastikas. It was an odd time to be studying poor art, he decided.

Then from the corner of his eye he saw something that made his heart sink. It was a brief flash of light two-miles in the distance on the two-track pasture road than ran on the lip of the divide. Light on a windshield again. Then he saw motion moving northward, which meant the vehicle was minutes away from arriving at the corrals. Harlan Boothe, Anne, and Gabby were not taking the jeep trail home. They were coming back.

Ezra knew his one chance was to get the big guy alone. He still had a clip-on pocketknife, a Kershaw Flipper with quick-assist opening, in his right front pocket. He'd trust the Lord to provide an opportunity. All he needed was a target. If he couldn't reach the knife he hoped his martial arts training would return. One punch to the throat was all he needed. There was no question he would kill this man if given the opportunity. He'd do so in a heartbeat.

Ezra looked at Nickie. "Let me out," he said. "And I will take you to where you can get cell coverage."

"No," Nickie shouted. "No games, old-timer. I ain't lettin' none of you out. You tell me or I begin hurtin' people."

"Okay, okay," Ezra said. He looked at the skinny one for help. Jeremy's eyes were a listless pool of apathy. "There's Hydrocodone in my truck," Ezra whispered to him.

Jeremy's eyes came awake.

Nickie swung the gun around and pointed it at his cousin. "Forget it. We get it later. We got money coming, Jeremy. More money than you or I have ever seen."

"Boothe won't have money," Ezra said. "His money is tied up in banks and investments and securities."

"Money," Nickie said. "He'll have more in his wallet than we got. And credit cards. Besides, we take him to an ATM machine and we make it sing and rain."

"But you have to call him."

Nickie pointed the revolver at Ezra. "Tell me, old man, or I shoot you first."

"The loading chute," Ezra said.

"The what?"

"See that structure behind you that's up off the ground. That's how we load cattle into trucks. The two big poles at the end are 15 feet high. Get on the catwalk, then climb the planks to the top of the poles. Pull yourself up on top and stand there. That's what we have to do when we need to make a call."

Nickie looked at him incredulously. "You're lyin'."

"No, we don't do if often, only when we have to. Look at it. You're high enough to get a signal up there. It's all easy except that last part."

Nickie looked at Jeremy. "What you think?"

Jeremy pantomimed that he didn't know.

"Damn dummy, why I ask you?" Jeremy started for the gate to get a better look.

"Give your gun to Jeremy," Ezra said. "It's dangerous to climb with a gun."

Nickie turned and looked at Ezra with ancient eyes. "Nice try, old-timer, but I'm takin' the gun. I can shoot you from up there. I ain't givin' the gun to Jeremy." He reached to the wall where a host of branding irons hung from nails. He picked one and handed it to his cousin. "They move," he said. "And you start whackin' 'em. Hit their hands, hit their faces, hit anything you can, but don't get near enough to the chute so that they can grab you. You got that?"

Jeremy nodded in agreement.

Nickie gave Ezra a hard look, stuck the revolver in his waist band, then turned toward the loading chute.

Ezra moved his right hand slowly to the pocket. He felt the stainless steel clip but it gripped the denim firmly. He had some trust with Jeremy. If he bid him closer he might come. But first he needed to get the knife free.

He stared at the skinny, voiceless young man. Could he kill him? Yes, he told himself, if he did so in his mind first. He had to look through him, as if he were only a piece of sheer paper.

Jeremy held the branding iron raised like a child playing his first game of Tee-Ball. He tried to watch all four prisoners at once, which was a strain, because all he really wanted to do was go to sleep.

To Jeremy's right, Landau ran his arm down his side, then reached out with his fingers and gripped the gate. The metal felt cool and smooth in his hand as if it welcomed his touch. He watched his captor closely. He'd made up his mind. When the big guy was busy climbing the chute, and when the little guy looked toward Ezra, he would make his move.

It was only a matter of minutes. Seconds, even.

CHAPTER FOURTY

Barney sailed down the county road with a heart as light as a feather and the fingers of his right hand dancing on the SUV's console, stabbing button after button, in attempts to make the radio work. Finally, he got some static. A few pokes more, and a country-western station came on reporting area news: the ranch woman from Brockway was out of intensive care, and her husband had confessed to the beating. The report of the assault being perpetuated by two strangers in an older model pickup had been false.

"Shoot," Barney said. He hated to hear about men hitting their wives. He punched more buttons and landed a religious station. *Come on, radio. I need to listen to some NPR. I need to hear the people I work for.*

Finally he got a station without music. It played a drama about a private eye named Guy... something-or-another. Barney couldn't make out the last name. The more he listened, the more he liked it. *This has to be NPR,* he thought. Public Radio was growing on him. Barney wanted the NPR gig and was confidant he had it. Why else would they ask to see him? Rejection could have been done over the phone.

Then his feathered heart dropped like a stone. Maybe they hated his program so intensely they wanted to tell him in person.

He slowed for a brood of sage grouse chicks crossing the road near a sharp curve.

Cute little rascals, he thought, *and good-eating when smoked.* Barney had neither shot nor eaten sage grouse, but he'd been told to smoke them, otherwise, they tasted like sage. As the last chick scurried by, a pickup sped around the curve, nearly side-swiping Barney, and leaving him sitting in a cloud of dust.

"Dang," Barney said. "That guy nearly creamed me." When the dust cleared he checked on the chicks -- no feathers in the road so he guessed the little fellas made it. He knew the truck. It was Corey Boothe's. He wondered where it was going and what the rush was.

His ring tone of *Ghost Riders in the Sky* sounded. He was surprised he had coverage.

"Hello," he shouted. A man's voice was dim amid the static. It was NPR.

"Phonograph?" Barney said. "No, I don't have a phonograph." He paused and strained to hear. "Oh, *photograph.* What? You need a photograph? Wait a second, okay. Just hang on."

Barney rushed to the top of a nearby knoll, his big feet pushing down a small avalanche of brittle clay with each step. "Hello? Can you hear me better now? Okay. You want a photograph of me? You have a photographer in town waiting? Okay. What am I wearing now? I'm wearing a shirt and jeans and a cowboy hat. Oh, and I still got my chaps and spurs on.

"That's okay? Good. My horse? No, I don't have my horse with me, but I could stop at my house and get my dog. Would that be okay? Great. Be right there."

Barney was beyond tickled. He was getting a contract, and Kitty would be in the promotional photo. He slid down the hill and rushed to the truck. He had to go get Kitty.

Nicholas was agile for a big man. He leapt onto the catwalk with ease and started climbing the five cottonwood planks like they were the ladder of success. Get high, get a signal, and a billionaire would drop into his hands like a wounded sparrow. With money in the pocket and no witnesses left, he and Jeremy would return to Vegas and disappear into the criminal underworld. The chute's anchor posts rose almost four feet above the top planks and were thirty inches in diameter, though the far one looked slightly wider. He crossed over to it. He boosted himself to the top and balanced on his knees before rising. He was almost 15 feet in the air. Nickie pulled out Corey's phone and punched the grandfather's number.

Ezra's body resisted him. The more he strained to unclip the pocketknife, the more his shoulder and hand flared with pain. Jeremy was getting droopy again. If he could reach the knife, Ezra was sure he could lure Jeremy close and kill or disable him. He'd release himself somehow and charge the big guy with the branding iron and knife. It would take more than shots from a .22 Magnum to stop him from saving Anne and Gabby.

Using his left hand, Landau began inching the chute's endgate open, but dried manure in the track impaired his progress. Landau was amazed to see the big man obtain his perch on the pole. Ezra, Landau guessed, had sent him up there hoping he'd fall.

Jeremy's head jerked and his eyes opened. He'd almost drifted to sleep. Nickie wouldn't like that. He looked at his prisoners. They appeared as a single mass of flesh and fear. Then he noticed the handle on the endgate seemed different. He stepped over and pushed on it. The gate slid three inches to a tight closure. Jeremy stared at Landau, raised the branding iron, and shook his head. "No-no," he said.

Ezra had his fingers on the clip, and it was slightly yielding. He felt the knife lift in his pocket. Then his hand spasmed and his shoulder contracted. He hit his lip to keep from yelling in pain. His hand released the clip.

The Range Rover traveled the divide to the east fork of Dead Man Creek then began ascending the bench where the corrals sat. The three passengers rode in silence. When Boothe's phone sounded he looked at the screen.

"Corey's calling," he said, and instinctively stopped the Rover. "Hello."

"This Boothe?" a gruff voice asked.

"Who is this?"

"I got the baby boy, Mr. Billionaire," the voice said.

If there was an opposite to *epiphany*, according to Henrietta Wallace, it was the state her husband dwelled in. Cluttered cloudiness, not unexpected insight, kept Barney bumping from one random activity to another, usually stubbing his toes along the way.

But today Barney Wallace had an epiphany.

It struck just as he was turning from the county road onto the oil. *Kitty was not at home. Kitty was back at the corrals with the crew.*

Kitty had to be in the photo. If he was going to ride a sudden wave of success, he wanted Kitty beside him. He jammed Landau's rental in reverse, spun around, and roared back down the Dead Man Road, driving faster than normal because the photographer was waiting.

Ezra had a new plan -- the chute bars he'd consider earlier - but it's success depended on the four executing it together. The ancient cattle chute didn't have side doors for releasing stock. On each side, at about knee-level, it had a thick plank that dropped down, but its latches couldn't be reached. From waist-height up, the chute had thick, rounded bars held in place behind a roller. He'd considered the bars earlier, but only individually. If each person grabbed a bar and pushed, they'd create an opening several could tumble through. If Jeremy swung the branding iron, two or three of them might be disabled, but someone would get away.

The problem was communicating the plan to the others and synchronizing it.

"Bars," he whispered to Doyle.

She didn't hear him.

"Bars," he said again, slightly louder.

Doyle appeared catatonic.

"Bars," he said, and nudged her with his leg.

The branding iron crashed against the side of the chute. "No talking," Jeremy said. "None of you talk." He put the iron down and leaned on it like a crutch while holding his side with his left arm. Sweat poured from his forehead. Jeremy looked very ill.

Ezra glanced at Doyle. She hadn't flinched when the branding iron struck the chute inches from her face. Ezra frowned. Doyle would be no help. Through the head catch he glimpsed Simon standing hipshot at the fence, one hind leg cocked and his head down. Behind him he heard the stirring of the mares, but horses didn't matter. Ranches didn't matter. His own life didn't matter. Only saving Anne and Gabby mattered.

The faster Barney drove, the more he realized he'd never wanted to be famous. The money NPR would pay him wouldn't be that much -- though enough for Mrs. Wallace to get her kitchen remodeled -- but the exposure could be huge. He'd sell more cartoon books and calendars. He might get invited to Elko. Who knows? He could even be invited onto a late-night television show.

Success brought one problem. Technology. He had no web site, Facebook page, or Twitter account. But surely that wasn't a problem more money couldn't solve. But would money change him? Could he follow his own adage of never using money to measure wealth? What would he do with more money? He wouldn't buy a ranch -- too much work at his age -- but he would purchase more acreage and construct a really nice roping arena. If he splurged on anything, it would be an insulated and air-conditioned dog house for Kitty. Kitty deserved it, and besides, the old dog's flatulence was becoming too much to bear in the house.

Ride fame like a bronc, he told himself. Sit back and spur. If he got tossed, he got tossed. Roll with it. If money and honors came, a good time would still be riding fine horses beside friends like Ezra and Joe.

He wondered how Joe was doing? He really needed to get to the hospital and see him, but life had been a bit hectic. Maybe tomorrow. He turned off the county road and onto the two-track that led to the corrals.

"What are you talking about?" Boothe said into his phone. The reception was bad. He could barely hear the stranger.

"We got your grandson," Nickie said. "You get back to the corrals and we'll trade him to ya."

"Who are you?"

"You don't need to know." Nickie turned the phone off and put it in his pocket. It was hard balancing on the post and a long way to the ground. He had to get down. Then to the east, where a road curved down a draw, he glimpsed something that seemed out of place. It was too shiny to be a bare spot of ground. It was the roof of a vehicle. It had to be Boothe. He smiled. His ATM was nearer than he thought.

But before he could begin his descent he saw another vehicle, a dark SUV speeding down the ridge from the north. It was coming so fast the driver had to know something was wrong.

Nickie didn't have time to climb down the planks. He reached into his pants, pulled out the revolver, and took a two-handed aim at the newcomer.

As he descended the ridge to the corrals Barney saw the object on the post and knew things weren't right. Who would be standing on top of a loading chute post? Whoever he was, he was huge; but why was he there?

He realized he saw no one else. The vehicles were present and the horses were in the corral, but where were Ezra, Garcia, Peter, and Doyle?

He saw the man on the post pull something up and extend his arms. He was pointing a handgun.

At 30 yards Nickie fired. The bullet hit the top of the windshield. Barney heard a pop and the twang of a ricochet and saw the glass crack. The shooter leaned forward for another shot. Barney had been slowing down, but now he turned the vehicle toward the chute and accelerated. The SUV hammered the post Nickie was standing on casting him forward. The SUV's airbags deployed. Nickie landed on the vehicles's roof, caving it in.

In an instant's time, Ezra heard a pop, whistle, crash, boom, and a dull thud. The pop was the .22 Magnum, the whistle a ricochet, the crash was the SUV striking the pole, the boom was the airbag deploying and the thud was Nicholas Pratt landing face-down on the wreck's roof.

Ezra glared at Jeremy who stood transfixed and staring in the direction of the chute. "It's over," Ezra said.

Jeremy turned slowly. His face showed a dull resignation.

"The lever," Ezra said. "Open the head catch."

Jeremy dropped the branding iron, reached up and pulled the lever that popped the two-pieced head gate open.

Though stiff and sore from being cramped, Ezra jumped from the chute, went around Jeremy, pulled the rear gate open for Landau, then rushed from the pens toward the crash. As he ran, he saw the Range Rover arrive from the east, but he knew Anne and Gabby were fine. Barney was the priority. The SUV's front end was crushed, the windshield shattered and the roof caved-in, but the door wasn't sprung. Ezra pulled it open. Barney lay unconscious, a deflated air bag in his lap. His face was swelling and blood streamed from his nose. Peter and Garcia arrived at his side. "Help me pull him out," Ezra said. They tugged on Barney in sections until they had him out and lying on the ground.

Anne instructed Gabby to stay in the vehicle, then she ran toward Ezra and Barney.

Ezra waved her away. "Go check on Corey," he yelled.

"His grandpa's with him," Anne protested.

"Check on him," Ezra said. "He may need help. And keep an eye on Gabby."

Garcia was trembling and his face was white. "Is Barney dead?" he asked.

"He's just out cold," Peter said. "Get some water, Garcia."

Ezra saw Doyle stumbling toward her vehicle. She picked her backpack from the ground and tossed it in the front seat.

Landau climbed up on his rental and checked on Nickie. The big man was sprawled across the dented hood with his head turned to the side. His eyes were open.

"He's dead," Peter reported.

"Peter," Ezra said. "Take the Ranger to the ridge and call 911. Tell them we need an ambulance and the sheriff." He looked toward Anne, who was bending over Corey. "Make that two ambulances," he said.

Garcia arrived with a bottle of water, and Ezra poured a steady stream over Barney's face. Barney sputtered as the water splashed across him, his eyes opened to tiny slits and he tried to raise himself. Ezra held him down with one hand.

"Ezra," Barney said weakly. "Where's Kitty?"

"Kitty's fine," Ezra said. He heard an engine start. Peter had already driven off. This was Doyle leaving.

Ezra jumped to his feet and stopped her. Doyle sat behind the steering wheel staring blankly ahead.

"Adrienne," Ezra said. "Where are you going?"

"Leaving," she said flatly.

"You can't leave," Ezra said. "The Sheriff will need a statement and a doctor should check you out."

"Canada," she said, and she tromped on the gas. The vehicle spun and jumped forward. Ezra watched it speed away.

Anne ran to Ezra. "How's Barney?" she asked.

"He's coming to. The air bag beat him up pretty bad. How's Corey?"

"He's alive but he needs attention."

"Peter's calling for help."

"Ezra," Garcia called. "Barney wants to talk to you."

Ezra bent over the cartoonist.

Barney looked up but couldn't see. "Ezra," he mumbled. "Kitty and I ... have to get to town... for photos ... N-P-R."

Ezra humored him. "That's a great idea," he said. "You clean up a little, and I'll turn your dog loose."

Ezra reached under the chute and unfastened Kitty's chain. The dog bounded joyfully to its master and began licking his face. Ezra searched around the wreckage until he found the revolver. He picked it up and walked to the pens. He didn't think Jeremy would be a threat but he had to make sure. He stepped through the man-gate with the Taurus cocked, but there was no need. Jeremy Pratt lay on the ground. Snoring.

And talking in his sleep.

EPILOGUE

The following morning Ezra returned to the corrals to load the mares for the sale in Billings. Anne had taken Peter to the hospital to say goodbye to Barney and Joe, then Peter was riding with Ezra to Billings to catch an evening flight home. As Ezra approached the corrals he was surprised to see a vehicle there. It wasn't Peter's wrecked SUV -- a tow truck had hauled it away previously -- it was Doyle's SUV.

He backed up to the loading gate beside the chute, literally driving over the site of the wreck. Shards of glass, plastic and metal littered the ground. He got out, walked around the loading chute and found Doyle sitting on the catwalk by the alleyway.

"Adrienne," he said. "What are you doing here?" Her hair was unkempt and her face was haggard. She appeared not to have slept all night. She had, though, changed her soiled pants.

"I had to come back," she said. "I don't know why. I guess I just couldn't run."

"That's good," he said.

"It's okay that I'm here?"

"Sure. Stay as long as you want."

"Where's Peter?"

"Anne took him to the hospital to say goodbye to Barney and another friend of ours."

"He's leaving?"

"He's flying out of Billings this evening."

"Is Barney okay?"

"He has a broken nose, black eyes and a couple broken ribs. They kept him overnight for observation. He did miss his NPR photo shoot."

"The young guy? The redhead?"

"He took a few day's leave from work to spend time with his parents."

"Boothe and his grandson?"

"I'm not sure. Corey was flown to a hospital in Denver for brain surgery."

"And the, uh...you know, the..."

"The skinny guy? Jeremy?"

"Yes."

"In custody."

"The big guy died?"

Ezra nodded. "Broken neck."

"Okay," she said. "I guess I can go now."

"Where will you go, Adrienne?"

"I'm going to go...someplace...to be taken care of. I think I've had a nervous breakdown."

"Will you be okay? Getting there, I mean."

"Yes, I'll be fine." She jumped down from the catwalk and stared at the pens. "We're all a part of something, aren't we? All of us."

"Yes," Ezra said. "We're all connected."

She looked east toward the badlands. "May I take the scenic drive home?" she asked.

"Sure." Ezra noted that she'd referred to his place -- the bunk-house, in particular, he thought -- as home.

She turned, walked to her vehicle, and got inside. The engine started. Then her window rolled down. "Did I thank you?" she asked.

"For what?"

"For letting me help gather the mares."

"Yes, you did. And Adrienne," Ezra said. "Please know you are welcome back anytime."

She nodded, the window rolled up, and Doyle drove away.

Ezra loaded the mares with a cold practicality. He didn't look at the horses closely, but he felt their confusion and concern. Still, they loaded easily, and he closed the trailer's end-gate.

He was getting in his truck when Anne pulled up with Peter and Gabby. Peter stepped out with his bags.

"I was going to pick you up at the house," Ezra said.

Peter nodded at the pens. "I wanted to see this place one more time," he said.

"How's Barney?" Ezra asked Anne.

"They're releasing him this morning," she said. "Joe, too. Joe said he didn't get any sleep last night because of Barney snoring."

Ezra smiled. "We have a cure for that," he said.

"Barney's cracking jokes," Peter said, as he loaded his bags in Ezra's truck. "He said the last time he got two black eyes from an air bag, it was for sassing his mother-in-law."

Anne and Gabby drove off and Ezra and Peter followed them out. There was silence in the truck as Ezra drove slowly and carefully down the pasture road. At the fence line beside the county road he stopped and Peter closed the gates behind them. They were still silent as the truck and trailer rattled down the Dead Man Road to Highway 59 North. They drove past the Riley ranch, through town, and followed a frontage road west to the Interstate. Once on the two-lane, Ezra picked up speed, set the cruise control, sighed, and leaned back.

"Doyle was at the corrals when I got there," Ezra said.

"She was? What was she doing?"

"Closing gates," Ezra said. "Just like you. She said she plans on going somewhere to be treated for a nervous breakdown."

"She'll need to," Peter said. "She'll get more bad news. Lars Anderssen was killed last night in Manhattan."

"Killed? You mean, murdered?"

"Supposedly a carjacking that went wrong."

"But, you think-- ?"

The journalist shrugged. "Who knows? If there was a hit, maybe it was on him."

"Doyle talked about some people, and she said it with a certain emphasis. *Some people.* I take it these are the people who were behind her and Anderssen. Do you know what she's talking about?"

"Just rumors," Peter said. "But I suspect they exist. Globalists. Billionaires. And defiantly anti-Israel like most of my friends in New York."

"Doyle told me they were against the EEEP program, but she suggested I take it because it would delay their plans."

"Are you going to do it?"

"Probably. Boothe's motivation for buying the ranch is gone. Doyle thinks the program will offer some protection for what's coming, whatever that is."

"You can't believe people who are having a nervous breakdown."

"I know. Still, I'm only 61. What do I have to do for the next seven years except work my butt off installing ranch improvements, filling out paperwork, and dealing with bureaucrats?"

"If you're lucky, Garcia will stick around."

"I hope so."

"Do you think the sage grouse will be listed?"

"Probably. When I was a kid, I wanted to be a naturalist. My favorite author was Ernest Thompson Seton. Today you never even hear the word naturalist. Everyone is an ecologist or an environmentalist. And those terms scare me."

"You think the listing of the sage grouse is a ploy?"

"It's a land grab. There is habitat loss, but much of that was created by the government's own farm policies 30, 40 years ago. West Nile Virus is a factor but they can't quantify that. A main problem is predators. Sage grouse are big, slow, and dumb. They're on the bottom of the food chain, but the feds won't even consider predator control."

"If they can't survive, maybe they should go extinct."

"That's very Darwinian of you, but none of us want that. What we want is for urban idealists to stay out of rural affairs. In urbanization lies the ruination of the world."

"Thoreau quoted backwards?"

Ezra took his hands off the steering wheel and rubbed them. "Actually, I attribute that to the famous Barney Wallace," he said.

"What are you going to do about your hands and your shoulder?" Peter asked.

"Soldier-on, cowboy-up. You know, all that tough macho stuff."

"Have you been tested for carpal tunnel?"

"No," Ezra said. "It's never even come up."

"With all the writing you've done that's what the hand problem could be. It might not have anything to do with your neck."

Ezra stared at the road thoughtfully. Then he smiled. "The horse wreck on Pedro is a better story," he said. "It beats the heck out of saying I got hurt rewriting novels."

"Whatever happened to that horse?" Peter asked. "The bad Oswald."

"I sold him to a rodeo string."

"Is he good?"

"No, he's dishonest and dirty. He didn't even make a good bronc."

"I'm glad I didn't meet him," Peter said.

They rode in silence for a few miles, each in his own world.

Finally, Ezra said, "Speaking of stories, the incident yesterday. Is it going to be in your article?"

Peter shook his head. "No. It had nothing to do with horses. My article is about horses."

"I admire you for that," Ezra said. "Do you feel you have everything you need for your story?"

"It's all in the trailer back there. When you drop those horses off at the sales barn my story is over."

"You don't approve of what I'm doing, do you?"

"I understand what you're doing," Peter said. "I don't need to approve. I just wish there was a better way."

"I called the managers of the sales barn. I told them to get on the phone to any breeder that might be interested in a good mare or two. There's always a chance."

"When Lynne died his mares went to breeders, didn't they?"

"Most, not all. But the market has fallen more since then and there's no end in sight." "And horse slaughter houses is the answer?"

"It's part of the answer. Slaughter is a nasty business," Ezra admitted. "But, it's a necessary one. More horses suffer without it than because of it."

"I suppose we should talk about something else," Peter said.

"We could talk about what really brought you here," Ezra said. "And it wasn't horses."

Peter turned his head and looked at him. "What do you mean?"

"Don't be coy, Peter. You're going to tell me because things changed yesterday. Each of us has been given a chance to reconsider our priorities."

"So, have you known all along?"

"I had suspicions. I still don't know the details."

Peter stroked his trimmed beard and frowned. "Barney told me a story about Lynne getting a phone call from a woman back east some years ago."

"Yeah. Lynne told me and I told Barney."

"The woman who called Lynne was my mother."

"Your mother?"

"I came in the room while she was on the phone. It was a short conversation. When she hung up I asked her who she'd been talking to. She was reluctant to talk about it, but, after all, I am an investigative journalist."

"She met Lynne at the Madison Square Garden Rodeo?"

"Nineteen fifty-nine. She was sixteen years old and was totally smitten."

"There's more?"

"My parents separated just before I was born. I don't know the details because it was a forbidden subject. My father was business-driven. My mother was more adventurous and fun-loving. During the separation she went to a dude ranch upstate."

"You think she went to meet Lynne?"

Peter didn't answer.

"You don't think you're Lynne's son?"

Peter shook his head. "No, though at first I was probably hoping. I'm my father's son. I'm just nothing like him."

"Did you ask your mother about the dude ranch?"

"No, and I don't plan on it. When she made that call she was a grieving widow reaching out for the impossible. She doesn't know that Lynne has passed away, and I don't plan on telling her."

"Lynne won't be in your story?"

"No. I can't do that to her, but he'll be the spirit behind the story."

"You should have told me from the beginning, Peter. There are things I would have shared."

"I didn't want to hear about Lynne that way," Peter said. "I didn't want him to be personal. I wanted him to be an idea, a myth, a legend, and I wanted to see the country he loved, the people he enjoyed--"

"The horses he rode."

"Yes, the Oswalds."

"When you came did you know Lynne had already passed away?"

"No. I discovered that here after researching your articles."

"But why such a fascination with him?" Ezra asked. "You put a lot of effort into this. Money, time, travel, and doing a horse article you probably didn't have that much interest in."

"I was haunted. I had to know why my mother would look for some-one nearly 60 years after they'd met. What kind of man inspires that? All my life I thought my mother had a secret. It was a mystery I had to solve. Haven't you ever been haunted by someone or something?"

"Not by anything finite."

"What do you mean?"

"I'm passionate about many things -- land, good writing, good horses -- and I'm curious about many things, but I'm only haunted by the eternal. Scripture haunts me. Everything else is temporal. It all passes away with time."

"You're kidding? You mean you're only haunted by Bible verses?"

"By the Word? Yes."

"Which verses?"

"Ephesians 2:10 is one."

"What does it say?

"It says we are His workmanship created for good works. In the Greek, the word, workmanship, is *poiema,* from which we get the English word, poem."

"So that's why you're so particular about poetry?"

Ezra grinned. "That's what our life is meant to be. We are a poem written by God. We are meant to have a message of beauty and truth delivered with musical precision. We edit our lives to conform to His poetic intentions."

Peter shook his head. "Barney was right. You swim in deep waters. I might want to stay in the shallows with Barn Wall."

"Trickles and ripples," Ezra said.

"Chuckles and giggles," Peter added.

They rode in silence again, the miles sped by, and soon they were on the outskirts of Billings.

"I can call a cab from the sales barn," Peter said. "There's no rea-son for you to pull this trailer through Billings traffic."

"I'd appreciate that," Ezra said. "I'm not one for city traffic."

Ezra pulled into the sales yard and picked his way carefully through a melee of pickup trucks, eighteen-wheelers, trailers, people and horses. He got in the line for the unloading alley behind other trucks and trailers. A yard man with a consignment pad came to his window. "Whadya got? he asked.

"Eight registered Oswald mares," Ezra said. "The papers will be in the office, but they sell as loose horses."

The man scribbled the information down and handed the pad to Ezra who signed it and handed it back.

Then Ezra and Peter stepped out and watched as another yard man opened his trailer gate and jumped the mares out. They stirred in confusion. A day ago they were miles from people, traffic, and other horses. Now they were surrounded by pens, humans, and hundreds of horses. Simon's dam stopped in the swarm. Her long, lean neck led to a refined, straight head and gentle, questioning eyes that looked straight at Ezra.

He shivered trying to shake off the impulse.

Peter noticed his conflict.

The yard man began opening an alley gate to send the mares to their holding pen.

"Wait," Ezra said, raising his hand. He stepped into the unloading pen, sorted Simon's dam out, and jumped her back in the trailer. Peter closed the trailer gate for him.

"You'll have to go change your check-in sheet and get a new brand inspection," the yard man yelled.

"I know," Ezra said.

Peter looked at him without saying a word, but in the journalist's dark eyes, Ezra saw the vast prairie sky, the ruggedness of badlands, and the freedom of horses on the run. He also saw branding fires, men laughing, and loops cast straight and true. Whatever Peter Landau had come searching for, Ezra decided, he had obviously found.

He answered the question the reporter hadn't asked.

"For Lynne," Ezra said.

----- the end -----

Made in the USA
Charleston, SC
26 April 2014